Praise fo

THE TRAI

"In *The Traitor's Daughte*   bo-
rators and resistance fighters in an occupied   out
against the backdrop of an impending cataclysm that could
render all of their machinations irrelevent. Compellingly
complex motivations and character dynamics mark Paula
Brandon's welcome debut."

—JACQUELINE CAREY, *New York Times*
bestselling author of *Naamah's Kiss*

"Paula Brandon's *The Traitor's Daughter* is a dark, rich feast,
rife with plagues, kidnappings, political intrigues, bloody
crimes, bloodier revenges, arcane upheavals, and the threat
of zombies."

—DELIA SHERMAN, author of *Changeling*

"I love a fantasy world so solid that I can breathe the air, smell
the earth, and truly feel the touch of the magic. The world of
The Traitor's Daughter is all of that and more. In this world,
the solidity masks a nightmare: an approaching inversion in
the conditions of magic that will change *everything*. To create a reality so convincing and destabilize it with a threat so
dizzyingly profound—what an achievement! Here's a story
to enwrap, enchant, and sweep you away. This isn't reading,
it's full-on living! A flawless all-round performance!"

—RICHARD HARLAND, author of *Worldshaker* and *Liberator*

"Brandon's debut, the first in a projected trilogy, is an impres-
sively imaginative epic disguised as an unassuming romantic
fantasy. . . . While the revolutionary and romantic threads
are engaging, it is Brandon's multilayered narrative that
makes this novel such an immersive reading experience. Rich
world-building, relentless pacing, and some tantalizing sub-
plots suggest that Brandon is an author to watch."

—*Publishers Weekly*

By Paula Brandon

The Traitor's Daughter

The Ruined City

The Wanderers

THE
RUINED
CITY

THE
RUINED
CITY

Paula Brandon

SPECTRA

BALLANTINE BOOKS
New York

A Spectra Trade Paperback Edition

Copyright © 2012 by Paula Volsky

All rights reserved.

Published in the United States by Bantam Books, an imprint of The Random House Publishing Group, a division of Random House, Inc., New York.

SPECTRA and the portrayal of a boxed "s" are trademarks of Random House, Inc.

Library of Congress Cataloging-in-Publication Data

Brandon, Paula.
The ruined city / Paula Brandon.—Spectra trade paperback ed.
p. cm.
ISBN 978-0-553-58382-3 (pbk.)
eBook ISBN 978-0-345-53237-4
I. Title.
PS3602.R36R85 2012
813'.6—dc23   2011035597

Printed in the United States of America

www.ballantinebooks.com

2 4 6 8 9 7 5 3 1

Book design by Mary A. Wirth

THE
RUINED
CITY

PROLOGUE

"Are you asleep?"

Grix Orlazzu lay with his eyes closed. His breathing was deep and regular.

"Come, this is useless. I know you are not asleep." The automaton's metallic tones scraped the atmosphere. "You cannot deceive me, Leftover. Open your eyes."

Orlazzu produced a muted snore.

"This is false. This is treacherous. This is organic. You will admit that you are awake!"

A steel-jointed finger poked Orlazzu's shoulder. For the life of him, he could not contain a curse, which killed all hope of further pretense. He opened his eyes to confront the glassy scrutiny of his creation.

"What time is it?" Orlazzu yawned widely.

"Time to get up. You have lain there on that pallet long enough."

"We inferior creatures of flesh and blood need our rest, you may recall."

"You have had four hours of rest. You cannot pretend that does not suffice. Come, enough of this sloth. Get up now, Leftover. You will get up *now*!"

Orlazzu sat up. For a moment his gaze traveled the room, its modest limits faintly visible by dawn light, before coming to rest upon the sturdy figure of his own mechanical double. The automaton returned the regard unblinkingly, and—not for the first time—Orlazzu repented his own failure to furnish his creation with functional eyelids.

"Well?" the automaton prompted.

"Well, what? What do you want now?"

"Your attention. Your regard. Your conversation. You will talk to me."

"About what, exactly?"

"My thoughts. My feelings. My inner self."

"Your inner self consists of gears, cogs, springs, and clockwork, driven by arcanely generated pulses of energy."

"And yours consists of imperfectly organized ooze, but I make allowances for your deficiencies. I do not despise you for them. I am still willing to confide in you."

"I haven't asked you to confide."

"You will listen. It is your duty. I wish to discuss my feelings of loneliness and isolation, the result of your neglect. You have not made me feel welcome—you *never* have."

"Correct. You are not welcome. Why don't you leave?"

"You are impertinent, Leftover. Not to mention insensitive, inferior, and generally reprehensible. I will not be pushed out of my own home."

"*Your* home?"

"I have come to regard it as such. I have developed a deep and abiding affinity for this humble cottage. Modest though it may be, yet it is my true and rightful place."

"Very well. You keep it, then. I'll go."

"Without me? Never. I will not allow it."

"You will not *allow*?"

"I am stronger than you, Leftover. I am faster, greater in endurance, and far more intelligent than you. We both know that I am more than your match. And I will not *allow* you to shirk your sacred responsibilities."

"Those sacred responsibilities including unlimited endurance of soulful chitchat?"

"Chitchat? How dare you? Have you any idea how *condescending* that sounds?"

"I believe I do, yes."

"I will not endure such contempt, such indifference! You will display the proper interest and concern that any creator owes his creation. You will acknowledge your obligation, recognize my needs, and strive to fulfill them to the best of your ability. I will settle for no less! Do you hear me, Leftover? You will do right by me!" The automaton's voice had risen to a metallic shout, but its face, limited in flexibility, barely changed expression.

Orlazzu studied his unruly double in silence for a moment, concluded once again that he could not bring himself to destroy the mechanism, and inquired mildly, "You view my obligation as permanent in nature?"

"No, for your term of existence is limited. But make no mistake, you will use your time properly."

"I see. Yes, I see clearly. Very well, Grix. You leave me no choice, and I must yield. This is your home, our home, our abode of inexpressible togetherness. Here I shall dedicate all the resources at my command to the furtherance of your happiness. What have you to say to that?"

The automaton eyed its creator in silence.

"That's what you want, isn't it?" Orlazzu prompted.

"That is what I demand. But you concede very readily."

"How can I fight the inevitable?"

The automaton's internal mechanism whirred. An erratic succession of beeps suggested mental disquiet.

"Right, then." Orlazzu rose from his narrow bed. The quality of light in the room told him that dawn had broken. "I must step outside for a moment, in the manner of organic humankind—"

"The details are unnecessary. I recognize your weakness."

"And then I need to collect some fuel."

"You've fuel enough already."

"Not so. Remember, it must season. You may assist me, if you will."

"Assist in what manner?"

"Gather sticks, chop wood—"

"I? I possess talents and intellect of the highest order. You would set me to menial tasks?"

"Necessary tasks."

"Necessary for you, Leftover. I have no need of fire, hence no reason to gather bits of wood. It is not as if I were some *servant*."

"You'll not come for the sake of fellowship? We could discuss your feelings."

"We will discuss them upon your return. Do not expect me to drudge for you. I have learned to assert myself."

"I applaud your progress. Excuse me for the moment, then. I'll return shortly." Pausing only long enough to wrap himself in his oilskin cloak, Grix Orlazzu exited the hut, shutting the door behind him.

He emerged into a dim world filled with mist and cold moisture. The weak light of early morning just barely managed to find its way through the fog. The tufted grasses underfoot were dank and dead, the low shrubbery leafless and skeletal. For all of that, his surroundings were intensely charged. Almost he imagined that he could feel the power of the Source vibrating through the ground and tingling through the air, to raise the gooseflesh along his forearms and stir the hairs at the back of his neck. Closing his eyes, he opened himself to the Source, and in that unguarded moment felt the vast intangible presence of the Other pressing hard on his intellect. An intimation of ancient intelligence too alien to comprehend, a sense of measureless will spanning the ages, and then he slammed shut the gates of his mind, excluding the intruder.

Orlazzu opened his eyes. He was breathing hard, as if he had run a race, and his heart was pounding. He came within a nervespan of ducking back into the shelter, whose arcane reinforcements were proof against all attempted incursion, then considered the consequences and quelled the impulse. He was capable of resisting the Other. It was largely a matter of vigilance.

Two minutes of brisk hiking carried him over the crest of a rise and down into a hollow hidden from the hut and its glass-eyed tenant. There sprawled a dense tangle of brambles, and beneath the spiked branches lay a pile of dead leaves. Plunging his hand wrist-deep into the leaves, he dragged forth the sack that he had hidden in that spot some twenty-four hours earlier. Within the sack reposed his most essential belongings—a clutch of arcane instruments and substances, a few mundane tools, the best of his books and manuscripts, and a few days' supply of food. Little enough, but they would serve.

Sack slung over his shoulder, Orlazzu fled into the fog.

ONE

Aureste Belandor's eyes moved from the still body on the bed to the still body on the floor, and back again. His brother Innesq lay white-faced, blue-lipped, and apparently dead of exhaustion. Newly awakened from his coma, weakened and drained, Innesq had been unfit for arcane endeavor. The intense exertion required to halt the plague-crazed guard's rampage had cost dearly. Rigid on the floor sprawled the corpse of the young guard Drocco, bones shattered and skull fractured by the blows of the poker wielded by his master—his loss negligible in itself, yet threatening enormous inconvenience. For an instant the Magnifico Aureste stood paralyzed, prey to uncharacteristic indecision. The moment passed, and he was himself again.

Applying two fingers to his brother's neck, he discovered an erratic and dangerously weak pulse. No matter. Innesq was not about to die; Aureste Belandor would not permit it. He yanked the bellpull beside the bed, and a Sishmindri answered the summons at once. The amphibian's air sacs fluttered at sight of the dead guard.

"You are called Zirriz, are you not?" Aureste demanded, business-like as if he conducted ordinary household affairs.

The hairless greenish head bobbed.

"And you frequently assist Master Innesq in his workroom?"

"I obey," the Sishmindri reported.

"Well, Zirriz, Master Innesq has overexerted himself and suffered a relapse. It is your task to restore him."

"How?"

"You will find a way. Do not pretend ignorance, as you

value your green hide. His illness is arcane in nature. As his assistant, you must have received instruction, learned what to do in the event of an accident or emergency. You will use that knowledge now."

There was no immediate reply. Zirriz advanced to the bedside, studied Innesq's blue-white face, then took up one lax hand to examine the fingertips at some length.

"Need leech-man." The Sishmindri laid Innesq's hand down.

"No. The doctors are charlatans, they know nothing. The responsibility is yours. Save Master Innesq's life and you'll be rewarded. Fail, and I will lock you in a small iron cage where you will starve to death at leisure. Now get to work."

Zirriz stared, his thoughts—if any—unknowable. At last he replied, "Need dust."

"Then get it. There is plenty to be had."

"Cure. For sickness. Magic."

"An arcane restorative? Good. Where is this to be purchased? I'll pay any price."

"Made. In workroom."

"Did any of this dust survive the fire?"

Zirriz's brow ridges flexed. Clearly he did not know.

"Go and see." Aureste controlled his impatience with difficulty.

Zirriz made for the exit.

"Halt." The command was obeyed, and Aureste's hand sketched a gesture encompassing the corpse on the floor. "You will remove this carrion." He felt the weight of unspoken questions, and his mind sped. Drocco carried the plague, whose discovery consigned Belandor House and its inhabitants to the deadly limbo of the quarantine. And yet—a quick glance served to confirm—nothing in the victim's outward appearance revealed contagion. His death wounds were gapingly apparent, their red testimony sufficient unto itself. Prompt disposal of the corpse should guard the potentially catastrophic truth.

The amphibian was staring, his comprehension open to question.

"The fool was roaring drunk," Aureste found himself explaining. "He drew his weapon and suffered the consequences. Now get him out of here. Cart his carcass to the nearest dunghill, or to the Allwights if you prefer, and leave him there. In any case, get rid of him. Do it now."

"Cannot," the Sishmindri replied, unbelievably.

"What do you say to me?" Aureste's gaze roved in search of a whip.

"General Order Fourteen."

Of course. Governor Uffrigo's infamous decree, with which Aureste had reluctantly familiarized himself in recent days. General Order Fourteen, which imposed an early curfew upon Faerlonnish nationals and their Sishmindri chattel alike. General Order Fourteen, which mandated the confiscation of any Faerlonnish-owned Sishmindri found out upon the streets after the hour of ten. In the event of discovery, the dead guard—a person of no importance—could be explained away with relative ease. But the Taerleezi authorities would immediately seize the amphibian, a commodity too valuable to sacrifice.

"Very well." He released the concession grudgingly. "Carry him hence at dawn, then. In the meantime, summon such assistance as required and have that thing removed from my brother's chamber."

Zirriz stooped to inspect the corpse and reported, "Not dead."

"*What?*"

"Still moving."

"You are lying or dreaming." Mastering vast repugnance, Aureste approached to stare down into the dead man's face. Drocco's eyes were wide open, and the lids twitched perceptibly. Apart from that minuscule motion, he was rigid and motionless, held fast in Innesq's arcane toils. Could such bonds ever break? Did the—he groped for the term his brother had used—did the *Overmind* look upon him through those staring eyes?

He suppressed a thrill of almost superstitious horror. There was no cause for fear. Innesq's intangible restraints would hold firm until the guard's body turned to dust.

"It is a final spasm of the muscles, nothing more," he decreed. "He's finished." He paused, daring contradiction, of which there was none. "Now do as you are bid, and keep me informed of your progress." Averting his eyes from the embarrassment on the floor, Aureste departed, making his way through the smoke-blighted corridors of the north wing to the chamber now serving as his makeshift study. As he went, the signs of the recent fire were everywhere about him: blackened frescoes and hangings, cracked and wounded stained-glass windows, empty mirror frames, moldering waterlogged carpets, gilt-peeling furniture, broken porcelains—and all of that was here in the north wing, whose damage was minor compared with the devastation of the central section and the south wing. Belandor House, site of privilege and grandeur, *his own house,* had suffered a blow from which it would be slow to recover, if it ever recovered at all. But the building and its contents were feathers weighed in the balance against the attack upon Innesq—an attack that might yet prove fatal.

Aureste repelled the thought, expertly substituting tastier objects of contemplation, chiefest of which was vengeance. The author of the outrage, or at least its principal perpetrator, presently languished in prison—a circumstance offering boundless opportunity to the creative enemy.

Mere minutes earlier, Innesq Belandor had explained the urgent necessity of establishing a truce with Vinz Corvestri. The cleansing of the Source, whose imminent reversal threatened the Veiled Isles—and perhaps the lands beyond—with uncanny catastrophe, demanded the combined talents of some half-dozen arcanists. Corvestri was an indispensable member of this group, his contribution essential. And Aureste had accepted the truth of this, even at the cost of unusual remorse. For once he had genuinely repented his own actions. The rush of guilt and shame was still fresh in his mind, but already it was beginning to recede. Perhaps Innesq had exaggerated. Perhaps sickness and exhaustion had clouded his intellect, or maybe he had simply been mistaken.

Reaching his study, Aureste shut himself therein and commenced a tigerish pacing. His eyes, shadowed with sleeplessness and heavily bloodshot, reflected reddish glints. The accumulated fury, fear, and frustration of recent days burned along every nerve. A leisurely vivisection of Vinz Corvestri offered some hope of relief, but this solace was denied him. *For now.*

For now, he would seek distraction in labor. Seating himself at the plain, small table that now served as his desk, he attempted to fix his attention upon the catalog of domestic damages compiled by his brother Nalio.

Nalio had been so proud of his precious lists, and not without reason. Beyond doubt, the youngest Belandor brother displayed a true talent for minutely detailed clerical work. Such painstaking skills were needed in the world and deserved their credit. Accordingly, Aureste strove to apply himself, but the endless review of ruination failed to hold his attention.

Two faces filled his mind's eye—the only two that mattered. Innesq's, lately so alive with purpose, but now bluewhite and empty—perhaps forever. Beside it Jianna's, so nearly found, but now lost again—perhaps forever. The rage with which he habitually deflected fear and grief threatened eruption then, and he focused it all where it belonged—upon the soft-bellied form of Vinz Corvestri. With whom he was now required to cobble some sort of truce.

It was absurd. Corvestri was marked for death by slow torture. No truce was possible, now or ever.

But Innesq had insisted. *Make peace . . . Or all is lost,* he had declared, leaving little room for argument. Well, should he ever emerge, faculties intact, from this latest coma, then his wishes would be granted. Until that time Vinz Corvestri remained imprisoned, preferably in the darkest, coldest, rankest dungeon that the Witch had to offer. His miserable life was safe for the present. In the event of Innesq Belandor's death, however, Vinz Corvestri's stay of execution lapsed. Nor would his arcane skills save him, precious though they might be to the world and everyone in it. There would be no trial, no judicial delays and nonsense. Corvestri would die at length, in the manner of Onartino Belandor. And this time, Aureste would relish the spectacle.

The prospect was less consoling than he expected. Innesq's gasping whisper haunted him. *Adepts must gather. Work together as one . . . We need them.* The voice was not to be excluded, but might be disregarded, superseded by other matters. Aureste bent a blind gaze on the paperwork before him. In his imagination, he walked the Alzira Hills in search of Jianna. She was alive. He forced himself to believe it. He could see her face, he could almost hear her voice. She was out there. Somewhere.

· · ·

"We must put an end to the Governor Anzi Uffrigo," observed Celisse Rione calmly, as if stating the obvious, and her listeners eyed her in silence. "The Viper should have been removed years ago. We've been remiss, and it's time to correct our error."

Jianna wondered if the others shared her own amazement. Her gaze swept the circle of individuals seated on the logs positioned about one of the various small cookfires dotting the Ghostly encampment. Beside her sat Falaste Rione, his face visible to her in profile, his expression, if any, impossible to gauge. Next to him, was Trox Venezzu—youthful, scruffy, with a bowl of stew in his lap, his spoon suddenly stilled on its way to his mouth. Similarly motionless and watchful sat all of the others, with the exception of Poli Orso, leader of this rustic branch of the Faerlonnish resistance force, and master of the camp. Orso, an elder of the group at age thirty-two, was short and stocky of build, with a broad face, blunt features, unhurried countrified speech, and an expression of bovine serenity suggesting untroubled digestion. Anyone meeting him for the first time might have taken him for a slow-witted yokel. It had taken Jianna but a very brief term of residence, however, to recognize the respect that Poli Orso commanded among his followers, and to note the sharp intelligence lurking behind the dull façade.

Orso swallowed a mouthful of stew without haste, then replied tranquilly, "Not real, my girl. Fancies. Just like it was the last time you pushed for it."

"Things have changed," Celisse returned.

"Have they, now?"

"You know it. You know what the Taers did at Ironheart. The guilt lies with Uffrigo. His crimes can't go unpunished forever. It will destroy Faerlonnish spirit."

"So now you're talking for the whole population, eh?"

"Our friends, the allies of the resistance, were slaughtered without mercy." Celisse ignored the other's barb. "Torture was employed. The stronghouse was destroyed, and I'm told that the Magnifica Yvenza was forced to witness the murder of her two sons, then driven out of doors to shift for herself in the wild. The magnifica is one of the greatest and most generous allies that we have ever known. She's true to our cause, she has shared all her resources and offered our wounded the protection of her stronghouse for years. Now she's been violated and despoiled. Our debt to her is great, and it's time to pay. The magnifica must be avenged and supported; she's owed no less. I suggest that we send word to her, offering her refuge and a home among us." Turning confidently to her sibling, she observed, "Brother, I know you will agree. And surely you must serve as emissary to Yvenza Belandor. She'll listen to you."

Jianna's amazement sharpened to alarm. Potential disaster had materialized out of nowhere. One moment she had been peaceably spooning her stew, imagining herself secure; the next, she confronted utter ruin. Yvenza Belandor's arrival would instantaneously blast the persona of "Noro Penzia" out of existence. Falaste Rione's female assistant of vague origins would stand revealed as Jianna Belandor, daughter of the notorious Magnifico Aureste. Perhaps she would be lucky and they would only hold her for ransom. More likely they would kill her, and ship her remains home to Vitrisi in a bucket. Beyond question, Yvenza would urge them to it. She'd demand Falaste's blood as well; certainly she hated him now. She would see to it that every Ghost within sound of her voice learned that Falaste Rione had chosen to betray his great benefactress for the sake of Aureste Belandor's daughter. She would contrive to suggest that he had conspired with the Taerleezis, somehow personally engineering the downfall of Ironheart. She would limn him as a traitor in league with the enemies of Faerlonne, and by the time she finished, the Ghosts would be ready to rend their erstwhile beloved physician limb from limb.

Jianna felt the color drain from her cheeks—an alteration camouflaged by the shade of early evening, and the ruddy glow of the cookfire. She kept her face and hands still, but could not control the instinctive jump of her eyes back to Rione's profile.

Nothing revealing there; not the slightest hint of discomfort or guilt. His manner was easy, the soothing quality of his voice particularly apparent as he replied, "It's a generous thought that does you credit, sister, but the magnifica will never consent. She'd view the offer as charity, which she'd die rather than accept. She might even take offense. You know this. You know *her*."

"I do." Celisse reflected briefly, then replied, "I'll grant your point. She won't live with us, now or ever. But the other thing's a different matter. She'll want justice, in pursuit of which she'll accept our support gladly. And this *you* know."

"Ironheart is gone, along with the Taerleezi force that destroyed it. For the moment at least, the true culprits stand beyond reach of justice."

"The true culprit is the Taerleezi governor," Celisse informed him. "Not the easiest target in the world, but scarcely beyond reach. It is simply a matter of planning and preparation."

The words and sentiments were so much at variance with her girlish appearance that Jianna's wonder deepened.

"You hold one man personally responsible for all Taerleezi crimes?" Rione inquired politely.

"I'm not that simple. But he is foremost among the Taerleezis, the most visible, the embodiment of their authority. His destruction carries symbolic weight. It will demonstrate their vulnerability, and for that reason, among many others, it must be accomplished. It *shall* be accomplished. Our cause demands this."

Jianna regarded the siblings in turn. The facial similarity between the two of them was striking, and they shared certain traits of mind and character as well. Intelligence, obviously. Resolve, great energy, dedication, selflessness. But their differences were equally pronounced. Celisse possessed a certain icy inflexibility of will most unlike her brother's open-mindedness. It was also becoming apparent that she owned something else that he lacked—ruthlessness.

"Celisse, stop and consider consequences," Rione advised. "Should the Taerleezi governor fall prey to a homegrown assassin, Faerlonne will suffer vicious reprisals. I don't know how many of our people will die, nor yet how many more will lose all they own, to end destitute and facing starvation. Uffrigo is a swine, but the cost of his slaughter outweighs the value."

"Not so." Celisse's voice was crystalline music, her face sculpted in marble. "It is something that must be done, and no price is too high. Those who lose their property or their lives are martyrs to the cause of Faerlonnish freedom, and their sacrifice will never be forgotten. True patriots will pay the price gladly. Those who hold back, grudging the cost of liberty, are no friends or patriots, but creatures of the enemy, whose loss we need not mourn. Here there can be no argument."

"There can be plenty," Rione countered. "Difficult though it may be for you to believe, trust me when I tell you that a host of very good Faerlonnishmen would rather see their families safe than see the Governor Uffrigo dead."

"Good Faerlonnishmen place Faerlonne first. Fortunately for all of us, the decision doesn't belong to you."

"But I might have a word or two to say about it." Poli Orso reentered the conversation. "You paying attention, Celisse? Or have you grown too important to waste time listening?"

"I'm listening," Celisse returned expressionlessly.

"Then you should hearken to your brother, he's talking good sense. We'd all of us like to see the last of the Viper, but now's no time to make the move. Too many of our own folk would pay too dear for it. Patience. Our chance will come, never fear. Until that day, there's other matters to keep us busy."

"What other matters?" Celisse did not quite sneer. "We've sat idle in this glade for weeks. There have been no ventures, no accomplishments, no progress. This inactivity amounts to failure. It's a disgrace to us all."

"It's no disgrace that half our company's taken sick with the hot heaves."

"The sickness is falling off now. My brother will soon conquer it altogether."

"I hope so, but his work's not done yet. Use your head, girl. You want to stage a raid on the nearest Taer tax collector, with every other of our lads stopping along the way to spew? That what you want?"

"What I want," Celisse stated with chill clarity, "is to serve the cause of Faerlonnish freedom by any and all available means. What I do not want is to see that cause undermined by the weakness and timidity of irresolute men."

Jianna caught her breath. There was no discernible limit to this young woman's effrontery.

And it seemed that even Poli Orso's apparent placidity had its breaking point, for his eyebrows drew together into an uncharacteristic frown, and his voice was unwontedly sharp as he warned, "Enough of that. I'll not have morale ruined by a green girl with big ideas, a big mouth, and little common sense."

"I am no green girl, as all here well know. I've fought and more than earned my right to be heard." Celisse almost appeared pitying. "And I'm sorry that the truth offends you, Poli Orso. Perhaps if you were true to the cause, honest with yourself and with others, then you could hear the truth without flinching."

"Your truth is filtered through cheesecloth dyed the color of your own choosing." Orso shook his head. "And you don't even know it. But know this. You're a good girl with a brave heart, and everybody sees it. But that gives you no right to run folk down, stir things up, make trouble where nobody needs it. You're doing more harm than good. If it's so bad here, then maybe you'd best be off on your own, where you can have everything your own way."

"And if I should choose to leave," Celisse returned deliberately, "how many of our group would elect to follow me?"

"Why not ask 'em?" Orso invited. "Take a vote, if you're minded. The answer might teach you a good lesson."

"One of us would learn. But don't worry, Poli Orso—I won't weaken our force by splitting it. For now, I merely state a clear and indisputable fact—that it has become necessary to eliminate the Governor Uffrigo. I trust you will consider it." Straight-spined and ice-faced, she departed the firelit circle.

A low hum of uneasy conversation arose in her wake.

"Where's she going?" Jianna whispered.

Rione shrugged.

"Is she in trouble now?"

"No."

"She can talk to the commander that way? Without punishment?"

"The Ghost Army hardly maintains traditional military discipline," he replied in a low tone meant for her ears alone.

His smile warmed her more effectively than the fire, and there was no obvious reason for it. There was nothing so very extraordinary about his smile. It made her think of summer sunshine kindling life in a garden, but there was nothing remarkable in that. Nevertheless, she suspected that she would never tire of watching his expressions.

"She won't do anything—rash?" she inquired, less in true concern than in simple desire to hear more of his voice.

"There's little she can do. Orso spoke truly. These men won't follow Celisse's lead. She's respected, but she's young, female, and her zeal is accounted extreme, even among the Ghosts."

"She was right, though, when she said that you'll soon put an end to the sickness. The Ghosts will be back about their business in a matter of days, wouldn't you say?"

"Some of them, yes."

"And they'll want to change their campsite, won't they? They've tarried in this place too long as it is. They'll want to move?"

"As soon as they're fit to travel."

And then you can take me back to Vitrisi. She did not dare to speak the words aloud; it would somehow bring bad luck. He *would* take her back home—he had to. There was nobody else. She could hardly travel on her own through the Alzira Hills. Without a guide or protector, without money or a weapon, she would be picked off within hours if not minutes. Of the healthy and ambulatory Ghosts, none would take the time to escort her. She did not want any of them, anyway.

As for Falaste Rione himself, since the afternoon of his arrival, his attention and energy had focused exclusively upon the care and treatment of his patients. He would never dream of leaving those in need, and that sense of duty was one of his many attributes that she admired. She even shared it, to a certain degree.

Those sad invalids, with their fevers and chills, their agues, regurgitations, and bloody fluxes—not to mention their endless catalog of ordinary injuries and maladies, the fruit of their hardscrabble existence—they were surely to be pitied. And all of them were so appreciative of the care they received, so grateful for the smallest act of ordinary kindness. The thanks she had received for simply distributing dippers of water had brought the tears to her eyes more than once. No, she did not wish to abandon them, not so long as they truly needed her. More to the point, she did not wish to abandon Falaste Rione, so long as *he* needed her; or, honesty compelled her to admit to herself, so long as she was genuinely useful to him. Her indispensability was open to question, but her usefulness was indisputable.

And so she had changed dressings and cleansed open sores, mopped vomit and emptied bedpans throughout the recent days and nights, temporarily banishing thoughts of home and family. But it would end soon, as she had known that it must, and now she could afford to let her mind fly back to Vitrisi, with all its vitality, color, and meaning. Belandor House. Home. Family. *Father.* His grief on her account must be terrible, but very soon she would be with him again; he'd see that she was safe and well.

And then? Her expectations beyond the point of reunion were fuzzy, but they included living in Vitrisi for the rest of her life, and somehow or other Falaste Rione would be there too, perhaps as the Belandor family physician, like his father before him. Yes, that would do very well. But she would have to get him there first, and—given his devotion to the welfare of his patients—frustrating delays were inevitable, unless she could manufacture some compelling persuasion.

And then, quite abruptly, an amorphous uneasiness hovering about the edges of her mind solidified, and she did not need to manufacture anything. It was real and too immediate for comfort.

"I need to talk to you. Alone," she told Rione quietly.

He looked into her eyes and his brows rose. He nodded.

Rising, she walked away from the fire and he followed, both oblivious to the knowing smiles of their companions. When they were out of earshot of the others, they halted, and she turned to face him. They had reached a small stand of trees at the edge of the campsite. She could discern Rione's outline by starlight, but the night masked his face. The breeze carried the aroma of the Ghosts' stew pots, but her appetite had died.

"I'm worried," Jianna announced without preamble. "You remember, the night we fled Ironheart, you told me that we'd be safe from pursuit among the Ghosts. So far as that goes, you were right. When the news came that Ironheart had been destroyed, Yvenza dispossessed, and Onartino and Trecchio killed, I felt safe. I fancied that neither of us had anything more to fear—as if Yvenza were as dead and silent as her two sons. I wasn't thinking.

"But tonight, your sister opened my eyes. She spoke of bringing Yvenza here, and we both know what that would mean. You quickly shot arrows into that idea and I was relieved for a matter of seconds, until I realized that it doesn't matter that Yvenza isn't actually *here*. She's alive out there, she still has a voice, and she's certain to use it. She'll tell the world what you did for me, and she'll make it sound like a crime— your crime rather than her own—and people will believe her. I don't know how long it will take, but sooner or later the word will make its way to this camp. Even if the camp moves, the news will find it, one day. That's ruin for both of us."

"Yes. I've been wondering lately how much time we have left." His voice was unruffled as always.

"You never spoke of it. You meant to spare me the worry?"

"No need to speak of it. I knew that you'd see it for yourself, all too soon."

"It took me long enough. But now I know, and we both see that we can't stay here. It's time to go, time for you to take me back home to Vitrisi. Please, Falaste—I want to go home."

"I know. And so you shall, but we can't leave quite yet. Some of the boys are still too sick. They rely on us, there's no one else."

We, he had said. *Us.* It was music, but even so—

"Yvenza," she objected.

"No immediate threat, I believe. You don't know her as I do. The magnifica does not strike carelessly or at random. She'll wait for a strategic moment, and she'll want to be present, if possible, to witness the results."

"What a disaster that woman is!"

"Not entirely. But she can be very hard, and my betrayal has angered her deeply."

"You did nothing wrong, you only offered help where it was much needed. She's the criminal."

"The magnifica is unlikely to view the situation in that light," he replied drily. "I think it safe to assume at this point that I've supplanted you as the chief object of her wrath—a distinction I'd happily forgo."

"You may not need to." The words popped out of their own volition. Jianna was aware of some confused impulse to console him. He stood silently awaiting enlightenment, and there was no choice but to continue. "There's something that you don't know. Remember when Trox came with the news of Ironheart's destruction, and he spoke of a Faerlonnish presence among the Taerleezis? He even mentioned stories of a Faerlonnish commander. And I've heard those same stories repeated several times since then."

"So have I, but I haven't placed much faith in them."

"You should, though. They're true." Unconsciously she lowered her voice. "It was my father."

"Where have you heard this?"

"Nowhere. Nobody had to tell me. I knew."

"How?"

"Because I know my father. Throughout the days I spent at Ironheart, I always knew that he'd come for me. I was surprised and worried that it took him as long as it did, but I never doubted his will, and I was right. He was late, but he finally came. And he made them sorry."

"I know that was what you longed for night and day, but how likely is it? To begin with, how could he have known where to look for you?"

"He'd have found me, somehow. Perhaps Uncle Innesq helped. Uncle Innesq has the knack, you know."

"I've heard something to that effect. But even so—Ironheart was assaulted by Taerleezi troops, very well armed, even equipped with artillery. No Faerlonnishman could gain access to such resources—not even the Magnifico Belandor."

"He'd have found a way. Once he's set his course, nothing stops him. Perhaps he needed to spend a lot of money, but he'd have done that—for me."

"That last I believe."

"So you see, Yvenza will be so busy hating my father, and my father's daughter, that she won't have that much hatred left to spend on you. Unless I underestimate her supply."

"I reserve judgment. Still, if you're right, one detail of the account is clarified. We've heard that Onartino and Trecchio were tortured. If so, what information was sought? The Taerleezis had little to gain, but Aureste Belandor would have demanded the whereabouts of his daughter. There's an explanation."

"But not the right one. My father would never countenance the use of torture, not even upon such a pig as Onartino. He's a good man; it's not in him to do it." There was no answer, and Jianna was impelled to insist, "If it actually happened at all—and we don't really know that it did—then the Taerleezis were responsible. We've both seen their handiwork. I tell you, my father had nothing to do with it."

His silence continued and, for the first time, she felt doubt gnawing at her heart. Before she could analyze the unfamiliar sensation, he answered, rather slowly, as if choosing his words with care.

"You're right, we don't know exactly what happened. We hear these stories at second hand, and they're bound to contain distortion. Let's consider instead the matter at hand. We agree that it won't be safe for the two of us to remain in this place for very much longer."

"You've lost the friendship of Yvenza because of me, and now I'm about to compromise your position among the Ghosts as well. You've saved my life, and I repay you by destroying yours. How you must wish you'd never met me!"

"Stop driveling, woman. My decisions were entirely my own, and I regret none of them."

"You don't? Really?"

"I'll take you back to Vitrisi," he changed the subject calmly. "All the way to Belandor House itself."

"Oh, Falaste, thank you! I can hardly believe it! When can we go? Tomorrow morning? Early!"

"Slow down a little," he advised, and she could hear the smile in his voice. "Remember the sick lads. Let's give them a few more days. We can afford it, and they need it. When the contagion is fully contained, we'll go, I promise."

He had promised, and his word was gold. She was going home. The hope and happiness that filled her were almost frightening. Foolish tears prickled her eyes.

"A few more days," she agreed, and swallowed hard. But her gain represented his great loss, and he must surely feel it. Still driven by the urge to console or encourage him, she observed, "And you know, when we reach the city and my father hears all that you've done for me, he's going to be vastly indebted. He'll want to—" *Reward you,* were the words that popped into her head, but they struck the wrong note, turning her rescuer into a servant or hireling. "He'll want to demonstrate his gratitude. I do hope you'll allow him to do something for you. Really, he could do a great deal." *He could offer you a permanent position at Belandor House,* she elaborated mentally. *And he will, I promise.*

His reply astounded her.

"I won't meet the Magnifico Belandor."

"What? But of course you'll meet him. You must."

"That isn't possible."

"But he'll want you to," observed Jianna, as if this settled the matter. "And *I* want you to."

"No."

"I don't understand. Why will you not?"

"To seek out such a man as Aureste Belandor—to be received into his home, to exchange courtesies and pleasantries with him—would damage my standing in the eyes of the resistance beyond hope of recovery. Once I'm perceived as the magnifico's friend, guest, satellite, call it what you will—then their trust in me is destroyed, and that is something I don't wish to sacrifice."

"What kind of real trust is destroyed as easily as that?" Jianna demanded, scowling. "Are you saying that you can't exchange a single word with my father, can't even step over the threshold of our home, without fear of *contamination?*"

"Know that I don't mean to pain or offend you. But your father is a great enemy of the Faerlonnish resistance—"

"He isn't, he cares nothing at all about it! He just wants a pleasant, happy, comfortable life for himself and his family. Is that so wicked?"

"Depends on what he's willing to do to secure it, but that's a discussion for another day. For now, only understand this— when I leave you in Vitrisi, I must return to the Ghosts armed with some hope of finding a welcome among them."

"Leave—" It came like a sudden slap. Surprised and unnerved, she floundered in search of sound objection. "But I thought you just agreed that you can't stay here."

"*You* can't stay here, and we must see to your safety. But I can still make my peace, and I mean to do so."

"Can you, though? Will these paragons of moral purity pardon your crime of assisting Aureste Belandor's daughter?"

"I believe so. I'm of some use to them," he returned equably. "At least I hope so, for it's more than the plight of the Ghosts that draws me back. I must keep an eye on my young sister."

"You sound worried."

"You heard her just now. When she holds a strong conviction, it fills her completely, leaving room for nothing else. At such times, she knows no limit or restraint. There's nothing in the world that she wouldn't risk or sacrifice for the sake of her beliefs."

"But you said just now that there's little she can do."

"Little in terms of disrupting the camp or splitting the force, for the boys won't follow her. But she could take it into her head to attempt something on her own."

"Attempt what? She's only a young woman, without rank or noble kin, money or influence. What could she do on her own?"

"Destroy herself, I fear. I'm her older brother and her only family. It's my task to offer such guidance and protection as she can be persuaded to accept."

"I suspect she doesn't accept a great deal of either."

"You are right. But she does pay me the courtesy of listening, and sometimes she can be swayed, or simply calmed. She needs my influence now, I believe, and so my sojourn in Vitrisi will be brief."

Perhaps, thought Jianna.

"In the meantime," Rione mused, "I can only hope that nothing will happen to touch off one of her explosions."

• • •

It was high noon, but the streets of Vitrisi were dim and discolored, veiled in winter fog laced with heavy smoke. The smoke and the meaty odors that it carried were pervasive these days, masking the ordinary scents of the city, overwhelming the salt tang of the sea. Swelling the dark breath of the great funeral pyres that burned night and day was the smoke of innumerable incense burners and herbal fires employed to ward off the pestilence. The utility of these secondary blazes remained unproven, but their contribution to the general atmosphere was undeniable. Everywhere, the sharp prophylactic perfumes mingled uncomfortably with the airborne remnants of the dead.

The pungent miasma infiltrated every cranny and crevice of the city, from the twisted narrow lanes of the Spidery, to the respectably sedate parks and courtyards of the center, to the elevated mansions of the august Clouds, and then went even farther, pushing beyond the warehouses and taverns of the waterfront, out into the harbor to shroud the colossal figure of the Searcher, obscuring his bronze features and dimming the light of his great lantern. All Vitrisians, both human and other, seemed to bend beneath the atmosphere, whose weight and sad density lent them the insubstantiality of ghosts. Sound was likewise smothered beneath the charcoal pall. The rumble of wheels and the clop of hooves on cobbles, the sigh of the sea breezes, the tolling of bells, the clank of hammers on anvils, the crackle of fires great and small, the screeching of gulls and Scarlet Gluttons, the barking of dogs, and above all, the vocal babble of humanity—all was suppressed in volume and oddly remote. The air was harsh and cold, but riddled with unexpected pockets and puffs of warmth, carried from the insatiable pyres.

There was no escape from the smoke. Respecting neither power nor privilege, it pressed its weight against the walls and windows of the Cityheart itself, seeping in through invisible breaches to claim the stronghold of the Taerleezi conquerors as its own. The adjoining Plaza of Proclamation and its tributary avenues were likewise swathed in grey, their inhabitants veiled in deep anonymity.

And therefore, the eccentricity of two dim wavering figures

initially went unnoticed. They were similar in size, shape, and slightly hunchbacked posture. Their skulls were flat and hairless, their golden eyes prominent, their air sacs flaccid. Both were identically liveried in purple velvet heavily embellished with gold, these colors identifying them as property of the Governor Anzi Uffrigo's household.

The two Sishmindris were making their way across the plaza toward the Cityheart, their owner's residence. A commonplace sight; many liveried amphibians traversed the area at all hours of the day and night. This particular pair, however, were distinguished by their curiously unsteady gait. Both wobbled and staggered for all the world like drunken human beings. But they were not drunk. It had never been necessary to pass a law officially forbidding Sishmindris the pleasures of wine; no power in the world would induce the creatures to swallow alcohol.

On they pressed, stumbling, now clinging to one another for mutual support, great eyes vacant and seemingly blind. And still they attracted little attention, for the human world was frequently unseeing, until one of them faltered and fell. For a moment he lay motionless, then his limbs began to twitch and jerk, his head thrashed from side to side, and a spray of blue-green froth bubbled upon his lipless mouth. At sight of this, his companion raised a croaking outcry, easily recognizable even to those unfamiliar with the amphibian tongue as an expression of distress, and the interested citizens began to gather.

"Rabies," opined an onlooker.

"Or worse," came the ominous reply.

As if in confirmation of unspoken collective fear, the fallen Sishmindri began to tug at the purple velvet garments that seemed to be suffocating him. Presently he managed to tear them away, exposing a dry-skinned, feverish body marked with distinctively tri-lobed dusky carbuncles; the signature of the plague.

A gasping agitation stirred the circle of human witnesses,

for this evidence offered absolute proof of a truth long suspected but never before verified—that the amphibian Sishmindris were susceptible to the human disease. They could contract the plague and presumably spread it. There was an instinctive shrinking withdrawal from the potential source of contagion.

The glazed golden eyes of the standing Sishmindri roamed from face to frozen face as in search of aid. A fervent but unintelligible chain of syllables rasped out of him. He stretched forth a web-fingered hand, and the nearest humans backed away. Throwing back his flat-topped head, he loosed a delirious croak that rose to the level of a scream, then tottered and fell prone beside his companion. His body commenced to jerk.

For a long moment the staring citizens stood frozen. Action was called for, but dangerous, and nobody ventured to approach. Soon, however, some pragmatic individual found a way. There was a speeding blur of activity, a couple of sounds better unheard, then a cheap taped hilt protruding from a heaving greenish chest. Some decisive individual blessed with good aim had thrown a knife. Within the space of as many seconds, another half-dozen knives followed, and three of them hit their targets. The wounds appeared mortal, but the plaguey amphibians refused to die.

The supply of immediately available blades was exhausted, but there were other weapons to be had. The Plaza of Proclamation was kept indifferently clean, these days. Refuse and rubble lay strewn everywhere. Stones, brickbats, and broken bottles came readily to hand. In an instant, these missiles were pelting the Sishmindris.

The flying rocks did their work, and the doleful outcry subsided to a feeble croaking, inaudible above the fierce shouts of the citizens. The uproar drew the attention of the guards stationed at the nearest Cityheart entrance, and a pair of them approached to investigate. Thrusting their way to the center of the human clump, they caught the gang of Faerlonnish nationals vandalizing the governor's property, and drew their swords at once.

"Clear off, you lot," one of the Taerleezis bellowed, making himself audible above the din. "Out of here, or face charges."

Vociferous protest followed, but the overlapping, some-times incoherent attempts at justification fell on deaf ears. The Taerleezi guards saw only a pair of valuable Sishmindris, clothed in the livery of the governor's household, fallen victim to senseless Faerlonnish violence. The wretched creatures—glistening with blue-green fluid, cut, bruised, swollen, and maimed almost beyond recognition—still stirred feebly, but appeared unsalvageable. Even as the disgusted guards looked on, a rock flew from the crowd to strike a greenish head. The Sishmindri quivered and went still.

It was outright mutiny, and it had to be quelled. Turning to the nearest citizen, a stout and threadbare laborer, one of the guards dealt a sweeping backhanded blow to the face with the flat of his sword. The victim dropped to the pavement. He had not flung the most recent rock, but he was identifiable by his manifest poverty as Faerlonnish, and for the moment that was enough.

Protest roared; stones and bottles flew at Sishmindris and Taerleezis alike. One of the soldiers went down, bleeding from a head wound, at sight of which his companion thrust steel through the nearest set of Faerlonnish vitals, whose owner was young and female. At that instant the gathering of outraged citizens coalesced into a mob. A dark roar thundered through the Plaza of Proclamation, and set the Cityheart win-dows to rattling. A boiling human tide overwhelmed the two Taerleezi guards, and the pent rage of decades found murder-ous release. Moments later the guards at the Cityheart en-trance were likewise annihilated. Still seething, the tide flung itself against the heavy door, which was locked and barred.

For some minutes longer they remained there, some screaming threats and imprecations at the Taerleezi governor immured within, some flinging rocks and refuse. It ended when a sizable squadron of helmeted Taerleezi soldiers rounded the edge of the Cityheart and marched into the Plaza of Proclamation. The wiser among the Faerlonnish rioters immediately retired. The foolishly heroic stood their ground.

The Taerleezis issued neither warning nor command to disperse. Advancing smartly in close formation, they cut down all in their path. Attempted resistance was inexpert and ineffectual. Within moments, some ten or twelve Faerlonnish lay dead on the pavement. The rest fled for their lives.

It was not to be supposed that so flagrant an affront to Taerleezi authority would go unpunished. Two hours later Taerleezi troops in full battle regalia descended upon Rookery Grove, a neighborhood of modest homes and shops adjacent to the Plaza of Proclamation. Taken by surprise, the residents offered little opposition as the invaders burst in, taking tenement after tenement by storm, and herding male Faerlonnish above the age of ten out into the street, where all were systematically butchered and decapitated. Some two hundred bodies were left in the street for the locals to dispose of as they saw fit. The heads were mounted on poles and arrayed in neat rows at the southern end of the Plaza of Proclamation, to serve as a reminder to all.

TWO

The term "solitary confinement" was a misnomer, perhaps applied ironically. There was nothing in the least solitary about Vinz Corvestri's confinement. He shared his tiny space with a host of companions: some four-legged, some six-legged, some indeterminate of appendages, all of them unwelcome. He could hear them rustling and clicking, too near at hand. Sometimes their movement stirred the damp straw on which he lay, and sometimes they scampered or scuttled across his body, the tickling contact always causing him to jerk, no matter how often he felt it. Sometimes they stung, and then he hit at them. Usually they escaped, but when they didn't, and the small creatures exploded juicily against his skin, the sensation was worse than a sting.

He never saw them, however. He never saw much of anything, for the darkness was intense. Once upon a time, not so very long ago—or perhaps it had been long ago, it was impossible to judge the passage of time while buried alive—he had possessed the ability to draw upon the vast potential power of the epiatmosphere as a source of light, whenever he wanted. Or, when he preferred, he had been able to achieve a temporary capacity to see clearly without benefit of illumination. He could not do these things now, however. For uncountable days and nights he had been denied use of the powders, draughts, lozenges, and assorted inhalations upon whose properties he customarily relied for mental enhancement. And even had he enjoyed access to such substances, he could never have achieved the inner clarity and focus so essential to the practice of the arcane art; not here in this black hole of a dungeon, with its rats and its crawling things, its reeking atmosphere faintly tinged with smoke, its puddles, weeping walls, and its deep chill. Not here, where he was perpetually hungry and cold, often sleepless, and always afraid. In this place he was helpless as any ordinary prisoner.

He was not ordinary, however. He was a magnifico of Faerlonne, head of one of the Six Houses, and as such a personage of some consequence, even to his loutish Taerleezi captors. Or so he often told himself; and not without some reason, for what else could explain the clearly preferential treatment he had received? Despite his extreme wretchedness, he was fortunate by comparison with most others, for—unlike those anonymous fellow captives—he had not been tortured; at least, not technically. He had been subjected to countless miseries and humiliations. He had suffered through hours of threatening, abusive interrogation. He had been bullied, screamed at, reviled and mocked, deprived of sleep, slapped, shoved, spat upon and urinated upon—but he had never been whipped, beaten, or maimed. He was achingly hungry, but not literally starving; chilled to the bone, but not literally freezing. He had once been conducted to the prison's deepest levels, there to behold the instruments of torture—but those instruments had never touched his flesh. Bad as it was, it might have been far worse.

He wondered whether anyone had dared to intercede on his behalf; his family, perhaps. During the term of his incarceration he had received neither visitors nor messages from the outside world, and had expected none such to be permitted. Sitting there alone in the dark silence of his living tomb, however, he could not help but wonder whether he had not already been forgotten by all who once knew him. Perhaps he had received no greeting or word of encouragement because none had been sent. His wife, Sonnetia—would she spare so much as a moment's thought for him? Or had she quite dismissed him from her mind? Well, perhaps she had, but one thing was certain— young Vinzille would not. His son's affection was deep and true. On this point, if few others, Vinz was genuinely secure.

For a while he sat very still, head filled with recollections of the happy times he had shared with Vinzille in the workroom. But the miseries and terrors *would* worm their way back into his thoughts, despite all his efforts to bar them. His teeth would chatter, his hands shake, no matter how he tried to still them. And then all of it flew from his mind as the cell door opened and the light from the corridor burst in upon him.

The onslaught took him by surprise. He had heard no tap of approaching footsteps. The stone walls and heavy cell door muffled nearly all external sound, thus intensifying the prisoner's sense of utter isolation; by design, no doubt. The lantern light was moderate, but dazzling to Vinz's unaccustomed vision. He shut his eyes and turned his face away.

A thud of boots on the floor, and then their hands were on him, hauling him to his feet. He offered no resistance. Nor did he ask them where they were taking him. He already knew.

Out of the cell, along the damp corridor, and up a narrow flight of stairs they steered him, Vinz still blinking against the light, mute and passive in the hands of the two guards, the iron fetters that confined his ankles clanking with every short step. Another few feet, then they thrust him through a familiar door into a small, grim room.

The place was bare as always save for a table laden with notebooks, ledgers, and writing materials. At the table sat three men. Their names and titles were unknown to Vinz, but he recognized their faces, having confronted them often enough. The one on the left, with his long visage, long upper lip, and drooping eyelids, looked like a sleepy horse, but that appearance was misleading; he was very much awake. The one on the right— chubby, elderly, silver-haired, and pink-cheeked—might have been taken for a benevolent grandfather, but for his palely depthless, blind-looking stare. And the one in the middle— burly, black-thatched, and red-faced—glowered like some hard-drinking village bully. All three of them wore the shoulder sashes and brass insignia of minor Taerleezi officials.

Vinz knew what to expect, and the meeting held no surprises. The interrogation began, consisting of the same questions that he had heard and deflected so many times: Who were his accomplices among the criminals of the Faerlonnish resistance—what names could he supply? Who were the leaders—what names? What were the plans? What were the targets? Had the Magnifico Corvestri taken part in the attack upon the Palace Bonevvi, as the evidence clearly suggested? Could he identify his fellow culprits, thereby diminishing his own guilt? What about the attack upon the Oats Street Armory? The magnifico had been there, along with—who else? What names? What *NAMES*?

The voices hammered.

In earlier interviews he had striven to defend himself, answering all questions put to him at earnest length. He had been stalwart in his denials, composed and lucid in his explanations. He had even ventured to hope that his eloquence might favorably impress the interrogators.

Such hopes were vain. They had not troubled to contradict or refute him. Indeed, he might have thought them deaf, had not the horse-faced individual periodically shifted his somnolent gaze from the prisoner's face to the notebook on the table before him, wherein he scribbled the occasional observation. They had always permitted Vinz to speak uninterrupted. Then, when he was done, they had simply repeated their questions.

He had attempted to parry with questions of his own concerning the nature of the charges and evidence against him, but these drew no response. Thereafter he had lapsed into silence and apparent vacancy.

His silence in no wise discouraged the Taerleezis. Their queries and accusations flew like arrows, but presently a new string of syllables added itself to the bombardment: *Your silence, denying nothing, equates to a confession of guilt.*

In better times, the arrant injustice would have infuriated him. Now it hardly seemed to matter. He said nothing, and the threats proliferated along with the indignities, yet his skin remained whole, for the most part. The voices were beating at his ears, and he performed an internal operation that he had lately developed—mental removal. The discipline of a lifetime was not wholly lost, even here, and he achieved success with relative ease. The grim chamber and its noisy tenants faded from his consciousness, and he walked green meadows in the company of his son.

A sharp slap across the face recalled Vinz to confused reality. The hands of the guards were on him again, and they were not exactly hurting him, but they were busy, and it took him a moment to understand what they were doing. The sudden chill of the atmosphere upon his exposed flesh cleared his mind. They were tearing his garments away, using the points of their daggers where the fabric refused to yield. Within seconds they stripped him bare of all save iron fetters, and one of the interrogators was intoning piously: *Decency is a privilege that you have failed to earn.* Then someone threw a bucket of cold water over him, and the guards were guffawing.

This latest humiliation was indifferently effective. Vinz was conscious of physical discomfort underscoring dull misery. He seemed to have lost the capacity to feel much else. Apparently the Taerleezis recognized his present imperviousness, for the interview concluded abruptly, and the guards removed him.

Down again to the lower level of the prison known as the Witch. Back into his tomb of a cell. The door clanged shut, and the darkness swallowed him.

He sat very still, eyes wide in the dark. Soon he started to shiver. That, in addition to the chattering of his teeth, recalled him to a sense of his own damp nudity. He was very cold, but unhurt, and once again he wondered at the comparative restraint of his captors. But then, he reminded himself, they had no real need of a confession to justify his conviction and execution. That packet of letters they had discovered in his home on the evening of his arrest furnished all the proof the law required.

He had never been allowed to see those letters, and could only speculate as to their contents; just as he speculated endlessly as to their origin. Beyond doubt they were forgeries, planted in his study by some enemy bent upon his ruin. An enemy enjoying access to Corvestri Mansion, probably by way of a servant or Sishmindri. The suspicions scuttled through the dark of his mind as the rats and insects scuttled through the dark of his cell, but always sought the same recurring conviction. The woman Brivvia, who had been spied entering and leaving Belandor House more than once; the woman who was personal maid to his wife.

He thought about his wife now. It seemed he could not stop himself from thinking of her. The Magnifica Sonnetia, with her beautiful, fine-boned face that he could not read. Sonnetia, with her perfect composure, perfect manner, and perfect deportment covering . . . he knew not what. Sonnetia, with the mind and heart he could not fathom. Had she dispatched her maid to Belandor House?

His shivering intensified, but that was natural enough. His naked flesh was still wet, and it was very cold in his cell.

• • •

"This has continued too long. You must wake up now. It's your duty, and you are needed. Wake," Aureste commanded.

There was no response. Innesq lay still in his bed, unconscious, unreachable as ever, neither dead nor truly alive. Unlike those around him, he suffered nothing of fear or grief. Aureste resisted the impulse to drive his fist into the peaceful white face. But he needed to drive it somewhere. His dark eyes, burning within their deep sockets, lifted from the bed to the form of the nearest victim.

"You have failed," he observed, with a sensation almost approaching pleasure.

"No," replied the Sishmindri called Zirriz.

"No? My brother is awake, then? He's conscious and mentally whole? Somehow I failed to observe it."

"More time. Find magic dust. Then good."

"You've had time enough. What did I tell you would happen if you failed? Well? Do you remember?"

A deep tremor rippled the amphibian's facial muscles.

"I see that you do. Speak, then. What did I promise?"

"Hunger and death."

"You have earned both."

No reply. The Sishmindri simply stared at him, eyes goldenly blank, and Aureste's ire heated. Zirriz did not beg or bargain. Offering neither excuse nor self-justification, he simply awaited his doom with the quiet impassivity of his kind. There was no satisfaction to be had from him. The threatened execution was largely bluster—a healthy, well-trained Sishmindri was simply too valuable to kill outright. But there were lesser punishments perhaps affording a certain measure of enjoyment.

A braided leather whip armed with a cluster of lead pellets at the tip lay coiled on the chair beside the bed. Aureste had absently dropped it there some twenty-four hours earlier, in unconscious anticipation of this very moment. The whip seemed magically to leap to his hand. He plied the lash with vigor, and the lead pellets ripped a long gash across Zirriz's brow.

The Sishmindri instinctively threw a protective arm across his eyes. A vicious rain of blows tore his livery to shreds and beat him to the floor, where he crouched in shuddering silence.

And still no satisfaction. The creature refused to cry out. His blue-green blood was streaming from dozens of crisscrossing cuts, he was swaying upon the verge of collapse, but no sound escaped him.

Some demon stirred to life in Aureste's brain then, a deadly resolve to break his victim, increasing the speed and force of his blows. The lash was now tearing long strips of greenish flesh from Zirriz's back, no doubt marring him forever and considerably reducing his value on the open market, but the Magnifico Aureste was beyond caring. For a time, his awareness of his surroundings all but lapsed. And then came a sound refreshing as springtime rain—a muted croak of agony—followed by Zirriz's collapse into unconsciousness.

The world resumed reality. His chest heaved and his arm ached. The Sishmindri lay motionless in a blue-green pool at his feet. He did not know whether the amphibian still lived, and for the moment did not care. A sense of weary disgust filled him and he tossed the whip aside. Then, with reluctance, almost as if afraid of what he might confront, he turned his eyes to the bed.

He *was* afraid, Aureste realized. For reasons best known to himself, Innesq Belandor valued and esteemed the Sishmindris. To see one of his favorites so savagely abused would shock, grieve, and offend him. He would disapprove; he might even withhold forgiveness.

That last possibility was insupportable.

He might have spared himself the worry. His brother lay comatose as ever, and disappointment twinged across Aureste's mind. Some part of him below the level of consciousness had hoped that a violent outrage, an assault upon his deepest sensibilities, might blast Innesq from slumber. But violence was as useless as pleas, commands, and exhortation.

He had seriously damaged or destroyed a costly piece of property, to no purpose. Zirriz lay motionless as Innesq, a silent embodiment of reproach.

Aureste yanked the bellpull and a Sishmindri answered the summons promptly. Another male, clothed in livery, and—but for the brown mottling upon the skin of his pate—a near double of Zirriz. He did not recall the creature's name and did not want to know it.

"Remove him," Aureste commanded, pointing at the fallen amphibian. "Tend to him if he is still alive, dispose of the remains if he is not. Call such assistance as you require, but get him out of here."

There was no answer. The Sishmindri was staring at the limp form on the floor, and his great eyes were full of something that few humans knew how to read.

"Well, do you understand me?"

"Yes."

"Then look to it." Aureste exited the chamber, stalking swiftly through the north wing corridors to the sanctuary of his makeshift study, where he seated himself at the worktable with a sigh. His body, mind, and spirits all seemed iron-weighted. A draught or three of strong spirits might have lightened the load, or at least distanced it, but he resisted the impulse. What if Innesq awoke, to find his brother—distanced? Better by far to lose himself in work.

The binder containing Nalio's lists of destruction lay on the table before him. He opened it and tried to apply himself, but the catalog of ruined rugs, burnt bedding, and shattered chandeliers soon sent his mind wandering along uncharted paths. He was a little uncomfortable with himself, he realized; an unaccustomed sensation. Inappropriate as well, for he had every right in the world to beat his own Sishmindri, and Zirriz had deserved a good hiding or worse. He had failed his master, after all.

A light tap on the closed door broke his reverie.

"Come," he commanded, and another Sishmindri appeared. Female, this time. Empty-faced, like all of them, but something in the hunch of her shoulders made him wonder if she knew yet what had happened minutes earlier in Innesq's chamber.

Of course she knew. By this time every Sishmindri in the house knew. So much the better, the lesson would make better servants of them.

"Woman here," the Sishmindri announced.

Brivvia again, he supposed. His brows drew together. He had no further use for her at present, and if she thought to extract additional payment from him, she was sadly mistaken. It was on the tip of his tongue to order her ejection, but then he decided to deal with her personally. He would make short work of Brivvia.

"Admit her," he ordered.

The Sishmindri bowed and withdrew. A moment later a cloaked and hooded woman stepped into the room.

She had been making good use of the money she'd had from him, was his first thought. She had exchanged her cloak of dreary grey-brown frieze for a much better garment of fine wool, colored the almost black-green of pine boughs at twilight. The change suited her, even seemed to lend her extra height and grace.

She pushed her hood back to reveal rich chestnut hair, *not Brivvia,* then his breath caught as she turned to confront him squarely and he looked into a face he had not viewed at close range in half a lifetime.

"Sonnetia?" he murmured, half doubting his own vision.

"Magnifico. It is good of you to receive me, uninvited and unannounced," Sonnetia Corvestri returned very correctly, as if seeking refuge in formality.

Her voice was a little lower in pitch than he remembered, but still melodic. The hair was a little deeper in color, as if the bright streaks once painted by the sun had darkened with the years. And her face—it had lost something of its youthful softness, the bones were more prominent and the mouth firmer—but it was surprisingly unaltered. Something stirred inside him at the sight of it, a kind of wonder that he thought had fled his mind years ago. For a moment astonishment paralyzed his usually ready tongue and he sat staring at her.

"I should like a word with you, if it is convenient," Sonnetia prompted quietly.

"Ah, forgive me, Magnifica." His trance broke and he rose to his feet. "You've taken me altogether by surprise, and I neglect courtesy. Pray be seated. May I offer you refreshment?"

"Nothing, thank you." Choosing the chair nearest his worktable, she seated herself, her back very straight.

He resumed his own seat, his thoughts in disarray. What in the world could have induced her to step over his threshold? Was she really as calm as she appeared, or was her heart beating as quickly as his own? How could she still be so beautiful, after so many years? Aloud, he inquired simply, "How may I serve you, madam?"

"I know that my visit must be as unwelcome as it is unexpected, but I ask you to listen to me with an open mind. It's to your own advantage, as well as mine, that you do so."

"Your visit is not unwelcome, and I'll listen willingly."

"Good. Then I'll not waste your time with preliminaries. You know that my husband has been arrested?"

"All the city knows it."

"He lies in the Witch, charged with . . . many things. The sum of all is that the Taerleezi authorities believe him to be deeply involved in resistance activities."

"While you, his wife, believe him innocent."

"The question of his true guilt or innocence doesn't greatly concern me. He's my husband and the father of my son. I want him freed, and the charges against him dropped."

"No doubt all of his friends and family share your sentiments."

"Not to the same degree. The future of my son hinges upon his father's fate. You've a child of your own. I believe you understand me."

"Your concern for your son, yes. Magnifica, accept my sympathies."

"It isn't your sympathies that I've come for. I want your assistance."

"You speak very plainly."

"I urge you to do the same."

"As you wish. Plainly then, I am honored to assist you. You've only to name the sum."

"Sum?"

"The Magnifico Corvestri's absence imposes hardship upon your household. That is a great misfortune. Neither you nor your son shall want, however. You may rely upon me to safeguard your security and comfort."

"What collateral would you demand, Magnifico?"

"Nothing beyond your goodwill, madam."

"This liberality exceeds measure," she returned drily. "Happily, I am not obliged to exploit your generosity. I've no need of your money."

"What can I offer, then?"

"Influence. You've the ear of the governor. Use your influence on my husband's behalf. Liberate him."

Aureste studied her. Clearly she had failed to identify him as the author of her husband's ruin. Nor was she aware of the part that Vinz Corvestri had played in the attack upon Belandor House, else she would never have come to him with such a fantastic request. Even so, could she truly imagine for one instant that he would lift a finger to assist his own enemy? Had decades of connubial ennui dulled her once keen wits?

Assuming an expression of benevolent regret, he replied, "I fear you greatly overrate my importance. It's true that my business dealings with the Taerleezis lend me a certain utilitarian value. The governor is civil enough, because it's worth his while to be so. But my influence with him is nil, and my words carry no more weight than those of any other Faerlonnishman."

"I do not believe that."

"Ah, Magnifica." He permitted himself a rueful smile. "I know how the world speaks of me, but you mustn't credit all that you hear. I am only another member of an oppressed population—rather more fortunate than some, yet essentially dust beneath the Taerleezi heel."

"Never. We once knew each other well, Magnifico. Perhaps you have forgotten, but I have not. Many years have passed, but I don't think that you've changed at all. The Aureste Belandor I once knew could and would have overcome all obstacles to achieve any goal, once he perceived the reason for it."

"What reason could possibly exceed my sincere desire to oblige you?"

"Oh, I think we can do rather better than that. Tell me, is it not true that your younger brother Innesq Belandor has lain gravely ill for some days now?"

"Where did you hear that?"

"Where does one hear anything? Is it also true that Innesq's malady is arcane in origin?"

"I'm no judge of such things." His mind raced. Her point was already clear to him.

"No physician has been able to cure him, no treatment has restored him?"

"Not yet, but it's only a matter of time."

"Well, then. For your brother's sake, will you not cut that time short?"

They exchanged glances of pure understanding. Nothing more needed to be said, and he recalled that few spoken words had ever really been necessary between the two of them, but he wished to prolong the interview, and therefore he invited, "You have reason to believe that your husband—?"

"An arcanist of the first rank. One of the finest in all Faerlonne, as even you must grant. Altogether capable of addressing arcane ills—I can attest to this. And quite probably the best hope open to your brother."

"You personally pledge the best skills and efforts of Vinz Corvestri?"

"In exchange for his freedom and safety, yes."

"What exactly do you expect me to do?"

"Succeed, Magnifico. Only that. On the day that my husband walks out of prison, he'll present himself at your door."

Her husband was unlikely to walk out of prison on his own two legs. More likely, he would have to be carried. And after that, he would need a long period of recuperation before he was fit to apply his arcane talents to any project, great or small. The thing was impractical. Aureste's flash of interest began to wane. Aloud, he observed solicitously, "The Magnifico Corvestri will no doubt wish to rest and refresh himself at length before attempting arcane exertion."

"That won't be necessary. You are thinking that he's been brutalized, unnerved, perhaps injured in prison, and thus rendered useless to you. Not so."

"You seem certain. You've seen for yourself?"

"No, they've permitted him no visitors."

Not a tear in her eye, not the smallest sign of distress. Aureste observed her detachment with distinct satisfaction.

"But I can be sure that he's suffered no extreme mistreatment, as I've taken steps to spare him the worst of it."

"Steps?" Aureste encouraged, fascinated by her coolness and ready comprehension.

"Large sums of money, properly distributed, protect my husband, up to a point."

"That would be the best way, but I didn't realize that you possessed the means."

"I had the Steffa jewels. I showed them to you once, long ago. You probably don't remember."

"Of course I do. I recall a remarkably fine sapphire-and-diamond necklace. There were bracelets, several rings, brooches, shoulder stars, knee sparklers, a tiara—all very old, very splendid. You sold them?"

She nodded.

"They were family heirlooms, were they not? Prized property of House Steffa through many generations?"

"Very many, and we managed to hold them through the wars and after, until they came to me by direct descent. I had thought to bequeath them someday to one of my male cousins, thus restoring them to Steffa hands, where they belonged. But circumstances dictated otherwise, and now they're gone. It was necessary."

She spoke with her customary composure. A stranger would have thought her perfectly unmoved. To Aureste, her regret was obvious and poignant. Whereupon he found himself seized with an impulse worthy of some moonstruck adolescent, to track down the Steffa jewels, purchase them at any price, and return them to her on a golden charger. It was more than her dolt of a husband could possibly give her.

"So you see, both your brother and my husband stand to

benefit. It's best for all." Sonnetia paused in expectation of a reply. There was none, and she added, "I hope you agree."

"I do agree." The words came hard. Every particle of him longed to consign Vinz Corvestri to the rack and heated pincers. "I can't promise success, but I'll do all in my power to assist your husband."

"Then he is as good as free, and your brother will soon be well. I believe we understand one another."

We always did. Aureste inclined his head.

"Magnifico, I thank you for your time and attention. You have been generous with both." Sonnetia rose from her chair.

Aureste stood at once. She was about to leave, and for a moment he vigorously cast about for some means of holding her, but there was none. Their business was concluded—presumably for life. Once she walked out of the room, he would probably never exchange another word with her. He wanted to plant himself squarely athwart her path, blocking her exit. Instead he declared courteously, "I will see you to your carriage."

"Thank you, no. I came on foot and alone. Best by far that my visit goes unnoted."

"As you wish. Farewell, then. I've enjoyed speaking with you again, however briefly. Permit me to observe, Magnifica, that the years have scarcely touched you. You are remarkably unchanged."

"You have not observed closely." A slight smile touched her lips and then she was over the threshold, out of the room, and the door had closed behind her.

Gone again. And carrying with her his promise to rescue her damnable husband. He would keep that promise, for his brother's sake. But then—when Innesq was well and strong again—perhaps it would not be too late to readdress the matter of Vinz Corvestri's punishment. And it was not likely that Sonnetia Corvestri possessed a second set of heirloom jewels to sacrifice in her husband's defense.

What a woman she was, and what a wife. Far too fine for Vinz Corvestri. Who would not enjoy his undeserved good fortune for very much longer—but that was a happy thought for the future. For the moment, Corvestri was reprieved, and the mechanics of his removal from prison had yet to be designed. *I want him freed, and the charges against him dropped,* Sonnetia had specified, which precluded a simple escape and flight. Corvestri's name had to be cleared. *For the present.* Not the easiest task, but hardly impossible.

Aureste commenced pacing to and fro. The strongest evidence against the prisoner—in fact, the only real evidence, provided the craven hadn't been terrorized into some sort of confession—resided in the forged documents, planted in his home, discovered by the Taerleezi guards, and currently reposing within a padlocked chamber deep in the heart of the Witch prison. Without them there was no remotely reasonable case, even by Taerleezi standards, against Vinz Corvestri. Those documents had to vanish.

How to reach them? Aureste's strides lengthened. The schemes popped like small powder charges in the fire of his mind. A simple matter, really. No need of arcane wonders, gymnastic miracles, or mathematically precise planning. It was merely a question of petty bribery. A few coins in the pocket of a hungry turnkey or a corrupt official, and the thing was done. And he knew several thoroughly corrupt officials . . . Presently, a pungent odor blurred his cogitations. He became aware that it had been with him for some time, but it took another moment to identify the source.

A spattering of viscous fluid moistened the edge of his right sleeve. He inhaled deeply and his nostrils flared in distaste. He was wet with Sishmindri blood, fresh from Zirriz's wounds. The stains were nearly invisible against the dark quilted fabric of his doublet, and yet he could not help but wonder whether Sonnetia Corvestri had noticed them.

THREE

It was a bitter winter's day, but the denizens of that rancid section of Vitrisi known as the Spidery did not have to suffer the cold. Not that many of them could afford the price of fuel to heat their rented rooms or squatters' dens, but this year there was no need to purchase wood or coal. This year, the city provided plenty of warmth at no cost.

At the western edge of the Spidery yawned the Pits, ancient quarry and site of major disposal. Throughout the centuries of Vitrisi's life, the Pits had swallowed huge quantities of waste. The deep natural limestone craters seemed limitless in their capacity; no offering had ever truly taxed them. This year, however, matters had changed. This year, the largest public pyre in the city burned at the bottom of one of the shallower excavations.

The fires blazed incessantly, by necessity. There were so many bodies. So many victims of the plague, such huge quantities of meat, fat, fabric, and bone. So much matter to consume, and such great stores of fuel required. The spectacle was grim and the stench troubling, but the audience was always large. The men, women, and children of the Spidery huddled day and night about the public pyre. Some had even constructed tiny makeshift shelters or pitched small tents about the perimeter.

All present knew the dangers of smoke-borne contagion, and all were willing to accept the risk for the sake of the delicious warmth.

Throughout the morning, the day's business proceeded normally. A mule-drawn cart laden with corpses arrived at the customary hour. The Deadpickers—odd figures in their masks, gauntlets, and protectively padded garments—disembarked to lead their reluctant team along the steep rocky path that circled its gradual way down to the floor of the excavation.

By this time, the fire was burning low. The Deadpickers took advantage of the lull to heap their cargo onto the pyre in layers of corpses alternating with layers of straw, oily rags, and kindling. This done, they grabbed faggots and logs lying at the bottom of the wagon and tossed them onto the blaze, which roared into renewed life. The drain upon local and civic resources required to maintain these perpetual fires was vast—a matter never considered by shivery Spidery denizens. Someday, perhaps in the near future, the supplies of timber, coal, and peat were bound to fail. But it had not happened yet and, for the present, the locals basked.

The flames cavorted, the corpses blackened, the Deadpickers prepared to depart. All followed the usual pattern, as the Vitrisians had learned to expect. And then came an unwelcome innovation.

One of the corpses lying at the top of the heap sat up slowly. Several spectators screamed. Those nearest the pyre milled in confusion, torn between the urge to assist a hapless victim prematurely consigned to the flames, and the natural fear of fire and pestilence.

The individual, whose gender was impossible to judge, presented a shocking spectacle. His or her hair was gone, facial features lost, digits charred to bony sticks, winding sheet ruddy with fire. He or she was clearly beyond help, and it could only be hoped that a swift death would cut the wretch's agonies short.

But death seemed unwilling to oblige. As the citizens watched in mounting terror, the object of attention swung his or her legs carefully out to the side and then, like a child at play, slid down the human heap. Straight through the roaring flames he or she bumped and bounced, with never a cry of pain. At the bottom the barely human figure hauled itself laboriously upright, to stand hesitating among the fiery logs.

For the moment, the wonder of the spectators superseded alarm, and they watched in paralyzed silence.

The ruined individual turned what had once been its face and eyes this way and that. After a moment, it lurched from the fire to advance upon the crowd. Small flames danced along its shoulders and licked the remnants of its winding sheet. Fine flakes of blackened skin and fabric drifted from its limbs in miniature storm clouds. The citizens retreated. Many turned and sprinted for the path. Among those remaining, fresh screams broke forth as a second corpse sat up amid the flames. This one was identifiably female, with streaming grey hair frizzled by the heat, and sober garments half burned away, but otherwise almost intact. As she slid down from the summit of the pyre, then stood to follow in the halting footsteps of her predecessor, it could be seen that only the whites of her eyes showed beneath her drooping lids. Her jaw hung slack, and the cast of her face was distinctly blue. Her inclusion in the pickers' cargo had been no mistake. She was unmistakably dead, or perhaps more properly termed undead. Such was the expression used in the accounts of the worst of all plagues, the pestilence of legend known as the "walking death."

The tales were so ancient, so shrouded in myth and superstition, so rife with exaggeration and impossibility that many contemporary rationalists had simply dismissed them. The skepticism had persisted through weeks of rumor, speculation, and increasingly frequent claims of undead sightings. The present spectacle dictated reconsideration, however. And if it was true that the dead plague victims could rise and walk, then other aspects of the old stories might also be true. The apparent intent of the undead to spread disease, for example— perhaps a reality. The stubborn animation of the corpses, proof against almost any damage short of utter dissolution— perhaps true. And then, those unsettling stories of silent, shared understanding among the walkers—perhaps even they, too, contained some truth.

When a third smoking remnant dragged itself from the

pyre, the courage of the witnesses failed and nearly all fled the scene. Only a handful of the coolest ascended to the rim of the excavation and there remained to watch at a safe remove.

For a time, the three undead stumbled about in apparent aimlessness, their steps wavering and uncertain. But soon their mastery of their bodies increased and their movements acquired assurance. When they could walk without faltering, the three turned as one and made for the path. Though their pace lagged, their aspect was oddly purposeful.

The alarm of the spectators deepened. Laying hands on the limestone fragments strewn throughout the vicinity, several citizens commenced a bombardment. Rocks rained down on the undead, briefly retarding their progress. One sizable chunk struck the head of the grey-haired woman, smashing her to the ground. For a moment she lay as if truly dead at last. Then her skinny arms lifted to shove the rock aside, and she rose to her full height. Her skull had been crushed, reducing most of her head and all of her face to pulp, but these injuries hardly impaired her. Her eyes were gone, but she seemed to experience no difficulty in finding her way, as she followed in the wake of her smoldering companions.

At this, the nerve of the lingering citizens broke, and all retreated. The undead appeared unconscious of human activity. Silent, unhurried, inscrutable, the three of them made their unopposed way up the path. Upon reaching the summit, they paused at the edge of the pit as if in voiceless conference. For long moments they stood motionless as mundane corpses. Then, ruled by shared or simultaneous impulse, they resumed walking. They were headed east, toward the heart of the teeming Spidery. Their pace was steady and their intent, if any, a mystery.

· · ·

Vinz Corvestri did not understand how it came about, and deliverance took him quite by surprise. When his cell door squealed open and the guards marched in to unlock his fetters and present him with a set of fresh garments that he dimly recognized as his own, he knew that he was not about to face another routine interrogation. His first thought was that they had come to drag him off to execution, and he went limp with fear. But the law, even Taerleezi law, granted him a trial of some sort, and there had been none. Not that it would have been anything more than an empty formality at best, but it would at least have given him time to prepare, time to assume a dignified demeanor.

No room for dignity now, not with hands shaking so badly that he could hardly manage the fastenings of his own clothes. He dressed himself at last, under the guards' unblinking regard. Then they were trundling him out of the cell, along the corridor, up the short flight of stairs, at the top of which they steered him left; not right toward the interrogation chamber that he knew, but left. Toward the scaffold? His steps faltered then, and he might have fallen had not the grip of the guards held him upright.

"Don't look so green, Magnifico," one of them advised with undisguised amusement. "You're the lucky one today."

Lucky one? What did the ruffian mean by that? Not trusting his own voice, Vinz raised his brows in mute and miserable inquiry.

"You're going home," the guard informed him.

Home. The pang that shot through him was almost painful. For an instant wild hope flamed, before he realized that they were mocking him, and then a rush of desperate anger restored his courage. He replied with an obscenity that set both guards roaring with laughter.

"He don't believe it," one of them observed.

"Would *you* believe it?" countered the other.

"Nah, but then, I don't have big friends."

"Choice friends. Don't it make your mouth water?"

What are you talking about? Vinz wanted to shout at them. He controlled the urge, and finally they came to a place that he remembered. It was a chamber of moderate size, its walls lined with shelves loaded with ledgers, its central space occupied by a big desk, a chair, and a manifestly indifferent individual. Here he had been conducted upon the evening of his arrival, here his name and the date of his arrest had been entered into one of the ledgers by this same bored Taerleezi, who had then consigned him to a cell, whose number had also been entered. And now the process seemed to be reversing itself.

"Name?" the officer inquired without interest.

Vinz furnished the required information, and the other jotted it down neatly. Several perfunctory questions followed until the prisoner, unable to contain his bewilderment, finally blurted out, "What does this mean?"

"Don't you understand?" The officer appeared mildly surprised. "You're being released."

"No, no I don't understand. What of the charges against me?"

The officer consulted one of his notebooks without haste, then reported, "Dropped."

"Dropped? How? Why?"

"Lack of evidence, it says. No case."

"But—I'd been told there was strong evidence. Written evidence. I was never allowed to see it, but—"

"No evidence. If it ever existed, it's gone now."

"Gone where? How?"

"Who knows? Mislaid, pinched, or accidentally discarded, maybe. Looks like you're one lucky little Faerlonnishman with some good friends out there, eh?"

Good friends? The Taerleezi seemed to imply that somebody had exerted some sort of influence on his behalf. It must have been Lousewort and his allies of the resistance. Somehow they had broken in and stolen the incriminating documents. He would not have believed them capable of penetrating the Witch itself, but they must have succeeded, for who else could it have been? Unless, by some unlikely chance, the "accidental" loss of the evidence really *had* been an accident.

The formalities were swiftly completed, whereupon Vinz was conducted from the building, across the grim walled courtyard, to a small side gate through which he was neatly ejected. The gate banged shut behind him.

It was morning, but hardly seemed so, for the air was very dark with fog and smoke, cold and harsh with winter's chill. The glow of the rooflights overhead scarcely reached ground level. The streets were wakeful, but still relatively quiet. Lanterns glowed behind a few shuttered windows. The wagon vendors were setting out their wares, but the customers were not yet much in evidence. A beggar asleep in a nearby doorway had not yet been chased from his refuge, and the night's ice on the nearest public trough had yet to be broken.

Vinz gazed about, still mystified, and stunned by the suddenness of it all. He breathed free air and enjoyed free movement for the first time in—how long? He did not know. The days and nights had blurred in the bowels of the Witch. The actual number did not matter; his term had seemed endless. But it was over now, and he found himself at a loss. Where to go, what to do, now that he could go anywhere, do anything?

Home, certainly. But Corvestri Mansion stood halfway across the city, and he—a titled magnifico, head of a House of the Six—had no money to hire so much as a donkey to carry him. The master of House Corvestri would have to walk.

He turned north toward the Clouds, to encounter a blessedly familiar object: his own mildly battered carriage, emblazoned with the Corvestri arms, drawn by a pair of respectable bays. And there in the box sat his own slightly untidy coachman, waiting to carry him home. Foolish tears scalded his eyes at the sight. He dashed them away and approached. The coachman greeted him with appropriate respect, the first he had received in too long. The door opened. He climbed in and seated himself beside his wife.

He made no attempt to kiss or embrace her. He had not bathed or shaved in days. No doubt he was repulsive, despite the clean clothing, and he did not wish to disgust her. Probably this was a wise choice, for she herself never offered to touch him, but welcomed him with courtesy as soft, cool, and impenetrable as the fog.

The carriage moved off amid grinding rumbles. Vinz studied his wife at length. He had not viewed her by morning light in a long time, and the present cold grey illumination revealed the slight sharpening of her features, and the dwindling luminosity of her fine skin. It would be easy, so easy, for an arcanist and magnifico of Vitrisi to find a younger, fresher female, glowing with gratitude and admiration. Someone to appreciate him, someone to see him as he deserved to be seen.

He scarcely found himself tempted. There was only one woman whose opinion mattered.

He asked her for news of Corvestri Mansion, and she answered at length. Some minutes passed before he could bring himself to voice the questions of greatest significance. But at last he asked about Vinzille, and learned that the boy did not yet know of his father's release. She had not told him, Sonnetia explained quietly, for fear of disappointing his expectations in the event of . . . mishap.

So she had not been quite certain of his liberation. The question hung in the air. He could no longer delay asking it.

"How was my release obtained, madam?" Vinz inquired.

She told him, and her answer exceeded his worst imaginings. The Corvestri carriage clattered on through the streets of Vitrisi, and Vinz learned that his wife had sued for assistance to none other than the Magnifico Aureste Belandor. Apparently she had marched straight into Belandor House, confronted the beast in his lair, and somehow obtained a promise of aid; by what persuasive means, Vinz did not dare to consider. She had not known exactly how the Magnifico Aureste would deliver her husband, but she had never doubted for one moment that he would find a way.

Your faith in him is touching. Vinz suppressed the sarcasm with difficulty. The thought of his wife alone in the presence of Aureste Belandor jabbed like a scorpion's sting. He did his best to push the image away, for he needed to listen. She was still talking, and he soon received the answer to the most sinister of unspoken questions: the nature and extent of Aureste's price.

She had pledged her husband's arcane skills in payment for his freedom. Vinz was now obliged to present himself at Belandor House, *this very day,* there to effect the awakening of the mysteriously comatose Innesq Belandor.

Well. It might have been worse. The task lay within his power, probably. But still—he wondered whether Sonnetia or Aureste appreciated the irony of the situation. Surely neither recognized him as the author of Innesq Belandor's misfortunes. Or perhaps—the disturbing thought came unbidden—Aureste simply found it expedient to grant his enemy a temporary reprieve.

In due course they reached Corvestri Mansion, where his reunion with his son banished all other considerations, for a time. And then for a hot bath, and a big hot meal, and after that luxurious hours of dreamless sleep upon a soft mattress; the first sound sleep he had enjoyed in many a day.

He woke in the late afternoon. He lay in his generous bed, in his comfortably warm chamber. The linens were fresh, the blankets dense, and a respectable heap of coals glowed on the grate. He himself was clean, well fed, safe at home, and free. For a few drowsy moments, Vinz luxuriated in the unaccustomed sense of well-being. Something gnawed at the edges of his satisfaction, however, some recollection that he wanted to exclude.

It ate its way into his conscious mind all too quickly. His present contentment came at a price, and payment had now fallen due. He was expected to present himself at Belandor House, there to revive Innesq Belandor, this very day.

As a matter of debt and honor, the thing could scarcely be postponed, much less denied. Accordingly he forced himself from the bed, dressed without assistance, then rang to order the carriage, only to learn that the vehicle stood ready and waiting at the door, by order of the magnifica.

At times her efficiency was almost too commendable.

A small, bitter draught fortified him against the impending arcane exertion. It had been weeks since he had last tasted such a preparation, and its effects were potent. A pleasurable current swept his mind and body, while his internal vision sharpened a hundredfold. His spirits lifted. He almost felt like himself again.

With a firm step, he made his way to the waiting carriage. He took his seat, the door latch clicked, the driver's whip snapped, and he was on his way.

There was no real need to use the carriage. Corvestri Mansion and Belandor House stood within brief walking distance of one another. But the Magnifico Corvestri could hardly come trudging up his detested neighbor's drive on foot. Dignity—indeed, self-respect—demanded some suitable display of status. And so he was carried the short distance that he had walked secretly and alone the night of the assault upon Belandor House.

The memories of that night came back to him now, despite his efforts to evade them; the sights, sounds, and smells, the heat of the fire, his own terror and sickness. Disturbing, repellent memories. The last thing he wanted was a return to the scene of that nightmare, yet here he was, rushing toward it like some helpless swimmer caught in a current and heading straight for the rocks—an image too sadly emblematic of his entire life.

The journey was brief. The gracefully fashioned steel gates guarding Belandor property swung wide, and the Corvestri carriage clattered on toward the house. Vinz knew what to expect. He had heard and compared a dozen accounts of the fire damage. Even so, he had never seen for himself, and the image of Belandor House as it had always been—tall, imposing, magnificent—still held sway in his mind. He found himself curiously shocked to confront the reality of a blackened ruin. His first disbelieving impression was that of utter devastation. The tower crowning the central section had collapsed, and the roofless south wing looked worse yet. Great heaps of debris, some shrouded in oiled tarpaulins, rose here and there like exotic burial mounds. Surely Belandor House was ruined beyond hope of repair. Curiously mingled satisfaction and shame filled him.

The carriage followed the curve of the sooty drive, past the boarded-up wreck of the main entrance, to the north wing of the building, where it halted before a doorway seemingly free of damage. The north wing as a whole stood essentially intact, its visible wounds confined to broken windows, shattered rooflights, and dark smoke stains. He disembarked, advanced, passed a sentry unchallenged, and was admitted by a Sishmindri faultlessly liveried in the Belandor slate and silver. Evidently the family continued to maintain itself in some semblance of state.

He stood once again within Belandor House, in a gallery hung with smoke-sullied paintings. Light filtered in through cracked, dimmed windows. Almost unbelievable that he should find himself here again.

"I announce you, Magnifico." The Sishmindri bowed and retired.

Announce him? To whom? Was he about to confront Aureste Belandor, in the flesh? Despite the fortifying draught, uneasiness stirred his innards. And it was ridiculous, really, when every possible victory and advantage lay on his own side. He, after all, possessed trained arcane talent, a priceless commodity for whose sake his enemies had been forced to secure his release from prison. He was the husband of Sonnetia Steffa and the father of Sonnetia's son. He was the master of a great mansion—a bit shabby these days, but infinitely superior to the maimed remains of Belandor House. By most reasonable standards of comparison between the two Faerlonnish magnificos, Vinz Corvestri emerged as the clear victor.

But still, he did not want to face Aureste, who somehow wielded an undeserved power to intimidate. And what if his host insisted upon witnessing the arcane procedures? The thought of those pitchy malevolent Belandor eyes boring into him was intolerable. Despite all his skill and experience, he would never be able to perform under such circumstances. He might insist upon his need for privacy, but what if Aureste refused to comply?

As it happened, his concerns were groundless. Footsteps tapped, and he turned to face a dark-clad figure descending the stair. Not Aureste—too short, too rickety, face and hair too thin, but a Belandor unmistakably, with the family eyes and facial structure on a meager scale. This was the youngest brother, Nalio, perennially lost in the shadow of his siblings. And the unremittingly black garb? Vinz remembered hearing that the junior Belandor brother's wife had died during the attack—killed by fire or sword, it wasn't clear which. Presumably her husband mourned her. Guilt flickered about the edges of Vinz's mind. In a way, this was almost worse than facing Aureste.

"Magnifico, I bid you welcome," Nalio Belandor intoned, civilly but without warmth, much as he might be expected to greet the hereditary enemy of his House. His enunciation was excessively precise, his voice nasal and unimpressive as the rest of him. Clearly he suspected nothing of the visitor's involvement in the ruin of his home and the murder of his wife.

"I thank you." Vinz's assurance returned with a rush. He could deal with this person. His back straightened and his chin came up. He dared to speak with a hint of condescension. "I am informed that Master Innesq Belandor's plight is desperate. No mundane method suffices to restore him."

"That is so, Magnifico."

"Conduct me to him."

"This way."

Up the stairs and along a corridor to a chamber furnished with a big carven bed wherein reposed a very still figure.

"Leave me alone with him," Vinz commanded.

Nalio Belandor stared at him. Doubt and distrust narrowed the big eyes in the thin face. Vinz returned the gaze serenely.

"As you wish." Nalio inclined his head and compressed his lips. Evidently he had been instructed to defer to the visitor— upon this occasion, at least. "Should you require assistance of any kind, do—do—do not hesitate to ring."

"I thank you." Vinz waited. After a moment, the other turned and exited with obvious reluctance. The door clapped shut.

Approaching the bed, Vinz stared down into the waxen face of Innesq Belandor. Very like his older brother, Aureste, although inspection revealed the differences. Pity that it *wasn't* Aureste lying helpless in that bed. Pity that the stroke aimed at the magnifico had missed its target and caught a harmless innocent.

Harmless? Hardly. Here was an arcanist of dangerous talent, his abilities perhaps exceeding Vinz's own. And innocent? He was a Belandor, and they were all made of the same stuff. His resemblance to Aureste was scarcely coincidental. Even so, Vinz could not quite still the pangs of conscience. He had never heard anything but good report of Innesq Belandor. Moreover, he could not seem to forget the expression in Innesq's eyes at the moment the two of them had faced each other on the night of the attack—that look of calm, fearless comprehension. He could see it now.

Compunction gnawed. Deliberately he shut himself off from it. No time for distracting qualms. Right now, he needed to delve into the exact nature of Innesq Belandor's condition.

Rest and nourishment had served him well. The discipline of a lifetime came to the fore, and his mind cleared. His mundane surroundings fell away, his perceptions altered, and—for the first time in eons, it seemed—the inner light dawned, and he touched the power of the Source. The sensation, following long deprivation, was almost too glorious. Deep joy threatened to rock his concentration.

His skill and talent were still with him. When he rested light fingertips upon the unconscious man's brow and sent his intellect questing, the origin of Innesq's affliction revealed itself at once. Profound depletion, a dangerous drainage of strength and energy. Nothing more. Until that moment, Vinz had not known what to expect, for the effects of the arcane anomaly—*impossibility*—that he had precipitated on the night of the attack were incalculable. Anything or everything unimaginable might have befallen his victim. The problem that he confronted, however, was soluble.

The technique at his command enabled him to replenish Innesq, but the procedure was taxing and the long effort left him shaky. Legs suddenly weak, Vinz sank into the wheeled chair that stood beside the bed. His attention remained fixed on Innesq's face, white as the linen pillowcase, closed eyes shadowed in charcoal, no apparent change. Yet a change had occurred, something he detected by means of enhanced perceptions rather than physical senses. He recognized the invisible stirring of renewed life, and was therefore unsurprised when the other's eyes opened.

"Magnifico Corvestri," observed Innesq. His voice was faint but tolerably clear. His eyes were likewise clear: awake, aware, and filled with intelligence.

Vinz started. Skill and experience notwithstanding, he had not anticipated quite such a swift and complete recovery of intellect. Moreover, Innesq's expression was unnerving. He felt exposed beneath that serene regard, and it came to him then that Innesq must have seen straight through the mask to recognize him on the night of the attack—that Innesq knew everything. He wanted to bolt from the room, but instead sat as if paralyzed.

"We must put it behind us," Innesq whispered.

There could be no mistaking his meaning. Yes, he knew, all right. Vinz had not foreseen it, could scarcely believe it. He had blundered, but it was not too late to correct his error. A flex of his practiced mind could return Innesq Belandor to the comatose depths, and this time permanently. He drew a deep preparatory breath.

"Make our peace. Work together. The Six." The voice was feeble, but infinitely resolved.

"The Six?" Vinz stared.

"It's time. You see it."

Yes, Vinz realized. *Yes.* He did see it, but had never until this moment faced it squarely. For weeks—no, months—he had told himself that the moment had not yet arrived. The situation demanded investigation, analysis, consideration. Careful planning. Communication among all parties involved, exchange of ideas, consensus; in short, plenty of reassuring delay. But somewhere deep inside, he had known better, and with one simple remark, the man just awakened from a coma had dragged it out into the light.

"Reversal of the Source approaches," Vinz agreed.

"It is all but upon us. We cannot wait. We must call upon the others."

"Communication among the Six has generally lapsed."

"We shall renew it."

"The ban upon arcane practice has affected Faerlonnish technique. We have lost something of our skill."

"Not all of us. In any event, two of the Houses are Taerleezi, unaffected by the ban. Among the lot of us, we shall find expertise enough."

"How many of us remain, though? House Orlazzu is all but extinct. House Steffa is virtually dormant at present. My son Vinzille combines the best of Steffa and Corvestri, but he is only a boy. There are the two of us. Houses Pridisso and Zovaccio, on Taerleez, may perhaps furnish some talent. Apart from that, who is left?"

"There is a second promising Belandor adept we might enlist. As for House Orlazzu, I am not altogether certain. And there are possibilities beyond the Six."

"What, the lowborn incompetents, the pretenders, the tinsel-and-fustian magicians of the city? The cleansing of the

Source requires the combined talents of six accomplished adepts, and I fear they're not to be found."

"The presence of six is traditional, but perhaps not essential. We may make do with fewer." Innesq sat up in bed. "Whatever the task demands, we shall secure."

His voice was still weak, but he spoke with such absolute conviction that Vinz's courage and optimism stirred in response, along with dawning admiration. Maybe it was true, maybe it *could* be done. When Innesq Belandor spoke, it was remarkably easy to believe. But a short time ago, he had done his best to kill this man, missing only by reason of improbable—*impossible*—circumstance. Now he found himself blessing his own failure.

"I shall send word to my young kinswoman in the Alzira Hills this very day," Innesq declared. "She will be frightened and in need of some reassurance."

"It is too soon," Vinz told him. "You must rest and recover your strength."

"There is no time for that, I have lost too much time already. There are sustaining draughts in my workroom—ah, but I remember, the workroom has been destroyed."

A revealing flush warmed Vinz's face. Eyes downcast, he remarked, "You are welcome to use mine. You may regard it as your own." There was no reply, and he looked up to find Innesq's eyes fixed upon him. Once again there was understanding, but no accusation in those eyes, which seemed to see straight through to his center.

"I accept with thanks." Innesq stretched forth his arm. "Come, Magnifico. Will you not shake my hand? We are allies now."

Vinz clasped the proffered member gladly. A burden seemed to drop from his shoulders.

FOUR

"Allies? Have you taken leave of your senses?" demanded the Magnifico Aureste.

"My head is tolerably clear, I believe," returned Innesq Belandor.

"The evidence suggests otherwise. Let us forget for the moment that the little rodent's a Corvestri. For now, I'll overlook it."

"Generous."

"Harder to overlook is the role he played in the destruction of our home. It couldn't have been accomplished without him, and the guilt is largely his. Or have you forgotten that detail?"

"No more than I have forgotten the murder of poor Unexia and the servants. They were great crimes, it is true. But we must pardon them now."

"Pardon? That's pretty poetry."

"It is a necessity."

Muted morning light struggled in through the cracked windows of the north wing demi-council chamber, lately pressed into service as a dining hall. The two brothers sat at table, finishing their breakfast. Attired in his customary sober robes, and upright in his wheeled chair, Innesq ate with good appetite. His face, while still pale, had lost the deathly waxen hue. His eyes were alight at the bottom of shadowy sockets, and his voice was quiet but resonant. Only the slight languor of his gestures betrayed unacknowledged weakness.

Once again, disaster had been averted. Aureste's relief and pleasure were genuine, but did not embrace full pardon of the true culprit. Now that Innesq was safe, Vinz Corvestri's reprieve had lapsed.

"I see by your expression that you do not agree," Innesq observed. "But I tell you again that personal hatred is an indulgence that none of us can afford. We of the Six must pool our resources, else all of us are lost. For an instant, not long ago, you seemed to believe me, but now you have settled back into comfortable skepticism."

"Not so. Indeed, I do believe you. But Corvestri has dealt us a deep wound—nearly fatal to you—and the thought of some obligatory alliance with him and his House disgusts me."

"You must make up your mind to endure it, at least for a while. But come, it needn't be such a trial. You'll see little if anything of the Magnifico Corvestri during the next few days. The Distant Exchange whereby we send word to our counterparts of the Six will be performed within Corvestri Mansion. The magnifico has offered me full use of his workroom."

"After destroying yours. But truly, you can't mean to set foot in Corvestri Mansion."

"Wheels, in my case."

"The thing's impossible."

"The thing, as you put it, is essential. Understand clearly, once and for all. There is no time left for family feuds, tribal squabbling, personal rivalries, or other such pointless distractions. When the danger is past, those concerned may resume the games, should they so desire, but not before then. I am relying upon your good sense to support and assist me in this. If you cannot or will not, then I must proceed without you."

Aureste examined his brother, whose fragile appearance, gentle manner, and calm good humor concealed a will at least as strong as his own. He himself was acknowledged head of the family, but Innesq was the undisputed premier arcanist of House Belandor. In all matters arcane, Innesq ruled.

"I'll always support and assist you." Aureste's eyes dropped under the other's regard. To disguise his discomfiture, he continued, "But I must wonder if you don't overtax yourself. Surely it's too soon for exertion. You aren't strong enough."

"I was not strong enough yesterday," Innesq admitted, "as I discovered when I attempted to leave my bed. But now I have had a good night's sleep, a solid breakfast, and I am perfectly well. I am expected at Corvestri Mansion, and it is time for me to go."

"Go?" *Incredible*. "Pardon me, but how long is it since you have—gone—anywhere?"

"I can hardly say. But I am going now."

"Well. If you are truly set on this, then take the state carriage, it will best accommodate your chair. And at least two or three bodyguards, fit to deal with Corvestri treachery."

"A Sishmindri to assist with my chair will more than suffice. Zirriz is one of the strongest and ablest, but he does not seem to be available. When I ask for him, I am told only that he is 'gone,' which, among the Sishmindris, may mean physically absent, mentally deranged, dead, or spiritually diseased. I have not ventured to demand specifics, because—as you may know—the Sishmindris regard direct inquiry into such matters as intrusive. Do you know where Zirriz is?"

"Why, no." Aureste offered a faint, puzzled frown. "But if he's gone missing, then he must be found and brought home at once. Vitrisi is no safe place for a stray Sishmindri, these days."

"It never was, but what do you mean?"

"While you slept, there have been killings. It began in the Plaza of Proclamation, where a pair of Sishmindris belonging to the governor's household were attacked and slaughtered by the rabble, along with a few Taerleezi guards."

"There can be only one reason. The poor wretches must have contracted the plague."

"You've hit it. Those creatures carry and spread the disease. The governor avenged the destruction of his property—the massacre in Rookery Grove was designed to quell Faerlonnish enthusiasm—but all that it really accomplished was to drive the panic-stricken into the shadows. Since Rookery Grove, the public fears have fastened upon the Sishmindris, who are now turning up dead all over town. I don't know how many have been killed, but this I do know—there are plenty of Vitrisians fully in favor of wholesale extermination. If our poor Zirriz is wandering about out there, we'd do well to find him—for his own sake."

"And ours."

"True, his disappearance represents considerable financial loss." Aureste's tone of regret was perfectly sincere.

"That is not what I mean. The Sishmindris do not lack intelligence or strength. They submit to slavery perforce, but it is possible to push them too far."

"And then?"

"And then we might find ourselves confronting a true revolt."

"Splendid. Perhaps they might rally the horses and donkeys to a Pan-Bestial cause."

"You persist in underestimating these beings. I can only hope that you will not find yourself too rudely disillusioned one day."

"And if I do, I trust you'll be there to intercede on my behalf."

"I would try," Innesq returned mildly.

Shortly thereafter, to the wonder of all, Innesq Belandor departed his ancestral home. Attended only by a single Sishmindri, he traveled by carriage the short distance to his destination. His wheeled chair was unloaded, he was assisted into it, and then, for the first time in human memory, a Belandor crossed the threshold of Corvestri Mansion.

Vinz Corvestri was there to greet him, together with the adolescent son, Vinzille, the one described by his father as combining the best of Steffa and Corvestri. Certainly a promising youngster, weedy but well favored, with intelligence and curiosity lighting his greenish eyes.

The two of them conducted him by an obscure route to a workroom at least as fine as his own lost haven, and unmistakably older. This space had served the arcanists of House Corvestri throughout the generations, and the echo of their ambitions still rang through the atmosphere. Some of those past adepts almost seemed to speak aloud.

They seated themselves at the table, the boy including himself as if by habit, the father offering no objection. Preparations were quickly completed, and the Distant Exchange commenced. Young Vinzille's mind was immature and his technique unsophisticated, yet his talent was marked and his contribution noticeably enhanced the sending. Within moments the message was winging toward arcanists far and wide.

. . .

Grix Orlazzu came down into a rock-strewn hollow between hills, and there he stopped dead. For a moment he hardly knew what had halted him. Uneasiness, even suspicion, prickled along his nerves, and there was no obvious cause. His questing gaze traveled an ordinary misty vista. Then his mind recognized the subtle pressure of importunate intelligence seeking entry, and at once he raised barriers against the Other.

Moments passed. The pressure continued, and something of the visitor's quality managed to impress itself upon his consciousness. This call was almost comfortably familiar in nature. It came not from the Other, but from human minds much like his own. The minds of arcanists, linked and working together.

Instinct coupled with curiosity almost served to admit them. Then he caught the flavor of the message—an intimation of impending disaster, a plea for assistance.

Not difficult to guess the reason. These arcanists knew what was coming. They meant to cleanse the Source, and they wanted Grix Orlazzu's assistance.

They wouldn't get it.

He scarcely pitied the human tyrants of the world, whose greed and cruelty had wrought calamity everywhere. Surely they had earned their punishment.

Many of them, but not all.

And those who had not? The myriad blameless?

No concern of his. He did not wish them ill, but he was not obligated to help or defend them.

They would thrive or perish without him.

The shaky mental barriers reinforced themselves in an instant. The arcane call ricocheted off into the fog.

Grix Orlazzu resumed his trek.

．．．

The smell of sizzling bacon might have restored appetite to a corpse. In a certain sense, that was the function it was meant to perform. The hour was late for breakfast and early for the midday meal, but time did not matter when addressing the quirks of a ruined body and mind.

The sullen morning light of winter filtered down through the mists veiling the Alzira Hills, down through the bare-branched trees of the woods to touch the mouth of the little cave scooped into the base of the overhang shadowing the stream. A cookfire burned there, and beside it knelt Yvenza Belandor, frying the fragrant rashers. She wore her customary plain dark gown, beneath a winter cloak. Her hair was neatly ordered, her aspect purposeful. All in all, she appeared unchanged by loss or privation. Behind her, all but invisible in the shadows of the entry, Nissi sat cross-legged and motionless, luminous regard fixed on the fire.

Off to the side, in the midst of what passed for daylight, back pressed flat to the chilly support of the overhang, sat a still and broken figure. His large body was stingily covered in garments too small for him—breeches too short, doublet too narrow in the shoulders, too small in the chest, too short in the arms. But these items, former property of his murdered brother, Trecchio, were the sole garments available to a penniless outcast in the depths of the woods. They had been roughly altered to offer workable accommodation—both sleeves of the doublet slashed along their seams to allow passage of the bulky bandages protecting the left arm and the torn fingers of both hands; the breeches likewise sliced to pass smoothly over the battered feet. An assortment of additional injuries—burns, bruises, cuts, and worse—concealed themselves beneath the ill-fitting clothes. But the bandages wrapping the wounds that dented the beaten skull were whitely apparent. And nothing at all softened the wreck of the face— the lacerated lips folding oddly over a toothless gap, the smashed nose scarcely functional, and above all, the livid flesh surrounding the black pit of the burnt-out right eye. The remaining eye—the color of slush shot with blood—stared vacantly off into the mists.

The bacon was adequately crisp. Removing the strips from the skillet, Yvenza piled them onto a trencher, added a round of hard biscuit, and placed the meal before her son.

"Eat," she commanded.

He appeared unaware of her presence.

"I know that you hear and understand me. Do as you're told."

The cyclopean eye did not blink.

"You know the consequences of disobedience, boy. How many times must we repeat this sorry scene?"

A stranger observing the exchange would have thought Onartino Belandor deaf.

"As you wish, then." Grasping his jaw with one hand, she used the other to cram a rasher forcibly into his mouth.

Onartino offered no resistance. After a blank moment's delay he chewed and swallowed as if unaware. Another two rashers followed, then Yvenza paused.

"Now then. Pick up the next one yourself." She waited. Onartino neither stirred nor glanced in her direction. "Don't pretend you can't, we both know better. Do it."

He did not comply. Breaking off a fragment of the biscuit,

Yvenza stuffed it into his mouth. He chewed and swallowed. She inserted another morsel, and he ate it.

"You're like some worm that's been stepped on, boy. Where's your courage, where's your will? You were never strong on intellect, but at least you had some courage, or so I fondly imagined."

She grabbed his jaw. This time his mouth clamped. She slapped his face, heedless of the assorted injuries, and his one eye blinked. Her hand went to his broken nose and pinched the nostrils shut. His mouth opened and two bacon strips went into it. He chewed and swallowed both.

"Now show me what you're made of. Make an effort. Feed yourself."

He sat, good eye staring straight ahead.

Yvenza's lips assumed a contemptuous curve. Without further comment, she hand-fed him the rest of his meal, all of which he accepted passively. When the trencher was empty, she set it aside, rose to her feet, and extended her hand.

"Get up," she commanded. "Lean on me if you must, but move. Now."

Onartino appeared oblivious as ever.

"You've done it before. Now do it again. The white little girl called you back from the antechamber of death. I'll own that she did even more than that, for you've progressed further and much faster in recovery than would have been possible without arcane support. But you must do your part. You must work to recover your strength. You *shall* work, else find yourself some means of livelihood, perhaps one involving a tin cup. For I'll not have a crippled weakling on my hands." Evidently expecting no reply, Yvenza stooped, grasped her son's left arm and slid it over her shoulders, slipped her own right arm around him, and exerted force.

He sat inert, neither resisting nor cooperating. Powerful though she was, Yvenza's initial effort to lift him failed. Her eyes went to the still little figure seated just within the mouth of the cave.

"You—Nissi—come here. Lend a hand," she commanded.

The seated figure remained motionless. Nissi's eyes never strayed from the fire. In the dimness of the cave, her lips might have been moving, but no sound emerged.

Yvenza breathed a muffled imprecation. Tensing all her muscles, she exerted her strength and managed to raise her son to his feet.

He grunted. The quality of his breathing changed.

"You will walk," she decreed. She strode forward, drawing him along with her, partly by force, partly by willpower. He took a few uncertain, shuffling steps, and his grunt lengthened to a suppressed groan.

"Yes, I know, your feet hurt. You hurt all over. But that doesn't matter, it's nothing," Yvenza advised him. "It will subside as your strength returns. Now walk."

Leaning heavily on his mother's shoulder, Onartino took a short, slow step. Then another, after which he halted, gurgling for breath.

"Walk on," Yvenza directed. Shifting the grip of her left hand from his left wrist down to the bandaged digits lately bereft of fingernails, she squeezed hard. "Go."

A faint choking sound came out of him, and he resumed his shuffling progress. To and fro along the bank of the stream she steered him, until his increasing wobble convinced her that he had reached his true limit, whereupon she returned him to his former place on the ground beneath the overhang.

"Rest now. In an hour or so, you'll walk again," she informed him. "Soon your strength will return, and then you'll be fit to hunt the man who did this to you. D'you understand me, boy?"

She expected no reply, and was therefore taken by surprise when her son's swollen lips moved, and he spoke for the first time since the night of his interrogation.

"Hunt." The voice was unrecognizable; feeble and hoarse, enunciation altered by swelling, cuts, and loss of teeth.

"What's that you say?"

"Girl."

"What, his daughter, you mean? That's done; she doesn't matter now."

"Mine."

"Forget about that. It's the father we want. It always was, and now more so than ever before. Aureste Belandor is your quarry."

"Girl. Mine."

"Try to contain your stupidity. Work on strengthening your mind along with your body."

Onartino made no reply. His brief spate of loquacity exhausted, he relapsed into his former stuporous state; nor could all his mother's verbal prodding rouse him again. Presently she gave up trying. Her critical attention shifted to the cookfire, and thence to the depleted woodpile.

"You—Nissi," Yvenza addressed the still little figure in the shadows. "We need more fuel. See to it."

There was no reply. Nissi was unresponsive as Onartino, without his excuse of brain injury. Yvenza's lips thinned. A few long strides carried her to the mouth of the cave.

"I said we need fuel."

Nissi did not hear her. Absorbed in her unfathomable fancies, she was patently unaware. Her great pale eyes were fixed on the fire as if she saw meaning there. Her lips were moving.

Yvenza bent low to catch the words.

"I understand," Nissi whispered.

Yvenza's hand advanced as if to grasp the young girl's shoulder; hesitated, and drew back.

"I . . . do not know," Nissi told the fire.

Yvenza's eyes narrowed. She listened closely. Understanding dawned, and her expression altered.

"Perhaps. If . . . I can . . ."

There were two or three additional remarks, the barely breathed syllables unintelligible. Then Nissi exhaled deeply, bowed her head, and let her eyes close.

Yvenza allowed her to rest for a moment, then tapped her

wrist sharply, but not in a manner calculated to cause pain. The luminous eyes opened wide.

"Who was it?" Yvenza demanded.

"The nice one," Nissi confessed, caught and frozen in the other's gaze.

"Nice? Has he or she a name?"

"I have caught the echo of the name *Belandor* in his thoughts."

"Ah. *Ah*. You've engaged in arcane communion with an adept of our House?"

"We are not beneath the roof of Ironheart." The words were almost inaudible. Nissi's small hands began to shake.

"You needn't fear, child. I am not angry," Yvenza assured her. "Matters have changed. Look at me. No, don't stare down at the ground, look into my face, and hear me. The service you performed for Onartino proved once and for all that the true talent is in you. You belong to House Belandor, and it is folly to deny it any longer. When I watched you just now speaking by arcane means to someone far away, I finally perceived the nature of your gift, and recognized its potential as a matchless weapon. I've been shortsighted in the past, but that's over. From now on, you are free to develop and strengthen your talent. Be assured that I can think of endless uses for it."

"Free?"

"To practice and learn, yes. Now, tell me—the Belandor arcanist you've communed with—would that be a brother of Aureste's?"

"I . . . do not know."

Yvenza scrutinized the young face, and nodded. "Very well. Is this Belandor in Vitrisi?"

"He is in a wondrous city by the sea."

"Vitrisi."

"In a ruined palace. The great and beautiful house has burned. Angry, frightened people . . . did it. His workroom is gone. He is sad."

"He told you all that?"

"No. It was . . . around the edges."

"What was in the middle, then? What did he say?" The other appeared uncomprehending, and Yvenza's tone sharpened. "Come, I'll permit you to practice, but you must give back, you must contribute. Again, what did this Belandor adept tell you?"

"He said . . . said that we must gather to stop . . . the . . . terrible thing."

"What terrible thing?"

"I do not know."

"Don't make me ask you again."

"I did not understand. When I have sensed it, I have looked away. It was too big, I could not see all of it. It was a . . . change."

"Change in what?"

"Everything. All the world. All . . ."

"What sort of change?"

"Everything . . . goes back to the way it was, once upon a time. And it is no longer our world. We do not belong, there is no place for us, in these islands. And later, no place anywhere, he thinks."

"He doesn't know?"

"He fears, but speaks little to those around him. He is not sure, and does not wish to cause alarm and suffering. This is also . . . around the edges."

"What else was in the middle?"

"He said that the people like us must come together and work . . . as one . . . to stop the terrible thing from happening. He asked me to come. I told him that I am . . . not good enough, not strong . . . but he did not believe it. He asks me to come, he says that I am . . . needed." Nissi whispered the last word with an air of incredulity.

"Aureste's brother. I remember. Aureste set great store by that middle brother. One of his few weaknesses," Yvenza mused. "What did the arcanist tell you of this 'coming to-gether'? When and where?"

"As soon as may be. At 'the Quivers,' he told me. It is a high place, I saw, but . . . I do not know where."

"I do. Don't worry, I'll get us there."

"Us?" Nissi's enormous eyes grew impossibly larger.

"Surely. You are needed, are you not? Despite all your talent, you've small knowledge of the world, and you are scarcely fit to travel alone. I trust you recognize this truth."

The pale head bobbed.

"You require guidance and protection. I will furnish both. It is nothing less than a duty."

Nissi studied the ground.

"Tell your Vitrisi adept, 'the nice one,' that you set off for the Quivers tomorrow morning," Yvenza commanded. There was no reaction, and she elaborated, "It will be easy for us, we've little to pack. One of the advantages of beggary. We aren't quite destitute, though, despite Aureste's best efforts. I've a few coins and bits of jewelry about me that his Taerleezi scum overlooked. Enough to get us there, and that's all I need."

The ensuing silence stretched to such length that it seemed no reply was forthcoming, and then one came, almost inaudibly.

"Onartino?"

"We'll pass several of the hillfolk cottages along our way. I'll have one of the lads stay with him—feed him, clean him, change the dressings, and so forth. He'll be well enough." Again no response, and Yvenza pushed with her voice. "Go ahead, girl. Speak once more to the nice one. Tell him you're on your way. You needn't mention my presence just yet. And while you chat, I'll begin preparations. I'm looking forward to our journey, and to a meeting with Aureste's beloved brother. And perhaps—who knows?—to another meeting with Aureste himself. You cannot begin to conceive how eager I am to see him once again."

. . .

Preparations were swiftly completed, as promised. They consisted of little more than the stuffing of two sacks with provisions and scanty belongings. Yvenza retired early and slept soundly, her rest unbroken by dreams. She woke spontaneously at dawn and rose to discover Nissi, seated at the mouth of the cave and gazing stilly into the ashes of the dead fire. The girl might easily have sat thus throughout the night; she sometimes did so. A slight nudge roused her from her apparent trance.

Tea was brewed, biscuit toasted, apples sliced and fried. The simple meal was consumed in silence; the utensils were scoured and stowed. Through all of this, Onartino slept undisturbed at the back of the cave on the ledge that had once served as his bier, for his mother judged that ample rest succeeding ample exercise would hasten his recovery. She meant to wake him and feed him before departing, but was spared this necessity by the arrival of a gangling cottager's lad, bearing gifts.

He had brought a loaf of new bread and a clutch of old onions. Such offerings were frequently tendered by the local hillfolk to the displaced magnifica; no longer an object of fear, but still regarded with respect and scrupulously disguised compassion.

"Well, it's Prozzo's eldest." Yvenza greeted the newcomer with an exceptionally gracious smile.

"Magnifica." With a deep and painfully awkward bow, the youth presented his gifts.

"I thank you, lad." Accepting the little bundle, Yvenza passed it on to Nissi, who silently slipped it into the sack of provisions. "I'll not offer you payment, as I know from experience that you'll refuse. But I've another offer, perhaps more to your liking. Gainful employment, a paying job. What do you say to that?"

He respectfully requested particulars. She supplied them,

and an agreement was speedily struck. Prozzo's eldest son would occupy the cave for an indefinite term, during which he would tend to the damaged Onartino Belandor's needs, safety, and comfort, taking particular care that the patient should engage in a regular course of strength-building exercise. All of this, Prozzo's eldest promised to perform. In exchange for his services, he would receive immediate payment in the form of a silver ring with a purple stone. Upon the Magnifica Belandor's return, he would be given an excellent clasp knife, provided that he discharged his duties faithfully.

Prozzo Junior was profuse in his vows. Evidently satisfied, Yvenza drew the silver ring from some pocket hidden beneath her cloak and gave it to him, then hoisted the heavier of the two sacks to her shoulder and set off at brisk pace along the streambank. Taking up the second of the sacks, Nissi hurried quietly in her wake. For a couple of minutes they walked in silence, but they were scarcely out of sight of the cave and its occupants before Yvenza halted and turned to confront her pale shadow.

"Well?" she demanded.

Nissi likewise halted, at a safe distance.

"Come, what is it? I've felt your eyes pressing my back like a couple of great, moist sops."

Nissi made a couple of abortive attempts before she succeeded in producing a tiny sound.

"Onartino?" she asked.

"Safe enough. Prozzo's boy knows what will happen to him if he runs off or shirks. There's no need to worry."

Yvenza resumed progress, setting her course toward the north, with Nissi following close behind.

• • •

Daylight touched the rear of the cave, and Onartino Belandor opened his eye. For a time he lay motionless, empty gaze fixed on the stone ceiling arching overhead. Then his nostrils flared, his right hand twitched a little, and his face turned slowly toward the daylight. An unfamiliar figure stood silhouetted at the entrance. Onartino's eye blinked.

The figure advanced, resolving itself into a tall, skinny youth bearing an earthenware bowl.

"Good, you're awake," observed the stranger. "I'm Rol Prozzo, and the magnifica has hired me to do for you while she and the little white girl are away. Now see here, I've warmed you up a good mess of gruel. You have to sit up to eat it. Come on, I'll help."

Rol assisted his charge to a sitting position, back resting against the cave wall, then offered a spoonful of gruel. Onartino swallowed willingly. Another spoonful followed, and another, until about half the bowl had been consumed, at which point the boy observed, "Very good, Master Onartino, but better for you if you feed yourself. Come on, give it a try." He held out the spoon.

Onartino's right hand rose. His bandaged fingers closed on the handle. Slowly and uncertainly, he dipped a spoonful of gruel, raised it to his lips, and swallowed. Half the gruel went down his chin. The rest went down his throat.

"That's it. That's good," Rol encouraged.

The gruel diminished steadily. Soon it was gone, and Rol reclaimed the spoon.

"Just dandy, Master Onartino. At this rate, we'll soon have you dancing a jig. Now you just wait here while I see to that fire, and then we'll clean you up, eh?"

"Girl. Mine." The words were indistinct but understandable. Onartino's eye was fixed on the exit. "Hunt."

"What's that?"

"Hunt." Laboriously swinging his legs off the ledge, Onartino made as if to rise.

"Easy, now." Rol held him down. "You just bide a bit. First, the fire. Then a cleaning. Then we'll trot you around."

"Girl. Mine." Onartino struggled to rise.

"Stay *put*, now! You got to do what you're told. Your mother the magnifica has put me in charge. It's for your own good. You hear?" Deeming his point made, Rol released his patient and turned away.

Onartino's bandaged hand closed on the nearest fragment of rock. Dragging himself to his feet, he raised his arm.

Rol Prozzo spun in time to see the rock descending, but not in time to dodge it. The granite struck his skull with an audible crack, and he dropped to the ground.

For some seconds Onartino regarded the twitching figure at his feet. Presently he knelt with care and beat Rol Prozzo's head with the rock until all twitching ceased. Rising, he made his way to the mouth of the cave, where he paused, empty gaze sweeping the landscape. His one eye found the right direction.

"Hunt," said Onartino.

A fallen tree branch large enough to serve as a staff lay near at hand. He picked it up and turned his dragging footsteps west, toward Vitrisi.

FIVE

Celisse Rione stepped up onto a tree stump, elevating herself into visibility.

"Gather 'round," she commanded in a clear voice that carried through the camp. "I've news that everyone must hear. Gather 'round."

Her voice easily penetrated the canvas walls of the big infirmary tent, to be heard by the physician, the physician's assistant, and the few remaining patients. Jianna and Rione traded uneasy glances. Both moved to the entrance. Rione pushed the flap aside and they looked out.

A light layer of frozen moisture glazed the bare black branches. A haze of glinting frost lightened the cold-hardened mud of the campsite. A few scattered fires breathed grey smoke into the grey mists of winter. The canvas tents and shelters, once light in hue, had weathered and dirtied to a uniform dingy grey-brown. The patched and makeshift garments of the resident Ghosts had done likewise.

Color! thought Jianna, remembering Vitrisi with its stained-glass windows, rooflights, and flying pennants, its varied gardens, its costumes and equipages, booths and stalls, and above all its neighboring sea, of a thousand moods and expressions. Did these Ghosts haunting the foggy woods remember or know what was missing?

Celisse, simply clad in her gown and cloak the color of the tree trunks, stood very straight and very still upon her makeshift platform. Her face, young and grave, seemed to transmit inner light. Her immobility, together with the implied energy of her posture, easily drew all eyes.

Watching from the shelter of the infirmary tent, Jianna found herself inexplicably cold-fingered and clench-jawed.

The silence lengthened. Celisse finally allowed her blue-grey gaze to travel. What she saw of audience size and attentiveness must have satisfied her, for she began to speak.

"Friends and patriots, I've received news of an outrage," she announced, melodic tone conveying dignified sorrow. "Some of you will already have heard. To those who have not, let it be known—in the city of Vitrisi, the Taerleezi invaders have committed new atrocities exceeding all their past crimes, even those of the wars. There have been massacres upon at least two separate occasions. One occurred in the Plaza of Proclamation, where Taerleezi troops attacked unarmed Faerlonnish citizens too slow in obeying a command to disperse. At least a dozen of our countrymen were slaughtered in that place.

"Appalling as that was, far worse followed. Mere hours later, the Taerleezi soldiers entered the neighborhood of Rookery Grove, whose male residents were rounded up and driven out into the street, where they were slaughtered like cattle. Thereafter the corpses were mutilated—the heads cut off, mounted on poles, and left on display at the edge of the Plaza of Proclamation."

Celisse paused, allowing her listeners a moment to visualize the scene. A collective mutter of indignant revulsion suggested that the account was new to most of the audience.

It was entirely new to Jianna. Turning to Rione, she whispered, "Can this be true? Or is she making it up?"

"She certainly believes it to be true. My sister never lies," he returned in an equally low tone. "And she may well be right."

When the response subsided, Celisse continued, "Friends, we've suffered the tyranny of the Taerleezi beasts for decades. But in all my days, I've never heard of a crime blacker than this one. Is there anyone here who knows of anything worse?" She paused briefly, inviting reply, of which there was none. "I thought not. Listen to me. There comes a time at last when no being worthy of the name 'human' will accept further abuse. There comes a moment when self-respect, decency, and honor demand satisfaction. For Faerlonne and all of her children, that moment has arrived. If we love our country—if we love ourselves, and our sons and daughters—if we wish to continue regarding ourselves as a people of worth and value—then we must act. Otherwise, let us resign ourselves to the final destruction of Faerlonne. Let us bid our country farewell.

"I myself prefer to act," Celisse declared simply. "And I trust there are many among you who share my desire. What then can we do to avenge our murdered countrymen and our violated nation? How shall we strike fear into the hearts of the Taerleezis? I know one sure means of achieving this aim. I've proposed it in the past and been overruled—I now propose it again, and this time I'll not be denied. We must reveal Taerleezi vulnerability by striking at their highest and greatest. I speak of the Governor Anzi Uffrigo. He is a tyrant, a murderer, and an enemy of our country. We will now put an end to his career. The Taerleezis will quake, and all of Faerlonne will rejoice. Friends, are we agreed?"

Once again she paused for an answer. Her forceful but calm utterance, her composure and self-possession, were more compelling than any display of passion. Her aspect was confident. Clearly she expected enthusiastic assent to her proposal.

The response was less than she might have desired. An uneasy stirring animated the cluster of listeners. Leaden silence continued for some moments, until some young Ghost raised his voice in succinct objection.

"Reprisals."

"Perhaps. What of it? Are the deeds of Faerlonnish freedom fighters to be limited by fear?"

"How about by good sense?" another voice from the group spoke up. "Eh, girl?"

Jianna could not see the speaker from her present vantage

point, but recognized the unhurried tones of Poli Orso. The flush that darkened Celisse Rione's pale face was visible even at a distance.

"It is more than good sense—it is a vital necessity—to teach the tyrants that their worst offenses carry consequences. So great an outrage as the Rookery Grove massacre can't pass unpunished, else worse will follow. They must learn once and for all that Faerlonnishmen are not sheep for the butchering."

"They'll learn it, and the sooner the better," Orso countered. "But killing off the Viper be'nt the way to teach. Do this, and we'll leave the Taers no choice but to hit back hard, for the sake of pride. And for that, there'll be massacres that'll make Rookery Grove look like a tavern brawl. Will we do ourselves any great good with that? So we'll strike for our dead right enough, but we'll choose another target. That Taer tax collector sitting on his moneybags over at Worm Ridge— there's a good prize. All that silver he's squeezed over the last season might find its way back into Faerlonnish hands. The Taers would feel the loss right enough, and our own folk stand to profit."

The faces in the group about him brightened.

"Profit. Money. Prudence." Celisse's brows lifted. "Always Poli Orso thinks of such things. His care and extreme . . . caution are well meant, but they come at the cost of justice. We are Faerlonnish, all of us. Haven't we courage? Haven't we pride? Haven't we the strength and will to defend our nation?"

"More than one way of doing that. Doesn't do Faerlonne much service if we all throw ourselves off a cliff," Orso observed.

"We shall do Faerlonne the greatest service." Celisse's assurance did not waver. "And we won't stop to count the cost. We'll do this because we love our country and our compatriots more than we love ourselves. The true hearts among us will do what must be done." She let her eyes travel in search of kindred spirits. "Who's with me? Who's for Vitrisi, and action? Speak up now."

Silence followed, broken only by the nervous clearing of assorted throats. Celisse's demanding gaze swept the fidgety audience and fastened on a likely face.

"Trox Venezzu." She singled him out ruthlessly. "I take you for a lad of spirit. Have you the stomach for a dangerous mission?"

Following a protracted pause, Trox replied with audible discomfort, "I'd say the whole thing should be thought through, first."

"For how long, Trox Venezzu? Until the Taers have killed off half our people, and enslaved the other half? Would that allow enough time for thought? Or would you rather wait longer, perhaps until the world has forgotten that the island of Faerlonne was ever anything more than a third-rate province of Taerleez?"

No reply was forthcoming, and she selected a new victim.

"Illi Dunnzo. You've some red blood in your veins, I think. Are you for Vitrisi, and action?"

There was no answer. A moment later a scarlet-faced boy emerged from the group and made for the shelter of the woods.

"Zees Quiorno, then. Do you love your country, Zees? Are you a man? Will you come to Vitrisi?"

"Maybe. I'll let you know. Right now, I got work." Zees Quiorno departed abruptly.

"Benna Ciosso? You're a woman with the heart of a tiger. Shall we show these boys what courage is? Are you for it?"

"That I am not," returned the tiger in question. "This is dangerous foolery. Celisse, you fizzle like wet powder. Be good to yourself and the rest of us, and give it up."

"I thought more of you, Benna Ciosso. I thought better of all of you." Celisse's contemptuous regard chilled each of her listeners in turn. The slow gaze traveled from face to face, and then ranged farther, to the infirmary tent, where her brother and his assistant stood in the open entry.

For a moment the icy eyes bored into her own with an expression of such unequivocal animosity that Jianna resisted the impulse to step back into the shadows. Compressing her lips, she stared back. Eventually Celisse's eyes moved on, returning to objects of more immediate and intense displeasure.

"You are afraid for your own little lives. You are filled with such fear that it blots out all else. You are cowards, useless and unworthy." Celisse's voice and face remained calm and immeasurably cold. "I have lived among you for years, and that's what I think of you now. Is there anyone among you with spirit or heart to prove me wrong? If so, let him or her seek me out. If not, I've no use for any of you."

Head high, she stepped off her stump and marched away. Her listeners dispersed in muttering twos and threes.

"She's going to sulk in her tent?" Jianna inquired.

"Not the most sympathetic description," Falaste Rione returned.

"Well, you're right about that. I know you don't want to hear me speak ill of your sister, but she has some dangerous ideas. Happily, the Ghosts know better than to follow her. Think that solid snub she just received will teach her a lesson?"

"Perhaps." He smiled, but the vertical crease between his brows remained.

"You don't sound optimistic."

"Once she's made up her mind, Celisse isn't easily turned from her purpose."

"I know. Will of iron, and all that. Selfless dedication, intense patriotism, heart of fire . . . Immense self-importance, intolerance, utter humorlessness—oh, stop looking at me like that. All right, I'm sorry, I know, she's your sister. I can't help it. I've tried to like her, but she doesn't make it easy."

"I know that. But her intentions are of the best and highest."

"So are yours, but you aren't so *oppressive* about it. Sometimes I wonder how you and Celisse can look so much alike, and share so much, yet be so different."

"Sometimes, so do I. But not at the moment, when there are patients—er—languishing."

"Not very many languishing. Most are more like—lounging," Jianna told him, and it was true. The population of the infirmary tent had decreased dramatically. The power of the hot heaves was largely broken, and those few lately stricken with the malady suffered little of its earlier fury. Their lives were hardly threatened. Even so, they were miserable enough, and their sufferings still demanded care and attention.

Jianna worked hard, as had become her habit. The faces looking up at her smoothed and cleared under her ministrations. The experience she had acquired told her that every single one of them would live, and the sense of victory warmed her to the core. The hours passed quite happily, and then there was the midday meal, and more work, followed by a span of free time that she devoted to the mending and reinforcement of her deteriorating garments. During this time she never caught sight of Celisse Rione, which suited her well enough.

The day marched to its conclusion. The skies darkened from grey to charcoal, and preparation of the evening meal commenced. Jianna scraped carrots and chopped onions; small tasks to which she had grown accustomed. When the food was served up, she took her usual place at the usual fire, noticing for the first time the absence of both Falaste Rione and his sister. Rione was quite likely to come late to supper, or to skip it altogether, if a patient required attention. Such was not the case at the moment, however, and for the second time that day, uneasiness stirred inside her.

She ate, making abstracted conversation with the closest Ghost, while her eyes roved so incessantly that her companion soon grew impatient, and left off speaking. Jianna scarcely noticed. The minutes passed, and then Rione was there in the circle of firelight, face harder than she had ever seen it.

"I've just checked on Celisse," he informed the group at large. "All of her things are gone. She's cleared off."

A moment's silence greeted this announcement, and then Poli Orso spoke up, with some regret. "Can't say I'm surprised. The lass was that peeved."

Jianna's eyes were fixed on Rione's set face. Occasionally the working of his mind mystified her, but from time to time she felt as if his blood pulsed in her veins, and his heart beat in her breast. She felt so now.

"You think she's run for Vitrisi," Jianna heard herself state clearly. "You think she means to assassinate Governor Uffrigo."

Her listeners' attention crystallized. Somebody loosed a muted imprecation.

"I do." Rione turned to face her.

"All by herself?"

"Yes."

"Has she the smallest chance of success, on her own?"

"The very smallest. And the very greatest chance of destroying herself."

"You mean to stop her?"

"Yes. None of the sick lads here are in real danger, so I can be spared for a while. I'll leave tomorrow at first light. Noro, you may come with me or remain here at camp, as you choose."

"*Oh*. Well then, I'll come. I've a mind to see Vitrisi," she returned, trying hard to seem nonchalant. Inside, the surge of rising excitement threatened to smash all restraint. *Vitrisi*. Days ago he had promised to take her home, and she had never for an instant doubted his word. Nevertheless, the suddenness of it took her by surprise. She had prepared herself to accept delay, and now all at once they would be leaving this place tomorrow. And without pangs of conscience, for the sick lads were out of danger; he had just said so. She wanted to hop and shout. Instead, she sat still and fixed her eyes studiously on the bowl in her lap.

"You might want to take a couple of the boys along," Orso suggested. "Help you hunt the town."

"I know you can't spare them, and Celisse is most likely to let herself be found if I'm there on my own."

His refusal of the proffered assistance surprised Jianna, despite the adequately plausible explanation. What he said might be true, but it was equally true, she realized, that he would find it easier to accomplish his secondary task of returning "Noro Penzia" to Belandor House without benefit of Ghostly observers.

After that, he'd somehow track down his wayward firebrand sister and take her in hand, forestalling potential disaster. And then the siblings would rejoin the Ghost force, resume their resistance activities, and Falaste Rione would soon forget that he had ever been so unwise as to risk his own position for the sake of Aureste Belandor's daughter. He would try to forget that he had ever met her at all.

Let him try.

She would contrive to effect a meeting between Falaste and her father. Then the unassailably high-minded physician would see for himself. His own sense of justice would ensure recognition of the Magnifico Aureste's obvious virtue. A single, face-to-face meeting should accomplish all; and afterward, the good doctor might be persuaded to tarry in Vitrisi. For a long time.

Probably he would be glad to remain, once he arrived and saw the city again, for who could voluntarily abandon Vitrisi? The journey home would involve days of travel across the wintry countryside, but the prospect of much chilly discomfort did not discourage her at all. At the moment it seemed as if pure excitement would keep her warm throughout the trip, and it would begin *tomorrow at first light*.

. . .

"We have received replies," Innesq Belandor informed his two brothers. "A couple of them from Taerleez—from Houses

Pridisso and Zovaccio. The other, from our young kinswoman out in the wild."

"Really, I don't know that some untutored rustic waif of uncertain pedigree should be honored with the title of *kinswoman*." Nalio Belandor pursed his lips.

"If you trust in my abilities at all, then you must trust me when I tell you that she is of our blood," Innesq returned. "She is our cousin—a simple fact in nature, if not in law—and she possesses great natural talent. We very much need that talent now, and the young girl has forced herself to set aside a thousand fears in order to grant her consent. For this she deserves our respect as well as our thanks."

Nalio subsided with a frown.

The three siblings sat in the north wing's demi-council chamber/dining room. The remains of an excellent dinner lay on the table before them, for Belandor House's kitchen, at some remove from the main body of the building, had escaped all damage, as had its presiding chef. Save for the black mourning that Nalio wore for his murdered wife, the brothers were their normal selves.

"How reliable is any information garnered by way of Vinz Corvestri?" demanded the Magnifico Aureste. His black brows contracted. "This so-called communication occurred within the confines of his house, did it not? How shall we measure possible Corvestri influence?"

"Oh, there is no fear of that," Innesq returned, almost carelessly. "Vinz understands the importance of our undertaking too well to tamper."

"*Vinz?* How long have you enjoyed such informal intimacy with an enemy of our House?"

"Since the enemy became an ally."

"Surely you can't be so naïve. By all means, make such use of Corvestri and his resources as your purpose demands and his weakness permits, but don't commit the blunder of regarding him as an ally, a comrade, or indeed as anything other than a serviceable tool."

"Ah, brother, sometimes you oversimplify."

"Grant me patience! Do you truly imagine the enmity of generations dissolving upon a handclasp?"

"Do you truly imagine the self-interest of rational individuals incapable of overcoming ancient prejudice?"

"Just never turn your back on him, that's all I advise."

"We digress," observed Innesq. "I am trying to tell you that we have received affirmative replies from three sources. Ojem Pridisso of Iron Hill and Littri Zovaccio of Frinnasi will both embark from Taerleez within hours. Needless to say, they will use all arcane skills at their command to speed their own journey. As for young Nissi, she is already on the move. With the addition of Vinz and myself, that is a total of five arcanists of the Six."

"Didn't you tell me that you need half a dozen?" Aureste objected.

"That is the traditional quorum. An examination of the old accounts, however, leads me to believe that five should suffice. And who knows? Perhaps others will join us."

"What if it's the opposite? Suppose someone backs out, gets sick, dies, or simply disappears?"

"Ah, then we have reason to fear. I hold fair confidence in the combined power of five genuine talents, but that is the minimum. We cannot make do with less. But come, do not look so grim. Remember, this is no impossible undertaking. The cleansing of the Source by human agency has been accomplished in the past upon several documented occasions. Are we less skilled and determined than our ancestors? Can we not do what those who went before us have already proved possible? It is a challenge that others have met, and we shall do as well, or better. Will you believe that?"

"At the moment I'm concerned less with belief than logistics," Aureste told him. "These arcanists you've secured—are they coming here, to Vitrisi?"

"No, we have agreed to meet at the Quivers. It is thought that the Source's underground circuit throughout the Isles approaches the surface at that locale, but nobody truly knows. Whatever the reason, the site is undoubtedly infused with power certain to support our efforts."

"And how do you propose to travel? You're scarcely accustomed to gadding about on your own."

"I anticipate little if any solitary gadding. Vinz has invited me to travel with his party."

"Has he indeed? Now, there's generosity for you."

"Truly. His attendants will look after me well enough."

"No they won't. D'you imagine I'd allow it?"

"Allow?"

"Pardon me, I choose my terms poorly. I know too well that I can't stop you, once you make up that obstinate mind, but a moment's thought will surely persuade you. To begin with, consider the loss of personal dignity. You, a Belandor, abroad in the world without benefit of your own vehicle, horses, servants, Sishmindris, bodyguards, weaponry, provisions, and all other necessities. You, occupying a few spare inches in the Corvestri's second-best carriage, like some penniless spinster aunt. It won't do."

"He's right, Innesq," Nalio interjected. "Only think how it would look!"

"I believe the Belandor family honor capable of sustaining the blow," Innesq reassured them kindly.

"Appearances are scarcely the greatest cause for concern," Aureste continued. "Once you assume the role of Vinz Corvestri's passenger and dependent, you place yourself entirely in his power. You'll be out in the wild, far from family and friends, unprotected, and there he'll do as he pleases with you—torment or kill you for the sake of the hatred he bears our House, or perhaps he'll simply content himself with ripping the knowledge and arcane secrets out of your head, thus adding your wealth to his own mental hoard."

"These are idle fears. I assure you, Vinz fully comprehends the gravity of the situation, and he has set aside personal animosity, for the moment at least. I trust him for that."

"I don't."

"I am sorry to hear that, but I cannot afford to stay for your approval. There is no time to be lost, and I fear we have tarried too long already. Therefore, since I have made no arrangements of my own, I am obliged to embark with Vinz Corvestri tomorrow morning."

"No you aren't," Aureste informed him. "I feared something of this sort, so I've made arrangements on your behalf. There's the small brown carriage, which is light in weight and capable of navigating difficult roads. When the roads cease, there's a sedan chair for you. The guards and servants have been selected and they've received their preliminary instructions. The supply wagons are fully loaded and ready to move."

"Really, you are most efficient and generous, but I hardly think—"

"Rest assured, when we set forth for the Quivers, we shall travel in a style befitting two members of House Belandor."

"We? Pardon me, but surely you did not mean—"

"I mean that I'll accompany you on this expedition. You appear thunderstruck. I trust my presence isn't entirely distasteful to you?"

"No, certainly not. You have taken me by surprise, that is all. I must confess, I do not quite see your motive. What point in going, Aureste? What precisely do you expect to accomplish?"

"I'll safeguard Belandor interests. I'll see to it that you take no harm in the midst of the Corvestri vipers."

"No need. What will it take to convince you that the interests of Houses Belandor and Corvestri have currently merged?"

"You are brilliant and talented, but not a worldly man. You must grant my superior knowledge of the world, and listen when I tell you that it's fatal to trust in the honesty of our enemies. Don't trouble to argue the point. I won't abandon you to the questionable mercies of Vinz Corvestri, and there's an end to the matter. Tomorrow morning we head north toward the Quivers in our own party, among our own people. Resign yourself."

"I see that I shall not dissuade you. But what of your search for Jianna?"

"About to expand in a new direction. As we travel north, I'll question the locals and spread word of the reward that I offer."

"And if she returns to Vitrisi to find you absent?"

"If I thought that likely, then nothing would pry me out of this city. But weeks have passed, and I've given up hope that she'll simply appear at our door. Something prevents her. If I should happen to be wrong about that, however, then she'll be welcomed home by her uncle. During our absence, Nalio is left in charge."

"I shall—shall—shall not disappoint you, brother." Nalio's narrow face flushed with pleasure. "Your trust in me is not misplaced."

"I know it isn't." Aureste decided to throw his youngest brother a scrap. It was good policy, after all, to reward a faithful underling. "And while we are gone, you are authorized to proceed with the restoration of Belandor House. The work you've already done in cataloging damages and necessary repairs is outstanding. I know that the same care and discriminating judgment will shape the future of our home. Carry on as you've begun, brother, and we shall all find ourselves in your debt."

"I will—indeed I will!" Nalio's eyes shone. "I shall bring Belandor House back to its former self, and more. Give me just a little time, and you'll see!"

"I've every confidence in you. Where are you off to, Innesq?" Aureste demanded as the middle brother pushed his chair away from the table.

"My room. I must contact the others and inform them of our plans," Innesq replied. "The vehicles, you say, are ready to move?"

"Anytime you like."

"Very well. We shall depart tomorrow, at first light."

●　●　●

"First light" in Vitrisi at this time just barely exceeded no light at all. In the early morning, the heavy mists of winter blending with the ever-present pall of smoke held back the dawn. The streets lay in nocturnal darkness. The rooflights burning overhead barely penetrated the gloom, and there was only the solemn tolling of the hour from the bell tower at the bottom of Summit Street to confirm the arrival of the day.

Having breakfasted lightly in his own chamber, Aureste was dressed and ready to leave at the appointed hour. Warmly cloaked against the weather, he made his solitary way along the north wing central corridor, down the stairs, through the entrance hall, and out of the building, to discover the brown carriage waiting before the door, along with the loaded supply wagons, mounted guards and outriders liveried in slate and silver, assorted menials and footmen presently huddling for warmth. Aureste's practiced eye scanned the scene by the light of the carriage lamps and the links clutched in the chilly fists of a couple of servants—human servants, for no Sishmindris were to be included in this expedition.

His orders appeared to have been carried out properly. He nodded, satisfied, but could not arrest the flight of his memory to a similar scene of the not distant past: morning, sharp air, carriage and guards waiting at the door, ready to carry Jianna away. And they had taken her, and she had vanished, solely as a result of her father's choices . . . Not the time to think of it.

He realized that he had halted. Before he resumed progress, the whir of a well-oiled mechanism alerted him to his brother's arrival. Innesq was there, attended by a brace of those Sishmindris to which he was so unaccountably partial. Aureste caught one of the creatures watching him with its unreadable protuberant eyes, and an odd sense of angry guilt flashed across his mind. Resisting the impulse to turn his face away, he stared back coldly, and the Sishmindri's gaze fell. Only then did he allow his own regard to shift to Innesq's face, tranquil in expression, but haggard and terribly pale.

Tired, and still unwell. Unready to embark upon so demanding a venture, but nothing in the world would stop him.

Along with Innesq had come Nalio, a wholly superfluous presence. Presumably the junior Belandor deemed it appropriately dutiful to bid his siblings farewell.

But Nalio did not appear particularly dutiful. He was looking quite unmistakably—cheerful; happier than he had looked, in fact, since the slaughter of his wife. Contentment lurked in the curve of his lips and the luster of his eyes. There could be but one cause. It was the small measure of temporary authority, of course; clearly it had gone straight to his head. For the first and probably last time in all his life, he would rule Belandor House. And rule it at a critical juncture—at a time when hundreds or thousands of small decisions would be made, each decision imprinting itself upon the very structure of the mansion. Now he would be free to pore over his beloved lists and catalogs, to commune with architects, masons, carpenters, plasterers, artists, and artisans of every description, to his heart's content. His decisions of today and tomorrow might well resonate through the centuries. Of course he was happy. This was his finest hour.

Innesq's chair advanced to the carriage and halted. Courtesies and farewells were exchanged, then the attending Sishmindris deftly transferred their charge into the waiting vehicle. Thereafter the wheeled chair was collapsed in accordance with its cunning design and passed to the roof, where it was tied down by one of the human attendants. The amphibians retired in silence.

Aureste issued a mouthful of new commands to the guards, paused to take leave of the dewy-eyed Nalio, then climbed in and took his seat. The riders deployed themselves and the party embarked.

In recent weeks he had discovered the luxury of traveling about the city in anonymity. No such option existed now, in the midst of a group so large and conspicuous, but that substantiality furnished its own protection. In the presence of those armed guards, no rocks or refuse pelted the Belandor carriage; no insults or epithets erupted in its wake. They passed through the Clouds without incident, and the navigation of the White Incline proved similarly uneventful.

Aureste, unconsciously braced against some form of aggression, felt the tension seeping out of him. He let his eyes turn toward Innesq, whose own gaze was fixed on the passing cityscape. Dingy and dark it was, smothered in vapor, devoid of color, and at this early hour largely devoid of life, yet Innesq drank it in with obvious relish. Understandably so: it was unfamiliar to him. He had spent most of his youth and all of his adult life at home. His mind and inner vision had traveled unimaginable realms, but his body had remained sequestered within the confines of Belandor House—entirely by his own choice. Now circumstances had forced him to a different choice, and he appeared to be enjoying the novelty, achromatic though it was.

On along Harbor Way rumbled the carriage with its satellites, and gradually the grim air lightened a little, buildings began to distinguish themselves, and the street came to life. Human voices rose—the vendors were already at work—and above them, the cries of the Scarlet Gluttons. Innesq smiled at the sound, almost as if those discordant squawks possessed charm. Perhaps for him they did.

The smoky air was already scratching at the back of his throat. Almost unconsciously—so ingrained had the habit become—Aureste applied a handkerchief to his nose. The linen was scented with the musk of tunnel scitter—difficult to obtain and absurdly costly, but thought to offer the most powerful possible protection against airborne contagion, far outperforming the old-fashioned pomander. In addition to the treated handkerchief, he had taken to drinking infused chicory, and, thus doubly guarded, felt himself safe as a man could reasonably expect to be.

He saw his brother's gaze shift, and followed it through a gap in the warehouses lining this section of the street out to the harbor, where the Searcher loomed, just barely visible through the smothering mists. The colossus' bronze lamp, formerly so brilliant, now glowed faint as a dying ember. Never in all his life, not even at the height of the Taerleezi invasion, had he seen that light so diminished.

The carriage clattered on, and the Searcher receded behind it. Aureste fell into frowning abstraction, his mind busying itself with a thousand practical details of the journey. Innesq, captivated by the most mundane scenes of city life, watched Vitrisi flowing by. Some minutes passed before they found the way blocked by a barrier of recent construction, its raw planks flaunting the red X of the quarantine.

"Useless," observed Innesq. "They cannot contain this pestilence with barriers of wood."

"They can at least prevent the diseased rabble from troubling healthy citizens," Aureste returned. But in this he soon found himself mistaken.

A change in course, another few moments, and the street widened into a small open square containing a public well. Assorted neighborhood residents had gathered there, buckets empty and likely to remain so, for the way to the water was blocked by a group of the undead.

There were four of them standing beside the well—two men, a female child, and a being of indeterminate gender—their altered state revealed by the onset of decomposition, unmistakable even by the weak morning light. The Belandor coachman pulled up at once. The wagon drivers and mounted attendants did likewise.

Annoyed, Aureste looked out, and the reproofs died on his lips. The coachman's hesitation was excusable; the obstacle was considerable. Unwillingly fascinated, he studied the undead quartet. Deteriorating grey flesh, thin tufts of colorless hair clinging to pallid scalps, filthy rags swathing rust-jointed bodies, and then their eyes, milky and empty . . . But he did not wish to look at their eyes, and his attention shifted to the hapless locals, who huddled in frightened clumps. Witless sheep, confused and in need of leadership. But then, honesty compelled him to acknowledge, their situation was difficult. He could hardly fault their reluctance to engage the undead. As he knew from personal experience, the plague victims were nearly invulnerable to ordinary methods of attack. Their control demanded the skills of a true arcanist. Therefore he turned to his brother and asked, "Can you do something about this?"

Innesq said nothing. His eyes were fixed on the undead, his face bloodless. His lips moved, shaping inaudible syllables.

"We don't want another meandering detour, we've lost too much time as it is," Aureste persisted. "Clear them off. I know you can." Still receiving no reply, he added in a lower tone, "I've seen you deal with such things."

"Quiet," Innesq commanded.

"Take care, brother. Even you do not possess unlimited license."

"Do you not feel it? Is it not there in your mind and heart?"

"Feel what? What are you talking about?"

"The change. Surely you sense it. Push the trifles from your mind and let yourself perceive the world."

At such moments, Aureste deferred instinctively and without argument to his brother's superior knowledge. Shutting his eyes and employing a technique taught him by Innesq, he willed his intellect into a state of receptivity. Upon achieving the requisite clarity, he found himself curiously reluctant to open his eyes. More than reluctant—afraid. Formless dread threatened paralysis.

Nonsense. He opened his eyes, and his dread intensified. It took a moment to understand why; a moment to sort through a jumble of conflicting impressions. Initially he imagined himself transported to another world; or dreaming, or perhaps dead and finally confronting the eternal punishment with which so many optimistic enemies had so often threatened him. But no. Surely he was still alive, still in Vitrisi, still in his own carriage, with his brother sitting in the opposite seat. He was certainly in Vitrisi, for he saw the square, the well, the undead, and the cowed citizens; but saw them now in a different way, distanced and slightly distorted, as if they all belonged to some imaginary realm. They had no weight, no solidity, no home in the world of reality.

Nor did he himself belong to this place. He was an interloper here, unwelcome and unfit to live.

Aureste rejected the intolerable sensation with such ferocity that the world was shaken back into its accustomed aspect, or nearly so. A slight wavering of outline remained, which might have been ascribed to the heavy mists. That visual disturbance, combined with a sense of uncomprehending horror, told him that the anomaly persisted.

"What is it?" he demanded harshly.

"It is the will of the Overmind," Innesq replied in a whisper. His eyes never strayed from the undead quartet. Almost he seemed dazed, or perhaps awed. "It uses the physical resources of its hosts to generate its own thoughts and intentions, which are born of the old energy, the energy of the Reversed Source that once animated the ancient world. These sad puppets are the instrument by which the Overmind seeks to re-create its former home."

"You're telling me that those strolling cadavers over there are somehow causing this—whatever it is—this madness, this impossibility?" Aureste's gesture encompassed an injured universe.

"They are being used to cause it. In time, their cumulative efforts will influence the Source itself."

"Then destroy them here and now. Blast them out of existence. You have the ability."

The answer was delayed, and when it arrived, unwelcome.

"Pointless." Innesq shook his head. "Do not trouble to contradict me. It is possible that my skills might serve to lay those four unfortunates to permanent rest, but the task would impose heavy demands upon our time and upon my reserves of strength. We would lose several hours, and at the end, the accomplishment itself is negligible."

"Their removal wouldn't eliminate the disruption?"

"It might eliminate this one small pocket of disruption, here and now, but that is the equivalent of treating a single pustule of the smallpox. What you see before you is symptomatic. In order to effect a cure, we must treat the underlying cause, and the sooner the better."

Aureste nodded. He signaled the driver, and the Belandor coach rattled off along a new route, leaving consternated citizens and mute undead behind to settle their own differences.

· · ·

At about the same time, events of note were taking place elsewhere in the city. The section of Vitrisi known as the New Houses, which were now quite old indeed, was traditionally respectable in character and conservative in outlook. The denizens tended to embrace traditional Faerlonnish virtues, which included honesty, industry, thrift, and family loyalty. Their lives were modest, and few households kept more than a single servant. Nobody owned a Sishmindri. Quite apart from all question of expense, the amphibians were regarded as treacherous, dirty, and distastefully foreign. The recent identification of Sishmindris as carriers of the plague only served to reinforce prevailing local opinion.

Popular opinion had been ratified by the passage of a neighborhood resolution officially barring Sishmindris from the New Houses district. It signified little to its originators that their amateur legislation possessed no whit of official legitimacy. They were more than ready, as many fervently asserted, to fight to the death in defense of their homes, families, and innocent infants menaced by the Sishmindri peril.

This resolution was put to the test upon the wintry morning that a lone Sishmindri appeared within the neighborhood. The amphibian, sporting an armband that identified her as property of the Challosa household, was spotted trudging along Hay Street, which marked the western boundary of the New Houses. Her errand was unknown and irrelevant. Quite possibly she was unaware that she had ventured into forbidden territory, but this, too, was irrelevant. Ignorance scarcely mitigated the offense.

A party of the freshly established New Houses Guardians accosted her at once. Wasting no time upon warning or interrogation, the neighborhood protectors commenced beating her with their brand-new, iron-bound New Houses Guardians clubs. The trespasser's efforts to flee were neatly thwarted; she could hardly be permitted to spread plague far and wide. A few sound strokes beat her to her knees. Spreading her alien webbed fingers defensively before her face, she attempted speech, but a well-aimed blow drove the croaking syllables back into her mouth. The beating continued.

A curious thing happened then. Throwing back her hairless head, the Sishmindri loosed an unknown utterance. Something between a wail and a squeal, issuing in staccato bursts, it was a sound entirely unfamiliar to the ears of men.

The response was equally novel.

From out of nowhere, it seemed, jumped a pair of fully mature, sturdily built male Sishmindris. Amazingly, the creatures were unclothed, unmarked, and devoid of any identifying sign of human ownership. Even more amazingly, they were armed. One carried an ax, the other bore a sledgehammer. It might reasonably have been argued that the implements were mere tools of labor, suitable to Sishmindri use. In an instant this argument was conclusively refuted.

One of the rogue amphibians swung his ax, striking the nearest Guardian's neck. Blood spurted from the unmistakably fatal wound, and the victim fell. Almost at the same time, the second Sishmindri raised his sledgehammer and brought it crashing mightily upon the head of the nearest Guardian, who went down, dead before he hit the ground.

The human witnesses froze, disbelieving, for it was impossible. Sishmindris were submissive, passive, and cowardly. This was their nature. The spectacle of two such creatures taking up forbidden arms and turning them upon their human overlords was unimaginable. For a moment, reality wavered.

During this shocked lull, the two rescuers drew the crouching female to her feet, each taking one of her hands, and the trio fled down Hay Street.

The incredulity paralyzing the human witnesses yielded to fury, and the surviving Guardians set off in yelling pursuit. Within moments their number was increased by public-spirited citizens eager to join in the defense of the neighborhood, and soon a sizable gang bayed on the heels of the fleeing Sishmindris.

At first the long, leaping gait of the amphibians kept them well ahead of their pursuers. But presently the female began to falter; perhaps the beating had injured her. As the distance between fugitives and pursuers decreased, a new note of joyous anticipation sharpened the human voices.

A few yards farther on, an open alley offered escape from Hay Street. The Sishmindris sped for the shadows, thus removing themselves from forbidden territory. Ordinarily the chase might have ended then and there. But this case was remarkable. These Sishmindri had not only armed themselves— a capital offense in and of itself—but had actually succeeded in killing two human beings; and both martyrs New Houses Guardians, at that. Such a crime could not go unavenged.

Down the alley and through a tangle of twisting lanes known as the Briar Patch fled the three Sishmindris, with the citizens close behind—too close to evade, despite the tortuous complexity of the streets and walkways. The female was limping noticeably, slowing her male companions. But they, with the stupidity typical of their kind, failed to realize that their only possible hope of self-preservation lay in abandoning her.

They remained at her side, and the humans gained on them with every step.

Another sharp turn, and the citizens found themselves at the bottom of a cul-de-sac, confronting a tumbledown tenement whose door was crossed from top to bottom with a great red X. At sight of the quarantine symbol the citizens checked abruptly, for the most urgent bloodlust gave way before fear of the plague.

The Sishmindris displayed no such prudence. Speeding straight to the front door, one of them kicked it open. The three amphibians slid through, and the door banged shut behind them.

The citizens stood staring, thunderstruck for the second time within minutes. Nobody spoke, nobody moved. However keen their appetite for vengeance, not one among them dared to breach the red X.

But the Sishmindris had dared. Just as they had dared to take up arms against their natural overlords and commit double homicide. They were cowardly and irresolute, but they did not fear the plague. They were weak and submissive, but they seemed to be losing their natural fear of human beings. It hardly seemed possible, but it had been witnessed by dozens. Probably it had been some wild aberration, an isolated event unlikely to repeat itself within the next millennium. But it had happened, it was real, and the implications were disquieting.

SIX

It's happening. We're actually going. Jianna could hardly believe it. She sat astride a smallish, sturdy, black-maned bay—the first horse she had mounted since the day of her flight, capture, and ignominious return to Ironheart. A horse of similar quality carried Falaste Rione. Initially he had refused the loan of the animals, deeming the Ghosts' need the greater. But Poli Orso had insisted, citing the urgency of the mission, and in the end Rione had yielded, salving his conscience with a promise to hand the horses over to appropriate resistance activists in the city at the first opportunity.

Thus they were to ride rather than walk, and Jianna could not suppress her pleasure, but had the good sense to conceal it. It was not easy, for today the world seemed to offer encouragement. This morning the mists had thinned to the verge of transparency, permitting passage of tentative sunshine and affording a glimpse of pale blue overhead. It was not much, but sufficed to promise an eventual end to grey winter.

Most of the camp had turned out to bid their doctor farewell. The faces in the group reflected a warmth exceeding mere gratitude or courtesy, which only confirmed her expectations. She had long since noted Falaste Rione's ability to win friendship and respect wherever he went. What came as more of a surprise was the cordiality directed specifically at *her*. Perhaps it was only for the sake of the work she had performed as his assistant, but somehow it seemed more than that. The smiles, the handclasps, the expressions of appreciation and goodwill were heartfelt.

"You're a staunch lass, Noro Penzia," Poli Orso informed

her at the last moment. "And you're always welcome here, with Rione or without him."

Coming from a fugitive Ghost, such an invitation meant much, and it brought a lump to her throat. She would miss them, she realized; at least some of them. Perhaps they in turn would miss her a little. But these kindly sentiments were unlikely to survive the discovery of Noro Penzia's true identity.

Farewells concluded, and they rode from the clearing into the damp quiet of the woods. Within moments, all sight and sound of the Ghosts' camp were lost. Jianna's mind raced like a rain-swollen river. She was going home.

• • •

Ensuing days recalled the time she had spent traveling the woods with Rione following their flight from Ironheart. The same wet ground, the same stony trails and dead leaves underfoot, the same bare branches and dormant vegetation, the same long hours and monotony. But there were differences, now, and all of them welcome. Now, thanks to the generosity of Rione's friends, they rode rather than walked. Now they carried adequate provisions, necessities of all sorts, even blankets of lined and quilted oilcloth. Now neither one of them needed to feel the cold, for weeks earlier Benna Ciosso had produced a warm woolen cloak, only slightly moth-eaten, once owned by a female Ghost, long dead of unknown complaints. This garment now wrapped Jianna. Better yet, there were shoes, sturdy and sound, and only a little too large; a bit of packing in the heels had solved that problem. Rione had reclaimed his own cloak, and now both of them traveled in relative comfort. And finally, there was the world itself—still raw and chill of atmosphere, still muted in color, but almost insensibly changing. The knife-edge of the wind was dulling, the air softening, the mists lightening, the days lengthening, and the sky hinting at renewed color—quiet signs everywhere that winter was in retreat.

They were long, dull days, but not unpleasant. She was with Rione, she was traveling toward home, father, family, and Vitrisi. The discomforts and inconveniences of the journey were insignificant. From time to time a dark shiver at the bottom of her mind troubled her: *As soon as you're home again, he'll go away.* But she thrust such thoughts from her. When the time came, she would find a way to change his plans; she was Aureste Belandor's daughter, after all.

On a clear and unusually bright day, they emerged from the woods blanketing the hills to confront a broad, deeply rutted road that Jianna knew: the venerable VitrOrezzi Bond. They turned their course toward Vitrisi and presently passed a modest carriage drawn by a pair of greys, heading toward Orezzia. Its wheels rolled quite easily over a surface still coldly firm, but just beginning to soften to mud at the middle of the road. There was nothing remarkable about the conveyance, but it was the first proper carriage that Jianna had seen since the day of her kidnapping, a clear sign of civilization. She was back in the real world, and her spirits soared.

They traveled on through the afternoon, and during those hours spied a mail coach, a mule-drawn cart, and a quintet of mounted Taerleezi guardsmen. At the end of the day, when the light was failing and the atmosphere chilling, they came to an inn whose name, the Glass Eye, struck Jianna like a message from another life. For it was at this very inn that she had expected to spend the second night of her ill-fated journey from Vitrisi to the house of her betrothed in Orezzia. She had very much wanted to dine in the common room among the ordinary folk, she recalled. She had expected to find interesting novelty there. It all seemed inexpressibly remote and distant now, yet it had only been this past autumn.

And now, it seemed, that forgotten wish was about to be granted, for Rione suggested that they grant themselves the rare luxury of spending the night under a solid roof. Jianna assented readily, without questioning the expense. Throughout her entire life she had rarely been obliged to handle money and she had certainly never wasted a moment's thought on it. She did not think to consider it now.

They did eat in the common room with all the ordinary folk, and the single long table with benches on both sides, the communal pots and bowls in the middle, the elbowing and jockeying were not so novel after all. They reminded her of the servants' table in the kitchen at Ironheart, only bigger and noisier, with more crowding and worse manners. The food was adequately abundant, filling, and undistinguished. Conversation, however, was lively, for these travelers carried news and stories—all of indeterminate reliability, but absorbing nevertheless.

Jianna ached for news of Vitrisi. She inquired, and much information was forthcoming, little of it encouraging. Several Glass Eye patrons spoke of the plague raging in the city—of the spread of the pestilence, the inefficacy of the quarantine, the mounting fatalities, the ever-blazing pyres, the atmosphere of fear and despondency approaching desperation.

Exaggeration, thought Jianna.

They spoke of the increase in crime, violence, and generally erratic behavior; the correspondingly draconian controls imposed by the detested Governor Uffrigo; and the resulting popular resentment and unrest.

There's always popular resentment and unrest, thought Jianna.

They spoke of astonishing disruptions among the Sishmindris, who had been conclusively identified as carriers of the plague. In response to the reasonable and necessary measures introduced in the interest of disease control, the amphibians had turned vicious. Finally revealing their long-suspected strain of malevolence, they had banded together into predatory gangs occupying quarantined territory, whence they periodically issued to kill and plunder. Or so it was generally believed. In sheer self-defense, the decent human residents of the city had been forced to strike back, and now Sishmindris—even those in proper livery—were being killed in the street on sight.

Can't be true, thought Jianna. *Wild rumors.*

They spoke, too, in lowered tones, of the wandering dead—corpses unwilling to lie still, sometimes known to drag themselves from the pyre itself. Now these bodies were lurching around town in increasing numbers, and they were all but impossible to control, for their unseemly animation was proof against conventional weapons. Complete physical destruction offered the only sure means of halting them, but this goal was not easily achieved. Of late the undead had displayed a disturbingly intelligent tendency to seek safety in numbers. And where they congregated, certain sensitive or highly imaginative witnesses reported, the world changed and reality warped.

Lunatic fancies, Jianna told herself stoutly, but noticed that Rione was listening to these accounts with close, frowning attention.

After dinner there was nothing left but to retire to their respective chambers, at which point Jianna's appetite for novelty was surfeited, for she discovered then that she did not lodge alone. The room to which she was consigned contained two big beds, each accommodating four women. Had she traveled as Jianna Belandor, daughter of a wealthy magnifico, she would have enjoyed a private chamber with a soft bed for her own use and perhaps a pallet for a maidservant. Now she tasted the experience of the ordinary wayfarer—that is, one so fortunate as to sleep beneath the roof of an inn at all. She greatly preferred privacy. Even among the Ghosts, she had always had a pallet to herself. Still, it would not have been so bad had not one of her three bedmates needed to seek the chamber pot repeatedly throughout the night. The weary traipsing to and fro, the vibration of the lumpy bedding, the sounds and smells, woke her repeatedly. She was wide awake at dawn, and more than ready to abandon the dubious comforts of the Glass Eye.

The journey resumed, and around noon of the day after next, the air darkened. A dense blot loomed upon the atmosphere ahead, and Jianna caught the acridity of smoke on the breeze. At the inn they had spoken of Vitrisi's perpetual, smoke-belching pyres, and she had dismissed the accounts as exaggerations. Now she began to suspect that she had been mistaken.

Another hour of travel brought them to the verge of one of the villages clustering in the shadow of Vitrisi's ancient wall. This one, called Jiocco's Well, boasted a town square enclosing an exceptionally large public well, above which hung a sign of recent manufacture reading, GOOD HUMANS ONLY. A crudely daubed portrait of a Sishmindri marked with trilobed carbuncles of the plague, clasping hands with a human skeleton, underscored the message. An armed guard waited by the well, apparently prepared to enforce the edict.

Jianna recalled Jiocco's Well as a pleasant, bustling little community. Now the town center was all but empty, and several of the houses edging the square displayed boarded windows.

They rode on and the VitrOrezzi Bond brought them to the gates of Vitrisi, where, for the first time in her life, Jianna saw the way blocked by Taerleezi soldiers. They were not impeding egress, she noted at once. Apparently anyone and everyone could depart the city at will. Admittance was another matter, however. Would-be entrants—pedestrian, mounted, and in vehicles—had formed a line, and the soldiers were interviewing each in turn. Jianna and Falaste placed themselves at the end of the line, which advanced at fairly good speed.

Within minutes they reached the gate, where the bored Taerleezis on guard launched into a mechanical interrogation, clearly repeated countless times.

Names?

Rione answered truthfully.

"Noro Penzia," Jianna was surprised to hear herself reply, and Rione shot her a quizzical glance. It had slipped out easily, unthinkingly, through pure habit. But no, it was more than habit; her caution was founded in good reason. For one thing, her claim to the noble Belandor name would strike the guards as preposterous. They would see her as a dreamer or liar, there would be extra questions and delay, and they might just end by turning her away from the gate. Moreover, she had come to understand that the daughter of the Magnifico Aureste was a target in her own right—something she would never have believed in earlier carefree days.

Age?

Twenty-five and eighteen. Two accurate answers.

Condition?

"Physician," Rione declared. "And the lady is my assistant."

"Oh aye, and I'll lay odds she's got magic hands," volunteered one of the guards.

Jianna kept her face a blank.

Coming from?

Treating patients in the Alzira Hills. Another truthful answer, so far as it went.

Any cases of the plague among those patients?

None.

Any recent contact with plague victims? Shared lodgings with plague victims? Shared bed or board?

No.

State of health? Any recent instances of high fever, delirium or hallucinations, carbuncles, fainting, black bile, bloodspray, or invasive disembodied voices?

No.

Well, then. Neck and wrist check for telltale lumps.

Swallowing her outrage, Jianna bared the requisite anatomy. A quick inspection was completed, and the guards waved them through.

She was back in Vitrisi again. She had longed for this moment for months, but the reality scarcely matched her expectations. The streets, formerly so vital and colorful, were now thinly populated with humans and assorted animals, but no Sishmindris. There was not an amphibian to be seen. The merchants' booths were closed and shuttered, their pennants and streamers gone. There were no street singers, acrobats, or entertainers of any description in sight. Even the majority of beggars had apparently gone underground. Refuse bulked in heaps everywhere, and a haze of gritty smoke darkened, smudged, and discolored the world.

Jianna coughed. Her eyes watered and her throat scratched. *What's happened to my beautiful city?* She did not open her mouth to ask the question aloud, for fear of inhaling additional smoke, but not all voices were similarly stilled. There was one nearby, impossible to ignore, uplifted in some sort of chant or song. It was a pleasant, strong, rather hoarse voice, momentarily unidentifiable as to age or gender, and it seemed to be rhythmically reciting some sort of incantation, or perhaps it was only a list. Jianna listened.

" . . . *Concentrate of chicory, oil of blifilnut, essence of skorry and donkeyweed, star seeds, dried punia, mandragola, powder of shernivus, gingerroot mash with truni, milkweed pods, aromatic distillations—all pure, all good. Troxius medals, fine cast. Fegri charms, new made and strong. Draughts Sanguinarius, to fortify the blood. The Circle of Strength, impossible to break. The Secret of the Proportionate Progression, guarded for centuries by the arcanists, now revealed. Protect your health. Protect your families, save your children. Safety for sale!*"

The voice approached, its owner finally breaching the dense vapors, and Jianna stiffened at sight of an eerie figure voluminously cloaked in black, hands gauntleted, face shadowed beneath a wide-brimmed hat and guarded by a mask of odd design—black leather, with holes for eyes and mouth, dominated by a huge beak projecting half the length of a forearm.

"What is *that*?" She pointed discreetly. "Man or woman? And what's that thing on his or her face?"

"Woman, I think, but I can't swear to it," Rione returned. "Her clothing is fashioned to ward off contagion. That beak in the mask contains aromatic herbs meant to purify the air before it reaches the wearer's nostrils."

"Ingenious, but does it work?"

"I'm inclined to doubt it."

"Oh." She frowned. "What about the other things she's hawking? The powders, draughts, medals, and all the rest?"

"Useless, so far as I know. Toys and trappings of primitive superstition."

"You don't speak with such disdain of your own superstitions."

"I have none."

"Oh, really? What about the belief that your ritual of washing, scrubbing, or boiling everything in sight before performing surgery somehow helps? If that isn't superstition—"

"That, my little gadfly, is a reasonable conclusion based upon experience and observation."

"You started washing, and around the same time observed improved results. Does that necessarily mean that the one *caused* the other?" She teased for two reasons. One, she strongly suspected that Rione enjoyed it; the other, it helped to divert her attention from increasingly distressing sights and sounds of a stricken city.

Before he could answer, the hawker reached them.

"Safety, security, salvation," she or he offered with enviable assurance, extending a black-gloved palm upon which lay a bright object. "Newcomers to the city, be good to yourselves. Buy a medal of Troxius, beautiful detail, gold wash, scientifically proven power. Walk Vitrisi without fear. One diostre."

"A whole diostre for that? It's not even real gold!" Jianna objected.

"It's better than real gold, missy." The hawker's pleasant voice seemed to issue from the heart of a formless dark cloud. "It's health, it's hope, it's life. It's an anchor to hold you when the world thins out to nothing."

"When the world—what do you mean?"

"Haven't seen it yet? Don't worry, you will. And then you'll need something to hang on to, and you won't be thinking about the cost. One diostre, cheap at the price."

Jianna shook her head, the hawker faded back into the mists, and progress resumed. Another twenty minutes of travel carried them into a better section of town, where her spirits began to revive. Here the signs of disaster were not so prevalent. True, the streets were dim and smoke-strangled. Great red X's scarred several doorways, and there was still not a Sishmindri to be seen. Yet most of the houses seemed to be occupied, many windows glowed through the murk, and a few Scarlet Gluttons racketed from the rooftops. With but a little effort of will, it was possible to imagine an imminent return to normality.

This illusion expired as they turned a corner and, for the first time, Jianna beheld the undead. There they were: three molder-ing bodies, grey-fleshed and milky-eyed, but upright and ambu-lant, exactly as described. A deep shudder rocked her body, before the sight had fully impressed itself upon her understand-ing. A sense of wrongness filled her to the brim; a blurred recognition of some vast, silent change whose nature eluded yet terrified her. She swayed a little in the saddle, her flesh went clammy, and for a moment she thought that she was going to faint. Ridiculous, she had never fainted in her life. The horse beneath her snorted and quivered as if sharing its rider's qualm. She took a deep breath, and the dizziness receded.

The three undead seemed peaceable enough. They stood grouped closely together, bony fingers interlocked, hairless heads sweetly inclined toward one another. An occasional tremor shook one tattered limb or another. Apart from that, there was no motion and no suggestion of aggression. Even so, the aura of disruption was all but tangible.

Jianna's frightened eyes flew to Rione, whose own gaze was fastened on the trio. Without turning, he extended a hand, and she stretched sideways to grasp it tightly for an instant. The quick, warm contact braced her, and she was able to take in the entire scene: the incomprehensibly purposeful corpses, the gathering of scared but fascinated observers, and a lone voice—male, strong, and confident. Not a hawker; something or someone else.

"Friends, take heart," the speaker advised, his clarion tones ringing above the dejected mutterings of the onlookers. "There is nothing to fear from the Wanderers. I have discovered the secret of their unnatural vitality, and I have learned how to quell it."

Jianna's eyes sought the source and found it; a very tall, stout man, sporting a long violet cloak banded with rabbit fur and decorated with symbols worked in polychrome thread. His face was round and rosy. A narrow black mustache edged his full lips, and a wealth of glistening, carefully tended black curls framed his plump cheeks.

The pink face was familiar. She had certainly seen it before, and it took Jianna no more than a moment to recall the owner's name.

"Etris Cruzirius," she informed Rione. "My father once pointed him out to me, and told me that Uncle Innesq says Cruzirius is one of the few mountebank arcanists of the city who may actually possess a little talent."

Cruzirius's flamboyant appearance and theatrical manner hardly inspired confidence, but Uncle Innesq's judgment was reliable, and therefore Jianna watched with curiosity and some hope.

"Our city's cleansing commences here and now," Cruzirius proclaimed with glinting assurance. "Friends, clear me a little space, if you please, and honor me with your attention. For the best use of the arcane powers with which Fortune has deigned to favor me rests largely upon the trust and support of my observers and well-wishers."

It all sounded peculiar to Jianna. Uncle Innesq, a highly gifted, legitimate arcanist of the Six, never spoke of relying upon the trust or support of anyone. As far as she knew, he relied entirely upon his own talents, and preferred to conduct his arcane experiments in solitude. Still, there was room in the world for more than one method, and she was prepared to grant Etris Cruzirius the benefit of the doubt.

A path opened and Cruzirius advanced without perceptible

fear, never pausing until he stood no more than a dozen feet from the undead. There he halted to assume a dauntless pose, allowing his audience ample opportunity to wonder and admire. The three undead were similarly motionless, grouped in a silent colloquy. It was impossible to judge their awareness, if any, of the self-styled arcanist in the gaudy cloak.

Bowing his head, Cruzirius began to speak, so quietly at first that the cadenced syllables were inaudible. He made no use of the draughts, powders, or pills with which Uncle Innesq was wont to fortify himself prior to arcane exertion, and Jianna wondered at the omission, but strove to maintain an open mind.

Cruzirius spoke on, resonant voice gradually rising in volume until the incomprehensible words crashed on the atmosphere like waves upon an alien shore. There were gestures dancing to the music of that voice, arm sweeps extravagant as any actor's, and still Jianna wondered, for it was very unlike the concise grace displayed by Uncle Innesq upon the cherished occasions of her childhood birthday celebrations, when he had conjured transparent pastel fairies riding mythical winged beasts.

Her fellow spectators seemed not to share her doubts. The faces about her were rapt and respectful. Their awe was not difficult to fathom, for Cruzirius's voice possessed undeniable power. Her own pulses quickened responsively. Despite the vulgarity of his appearance and style, the man had some sort of genuine ability, she was certain. A curious electric tingle that she recognized shivered her nerves. She had felt it while watching Uncle Innesq at work, and she felt it now.

Cruzirius's practiced voice scaled the heights, and the surrounding mists seemed to thicken. Both arcanist and undead faded into the gloom. Jianna could see waving arms and billowing purple cloak; beyond them, three eerie, motionless figures. The air had gone indefinably bad. It did not stink or sting, but somehow seemed to have lost some of its life-sustaining quality. She drew deep breaths that failed to satisfy.

Others about her did likewise; distressed gasps could be heard on all sides.

Gasps gave way to shouts as the reality of Cruzirius's talent began to reveal itself.

Jianna leaned forward in the saddle, squinting to penetrate the veils of smoke and vapor. She could barely make out the three undead forms. They were no longer motionless, but stirring restlessly, as if troubled.

"They crumble, my friends!" Cruzirius proclaimed. "The dust claims its own. From the ground up, they crumble!"

Such a claim was not to be taken literally, yet the Wanderers were doubtless affected. All three were tottering and swaying as if on the verge of collapse. Presently one did collapse, and another, and then the last went down. She could no longer see them—too many bodies blocked her view—but the excited vociferation of the crowd implied success.

The quality of human outcry, along with the character of the atmosphere, altered quite abruptly. Shouts gave way to screams. At the same time, a sullen, bruise-colored glow lit the vapors shrouding the undead, and the air began to bite. Jianna dropped the reins and her hands flew to her face, which burned and itched as if stung by a million gnats. Her eyes watered, and the shrouded world swam. Her horse whinnied and shied, nearly pitching her from the saddle, and a startled squeal escaped her as her legs instinctively tightened on the mare's flanks. Hurriedly gathering up the reins, she resumed control of the horse, knuckled her streaming eyes, and looked about her.

Worse and worse. The glow lighting the mists had intensified to a glare, within which arced small bolts of angry luminosity. The undead were presently invisible, and Cruzirius nearly so, but the arcanist's voice rolled on richly. Few remained to listen. The coughing, watery-eyed spectators were retiring in droves. Jianna longed to follow them but, casting a glance at Rione, she saw that his interest focused intensely on the spectacle, and knew that he was unready to depart.

Moisture beaded her forehead and prickled under her arms. She was bathed in sweat, the product of alarm and excitement, she assumed, until she noticed that the raw air had warmed in excess of season and reason, leaping at a bound into high summer and beyond. It was far too hot for this time of the year, too hot for comfort, too hot to be endured.

"This Cruzirius fellow has bungled," she opined aloud and coughed, throat chafed by the scrape of unwholesome air.

Even in the midst of the uproar, Rione heard. Turning toward her, he began, "We'd best get out of—"

A new burst of unwelcome activity cut him off. The atmosphere immediately surrounding the fallen undead seemed to catch fire, so riddled it was with small, speeding bolts of radiant force. For a few seconds these missiles whizzed and circled within a circumscribed area, as if confined by an invisible wall against which they struck and ricocheted.

Etris Cruzirius's resonant vocalization ceased. A single incredulous exclamation escaped him. *"Impossible!"*

Breaking their invisible restraints, the brilliant spears of energy burst forth to fly in all directions. In a moment the air was filled with them. Where they struck flammable material, fire flared. Where they struck vital body parts, humans died. The ultimate fate of arcanist and undead was currently impossible to judge.

What was left of the crowd fled screaming. Jianna's terrified mare reared, and for the next few seconds, she strove hard to retain her seat and regain control. When she was able to dismount, she did so, seized the bridle, and quieted the trembling animal as best she could. Drawing the kerchief from her neck, she tied the cloth across the horse's eyes, for she had been told long ago that such measures enabled grooms to lead their intractable charges from burning stables, and the present situation seemed analogous.

Beside her Rione dismounted. She watched his eyes sweep the lightning-rent scene, and knew as surely as she knew her own name that he thought of staying to assist the injured. But it was madness; the victims were already dead, or nearly so. He could do nothing for them, and would only get himself killed if he lingered here. The thought was so insupportable that she plucked at his sleeve and, when he turned, threw him a shamelessly imploring look.

"Please, Falaste," she urged, voice soft but somehow audible through the surrounding din. "Take me away from here. Take me home."

He looked at her and his brows bent. Perhaps he was thinking of *her* safety. She hoped so. After a moment he nodded, and the two of them led their horses away from the site of the latest arcane disaster.

. . .

For a while there was no conversation. In silence they rode through the gloomy streets, each preoccupied with recent horrors. But when they reached the foot of the White Incline, Jianna's spirits began to stir. As they climbed, her sense of anticipation did likewise. Everything around her was changed much for the worse, yet at the same time inexpressibly dear and familiar.

Only minutes, now, she thought, and her mouth was dry with excitement.

They reached the top of the high bluff overlooking the sea, and now they were in the Clouds; underpopulated, dim and dirty of atmosphere, with the rooflights burning oddly in the afternoon, and more than one of the great mansions marked with red X's. But grand and imposing even yet, and above all, still hers.

As they neared the end of Summit Street, she unconsciously urged her mare to a trot. The last few yards, the last few seconds, seemed endless, but then the pale stone wall that surrounded Belandor House was rising before her, its wrought-iron gate firmly closed, as the magnifico would wish, and beyond the gate, *beyond—*

Ruin. Destruction. Devastation.

For a moment she thought it some visual trick of the wavering mists shaped by her own imagination.

No mistake. Belandor House had burned in the recent past. Not down to the ground, perhaps not beyond salvation, but the building had suffered immense damage. Jumping from her horse, she ran to the gate and gripped its bars with both hands. Her eyes rose in search of the central tower and found—nothing. The tower was gone. The remaining walls were charred and blackened, the ruined windows boarded. Even the grand front entrance, fully exposed to view by the collapse of the columned portico, was boarded. The south wing was worse yet—its roof entirely destroyed, its walls largely collapsed. Heaps of debris lay stacked atop the broken remains of a mosaic floor. The third main section of the building, the north wing, had not fared so badly, and was still probably habitable.

Jianna stared, momentarily numb with shock and disbelief. The anesthesia lapsed too soon as the implications of the scene sank in. Belandor House had burned, and the loss of property was massive—but what of lost lives? How had the residents fared? Father? Uncle Innesq? Kinfolk, guests, servants, and Sishmindris? *Father?*

She tore her gaze from the house. On the other side of the gate, a sentry stood watching her curiously. She did not recognize his face, which was square and dull. His slate-and-silver livery, ornamented with a medal of Troxius, was correct but a little baggy, not yet altered to fit him; he must have been engaged very recently. Catching his eye, she commanded, "Admit me."

His look of curiosity expanded to surprise. He stared at her, taking in her drab, slightly moth-eaten cloak, old shoes, and long hair falling in a simple braid down her back. His eyes shifted to Rione, who had come up behind her on foot, leading both horses. Clearly the newcomers were not beggars; just as clearly, they were not quality visitors entitled to respect or deference. He pondered a moment, then inquired, "What's your business here?"

"You are new and you don't recognize me." Jianna decided to forgive the fellow's ignorance. "I am the Maidenlady Jianna Belandor, daughter to the Magnifico Aureste. Open the gate, admit me, and bid a servant inform the magnifico of my return."

"Oho. You say you're *who*?"

"Tell the magnifico that his daughter has returned."

"Well, it would take a good set of lungs to tell the magnifico anything, these days."

"What are you saying? Has he been hurt? Is he—?" She could not bring herself to pronounce the intolerable word. "Explain yourself."

"What concern of yours, missy? Don't you know that nosy, cheeky little girls get walloped?"

"I've told you who I am." A few months earlier, she would have lost her temper and stormed at him. Now she was able to speak with an appearance of calmness. "If you refuse to recognize me, you're committing a blunder that you'll soon come to regret. For your own sake, answer my question. How fares my father, the Magnifico Aureste?"

"All right, the joke's getting tired. Or maybe you're not joking, maybe you're a proper loony. Either way, you got no business here. Clear off."

"You'd do well to believe her. She's telling you the truth," Rione interjected in his soothing, effortlessly persuasive voice. "I'll vouch for it."

"You will? Well, that makes all the difference." The guard nodded, with reverence. "And who might you be—the governor's son?"

Impudent ass! For a moment Jianna's temper threatened to slip restraint, and she fought hard for self-control. Anger would only make things worse. She needed to emulate Falaste's unruffled demeanor, but it was not easy. Wrathful words burned at the tip of her tongue, and might well have found exit had she not spied a familiar figure making its way around an angle of the building.

It was a Sishmindri, the first she had seen since reaching Vitrisi. The amphibian was carrying a basket of rubble toward the ruins of the south wing, with the evident intention of depositing his load atop existing heaps. Recognizing the distinctive pattern of mottling upon his hairless head, she shouted out his name.

"Ini!"

His head came up and he glanced around him.

"Over here!" She waved her arm, and his eyes found her. "It's Maidenlady Jianna—come over here!"

Setting down his burden, he obeyed. Seconds later he was there at the gate, staring at her with unfathomable golden eyes, but the distension of his air sacs revealed his surprise.

"Ini, you know me, don't you?" Without awaiting reply, she commanded, "Tell this blockhead who I am."

"Maidenlady Jianna. Magnifico's daughter," Ini replied without hesitation.

"For real?" The guard's jaw dropped. "You sure? If you're trying on some slimy hopfrog trick—"

"Truth," Ini asserted.

"You see," Jianna advised the guard gently, "you'd best open the gate without further argument."

Face scarlet, he obeyed.

"Thank you. Now, Ini, go inside and tell my father that I've come home."

"Magnifico gone."

"Gone?" Among the Sishmindris, the word embraced a variety of meanings, including death. Jianna moistened her lips and compelled herself to ask, "Where has he gone?"

"Away, with men to serve him, and many things to carry."

"Away where, and why?"

"Know not."

"For how long?"

"Know not."

"But he's alive and well?"

"He was."

Jianna shook her head, mystified and disturbed. She did not think to demand corroboration from the human guard standing near at hand. Instinctively, or perhaps on the unconscious basis of experience, she placed greater faith in the word of the Sishmindri, whose kind never lied. Her father believed that the amphibians lacked the intelligence and imagination to produce deliberate falsehood. Her uncle Innesq believed that lying violated their moral code. Either way, they were more reliable than humans.

"Very well. Then carry the word to Master Innesq. Tell him I am here."

"Master Innesq gone."

"*No!*" The tears sprang to her eyes. Innesq Belandor never ventured from home, and therefore, this time, the Sishmindri's meaning was unequivocal. Her brilliant and beloved uncle was dead. "He—he died in—" Her gesture encompassed the scorched ruins.

"Not dead. Away. With magnifico."

"Away?" Hope warred with incredulity. "Impossible. My uncle Innesq never leaves the house. He doesn't go anywhere, ever, except in his mind, and by way of his art."

"This time, he goes."

"*Where?*"

"Know not."

She hesitated, trying to take it in. Her father and her uncle Innesq were alive, but away from a wounded home. What or who was left?

Can't be. Please.

"Master Nalio?" she inquired with an effort.

"Ruler now," reported Ini.

It was difficult to imagine Uncle Nalio as ruler of a chicken coop, much less Belandor House. Still, if Aureste and Innesq were truly away, then Nalio would indeed inherit temporary command. Incredible, but inevitable. At least he would be able to furnish an intelligible account of all that had happened here in her absence.

"Very well, then. Ini, go tell my uncle Nalio that I have come home, with a guest. And send someone out to see to the horses." The Sishmindri bobbed a graceless bow and departed. "As for you—" Unconsciously adopting her father's authoritative manner, Jianna addressed the human guard. "You keep an eye on the horses for now. If anything goes wrong, you'll smart for it. Understand?"

"Yes, maidenlady." His face went redder than ever.

"Look to it." Drawing a deep breath to bolster her confidence, she turned to Rione.

"You reveal a new aspect of your character," he observed with an expression of mingled bemusement and amusement.

"Oh, well, sometimes one must be firm." She felt herself color a little. Concealing every sign of tension, she inquired easily, "Ready, then?"

"To take my leave, yes."

"That isn't what I meant."

"I know. But it's what I mean."

Exactly as she had feared. She studied his face, which was composed and seemingly tranquil, as usual. During the time she had spent in his company, however, she had learned to see beneath the surface, and now she beheld a wall of granite. He had set his course and he was not about to alter it. He meant to leave her—leave forever, without an instant's remorse or hesitation—and there was not a thing in the world she could do to stop him.

A great tumult of alarmed emotion boiled up inside her, and it was all she could do to stop herself from clutching his arm to hold him by force. Throughout the days that they had traveled together, she had known that this moment would arrive. But she had never allowed herself to consider its reality, for she had always managed to convince herself that, when the time came, she would find a way to stop him from going. At the point of crisis, when she really needed it, inspiration would strike and then she would produce words magical and potent as any ever uttered by the greatest arcanist.

And now her mind was empty of magical words. She was powerless to influence him. But Aureste's daughter would not give up without a fight.

"Oh, come, Falaste." She strove for a light, careless tone, and succeeded tolerably well. "Surely you can't mean to scamper off, just like that? Is that what friends do? You must come inside, at least for a meal and a little rest. Oh, yes, you needn't remind me of your grim resolve to avoid shaking my father's hand, at any cost. I haven't forgotten. But you heard for yourself, he's not here right now. So you see, you've really no good excuse."

"Jianna." He faced her squarely. "I told you days ago that I will not cross the threshold of Belandor House. I know you didn't believe that, but understand now that I am in earnest."

"Oh, but you—"

"Listen to me," he enjoined quietly, and she subsided at once. "Our journey has ended, and it's a happy ending for you. You've come back to your own home and your own family. Yes, the Belandor mansion has been damaged and your father isn't here to greet you—it's far from the fulfillment of your dreams—but these matters will mend. More to the point, you're safe and you're home. In a moment you'll walk into that house to resume the pleasant life of ease and comfort that you were born to enjoy. The events of the past months will fade from your mind like the remnants of a bad dream, and all will be as it was before.

"As for me," he continued, "I, too, resume my former life— that is, the drab ante-Jianna existence. Once upon a time it suited me well enough—perhaps it will again, in time. And the first order of business in that existence is to find my sister Celisse before she sets off some sort of firestorm. I can't afford delay, and therefore I take my leave."

"As easily as that?" she could not forbear asking. It would

have been far better to maintain an attitude of dignified indifference, but the words could not be contained. "All our time together, all the talk, the hardship and dangers we went through, and the work that we shared—did that mean nothing to you?"

"More than you can know," he replied gently, but his face was set and impervious.

"But you'll walk away, all the same?"

"There's nothing else for me to do."

Yes there is! she silently screamed at him. *You can come inside, you can stay with me!* She had not so thoroughly lost self-control that she uttered this sentiment aloud—particularly not in the presence of the guard, who stood a few feet distant, pretending to polish his Troxius medal, but patently eavesdropping. Instead, she asked quietly, "Where will you go?"

"To the Lancet Inn, near the Avorno Hospital. Should you wish to send word to me for any reason, I'll be there for at least the next several days."

And after that he would return to the Alzira Hills, and she would never see him again. This moment, here and now, was the final moment, and that concept was as difficult to encompass as some mathematical expression of impossibility. It felt like death, and she had no more words. The wide eyes she turned upon him were full of something like bewilderment.

"Be happy, Jianna. Good-bye." Remounting his borrowed horse, he rode off, leading her mare.

For a while she stood watching, but he never turned to look back. He might at least have spared her a glance. Her eyes filled with tears, which she dashed away impatiently. She had nothing in the world to cry about. She was safe. She was home.

Turning to survey the disfigured mansion, she located the nearest functional doorway. She squared her shoulders and walked toward it.

SEVEN

It hardly seemed like coming home. This north wing gallery, belonging to a section of the house that she rarely frequented, would have felt a little foreign at the best of times. And now—damaged, dingy, and smoke-stained—the place struck no strong chord of familiarity. Even the air, still laced with a faint tang of smoke, was alien to Jianna's concept of Belandor House.

Nevertheless, here was Uncle Nalio, attended by Ini, hurrying down the stairs to greet her, and he looked unchanged, save for the unremitting blackness of his attire. Mourning? *For whom?* He was staring at her as he came, eyes huge in his thin face, and she perceived his astonishment at her abrupt, unheralded resurrection. At the same time she was acutely aware of the alteration in her own appearance. She had left Belandor House accoutered like a young princess; she returned in the guise of an ordinary, commonplace girl. And for the first time, she wondered whether her experiences could have diminished or devalued her in some wholly unjust but nonetheless significant way. Had her father been there to greet her, the thought would never have entered her mind. But Aureste was absent. Falaste Rione's support had likewise disappeared, and Nalio Belandor's opinions had suddenly acquired unexpected importance.

"Hello, Uncle." Jianna offered an uncertain smile. *Awkward. Feeble. Embarrassing.*

"Niece Jianna." He halted before her, regarding her intently. They were of equal height, and their eyes were level. "It is really you. Until seeing for myself, I did not believe that it could be true. You are here, you are safe. Welcome, dear child. I bid you welcome to Belandor House."

The words were appropriate enough, but somehow annoying. He welcomed her as if he were the master of the mansion, graciously offering hospitality to a visiting kinswoman. But he meant no harm, and it was not exactly his fault that his manner had always irritated her. Therefore she submitted with good grace to a brief, dutiful embrace. He planted a suitably avuncular kiss upon her brow, and released her at once. She drew back a step, concealing her distaste.

"Where have you been, niece?" Nalio demanded predictably. "What happened to you? Why did you not send word?"

"I'll tell you everything," Jianna promised. "But it's a long story, and first, please, Uncle, tell me what's happened here. There's been a monstrous fire. Is everyone all right? Was anyone hurt? Where's my father, and Uncle Innesq?"

"No, everyone is not all right, not by any means. It was more than an accidental fire, niece. It was an—an—an organized assault, launched by the enemies of House Belandor. A number of servants and Sishmindris were incinerated or slaughtered. I have compiled a list of their names, should you care to educate yourself. Of infinitely greater import is the murder of your aunt, my wife Unexia. She—she—she is gone."

"Aunt Unexia—oh, it's horrible! I'm so sorry, Uncle Nalio!" Throughout the course of her life, she had rarely exchanged more than a few words of polite daily greeting with her uncle's thoroughly inconspicuous, almost anonymous wife. Yet her distress and sympathy were genuine enough. The mental image of a family member murdered by torch-wielding invaders was dreadful. Moreover, her uncle's grief invited natural pity.

"Thank you, niece. You display unexpectedly feminine sensibility, and it becomes you. I believe that I may safely express appreciation in Unexia Belandor's name."

Pompous fellow, can't he speak like a normal human being? The unkind thought rose unbidden, and she tried to push it away. Aloud, she inquired with quiet urgency, "And my father?"

"He has seen fit to withdraw."

Yes, I know that.

"My brother Innesq has embarked for the Quivers, there to meet with sundry great arcanists who wish to cleanse the Source. He is ill equipped to travel on his own, and therefore Aureste accompanies him."

"But Uncle Innesq never goes anywhere, not ever. I don't understand. Why would he go at all, much less now, when he's obviously needed at home?"

"He regards the present national plight as desperately in want of resolution."

"What, you mean they've gone off to find a cure for the plague?"

"That is incorrect. You must realize that the plague is merely a symptom of a greater underlying ill. It is clear to men of sound understanding that the Source has soiled itself, and the sole remedy resides in purification."

"How has the Source soiled itself?"

"What point in demanding a technical explanation certain to exceed your mental grasp? But come, you appear weary, disheveled, and travel-stained. You will wish to rest and refresh yourself before presenting me with a full explanation of your absence and silence, together with a detailed account of your actions. You have already observed that this north wing is the only section of the house that remains habitable. You will occupy one of the second-story chambers. There is one just across the hall from my own that will serve."

Just across the hall from Uncle Nalio? A little too close for comfort.

"Why don't I scout around a bit for an empty one that suits me?" she suggested.

"The one that I have chosen will suit you well enough."

"Am I not the best judge of that?"

"It is best by far that you accept my decisions without time-consuming argument, sulks, and tantrums." Nalio's brows and chin lifted. "I am, you will recall, acting head of House Belandor."

"Yes, I understand that, but—"

"Now, what did I just say about arguments and tantrums?" Nalio's upraised finger enjoined silence. His regard shifted to the mutely attentive Sishmindri. "Ini, conduct the Maidenlady Jianna to the chamber opposite mine. See to it that she is properly installed. Do not permit yourself to be distracted or delayed."

Jianna felt her cheeks heat. Her uncle spoke like a parent consigning some unruly, potentially deceitful child to the care of a governess. A tart reply quivered upon her tongue and she clamped her lips to contain it. Both law and custom upheld Nalio's borrowed authority, but it was only temporary. She could afford to let him enjoy his fleeting moment of glory.

"Niece, we shall dine together," Nalio decreed. "At which time you will relate all particulars and answer all questions put to you. For now, you may leave me."

"According to your will, Uncle," Jianna replied sweetly. *You obnoxious, insufferable little twit, you just wait until Father gets home.*

• • •

The room was one of those comparatively modest chambers that would formerly have been assigned to visitors of no great importance—obscure kinsmen, insignificant officials, or perhaps an exceptionally celebrated artist. Once upon a time, it would have struck her as insultingly humble. Now, following her term of residence among the Ghosts, the chamber with its polished wooden furnishings, finely carved stone mantel, good carpet underfoot, curtains and bed hangings of colorful crewelwork, seemed miraculously luxurious. It was not home, however. Not a single personal belonging marked the space as her own. In fact, she had never before crossed this particular threshold. Only once, during the course of a long-ago childhood ramble through the far reaches of Belandor House, she had come to this place, opened the door, stuck her head in, spied nothing remotely interesting, closed the door and gone away, never to return until now.

Jianna's eyes stung. It would all be better when her father and Uncle Innesq came back. Then everything would be right again.

I wish I'd stayed with Falaste! The thought flashed and instantly his face filled her mind: pale, fine, scholarly features— blue-grey eyes that saw everything—mobile lips that silently expressed so much—stubborn chin—and it seemed that all she wanted most in the world was to be with him again. But Falaste hadn't invited her to stay. Quite the contrary. He had delivered her to Belandor House like a parcel, then ridden away without hesitation and without a backward glance.

A couple of tears slid down her cheeks, and she wiped them impatiently. Falaste was gone and she had resumed her real life. The transition was unsettling, but she would accustom herself soon enough, and it was certainly all for the best.

Her eyes traveled the handsome, foreign chamber and found their way to the very small bundle of her personal belongings lying on the bed, where Ini had left it. Of course the Sishmindri had offered to unpack for her, but she had refused—her reluctance stemming from a curious sense of something that took her a moment to recognize as embarrassment. Her possessions were so meager, so shabby and makeshift that she was actually ashamed to let them be seen, even by a Sishmindri. Curious to find herself so aware of Sishmindri regard. Certainly her recent experiences had altered her in ways that she herself had yet to recognize.

She seated herself on the edge of the bed. (Soft. Lavender-scented. Richly patterned coverlet.) Another hour remained before dinner. In past years, she would have spent the time changing her clothes, selecting jewelry and ribbons, allowing a maid to arrange her hair. None of those options now existed. Certainly no luxury items reposed among her belongings these days. She unknotted the little cloth bundle, opened it, and surveyed the contents. One change of linen, one pair of knitted stockings, a roll of rags worn thin with repeated washings, a wooden comb, a wooden spoon, a twig with several lengths of thread wound about it, and a single, precious bone needle. Also a knob of brown soap, and a sliver of horn, pointed at both ends, serving as toothpick and nail pick. Not much there to work with.

Rising, she crossed to the washstand, above which hung a mirror—a small one by Belandor standards, but nicely framed in gilded carving, and once again astonishingly elegant by her recent standards of comparison. Studying her own reflection critically, she decided that Nalio's description of her appearance as "weary, disheveled, and travel-stained," had been insulting and only partially correct. So far as she could tell, she did not look particularly weary. Her hair and clothing were decently ordered. She was worse than travel-stained, however. She was filmed from head to foot with smoke-deposited soot. There was even a dark smudge of the stuff branding one cheek. No wonder the guard at the gate had failed to recognize her as the magnifico's daughter.

Removing her outer cloak, she uncovered a dress still reasonably clean, but mended and patched dozens of times, its once rich fabric threadbare and faded. No help for it; she owned no other.

The washstand offered a pitcher of fresh water, basin, lemon-scented soap, and lush towels. She cleaned herself as best she could, then combed her hair and plaited its dark length into a single thick braid, secured at the end with a length of twine. Once upon a time she had adorned her hair with exquisitely bejeweled and enameled combs. These days—twine.

There was a discreet knock at the door.

"Come," said Jianna, and Ini entered.

"Dinner now," announced the Sishmindri. "Master Nalio waits for you."

"I am ready. I'll find him—where?" Odd to be asking such a question, as if she were a stranger here.

"Eating place. Not real."

"Not—oh, you mean a makeshift dining room, set up after the fire?"

Ini blinked his golden eyes affirmatively.

"Lead me there, please." Strange, not to know the way. But the strangeness would wear off quickly, she told herself.

Ini bowed and departed, with Jianna at his side. He brought her along the corridor, down a flight of stairs, and then a few yards down another corridor to an arched doorway through which he ushered her with a graceless gesture. She paid him little heed, but the question shot across her mind, *What goes on in that hairless head of his?* Another peculiar mental twitch, and she could hardly account for it, but everything seemed awry just now.

The "eating place" looked to be a converted council or audience chamber, all but untouched by the fire, save for a few cracked windows. A good-sized table had been set up, and Uncle Nalio sat regally at its head, in her father's place; a sight that set her teeth on edge. Of course, as acting head of the household he had every right to be there. In any case, it hardly mattered, for there was nobody present to admire his new grandeur. He sat alone at an empty, oddly sterile board. The usual gathering of visiting friends, kinsmen, and business associates had vanished. Presumably all had departed in hopes of avoiding contagion, but where in the world would they find refuge? Across the sea, perhaps? Is that what it would eventually come to for everyone?

Nalio glanced at her as she walked in, his lips assumed an astringent pucker, and she was at once acutely conscious of her patched dress, scuffed shoes, and the twine in her hair. Ridiculous to fret over such trifles, but the expression in his eyes left her no choice. Averting her gaze, she headed for the chair at the foot of the table, the one farthest away from him.

"Not there, niece. I do not wish to shout the length of the chamber at you. Seat yourself here, beside me." It was a command.

Once again she swallowed an acid retort. His lordly tone was altogether ridiculous. Really, it was laughable, unworthy of her anger. Best to humor the little emperor, for now. She seated herself in the chair that he had specified.

Nalio was inspecting her openly and at leisure, at length observing, "We must remedy your appearance as best we can, without delay. You are a Belandor, and your present state ill becomes the dignity of our House. The loftiness of our standards expresses itself in our external aspect. This is a lesson that you must learn, niece."

"Yes, Uncle Nalio." *Oh, you pedantic, pretentious little pipsqueak.*

"We shall summon a dressmaker to replenish your wardrobe. You will also require a lady's maid of responsible character, adequate experience, and suitable years to serve as your personal attendant and chaperone."

What, you mean to sic some aging watchdog on me? We'll see. On the other hand, the promise of the dressmaker and the new wardrobe was exciting. Pretty clothes again, at long last. Perhaps looking like herself once more would help her to feel like herself, the Maidenlady Jianna Belandor, as opposed to some uneasy alien, belonging nowhere.

"I'll need someone who can do my hair." The smile directed at her uncle was suitably appreciative.

"That is not an unreasonable criterion." Nalio visibly relaxed and expanded. The interview was going well. "I am willing to allow this."

Allow. The arrival of the soup spared Jianna the necessity of reply. Just as well. No sense at all in picking a quarrel. The soup bowl and underplate were of fine, translucent porcelain, elaborately painted. The spoon was silver, heavy but gracefully designed. These were only the ordinary implements that she had used and taken for granted throughout her life, but she had never before noticed how beautiful and luxurious they were. Indeed, everything at Belandor House was beautiful, or had been so before the fire. And would be again, she silently promised.

The soup was rich and subtly seasoned, its flavor enlivened with floating herbs and petals. Whatever damage Belandor House had suffered in the recent past, its kitchen evidently functioned unimpaired. Jianna breathed an inaudible sigh. She had almost forgotten that such food existed.

Shellfish in wine sauce followed the soup. Then, breast of chicken garnished with half a dozen different species of mushrooms. There was newly baked white bread, fresh butter, a terrine of assorted vegetables, tiny preserved game bird eggs, salad of mixed greens, cream-filled pastries, and astounding hothouse fruits that tasted of summer. It was only an ordinary dinner by Belandor House standards, and it was magnificent beyond description. Jianna feasted, her enjoyment dampened only by Uncle Nalio's objectionable presence. He was eyeing her severely as she ate. The uncompanionable silence stretched, but at last he addressed her.

"Well, niece. You have enjoyed ample opportunity to refresh yourself and compose your thoughts. I trust you are now prepared to render a full explanation of your prolonged absence and silence."

"Very well, Uncle." She suppressed her annoyed reaction to his magisterial manner. His demand was entirely reasonable, in fact inevitable. Aureste himself would have framed the same request—but he would have stated it differently.

"It began about halfway between Vitrisi and Orezzia," Jianna commenced. "Our carriage was attacked by marauders."

"The carriage was discovered within days, along with the

dead bodies of its passengers, driver, and guards. Everyone was there except you, niece. Only you had vanished."

"They abducted me."

"So your father surmised. We could not fathom the absence of a ransom demand, however."

"They didn't mean to hold me for ransom. Their intentions were far worse."

She launched into a full description of the events following her capture by the outlaw Belandor clan. She spoke of Ironheart, its inhabitants, their hideous matrimonial schemes, and their connection to the Ghosts of the resistance. She spoke of the cruel treatment, the blows and threats she had received, and the menial work she had performed. She spoke of serving as assistant to Dr. Falaste Rione, an honorable physician and resistance sympathizer, whose father had once held the position of house doctor to the Magnifico Onarto Belandor. She described her rescue, the escape from Ironheart, the flight to the Ghosts' campsite, where Rione's medical skills were much needed, and whence no written communication had been possible. She described the ugly epidemic assailing the Ghosts, spoke much of Dr. Falaste Rione's talent and dedication, told of the doctor's ultimate success, after which he had finally been free to escort her back to Vitrisi and home.

Everything she related was entirely true, but some facts she deliberately omitted. She divulged nothing of Ghostly identities, hierarchies, plans, habits, resources, or whereabouts. She certainly made no mention of Dr. Falaste Rione's dangerous sister. Nor did she breathe a word of her own marriage to Onartino Belandor. She could hardly have brought herself to speak of it to her father, much less Uncle Nalio, and her sense of mortification was absurd, for she had nothing to be ashamed of. The so-called marriage had been a twisted travesty. It hadn't even been legitimate—not really—and of course, it had meant nothing at all. She had escaped unstained; she was the Maidenlady Jianna still. So she assured herself. Yet nothing could banish her rush of horror at the thought that—for the space of a day or two, between the wedding and his death—she had been Onartino's wife, and his property.

Nalio was pestering her with questions. He wanted details and specifics, particularly those relating to this Dr. Falaste Rione, with whom she had spent so much time. Who was this Rione person? What was his background, his credentials? Had he treated her with the respect due a member of House Belandor? He was clearly no gentleman, else he would have escorted her home to Belandor House and transferred her safely into the keeping of the acting head of the household.

"He did escort me home." Jianna strove for patience. "He just didn't come inside."

"I trust you made it clear to the fellow that he deserved a reward for his services?"

She felt the angry blood rush to her cheeks. "I think he was pressed for time," she returned obliquely.

"But how very extraordinary."

"Yes." She deliberately misinterpreted. "He *is* extraordinary." Oh, to pry him loose from this topic! She did not want to speak of Falaste Rione to Uncle Nalio, or to anyone else, for that matter. Somehow even the most commonplace, casual queries seemed invasive. Determined to change the subject, she plied her uncle with questions of her own, to which he replied at length. She verified, not to her surprise, that her father had been off upon some nameless jaunt at the time of the attack upon Belandor House. Of course. Aureste had at that time been launching his own assault upon Ironheart, of which Nalio appeared to know little or nothing. Hardly surprising—Aureste was not wont to confide in his youngest brother. Nalio knew only that Aureste had returned from that mysterious excursion frustrated, black-tempered, and distracted. He had undeniably applied himself to the healing of Belandor House, yet somehow, sometimes, his mind had seemed elsewhere. Nalio did not know why.

But Jianna did.

She fired off more questions and quickly learned as much as Nalio knew of his brothers' current expedition north, but it seemed that the verifiable facts were few. Innesq and others of his ilk were needed to scrub down the Source in some abstruse, unnatural manner that only arcanists could possibly understand. If they failed, egregiously unpleasant things would happen. But then, unpleasant things were already happening all over town. More and more Vitrisians were dying of the plague these days, but the dead refused to rest in peace; they had developed an unseemly fondness for aimless rambling. At least, it looked aimless, but who could really say? The dead themselves offered no insight, consistently refusing to answer all questions put to them.

The Wanderers, as they were often known, while displaying no violent tendencies, were nonetheless dangerous by reason of extreme contagiousness, combined with unwelcome sociability. Their taste for living company was so marked that a certain alarmist element of the population actually imagined the corpses engaged in an organized effort to spread the plague. This was nonsensical, in Nalio's opinion. The unfortunate remnants retained just enough of memory and feeling to long for contact with what had once been their own kind; it was nothing more than a final twitch of human instinct. Of course, "human instinct" could hardly account for the similarly gregarious behavior of the Sishmindri revenants. In all likelihood, the poor dead beasts simply demonstrated their continuing need and desire for firm human leadership, but again, the foolish alarmist element had taken fright. The result? There were sections of Vitrisi wherein Sishmindris were being slaughtered on sight—an appalling waste, in Nalio's opinion.

Uncle Innesq would find it appalling, too, thought Jianna. *But not for the same reasons. And Father?*

Rumor had it, Nalio confided, that certain presumably plague-crazed Sishmindris had turned feral, even going so far as to attack and kill their human overlords. Old wives' tales, to be sure. All but impossible to imagine the quiet, placid creatures capable of such behavior. But if by chance the rumors actually contained a grain of truth—if murderous Sishmindris haunted the streets of Vitrisi—then the threat was negligible, for they would never set web-toed foot upon Belandor property.

Nobody and *nothing* could possibly break in—not while Nalio Belandor was in charge. In addition to all of his brother's arcane safeguards—all of them reinstated and reinforced prior to Innesq's departure—there were plenty of mundane protective measures in place as well. Newly hired guards and sentries, formidably armed and stationed everywhere, indoors and out. Heavy locks of the most modern design, installed throughout the inhabited north wing. Hidden observation points. Cached weapons, secretly stored at key locations. An alarm system of bells and chimes. And then there were the fiendishly clever concealed *pitfalls*, designed to entrap and incapacitate intruders. He could not permit himself to enlarge upon that topic. The key element in the effectiveness of the pitfalls lay in *secrecy*. Suffice it to say, any would-be intruder was sure to encounter highly unwelcome . . . surprises, thanks to the vigilance and diligence of Nalio Belandor. In the past, security had been lax, and the results had been horrendous, but all of that had changed, under the stewardship of . . . Nalio.

To Jianna, it made little sense. It seemed that what was left of Belandor House had been transformed into some sort of a small fortress, not unlike Ironheart. Under the rule of Uncle Nalio, there were locks, bars, hidden pitfalls, innumerable regulations, and it was altogether unpleasant. There was no cause for real concern, however, for all of it was temporary. Aureste and Innesq would return within days, and then life would resume its accustomed aspect—at least, so far as possible within a largely ruined mansion overlooking a restive, fearful, angry, smoke-palled, plague-ridden, corpse-trodden city.

The meal was approaching its conclusion, and he was studying her with a thoughtful air that set alarm bells pealing inside her head.

"Is something amiss, Uncle?" she inquired, a shade too sweetly.

"All is adequately ordered," he reassured her. "Your return introduces an unexpected element, but we shall alter the design accordingly."

What in the world was he blathering about?

"I must decide what is to be done with you," he explained, evidently noting her look of incomprehension.

"What do you mean—*done* with me?" She frowned, puzzled and uneasy. "I've come home, that's all."

"I must determine the course best serving the interests of House Belandor," he announced, alight with noble resolution.

She did not understand what he had in mind, but he needed to be put in his place, and she replied very gently, "Surely it is my father's place to do so, upon his return."

"Surely. But who can say when that will be? My brother's absence may continue for weeks—months—years. During that period, whatever its duration, it is my bounden duty to act as head of the household."

She wanted to argue, but there was nothing to say. He was right.

"It is even possible," Nalio mused, "that neither of my brothers will return at all. I do not wish to alarm you, niece, but the world is often harsh and cruel. It is wise to consider all possibilities, one of which is that the burden I have assumed will be mine to bear for life."

Burden—you canting hypocrite! You'd like nothing better.

Perhaps her thoughts showed in her eyes, for Nalio's narrow face suffused, and he tilted his head back to look down his nose at her. "I will—will—will do my duty," he proclaimed. "And be assured that you—you—you will do yours."

"And what might that be?"

"When I have decided, I will—will—will let you know!"

"I see. As far as that goes, I believe I'll wait upon my father's will." Pushing her chair back from the table, Jianna stood up.

"Sit down this instant. This conversation is not over."

"Uncle, I bid you good evening." Head high, Jianna marched from the room. His voice was hammering at her back, but she did not stop.

. . .

Vitrisi lay well behind them. For long, monotonous hours, the Belandor carriage and its satellites traveled north along the Nor'wilders Way over rolling, mist-smudged terrain marked by little more than the occasional small farmhouse rising amid empty fields. The sky was colorless and the land correspondingly drab, but the stark, wintry countryside offered one signal advantage. Here, far from the busy pyres of the city, the air was blessedly free of smoke.

Clean air notwithstanding, the scene was dull, and the Magnifico Aureste soon lost all interest. Drawing forth a list compiled by Nalio, supposedly describing each and every weapon carried by the Belandor party, down to the last miniature palm-bodkin—he lost himself in practical issues of distribution.

Innesq Belandor did not share his brother's boredom. The hours passed, and his eyes never strayed from the passing landscape. Judging by the smile of almost child-like wonder and pleasure lighting his face, the sight of the world beyond Belandor House—beyond Vitrisi itself—was unlikely to pall within the near future. When night came and they halted to make camp, Innesq's interest did not wane. The sight of the servants pitching the tents clearly fascinated him. The care and feeding of the horses, the preparation of the evening meal, even the digging of a communal latrine seemed to hold him spellbound. When the heat rising from the cookfire punched an incorporeal fist into the mists hovering about the campsite and Innesq lost track of all else, Aureste gave up vying for his brother's attention. At some point Innesq would surely return to reality, but for now he was conversationally useless.

In the morning the journey resumed, and it was a repeat in almost every particular of the previous day's travel. So, too, were the following three days, but after that, the character of the land altered. Curves sharpened to angles, the grade of the road grew steeper, and the fields gave way to virgin moorland. The road itself—faint, narrow, ill defined—seemed more concept than reality. Progress slowed, and the carriage lumbered laboriously over land beginning to manifest hints of springtime mud.

The particularly teeth-rattling navigation of a stony stretch one sunless afternoon led Aureste to question his brother.

"With your great gift, would it not be a simple matter for you to—how shall I put it—facilitate progress?"

"Grant the horses the power of flight, perhaps?" Innesq inquired. "Or better yet, devise some means of compressing the next several days' time into the space of a single hour?"

"Either would do nicely, but my imagination isn't quite that fertile. I wondered only if you might not contrive to smooth the road a bit."

"Ah. That I might, but I will not."

"You could shorten our journey by days."

"The cost is too high. Remember, each and every arcane exercise exacts its price in strength and vital energy. These commodities replenish themselves, but time is needed. The task that I and my colleagues face demands the highest talents and skills of all. I cannot afford to spend my resources upon such serviceable feats as the smoothing of roads, kindling of fires upon damp wood, or renewing the freshness of spoiled food. For now, I must play the miser. You understand me?"

"Oh, certainly. Certainly." Aureste's attention returned to weaponry, and the scenery flowed by.

In the time that followed, Innesq maintained his resolution. When they reached Boundary Water and crossed by way of a bridge so ancient and rotten that the timbers groaned and split beneath the weight of the carriage, he offered no arcane assistance, despite his obvious sympathy for the nervousness of the horses. When one of a supply wagon's wheels sank in mud, he did not help. And when mutual accusations of theft exploded between a couple of the guards, and it lay within his power to locate the missing article of contention, he uttered not a single potent syllable.

To Aureste, it smacked of artistic affectation. His brother's powers seemed inexhaustible, and he perceived no great need of exaggerated economy. Inwardly he chafed at avoidable delays, but deferred as always to Innesq in all matters arcane.

They pressed north, and the way further darkened when they reached a region of tree-clad slopes. Here the road narrowed, worming a constricted path among the pines, whose tall forms blocked much of the tired light. At times the shade lay so thick and heavy that it became necessary to light the carriage lanterns at midday. Despite the dimness and difficulties, no serious mishap occurred, which was fortunate, for there were no locals to whom they could have turned for assistance—no villages, roadside inns, not so much as an isolated woodsman's hut. The region through which they passed seemed uninhabited; presumably the soggy hills offered little hope of profit to men.

Therefore, on the gloomy grey morning that they spied a sizable party on the road ahead, the sight was startling.

"Is it—?" Innesq Belandor inquired of his brother.

Leaning out the carriage window and applying a spyglass to his eye, Aureste surveyed the scene. Through the fog he descried colored pennants decorating and identifying the vehicles ahead.

"Black and plum," he reported, drawing back inside and setting the spyglass aside. "Corvestri."

"Ah, we have caught up with Vinz." Innesq's pleasure was innocent and unfeigned. "Excellent."

"I don't see anything particularly excellent about it." Aureste scowled, once again annoyed by his brother's casually cordial use of their enemy's given name. "I suppose it was inevitable."

"It was, and I trust you'll keep your choleric humor to yourself when we meet my colleague."

"Your colleague. May I remind you—"

"No need."

"Very well. Be at ease, then. I'll contain my urge to gut your esteemed colleague like a fish when we finally come face-to-face—which won't happen, I trust, before we reach our destination."

"That will be some days or weeks hence."

"In view of your refusal to speed our journey."

"Now that we have overtaken the Corvestri party, surely you do not mean to travel separately?"

"I do."

"Aureste, you are allowing your spleen to rule your good judgment. We and our allies should combine forces. That is best for all."

" 'Allies.' Applied thus, almost as irritating a term as 'colleague.' For the sake of our own comfort and safety, we shall maintain distance between ourselves and the Corvestri creatures for as long as it's practical to do so."

"It is not 'practical' at all. Despite all differences, surely you must see the benefits of—"

"Enough, brother. I safeguard the interests of our House, and you must accept my decisions, as I accept yours in matters arcane."

"You safeguard nothing, you merely express hostility. But I see that you are resolved, and I will not waste time trying to change that obstinate mind."

"Ah, such large tolerance. Mark me, you'll soon see that I'm right."

EIGHT

Jianna found the next few days distinctly enjoyable, and with reason: They were almost entirely given over to the replenishment of her wardrobe. A small squadron of dressmakers and seamstresses descended upon what was left of Belandor House, and with them they brought lengths and bolts of wondrous fabrics. Measurements were taken, needs and requirements discussed, Uncle Nalio's approval secured, orders placed, and the work began.

Jianna reveled in it all, but two aspects of the endeavor piqued her curiosity: conspicuous luxury, and remarkable dispatch. She was to receive a lavish assortment of gowns, two of them formal, gold-laced, and fit for the grandest occasion. There were petticoats of stiff brocade, chemises, lace-edged undergarments of linen, lawn, and silk. There was a silk-lined woolen cloak of sweeping amplitude. Hoods, scarves, ribbons, gloves, shoes . . . everything.

Given Nalio Belandor's intense concern with appearances, it was only to be expected that he would clothe his niece as befit a member of his House. Even so, the liberality he now displayed was surprising, particularly in view of the huge cost of Belandor House's restoration. Who, after all, would see all the fine new clothes, particularly the elaborate formal gowns? She expected to live quietly at home until her father returned, at which time she would inform him of her decision to remain in Vitrisi. During that interval, while the city writhed in the grip of the plague, she was hardly apt to receive either callers or invitations. What need of sartorial splendor?

Redundancy notwithstanding, the beauty of the new garments was irresistible. Such slippery, slithery, jewel-hued silks;

such stiffly gold-crusted brocades; such deep, delicious, densely piled velvets! She could hardly keep her eyes or her hands off them. And within the space of mere days, there was plenty to handle, and to wear, owing to the unusual speed of manufacture. The little seamstresses were lodged in one of the north wing's humbler cubbies, where half a dozen of them shared a washstand and slept on pallets scattered about the floor; for Uncle Nalio's generosity did not extend to the hirelings. They worked in shifts, night and day, and the big wooden chest in Jianna's appointed chamber was filling by the hour.

Under the present circumstances, what could she do with it all? And what could account for Uncle Nalio's insistence upon such super-swift labor?

Uncle Nalio wasn't so bad, really. A bit annoying, of course. A bit fussy, priggish, petty, and absolutely crammed with self-importance, these days. But well intentioned, conscientious, diligent, devoted to Belandor interests in general, and to the rebuilding of Belandor House in particular. He brimmed with remodeling plans, most of which she listened to at dinner, for Nalio was firm in his conviction that the proprieties must be observed, even in the most trying of times. And the proprieties demanded evening meals as stately as circumstance allowed, attended by all family members in residence. But now there were only the two of them.

How odd it was. In past years, most meals had been served in the family's private dining room—a smaller and more intimate space than the cavernous banqueting hall. At dinnertime the room had usually been crowded with immediate family members, more or less distant kinsmen, and visitors of varying rank. The Magnifico Aureste had always sat at the head of the table, with his two brothers immediately below him. Except when supplanted by a visitor of superior status, Jianna had come next, always seated next to Uncle Innesq. Then, to her left, and also directly opposite, usually sat attractive young people, clearly chosen with her pleasure in mind—clever, polished, stylish young people with whom she could trade news, jokes, and gossip; with whom she could, upon certain occasions, even engage in a little very decorous flirtation. In the midst of such conversational plenty, she had never needed to exchange anything beyond basic civilities with tiresome Uncle Nalio, and she certainly hadn't cared to. But now there was nobody else.

Initially she had regarded the prospect of conversation with him as an exercise in endurance, but she soon discovered how very easy—indeed, restful—it truly was. Any question concerning the repair of the house was enough to set his mouth in motion for the next quarter hour. The facts and figures came gushing out of him in torrents, and she could keep her wide eyes fixed on his face and her lips curved in an encouraging smile, while allowing her mind to wander along its own path. That path usually carried her to Falaste Rione.

Where was he now, and what was he doing? Had he tracked down his incendiary sister and dragged her back to the Alzira Hills, or was he still hunting? Was he safe and well? Recollections of his face filled her imagination: Falaste materializing out of the rain upon their first meeting; Falaste, working in the Ironheart infirmary; Falaste, sitting beside her in the sleet, with his cloak draped over the two of them. His smile, his eyes. Dozens of images glowed in quick succession, and such was their power that she would often lose track of Uncle Nalio's discourse. Then his purse-lipped silence and affronted scowl would alert her to her error, and she would manufacture another question to set him talking again, freeing her to return to her memories.

The days were largely filled with fittings, which once upon a time would have been exciting, and even now had not lost all appeal. But often as she stood there draped in damask, with the seamstresses buzzing about her, she would think of the work she had performed as Falaste's assistant, and suddenly the activity of the dressmakers and their human dummy seemed ridiculously trivial. Of course, their project was finite in nature. At the present rate, the new garments would be finished very soon, the workers would depart, and then—? What would she do with her time?

In the past she had never known loneliness or boredom at Belandor House, where family and friends lived in a palace overlooking the most wonderful city in the world. Now family and friends were gone, the palace lay largely in ruin, and the wonderful city had turned into a smoke-shrouded plague boil. What was there here for her, now? Uncle Nalio's company at dinner?

Of course, the bad times were bound to pass. Father and Uncle Innesq would come home in due course. The epidemic would subside, the wandering corpses would lie down, the smoke would clear, Vitrisi would resume normality, and Belandor House would rise again in all its splendor. It was only a matter of time, and she had time—more time than she knew how to use.

Perhaps she should take more interest in the repair of the house. It was an important matter of family concern, with which she, as an adult, ought to involve herself. True, Uncle Nalio possessed a rare conversational ability to drain all life from the most absorbing of topics, but she would listen for the ideas lurking behind his clouds of minutiae. At least, she would try.

Armed with this laudable intention, she presented herself at the makeshift dinner table. She was wearing one of her new gowns—lightweight wool in a shade of deep sapphire, with neckline, wrists, and buttonholes bound in scarlet silk; a simple, beautifully cut, and becoming garment. There were dark blue shoes with rosettes, and a wide silk sash with fringed ends, wrapped tightly to display her small waist. The promised lady's maid had not yet been engaged, and she had been obliged to arrange her own hair. With the aid of a mirror and a number of new silver pins, she had contrived a fairly credible twist. When completed, the image that looked back at her from the glass had been reassuringly familiar. Finally, she was herself again.

Uncle Nalio shared her opinion. When she walked into the dining room, he favored her with a smile of rare approval.

"Niece, you are much improved, and once again recognizable as a person of quality. I should no longer suffer a particle of shame in presenting you to the world."

"Thank you, Uncle." Jianna was proud of herself. She had managed to reply without sarcasm, temptation notwithstanding. All it took was a little self-control.

She seated herself at her usual place, on his left-hand side. Soup was served. For a time they ate in less than companionable silence, until Jianna compelled herself to inquire, "And have you chosen among the stonecutters yet, Uncle?"

"It is a delicate decision," he informed her, and proceeded to elaborate at length.

She tried to pay attention, but it was not easy. Her thoughts *would* gravitate to the camp of the Ghosts, and all that she had experienced there. Still, she needed to listen, it really was her duty. What was he saying now?

"But you do not wish to hear all of this," observed Uncle Nalio. "No doubt it is tedious."

She had let it show. She had let her attention slip, her boredom reveal itself, and now she had insulted him; exactly what she wanted to avoid. *Oh, bother.* Now he would complain and reproach, his face would turn red, and she would have to curb her temper and her tongue.

But Nalio did not look insulted or resentful. Quite the contrary, he was actually smiling at her with an aspect of roguish benevolence. The expression did not suit him. She hardly knew how to reply, but it didn't matter, for he was still talking.

"There are better things to fill a young woman's mind—eh, niece?" He seemed to aspire to jocularity, but he conspicuously lacked aptitude. "Come, don't stare as if you are stupid. Surely you divine my meaning?"

"I must confess, I do not."

"The recent preparations, the care, the attention, and the inordinate expense—have they suggested nothing?"

"They suggest your preference that your niece's appearance reflect the greatness of our House."

"A juvenile oversimplification, of course. I could not expect you to grasp the subtleties and complexities, yet you have happened upon the essential point. Yes, niece, you will serve as a representative of House Belandor, now that you are about to venture forth into the world."

"I've only just come home. Where exactly do you suggest that I venture?"

"Is this maidenly coyness?" He scrutinized her closely. "Upon my word, I believe that you are in earnest. It is my pleasure, then, to inform you of your good fortune. Niece, you are to be married."

"Someday, I trust." She smiled politely. He really *was* striving for humor. He meant well, but he shouldn't be encouraged.

"Sooner than that. The tradespeople will complete their work within the next few days. You will be properly outfitted, and then you will set forth for Orezzia."

"I don't understand." A certain internal quiver registered her realization that he was not joking.

"Surely your memory is not that feeble? Have you forgotten that you are betrothed to the Magnifico Tribari's oldest son?"

She recalled it well enough, but only as a distant memory. Part of the past, another life, with no present reality. *Ancient history,* she wanted to say, but instead replied courteously, "I've been absent for months. The Magnifico Tribari and his House must have dismissed all hope of the match long ago, and who can blame them?"

"Not so. House Tribari received the first half of your dowry long ago. The funds have not been returned, hence the betrothal continues unbroken. I have already dispatched a letter to the Magnifico Tribari informing him of your impending arrival."

The soup bowls were removed. The fish course was set before her: trout fillet in ethereal Cloud Sauce. She stared down at the plate. Her appetite had vanished. At last she replied, "It seems very hasty."

"Quite the contrary. The business should have been concluded months ago."

"But it wasn't, and so much time has passed, and now . . ." Her voice trailed off.

"Well, niece? Your point?"

And now things have changed! I don't want to go to Orezzia, and I don't want to be forced into another marriage. It's as if I were back at Ironheart. She could scarcely voice such thoughts, and therefore she answered, "Surely it would be best to wait for the Magnifico Tribari's reply. By this time, his son may have wed some other maidenlady."

"Nonsense. The betrothal was firm and legally binding. In the absence of a formal termination, the arrangement stands. Rest assured, you have not been supplanted in the young Tribari heir's affections."

But what if he's been supplanted in mine? Aloud, she replied respectfully, "That may be, Uncle. But perhaps the Tribari view of the matter doesn't coincide with yours. I think it would be wise to await reply from the Magnifico Tribari before I go hurrying off to Orezzia. In fact, I think it would be best to consult my father before taking action of any sort. He'd surely wish to judge for himself."

This time, Nalio's face did turn red—a rich, deep shade. "Aureste may be gone for months," he snapped. "And during his absence, I am master of Belandor House. I advise you to remember that."

"And I advise *you* to remember that you'll be accountable to my father, when he comes home. What d'you suppose he'll say if he discovers that you've packed me off to Orezzia before he's had a chance to see me?"

"I assume that he will laud my industry in carrying this marriage endeavor through to conclusion, at long last."

"No he won't. He'll want to know why you were in such a

great hurry to send me away. I'd like to know as well. Why, Uncle?"

"It is a matter of duty, necessity, family honor, and family connections. It is a happy coincidence that the Magnifico Tribari stands as patron to several of the finest artists and artisans in all the Veiled Isles. Once our respective Houses have been linked by marriage, the magnifico is certain to grant me the services of his protégés at nominal cost—or perhaps in his nobility, he himself will bear the entire expense. Our home will rise in renewed splendor. There now, is that clear enough for your understanding?"

"You mean to say you'd barter your niece for a clutch of painters and plasterers?"

"For Belandor House. I think only of Belandor House."

"And nothing of its human inhabitants?"

"It is hardly your place to question me. At present I stand in your father's stead, and I speak with the authority of the Magnifico Belandor."

Nalio's chin rose, and his narrow chest swelled grandly. He reminded Jianna of some small tree frog puffing itself up with air in order to intimidate would-be attackers, and the comparison triggered a sputter of laughter that she camouflaged poorly with a cough.

Nalio's red face darkened to purple and his mouth worked nervously for a moment before he added, with dignity, "I trust I may rely upon your willing compliance."

"No, Uncle Nalio. I'm afraid you may not." Swallowing her amusement, she spoke calmly and firmly. "I don't wish to vex you, but I feel that I must confer with my father before leaving Vitrisi. I'm certain that is what the magnifico would prefer."

"It is not—not—not your place to speak for the magnifico. That is my privilege."

"Then don't abuse it." The words slipped out, and she regretted them at once.

"You—you—you are an impertinent, undutiful flibbertigibbet!" His eyes flashed moist fire. "Your father indulged you shamefully. I have always said so, and I have always been right!"

"Please, Uncle. I don't wish to quarrel. I'll live here quietly until my father returns, and then the matter will be decided once and for all."

"The matter *has* been decided! By me, the acting head of the household! There is nothing more to be said."

"In that last, I defer to your will." She swallowed a mouthful of fish. "This trout is excellent. Do taste it."

Slamming his fork down with unnecessary force, Nalio surged from his chair to stand glaring down at his morally deficient niece.

"I will not endure such—such—such extreme impudence and insolence!" he informed her. "Perhaps your father would, but not I! Now that I am master, you will—will—will demonstrate proper respect and obedience. Do you understand me?"

"Quite."

"You will accept my decisions without argument. You will prepare to embark for Orezzia within a week's time."

"No, Uncle. I will not."

"This—this—this is unacceptable! Inexcusable! You feather-brained sauce-box! You coddled cosset! You mischievous, malapert minx! You will obey me, or suffer the consequences!"

"Really? What consequences?"

"Go to your room! Go to your room this instant!"

"I prefer to finish my dinner, first." Jianna applied herself to the trout, but managed to slant a glance up through her lashes, and saw her uncle's fist clench. She stiffened, but kept on eating. He would not dare to lay a hand upon Aureste's daughter. She had spent enough time in the company of people ready and willing to hurt her to know that she confronted no such danger now.

And sure enough, Nalio's fist came nowhere near her, but instead sought the table bell. A furious summons tinkled sweetly, and a Sishmindri entered, no doubt expecting to remove the fish course.

"Escort the maidenlady back to her chamber." Nalio paused a dramatic moment before adding, "And then lock her in."

Jianna stared at him, astounded for a moment, but rallied quickly. Addressing herself to the Sishmindri, whose mottling was familiar but whose name she did not know, she declared, "I will finish my dinner before retiring to my chamber. I'm certain that I express my father the Magnifico Aureste's will in telling you that your services are not required at present."

The Sishmindri blinked uneasily.

"Take her to her room." Nalio swept a gesture. "Now."

The Sishmindri hesitated a long, unhappy moment, before advising Jianna, "Maidenlady, come now."

"Presently." She sat still.

Scenting victory, Nalio directed, "If she resists, do what you must."

"Maidenlady. Please. Maidenlady."

She ignored the plea, and then the unthinkable occurred. A web-fingered hand closed on her elbow and tugged gently. The pressure was apologetic, more appeal than command, and yet he had actually dared to touch her. Jianna lifted outraged eyes to the Sishmindri's face, wherein she discovered nothing intelligible. For a moment she considered arguing, shouting, even struggling, but controlled all such impulses. Her angry expression, which should have daunted the creature, exerted no such effect. Evidently Nalio's displeasure was more to be feared than her own. Moreover, an adult male Sishmindri was strong, muscular, and quite capable of overcoming her resistance, should it actually come to that. Never in all her life had she conceived such a possibility, but she considered it now.

It was unbelievable. Prissy old Uncle Nalio could actually compel her obedience. And he'd do it, too. He was turning what was left of Belandor House into another Ironheart. She threw him a disgusted glance and met a glare of nakedly triumphant virtue. Jianna stood up, and the Sishmindri's hand withdrew itself at once.

"You'll have much to answer for," she informed her uncle, "when my father gets home." Turning from him, she made for the exit, her Sishmindri guard hurrying in her wake.

Behind her, Nalio's voice arose.

"Aureste will honor me, when he gets home. *If* he gets home. In the meantime, I am master here, and don't you forget it, you petted little cacodemon!"

• • •

For the next three days, the Belandor and Corvestri parties traveled the Nor'wilders Way decorously distanced from one another. Around sunset of the third day, when the tents had been pitched and preparations for the evening meal were under way, Aureste's game of chess with his brother was interrupted by the approach of a guard, who saluted and placed a folded message in Innesq's hand.

Innesq unfolded the missive, scanned the contents, and announced with apparent pleasure, "It is from Vinz."

"Really." Aureste's brows arched coldly. *Vinz.* "What does he want?"

"My presence. He invites me to dine with him."

"But how hospitable. Again, what does he want?"

"Not to poison me, I trust. Even you cannot convince yourself that we've anything to fear from him so long as we share a common goal."

"You underestimate the treachery of the weak. Trust me in this, I've seen it too many times. Despite his arcane talent and accomplishments that weigh so heavily with you, Vinz Corvestri is weak and stupid—"

"Not stupid."

"Not backward, but scarcely a first-rate intellect. Please, don't bother to argue. He's fearful and irresolute, and therefore not to be trusted by anyone, least of all by any member of House Belandor. You mustn't rely on his goodwill or place yourself in his power. The importance of your mission obliges you to protect yourself."

"You doubt the competence of his chef?"

"Very amusing. If anything, I doubt your competence to exercise caution. It wouldn't be so bad if I could be there to look out for you. Ah, but I wish I could be present to witness Corvestri's alarm when he first discovers that I am leading the Belandor expedition."

"He's known that since yesterday morning."

"Has he? Then I take it he's less concerned with arcane economy than you appear to be. Perhaps *he* will make himself useful and smooth the road."

"I doubt it. Vinz made no use of his personal resources to discover your presence. I mentioned it in my note."

"You sent Corvestri a note yesterday morning? Why?"

"It seemed the amiable thing to do."

"Excessively so. I don't like it."

"I suspected that you might not. And I fear that my acceptance of the invitation will only increase your displeasure."

"My displeasure together with my incomprehension. Why must you do this, Innesq? There's no sense to it. I believe it's sheer perversity."

"Scarcely that. I've no pleasure in plaguing you, but you must understand that my exchanges with Vinz serve a purpose. It will soon be necessary for him and me to work together in a particularly close and personal way—"

" 'As one,' you keep insisting."

"Yes. This will be easier to accomplish if all my colleagues come to share a certain degree of mutual confidence and comprehension. I am not certain that it will be possible, but we must try, and clearly the process must begin with Vinz Corvestri and me."

"It's clear that I can't dissuade you. Do me one kindness, then. When you go among Corvestri's people, don't go defenseless. Take along three or four armed guards, for the sake of my peace of mind, if nothing else."

"I shall need assistance navigating my chair along the road-way as far as Vinz's camp and back again. One of the guards may accompany me."

"Not enough."

"Even for your peace of mind, I can't accept more."

Shortly thereafter Innesq departed, inadequately attended by a single armed guard. Aureste watched, frowning, as his brother's chair made its way toward the cluster of lights that marked the site of the Corvestri camp. Presently the chair, its occupant and attendant vanished into the deepening gloom.

Aureste turned away and applied himself to mundane matters, but nothing held his attention. Visions of treachery filled his mind. Innesq, in all trusting innocence, lured into the enemy camp, captured and held hostage, or perhaps simply butchered out of hand. His betrayers would die to a man, but vengeance would scarcely soften the loss. First Jianna, and then Innesq. It did not bear thinking of, and he could think of nothing else.

Night fell, dinner was consumed, fires banked, sentinels posted, and those servants not immediately assigned to guard duty betook themselves to slumber. Aureste did not bother striving for sleep that was certain to elude him. For hours he waited beside one of the few fires still burning, and at length his patience was rewarded. The smooth whisper of a well-oiled mechanism alerted him, and a moment later his brother's chair rolled into the circle of firelight.

"Well?" Aureste demanded, noting with annoyance the other's look of pleasant tranquillity. "Well?"

"It was a most agreeable evening. The food was quite good, and the conversation equally so. I truly believe that Vinz and I are coming to understand one another. As you know, I regard such mutual accord as—"

"Yes, that's all very well," Aureste cut him off. "But there are more important matters. To begin with, can you give me some accounting of Corvestri's force?"

"It is all but impossible to quantify arcane force, but if I were to assess his general ability, I should probably say—"

"I mean, how many armed men does he command?"

"I could scarcely begin to guess." Innesq's eyes widened in mild surprise.

"Come, your powers of observation are remarkable. You must have noted guards and weaponry."

"Truly, I never heeded such things. My attention was elsewhere. If you desire specifics, I suggest that you simply ask Vinz. We should return his hospitality and invite him to dine with us."

"I would rather lie naked atop a nest of fire ants. Where *was* your mind, then? You mentioned conversation. They angled for information, I suppose."

"Certainly the boy did. It is only natural, at that age."

"Boy?"

"Vinz has brought his son with him."

"Stupidity. We've no leisure here to coddle children."

"Ah, young Vinzille Corvestri cannot be considered a child. He is quite extraordinary—I have never met a lad of such marked talent and promise. Even his appearance is exceptional. His Steffa heritage is quite evident, and his resemblance to his mother is striking."

"Is it? I should like to see that."

"Easily arranged. You need only return hospitality. Invite the entire family."

"Corvestri and son, you mean."

"And wife. Do not forget the magnifica."

"*Wife?*" He could not have heard correctly. "You're not telling me that the Corvestri imbecile has dragged his wife along with him into the wilderness?"

"Well, I do not know that 'dragged' is the appropriate term. The Magnifica Sonnetia strikes me as a lady of some character, and very much attached to her son. It is my belief that she wished to accompany the lad."

"Quite likely, but what of it? Corvestri needn't have consented. He permits his wife to expose herself to hardship, inconvenience, even danger, upon the basis of some maternal whim. What sort of husband is that? He doesn't protect her, he doesn't deserve her. Why did he allow her to come?"

"I must confess, I wondered about that. I observed the two of them closely, and almost it seemed that Vinz deferred to the magnifica as if through some sense of debt or obligation. It was an impression, perhaps only my fancy."

No it wasn't. So that was it. Sonnetia had demanded repayment of sorts for the sacrifice of the Steffa jewels and for her part in obtaining Corvestri's release from prison. No wonder her clod of a husband had found himself unable to refuse her—he was no match for her. A sense of admiration suffused Aureste's thoughts. She shouldn't be here, but at least she had won something that she wanted. *What a woman.* Aloud, he inquired inconsequentially, "And how did she look?"

"I am not the best judge, but I should say, very handsome."

"And did she seem quite—well?" His queries were increasingly inane, but he could not voice the questions that genuinely interested him. *Is she contented? Or is she restless and sick of her idiot husband? Did she ask about me?*

"So far as I could judge." Innesq was regarding him with that calm, straight look that always seemed to penetrate straight to his center. "You might see for yourself, quite easily. But no, I was forgetting, you are firmly opposed, even expressing a preference involving nudity and fire ants."

"Nor will I alter my decision. Socialize with our enemy if you must. I cannot stop you. But our respective parties will remain separate."

Two days later the Nor'wilders Way brought them to a narrow defile, where the road was blocked by a fall of rocks. Belandor and Corvestri servants worked together to clear the path, and thereafter the two groups traveled in tandem.

· · ·

It had been made clear that liberation from her chamber demanded unconditional surrender, and therefore Jianna capitulated, tendering Uncle Nalio her formal acceptance of all his decisions made on her behalf, together with her gratitude for his care and generosity. Thereafter her door was unlocked and she was free to wander about the remains of Belandor House as she pleased. She was also free to resume taking meals with her uncle, and in fact expected to do so, but this was not so difficult as she had feared, for Nalio was awash with magnanimity and disposed to forgive. There were no reproaches, no recriminations. He was still willing to discuss Belandor House repairs and renovations. He was likewise willing to discuss and display the newly arrived communication from the Magnifico Tribari, who expressed dignified delight at the prospect of greeting his son's bride in the near future.

The work on her wardrobe proceeded apace. Cutting and assembly were finished, fittings and alterations concluded, and the final finicking details of applied ornamentation were all but done. The big wooden chest in her room was now filled to overflowing with beautiful new garments.

It would be hard to leave them all behind. Impossible, in fact, for there were some with which she could not bear to part. The dark blue dress with the scarlet trim, for example. The sweeping woolen cloak. The silk chemises and embroidered stockings. The violet gown with its dramatic underskirt of black brocade.

And there was no reason to lose them all. It wasn't as if they were Uncle Nalio's gifts to her; they all came, only a bit indirectly, from Aureste. So she assured herself upon the quiet early-morning occasion that she spent stuffing a purloined pillow case with as many garments as it would hold. The jewelry came last and received special treatment. The little store of modest but good pieces—garnets, pearls, opals, and one fine ruby, set in gold—all went into a small pouch strung on a silken cord worn around her neck and tucked inside her bodice.

Then it was done, her rudimentary preparations completed. She wrapped herself in the fine new cloak, slipped her hands into the handsome new gloves, picked up the bulging sack, and marched out of the room.

It was just past dawn, but the servants were already about their business. One or two watched curiously as the magnifico's daughter went by, but none ventured to address her. Quietly, but without any effort at concealment, she made her way out of the house, then crossed the yard to the gate, which was locked and guarded. She spoke a commanding word to the sentry, who bestowed a startled glance upon her, but did not hesitate to obey. She went through, and the gate clanged shut behind her.

The air was dark and laced with smoke, but she could see well enough. She made her way along Summit Street at a steady, unhurried pace that she knew she could maintain for hours. Not so very long ago, the distance she intended to travel on foot would have seemed daunting; now, the prospect was hardly worthy of note. No more than an hour and a quarter or so of walking should bring her to her destination.

The Lancet Inn, near the Avorno Hospital, he had said. He would be staying there until he located his sister. Of course, he might easily have found her by this time. Falaste and Celisse might well have departed Vitrisi days ago. And if so?

Then she would take lodgings somewhere in the city. The sale of her jewelry would purchase room and board for weeks or months to come. There she would live quietly incognita, but she would keep her eyes and ears open. Eventually she would hear news of the Magnifico Belandor's return to Vitrisi. With Aureste reinstated and Uncle Nalio effectively neutralized, she would be free to present herself once more at Belandor House, where she would swiftly persuade her father to grant his word never to send her away again.

All of this was possible and attainable. She would carry it through if necessary, but hoped profoundly that the need

would not arise. With every fiber, she longed to find Falaste
Rione still in residence at the Lancet Inn.

The descent from the Clouds was an easy stroll downhill,
and the subsequent hike through various neighborhoods of
Vitrisi not nearly as bad as she had feared. Any number of
workmen or loiterers whistled and chirruped at her as she
passed, but she ignored them all, and nobody actually accosted her. Perhaps that apparent restraint simply reflected the
current prevailing fear of physical contact with potentially infectious strangers.

She passed many buildings marked with the red X, and
twice her progress was impeded by palisades of raw new
wood, slashed with scarlet paint, marking the boundaries of
quarantined neighborhoods. To her relief, she encountered
none of the wandering dead. Only once she passed a swollen
corpse, unequivocally down and supine in the gutter, its choic-
est bits the subject of dispute among a flock of Scarlet Gluttons. Averting her eyes, she quickened her pace.

Street after street, with the smoky atmosphere heavy in her
lungs, caustic in her watering eyes. Many of the pedestrians
that she passed had elected to shield their faces with protective gear of varying levels of quality, ranging from cheap tal-
lowed rags, to oilcloth vizards with gauzy eye-flaps, all the
way up to costly full-face leather masks equipped with herb-
stuffed nasal projections and eyeholes glazed with ground
glass lenses.

They looked as if they were on their way to some nightmare
masquerade.

The morning was well advanced and the streets grimly alive
by the time she approached the Avorno Hospital. The austere
old structure, built in the last century to house lunatics, idiots,
moribund paupers, and the victims of assorted epidemics,
normally stood with its door wide open in mute declaration
of its charitable function. But today the door was shut. The
cobbled pavement before the entrance was littered with the re-

cumbent bodies of the sick and the dying. From time to time a desperate outcry arose, which drew no response from within. Presumably the hospital was full to bursting.

She did not venture to ask directions, but a little searching soon brought her to the Lancet Inn. It stood in a small side street, very near the hospital, as he had described. The inn itself was old and eccentric, with emphatic gables, curious bulbous rooflights, and a brass knocker in the shape of a winged rodent. The place was modest but well maintained, and under ordinary circumstances might even have seemed inviting. She went in.

The proprietress—in keeping with her surroundings, elderly and tidy—eyed the newcomer with instant suspicion, and understandably so. A woman—young, handsome, smartly dressed—gadding about on her own invited but one conclusion. Nevertheless, a possibly solvent customer.

"Yes, madam?" The old lady succeeded in keeping her tone civil.

"Dr. Falaste Rione, please," Jianna requested, then watched with interest as the other's face creased in a grimace of disapproval, apparently contracting to half its former size.

"Up the stairs to the second story, door's on the left. Dr. Rione is quite the gentleman—he has taken a room of his own," the proprietress confided, adding with a perceptible touch of significance, "You won't be disturbed."

"Is he in now?"

"Oh, I could hardly say. 'Tisn't my place to pry. My guests know that I never meddle, no matter what they do. Just so long as they pay their reckoning and don't bring the Taers down on me."

"Then I'll go on up, if I may."

"Suit yourself. 'Tisn't my affair. I never pry."

Jianna ascended a steep and narrow, old-fashioned stairway that smelled of lemon oil polish. Her heart was beating quickly as she climbed, just as it had throbbed with anticipation days earlier, as she had made her way along Summit

Street toward her beloved Belandor House, whose reality had scarcely fulfilled her dreams.

Quite likely, he wouldn't be there at all. She would have to wait, probably until he returned in the evening. No, she wouldn't sit around waiting, she'd use the time to find someone willing to buy her jewelry, and perhaps the violet gown as well. She really had no place to wear it. Decidedly, it was best to focus on practical matters.

Four arched doors opened upon the second-story landing. The one on the left would be his, but there hardly seemed any point in knocking, for she already knew that he would not be there. Her heart was truly racing now.

Her hand moved of its own accord to deliver a weak tap, easily missed or ignored. A quick footfall within, and the door opened.

And *there he was,* lean and pale-faced, regarding her in plain surprise, and her mind froze. For a moment she could think of nothing to say, and stood staring at him.

But her eyes must have been more eloquent than she knew, for he took one look and inquired at once, "What's wrong?"

"May I come in?" She found her voice.

He nodded and moved aside. She stepped into the room, and he shut the door.

"I didn't think we'd ever see each other again." She had no sense of her surroundings. Her eyes never left his face. For the first time she fully realized how much she had missed seeing it.

"Neither did I."

"Have you found Celisse?"

"Not yet."

"Do you think she knows that you're looking for her?"

"Why are you here, Jianna? What's happened?"

"My uncle Nalio has happened. He's in charge of Belandor House during my father's absence, and he's decided to pack me off to Orezzia for a speedy marriage."

"That's what you were traveling toward at the time you were abducted, was it not?"

She nodded without enthusiasm.

"And the match was arranged by your father?"

Another nod.

"Your uncle seeks to fulfill the Magnifico Belandor's wishes. What could be more reasonable and responsible?"

"Reason and responsibility have nothing to do with it! And I don't think my father's wishes have much to do with it, either. Uncle just wants to trade me off for the Magnifico Tribari's pet artists and artisans to work on restoring Belandor House. That, and he wants to put me in my place—he's wanted to for a long time, I suspect. But he's not going to get away with it. I'm no heifer to be bartered at market, particularly not by the likes of Uncle Nalio. I won't go to Orezzia."

"Stop and think. Is it wise to reject the plans made on your behalf by a father whom you trust, just for the satisfaction of defying your uncle?"

"That isn't it. My uncle doesn't matter. I just don't want to go."

"You were willing enough once, and not so long ago."

"It *seems* long ago. Anyway, things have changed. *I've* changed. I've come to realize that Vitrisi is where I belong. When my father returns, I'll tell him so, and he'll listen to me—he always listens. I know I can make him understand, once I have a chance to talk to him."

"I see. When your father returns. And what do you propose to do in the meantime?"

"Well, that's why I've come to you. I thought I might be your assistant Noro Penzia again, for as long as you're here in the city. I could help you look for your sister, or help if you treat any sick people, or . . ." Her voice dried up. His eyes were boring into her, and she was all at once acutely self-conscious, uncomfortable, and filled with not unwelcome suspense.

"No," he said.

"What?" She was not certain she had heard him correctly.

"Go back home. Now." His tone was abrupt, his expression

chill, his resemblance to his sister more pronounced than ever before.

"Are you cross for some reason? You sound vexed."

"Do I?"

"What have I done?"

"You've really no inkling how thoroughly you've disrupted my life, have you?"

"Why yes, I have. I know that I'm responsible for turning Yvenza against you, and for endangering your friendship with the Ghosts, and I've already told you how sorry I am, and how grateful for all that you've done—"

"I'm not speaking of those things that I chose voluntarily. But I never chose to become so used to your company that the world and everything in it seems flat and stale when you are gone. I didn't expect that, but I was growing accustomed, and might have succeeded in banishing you from my thoughts, had you not come strolling back in, blithely ready to resume our connection for a few days, or whatever period best suits your purpose."

"I—I thought you might be happy to see me."

"You thought nothing, you simply acted, primarily to spite your uncle. But you'll think now, and you'll think about this— I am not your useful tool, to be taken up or set aside at your convenience. You do not walk into my life, wreak havoc, walk away without a backward glance—then turn up a second time, cheerily prepared to repeat the entire sequence."

He did not shout, but he was unmistakably angry, something she had never before glimpsed. An almost perverse desire to see more of what lay behind his habitual composure seized her, and she fired back, "*You're* the one who walked away without a backward glance! That day at the gate of Belandor House, you left, and didn't look back once."

"Do you imagine that was easy?"

"It certainly appeared so."

"For such a clever girl, you are sometimes unbelievably obtuse."

"I'm not obtuse! Don't you call me names. If I don't understand you, it's because you're making no sense. You're in a perfectly foul temper, and I don't know why you're angry, or what you think I've done, or what you want of me."

"This." Pulling her close, he kissed her.

Surprise, excitement, and wild happiness burst inside her. In the midst of it, two realizations touched her dazzled intellect. One, that this was what she had wanted from the moment she had crossed his threshold. The other—that for the first time since reaching Vitrisi, she finally felt that she had come home.

NINE

The union of the Belandor and Corvestri parties was sound in theory, but sometimes problematic in execution. Not that the behavior of the principals involved—the family members on each side—was less than irreproachable. Punctilious courtesy reigned. Between Innesq Belandor and the three Corvestris, the courtesy was tinged with a genuine warmth that seemed to deepen from day to day. The Magnifico Aureste neither received nor expected similar cordiality. His infrequent exchanges with the Magnifica Sonnetia Corvestri were decorous and distant. Her son Vinzille was doubtless hostile, but scrupulously polite. As for the so-called leader of the clan—the Magnifico Vinz—he and Aureste scarcely acknowledged one another's existence. Beyond a few obligatory, rigidly correct formalities, the two of them had not exchanged a word, and in fact almost never came face-to-face.

This avoidance was not mutual, for Aureste never troubled to alter his course in the slightest. But Vinz always faded from view at first glimpse of his old enemy, generally seeking refuge in his closed carriage. The wretch was clearly afraid. On the face of it, this seemed unlikely. Vinz Corvestri, after all, was the seasoned arcanist whose skills should have imparted every advantage. But the Magnifico Aureste's instincts had always been preternaturally receptive to the slightest whiff of fear or weakness, and he knew beyond question that Vinz Corvestri dreaded the sight of him. The situation offered much by way of potential entertainment, and it was only the fear of his brother's disapproval that prevented Aureste from seeking out and subtly terrorizing Vinz on a daily basis.

He resisted the temptation, and the members of the two

enemy Houses traveled on in uneasy peace. But the same could not be said of their guards and attendants, whose minds did not appear to embrace the concept of tolerance. Trouble flared continually between the Belandor and Corvestri servants—at the brooks and streams where they paused to water the horses, replenish empty skins and bottles, wash linen; at the cookfires; among the tussocks and the swaths of scrub vegetation, where they gathered fuel; and above all, at the games of dice and cards that they played in the evening.

There tempers boiled, and complaints often expanded into accusations, insults, thence fisticuffs. And on one unpleasantly memorable occasion, a knife fight erupted between a Belandor guard and his Corvestri counterpart. The combatants were quickly separated, and the resulting bloodshed minor, but thereafter certain commands were issued to the servants of both households. There was to be no fighting, with or without weapons, under any circumstances. Personal insults or threats, conveyed verbally or by means of gestures or pantomime, were prohibited. And finally, there was to be no gambling. Games and competitions of various sorts were permissible, but there were to be no wagers placed.

Inevitably there was grumbling, but open complaint ceased following the announcement that the slightest infraction of any new edict would be punished by a thrashing of the utmost severity.

The next two days passed free of incident. The following evening, however, around sunset, when the tents were being pitched and the campfires kindled, a blast of profanity followed by a howling exchange of insults signaled an end to the brief détente.

The source of the uproar was discovered in the lee of a tall rock, behind which a pair of guards—one from each household—had retired to play at dice. The game had not gone well, and mutual accusations of cheating and questionable ancestry had escalated swiftly. The guards had come to blows, and the Corvestri man, finding himself disadvantaged, had snatched up a stone and beaten his opponent with it. The Belandor victim—dazed, badly bruised, and bleeding—would probably have died had the fight not been forcibly halted.

It was a clear case of insubordination. When the two culprits were haled before their respective masters, the Magnifico Aureste did not hesitate to order his erring servant stripped and whipped. It behooved his counterpart to issue a similar command. His eyes shifted to Vinz Corvestri.

Vinz sat in clench-jawed silence. The ruddy sunset air was cool, but his brow was damp with sweat. He looked miserable and perhaps ill. Seconds passed, and he said nothing.

Aureste grew tired of waiting. Orders quivered at the tip of his tongue, and he contained them with difficulty. It was neither his place nor his right to command the punishment of a Corvestri attendant, but punishment was essential, lest discipline and morale suffer.

But the seconds passed, and Vinz Corvestri said nothing. His lips quivered a little, but no sound emerged. It was plain that he knew what had to be said, and could not bring himself to utter the words.

The spineless fool. Aureste strove to control his rising impatience. It was not easy, for the interested spectators were beginning to stir, and something had to be said.

Vinz finally obliged. "You have done ill," he informed the culprit, as if concluding deep deliberation. "And your offense merits the harshest punishment. Should you repeat your error, know that you will be whipped soundly. There will be no further appeals, and no mercy. Do you understand me?"

"Yes, Magnifico." A fervent nod.

"Then return to your labors."

Clearly elated, the guard withdrew, and a low murmuring rustled in his wake.

"The rest of you—back to work." Vinz swept a regal gesture. He was obeyed, without alacrity.

Unbelievable. Aureste's annoyance heated to full wrath. The puling milksop Corvestri was worse than useless, he was a liability. He hadn't the nerve to maintain discipline or enforce orders; he was all but encouraging the guards to disregard commands. Worse yet—idiotic, actually—he had spared his own guilty servant punishment *after* the Belandor offender had been sentenced to a whipping. The blatant injustice of it was certain to rankle, understandably so. Resentment could lead to unrest, disruption, delay . . . all of which could now be laid to the charge of Vinz Corvestri and his pitiful weak stomach.

Aureste turned the full blazing battery of his dark eyes upon his bungling foe, but the blast of bitter unspoken contempt spent its force harmlessly upon its target's retreating back. Corvestri was already on his feet and moving away, most likely skulking off to hide in his carriage. Just as well. Had he remained within range, words would have flown like poisoned darts.

It was now necessary to oversee the Belandor guard's punishment—a distasteful task at any time, and doubly so now. Unavoidable, however. Aureste watched without enthusiasm as his servant—already bruised and battered—was stripped to the waist, tied to a tree, and whipped bloodybacked. When it was over and the whimpering unfortunate was finally released, Aureste was likewise freed.

Anger laced with deep disgust seethed in his mind. For the moment, he wished only to free himself of the campsite and its inhabitants. He wandered off, and the noise and stir of humanity soon fell away behind him. Within moments he found himself apparently alone in a quiet world, walking a region of eccentric stone outcroppings set amid grey-brown patches of bramble studded with the first budding hints of spring growth. The atmosphere was soft, the light veil of mists infused with the warm tints of the setting sun. Aureste drew the clean air—no smoke, no stench of charring meat—deep into his lungs, and gradually grew calm. He looked around him. The prospect was spare and austere, but not unappealing. At the moment he welcomed the silent solace of bare rock, moist soil, thorny shrubbery.

He did not know how long or how far he walked, but at last the silence of his surroundings and the dwindling of the light told him to turn back. The color had leached from the mists, and the world was sinking into grey oblivion. Disinclined to stumble his way over rough ground in the dark, he quickened his pace. But when he came again to the greatest of the tall stones, thrusting skyward among the huddling briars, he found that the world was not empty after all.

A solitary figure wrapped in a long hooded cloak stood at the foot of the highest monolith. Face, form, height, and color were all obscured, but Aureste recognized the other at once, upon instinct. His heartbeat quickened. He hastened forward and spoke aloud.

"Magnifica."

She turned to face him. Her face was still, and he had no idea what she was thinking. Then she smiled a little, almost as if unwillingly.

"How is it that I am not at all surprised to see you here?" asked Sonnetia.

Perhaps because you wanted to see me here? Aureste allowed himself the luxury of speculating. Aloud he observed, "It is an isolated, lonely spot, madam. Allow me to escort you back to family and fireside."

"It doesn't seem lonely to me. I find it peaceful. It's possible to collect one's thoughts here."

"Ah, you sound like my brother Innesq. Always he speaks of the need for silence and solitude in which to focus his mind."

"I shall take that as a compliment. There are few worthier models than Innesq Belandor."

"Strange words, coming from a Corvestri."

"I wasn't always a Corvestri."

"I haven't forgotten, and I'm glad that you have not." He

saw by the slight lift of her brows that he had perhaps over-stepped his bounds, and added smoothly, "For the Steffa tradition of talent and achievement is surely to be treasured by its fortunate inheritors."

"Magnifico, the passing years have enriched you with the skills of a diplomat," she observed drily.

"Not so. Should I possess such skills, I would know how to tell you—gracefully, respectfully, delightfully—that it troubles me to see you walking alone and unprotected in so deserted and unknown a place as this. I would know how to tell you without giving offense that I fear for your safety. And the magic of my persuasions would secure your consent to accompany me back to the campsite. Alas, I own no such skills, and must only express myself with the bluntness of the simple plainspoken man that I am."

Sonnetia laughed, the sound of it dancing among the stones, and for a moment the composed, formal Magnifica Corvestri gave way to the vibrant Sonnetia Steffa that he had known so many years ago.

"Simple and plainspoken." She shook her head, still smiling. "Oh, Aureste, there will never be another like you."

"No doubt all to the good." He had a sense that the moment was almost enchanted. For this one instant, time had slipped, and she was herself again, her real self, the Sonnetia to whom he had once upon a time revealed his heart and all that was in it—well, nearly all. He had never been one to ignore opportunity, and therefore asked, "What are the bothersome thoughts that you came here to collect?" There was no immediate answer, and he pressed on, "Are you troubled by the rigors and discomforts of travel? Or was it the quarrel between the guards, and the meting out of justice?"

"Justice? Say punishment."

"Very well, punishment. You question the necessity?"

"I question the brutality. It isn't necessary to punish disobedient servants so harshly. It's been my own experience that gentler treatment is more effective."

"At home, I daresay. Among soft and civilized surroundings, soft and civilized behavior is appropriate."

"And you imply that it is not so here."

"I more than imply, I state openly—it is not so here. That is an unhappy truth. Out here in the wilderness, so far from human aid, our safety depends upon our vigilance, readiness, and efficiency, which can be maintained only by means of discipline. The rules must be clear; they must be enforced consistently and impartially. Each man in our party must understand that disobedience inevitably leads to punishment. Once they accept and believe in this principle, they will govern themselves accordingly. Thereafter, excessive harshness is not often required."

"And it is upon this basis, I presume, that you fault the Magnifico Corvestri for his refusal to order a man whipped like an animal?"

"Fault the magnifico?" Aureste's eyes widened in apparent astonishment. "Have I spoken a single word against him?"

"Not aloud, perhaps. But the look in your eyes—the twist of your lips, the angle of your jaw, the set of your shoulders—these things shout to the world."

"Perhaps the world's powers of observation and interpretation are somewhat less acute than your own, madam."

"And perhaps not. You do no service to this expedition in slighting one of its leaders."

"I agree. Nor would I dream of offering disrespect or discourtesy to the Magnifico Corvestri," he declared, avoiding the direct attack that would have sent her flying to her husband's defense.

She studied his face. "Ah, yes. The non-expression." She nodded. "I remember it well."

"You seem to doubt me, madam. How shall I demonstrate my good faith? Will a display of conspicuous candor convince you? You shall have it, then. I'll confess that you're correct in believing me opposed to the Magnifico Corvestri's decision, but not for the reason that you may suppose. I take no pleasure in the sufferings of our servants. Yet the magnifico's failure to administer clearly warranted punishment may be seen as a form of falsehood. He has broken his word."

"What, you mean the warning that fighting among the guards earns corporal discipline? He simply elected not to carry out a threat, that is all."

"You know better."

"You cannot pretend to view mercy as a moral lapse."

"I can when the harm it does outweighs the good. How shall we fare if the men who serve us come to see that our word means nothing? If our promises of punishment are meaningless, then may not our promises of reward prove equally empty? In which case, why should they trust us, follow us, or submit to our authority? What is there beyond the certainty of reward and impartially applied punishment to rule them? And it is this very certainty that your husband's action has compromised. It was a grave error. But don't fear that I shall voice my complaint aloud to anyone other than yourself. I wouldn't sow dissension between our two households—there is enough of that already."

"I hope for all our sakes that you mean that."

"With all my heart." It was not precisely a lie, for he intended no major sowing prior to the expedition's conclusion.

"As for the rest, you are mistaken," she informed him. "Chop logic as you will, you cannot convince me that it is ever wrong to spare a man a whipping."

She spoke with apparent assurance, but Aureste easily caught the underlying uncertainty. Concealing his satisfaction, he returned, "Than I'll abandon the attempt. It's no place for a debate, in any case. Come, Magnifica, it's almost dark. Will you not return to the camp with me?"

She nodded, and they departed. It was not quite dark, but the world was veiled in shade, and therefore both of them quite overlooked the presence of Vinz Corvestri, who crouched behind a nearby boulder, listening intently to every word.

• • •

"Young. Medium stature, slender build. Light complexion, dark hair, grey-blue eyes. In fact, she looks a good deal like me," Falaste Rione repeated for at least the hundredth time. "Plainly dressed but well spoken, and resolute of manner. Her name is Celisse Rione."

"Haven't seen her," the keeper of the Black Sheep Inn declared.

"She's in the city, she'll need lodgings. If she should come to this place, would you let her know that her brother is looking for her? I'm to be found at the Lancet Inn, in Cistern Street, near the Avorno Hospital. Will you tell her?"

The innkeeper shrugged. Falaste and Jianna exited the Black Sheep Inn.

"You should've offered a reward," Jianna opined. "Then that fellow would have come to life."

"You may be right, but I don't know how much good it would do. The fact is, it's all but impossible to locate Celisse if she doesn't want to be found. I truly believed that she'd seek me out as soon as she learned of my presence in Vitrisi. She must know by now, but she remains hidden. I didn't expect it."

"Well, you can't be certain that she *does* know."

"Not certain, but it's more than likely. I've dropped my name at inns, cookshops, and market stalls all over town. By this time she must have heard that I'm here, and she knows where to find me, but chooses to remain hidden. Despite all our differences, we've always been close, and never before has she sought to avoid me. This is something new and disturbing."

Everything about that fanatical witch is disturbing, thought Jianna. *She doesn't deserve such a brother; he's too good for her.* Silently taking his hand, she gave an encouraging squeeze, and received the same in return. Her heartbeat quickened magically. She looked into his face, with its fine, well-formed features, its intelligence and humor, and wanted very much to kiss him again. Perhaps it was unmaidenly, immodest, or even immoral, but she could not help herself.

Her mind winged back to that first morning kiss. Hours had passed since then, but the sensations lingered. She could still feel the warmth flooding her veins, the excitement firing her nerves. And the joy—the glorious sense of rightness, potent as a magical draught—that too was with her yet.

There had been few words. "*. . . Not fair to you . . . ,*" he had muttered, and she had replied, "*I want to be here.*" Then another kiss that had set the world spinning, and another. She had wanted it to go on forever, but he had released her and stepped back. The broken contact had felt like an amputation.

"*Come, we're going out,*" he had decreed.

"*Not now—later!*"

"*Believe me, maidenlady, it had best be now.*" He had smiled, but his face had been flushed, and his breathing quick.

And so they had removed themselves from the privacy of his room, venturing forth to resume the hunt for the missing would-be assassin. And while they searched, she had thought of little beyond his lips and arms.

Did he share her feelings? Or was he too occupied with thoughts of his troublemaking sister to think about kissing?

"When you look at me like that, the thoughts fly straight out of my head," he told her. "You've no idea how distracting it is."

Oh, good! "Then I'll try always to look at you like that," she promised helpfully.

"Don't. You'll turn me into a shambling idiot, and deprive the world of a perfectly serviceable physician."

"Never. But can't the world allow the serviceable physician a little time to enjoy life, now and again?"

"Only a bright spirit like yours could think of enjoying life now, with the city disintegrating all around us. Someday, though. Someday for both of us, I promise."

"Oh, that's a promise I'll hold you to. In the meantime,

though, where do we go? More inns and cookshops? Bath-house?"

"Pointless, I fear. It's plain that Celisse is ignoring my invitation. She won't come to me, so I must hunt the harder for her. I can't do that without help, and I believe I know where to find it."

"Resistance people here in Vitrisi?" Jianna guessed.

"You're a little too sharp, Noro Penzia. Yes, that's right, and please don't ask for specifics. I've a distance to walk. Shall I see you back to the Lancet before I set off?"

"No, thank you. Widow Meegri will give me the fish eye." Widow Meegri was the elderly, tidy, and wordlessly disapproving proprietress of the Lancet Inn.

"Pay no attention. She gives everyone the fish eye."

"She thinks I'm some sort of—I can't say what."

"What she really thinks is that you're a customer willing and able to pay for a room to yourself. That's uncommon, you know. I've indulged myself on this occasion in hope of easing the way for Celisse to approach me, but privacy is a luxury usually reserved for the wealthy. Speaking of which, are you able to pay, or do you need help?"

"Oh, I've means," she returned vaguely, and felt the color flood her face. Eager to change the subject, she continued, "It's a pleasant enough chamber, but I'm not minded to sit alone in it for the rest of the day. I'll come with you, wherever you're going. Where *are* you going?"

"To Cutter Lane in the East Cross. I know someone there."

"Someone?"

"A very good fellow."

"Ghost?"

"Of the urban variety."

"Does he have a name? Oh, I forgot—I'm not supposed to ask for specifics."

"In this case, I honestly can't answer. I assume he has a name—people generally do—but I don't know it. I have only his alias."

"You know where he lives, though."

"No idea whatever."

"You know where he works?"

"Haven't a clue. Don't know the man's trade, or even if he has one."

"Then how'll he be found? Do we go to Cutter Lane and loiter there, hoping that your Ghost will appear to us?"

"That's what it amounts to. Last night I placed a copper inside the crack in the base of Duke Dalbo Strenvivi's statue in the Strenvivi Gardens. That copper signifies my request for an afternoon meeting. We make our way to The Cask in Cutter Lane, take a table, and wait for the phantom to materialize."

"And if he doesn't oblige?"

"Then I return tomorrow and try again."

"This doesn't strike me as particularly efficient."

"I've often voiced that very same complaint. So far, however, the Ghosts have failed to initiate reforms."

They set off together for Cutter Lane. It was a long walk, and the way was dreary, carrying them along murky, smoky streets wherein the ponderous mists were oddly tinged with diurnal lamplight. They passed many a doorway marked with the red X, and once they saw a Deadpickers' cart, heaped with cargo, rumbling on toward the Pits. Most of the pedestrians out on the street wore some sort of protective mask. Identities were lost, and human voices were muted. But Jianna scarcely noticed the ugly or even frightening sights and sounds. He had taken her hand, and they were talking as they went—talking ceaselessly about anything and everything, as if the two of them would never run out of words. She could hardly have described that conversation, it was so lengthy and rich, and it swooped so freely from topic to topic. But she knew that it was full of confidences, confessions, laughter, and dreams. And she knew without stopping to think about it that she had never in her life been so happy as she was that afternoon, walking through a suffocated, plague-racked city hand in hand with Falaste Rione.

Had she been on her own, she would have needed to ask directions. But Rione knew the way, so they walked and talked without pause until they came at last to Cutter Lane—an obscure back street in a nondescript section of the city; neither wealthy nor poor, handsome nor ugly, pleasant nor any more repellent than the times demanded. And there at the top of the lane stood The Cask, an undistinguished wineshop of no discernible character.

They went in and took a small table at the rear. Jianna scanned the room discreetly; moderate size, plain furnishings, waxed plank flooring, reasonably clean, dimly lit. She somehow had the sense that The Cask was always dim, even on the brightest of days, and always had been so. The patrons, in their own way, were equally dim; a knot of unobtrusively idle tipplers at one table, a couple of decently neat apprentices, a lone greybeard nursing his glass of wine, a few anonymously respectable tradesmen, and a trio of elderly women seated together and giggling over their gossip as if they imagined themselves young.

In addition to drink, The Cask offered a modest bill of fare. Jianna and Falaste ordered soup. The bowls arrived promptly. The contents were acceptable and ordinary. They spooned soup and talked on. Lost in his conversation and his eyes, and the clear line of his jaw, Jianna lost all track of time. She had no idea how long it was before a shadow glided across the table, the air moved, and the chair beside her was suddenly occupied.

She turned to look, but there was nothing remarkable to see. Just an ordinary man of indeterminate years, plainly dressed, medium size and build, forgettable bland face, nondescript to the verge of invisibility. If asked to describe him, she would have found it difficult—there were no distinguishing features.

"Rione. Been a while," observed the stranger. His intonation was difficult to place. He might have been a shopkeeper, an artisan, a gentleman's valet, a clerk—almost anything.

"I've been off in the hills up until a few days ago," Rione replied. "Good to see you, L."

L? Jianna's brows rose.

Rione answered the unspoken question at once. "Maiden-lady Noro Penzia, allow me to present my associate Louse-wort. L, the Maidenlady Noro is my assistant, and she's spent the last several weeks tending our ailing friends out in the Alziras."

"Maidenlady." Lousewort inclined his head courteously enough, but he was studying her closely, eyes a little narrowed and forehead creased, as if trying to catch a memory.

She felt like a child about to be caught in a lie, and it wasn't fair, for "Lousewort" certainly wasn't *his* legitimate name. Nonetheless, she could hardly keep from squirming beneath that faintly puzzled gaze. She smiled politely, met his eyes, and did not blink.

Mercifully, his attention shifted back to Rione. The two of them launched into a terse exchange of enigmatic, presumably coded information that seemed to describe recent resistance activity taking place within and without Vitrisi. Jianna understood every word touching upon the recent illness among the Ghosts of the hills, but most of the other references eluded her, particularly those alluding to "Matchlock's Fire Brigade." Thoroughly ignored, she grew restive. They were like children, she told herself; like little boys forming secret societies guarded by passwords and rituals designed to exclude the rest of the world, particularly the female half of it, whose members *weren't interested, anyway.*

The abruptness of its conclusion took her by surprise. One moment, they were speaking of "the final fruits of the Blue Rooster Enterprise," whatever that might have meant, and the next Lousewort was leaning forward across the table to inquire, with the air of a man getting down to business, "And what have we today, then?"

"You recall my sister Celisse?" asked Rione. The Cask's

healthy buzz of conversation made it easy to speak without being overheard, yet he lowered his voice.

Jianna's interest revived.

"Hard to forget her," Lousewort replied.

"You remember her zeal, energy, and courage."

"Admirable."

"Her virtues occasionally impinge upon vice. She's taken it firmly into her head that the Governor Uffrigo must be eliminated. Following an unsuccessful effort to drum up support in camp, she left without a word to anyone. Nobody expected her to do such a thing, so nobody stopped her. Perhaps I should have guessed, perhaps I should have paid more attention, but I was preoccupied with my work. I know my sister well enough, though, to be quite certain that she's come to Vitrisi determined to do the job on her own."

A low whistle escaped Lousewort. "That girl's a bolt of lightning," he opined.

"And likely to blast us all as she crashes in glorious ruin. I've been searching for days, and I haven't been able to find her." Rione shook his head. "I've dropped my name all over town, but she refuses to come to me. And now I must confess that I need help."

"My people will do all they can. Several of them would know Celisse Rione by sight. As for the others, we'll work up a good description. She shouldn't be so hard to spot, she naturally stands out. It is only a matter of time."

"Good. I needn't point out the consequences of her success."

"But her success is nearly impossible, isn't it?" Jianna interjected. The questioning eyes of her companions turned toward her, and she continued, "I mean—she's dauntless, daring, dedicated, and all that sort of thing, but when all's said and done, she's just one young woman, all alone. What real chance has she of coming anywhere near the governor? Uffrigo has all sorts of guards and attendants about him, hasn't he? What will she do, whip out a poniard and fight her way through an entire squadron single-handed? Isn't it far more likely that the girl will soon be forced to recognize the impossibility of her task? What can she do then but admit defeat?"

The two men traded glances. Neither replied.

• • •

The tangle of twisty little lanes known as the Briar Patch was bewildering at the best of times, and doubly so now. The narrow, unpaved streets, sunk in the shade of architectural projections almost meeting overhead, hoarded smoke, odors, moisture, and darkness. The dense atmosphere permitted vision only a few feet in any direction, and those few feet were likely to include exterior walls slashed with great red X's that often blotted out street names. Even those residents quite familiar with the area might easily have lost their bearings, and strangers were certain to suffer confusion.

Thus, not surprisingly, the lanes were comparatively empty, while those hardy souls venturing abroad went masked and muffled against contagion. The plague menaced all of Vitrisi, these days. Not even the highest and wealthiest enclave, much less this obscure warren, could regard itself as safe. Yet here, somehow, it seemed that the pedestrians were particularly vigilant. More often than not they walked in pairs or larger groups, and the eyes behind the protective masks were particularly active, sweeping this way and that, as if there were something more than disease to dread.

One young woman, however, did not fear to walk alone. Her step was confident and purposeful, her pace brisk. Her one apparent concession to the menace of the plague resided in the kerchief wrapped loosely about the lower portion of her face, covering her nose and mouth. Above the lattice-patterned fabric, her grey-blue eyes were alert and watchful. The eyes searched everywhere, and soon spied what they sought: an adult male Sishmindri, loitering in the gloom of a recessed doorway.

Everything about the amphibian was peculiar. He was naked, for one thing; unencumbered with livery or human garments of any description. Although seemingly healthy, he leaned upon a stout stick that might have served as a support, but might easily have been viewed as a crude and illegal weapon. Most surprising of all, he performed no bow or gesture of respect as the young woman approached. He stood straight and still, observing her inscrutably.

She halted before him. The two studied each other in silence, and still he neither bowed, nor dipped his head, nor even lowered his great golden eyes in subservience. The silence lengthened, and it was the human who was obliged to break it.

"I have heard," she announced in cultivated and melodic tones, "that your kind is free and proud, here in this place." There was no reply, and she pressed, "Is this true?"

He stared at her.

"If it is true," she continued, "then it is good, and I am glad. But your freedom is a sickly infant. You are surrounded on all sides by your enemies and oppressors."

"You go." He spoke at last, words thickly accented but comprehensible. "Go from this place."

"I will not go until I've been heard."

"What do you want here?"

"To ask and to offer help." There was no reply, and she continued, "I have heard that a leader has risen among you, and that he is called Aazaargh." The name she uttered emerged as something between a croak and a grunt. "I have heard that this is his real name, his Sishmindri name. If so, I am honored to speak it, however poor my pronunciation."

"What do you want here?" the amphibian repeated.

"I wish to speak to Aazaargh. I've an offer to extend to all Sishmindris enslaved and imprisoned within this human city of Vitrisi."

"What offer?"

"Your leader may hear it, if he will."

"Who are you?"

"My name is Celisse Rione. I am of the Faerlonnish resistance."

"You have the right to speak for them?"

"For those among them of courage and sound understanding, yes. Now, will you lead me to Aazaargh?"

For some moments he stared at her. She sustained the scrutiny unmoved.

"Come," he said at last. Turning from her, he set off along the lane, and Celisse fell into step beside him.

Soon they passed under a dilapidated archway into a garbage-strewn courtyard, through a gate into another lane smaller and darker than the last, and thence along a walkway too narrow to be called a street. As they went, there were fewer and fewer human pedestrians to be seen, and presently none. Sishmindris, however, increased in number. All of them were naked, and many bore weapons—not sticks or tools of ambiguous function, but knives, spiked clubs, spears, even two or three swords. Moreover, these implements were carried openly, even in the presence of a human observer. If anyone had cause to fear, it was doubtless the human. Alien golden eyes pressed almost palpably upon Celisse Rione. She appeared unaware.

They came to a tenement with boarded windows and a front door reddened with the mark of quarantine. There they halted.

"You fear the Invader," stated the guide, evidently employing his own kind's term for the plague.

"I am not afraid," Celisse returned, and saw the other's air sacs swell in surprise. "Lead on."

He complied, and they went into a dank street-level foyer containing an eccentric collection of big vats, washtubs, caulked barrels, and even a couple of metal bathtubs. All of these vessels were filled with water, and several of them occupied by Sishmindris satisfying their natural taste for bathing. All hairless heads turned as the human female entered. Water

sloshed audibly against the wall of many a vat, and protuberant golden eyes stared.

They halted.

"Wait," commanded the guide. Turning from her, he departed.

Celisse Rione stood quietly where he had left her, just inside the doorway. If she felt the pressure of universal regard,
she showed no sign of it. She neither fidgeted nor stirred. Her
face was calm and still. Only her eyes moved, deliberately
scanning the foyer, its contents and occupants. The contents
included piles of rocks, bottles, and bricks; supplies of sharpened sticks leaning against one wall; coils of rope, and lengths
of thick iron chain.

One of the Sishmindris climbed out of his bath, dripped his
way across the floor, and paused before Celisse, inspecting her
unabashedly in a manner that would, in normal times and society, have earned him a sound hiding. Celisse calmly mirrored
the expressionless regard. A second amphibian joined the
first, then another, and presently a Sishmindri semicircle
hemmed her in closely. And still she displayed no flicker of unease.

Soft splat of a web-toed foot upon the damp tile floor, and
her original guide was back again.

"Come," he commanded.

She followed him up a rickety stairway to a second-story
corridor, through an open door into a good-sized chamber
with heavy window curtains shut against the daylight. The
room was bare of human furnishings other than a row of
brimming washbasins ranged against one wall. Three naked
amphibians squatted on the floor. Their palms rested flat
upon the wooden planking, their knees were widely splayed.
One of them was the biggest Sishmindri that Celisse had ever
seen. His shoulders were uncommonly broad, the muscula-
ture prominent, his hands almost freakishly large. He would
never have found a place of much visibility in any fashionable

household, for he lacked stylish resemblance to humankind. His bulging eyes were set high on a very flat skull, and his lipless mouth split his face from air sac to air sac.

"You are Aazaargh?" Celisse inquired of the overgrown amphibian.

"Yes. What are your words?"

His accent was heavy. Only by dint of strenuous concentration was she able to understand and reply without a request for repetition. He was surely closer to a Sishmindri in its natural state than any other she had ever encountered.

"It is said," Celisse declared, "that you and your people have taken this section of the city and made it your own." Expecting no reply, she continued without pause, "This is a noble deed, worthy of honor. You have suffered vile injustice at the hands of men, you are the victims of countless crimes. Your courage now in liberating and defending yourselves is to be admired."

No reply. Aazaargh and his companions attended expressionlessly.

"But your daring and nobility are useless, and your efforts doomed to failure," Celisse stated dispassionately. "You are surrounded on all sides by the forces of men. In their own good time they will turn their attention to you, and then your dream of freedom will die. You cannot hope to conquer, nor can you hope to escape. Most of you will die, and the survivors will return to slavery."

"No slavery," said Aazaargh.

"Death, then." Celisse nodded her approval. "You are right. But what if there is another choice? You must understand that the ranks of the oppressed include humans as well as Sishmindris. All Faerlonnishmen, native to this island, presently suffer the tyranny of the Taerleezi invader. I will own that we have not suffered as your kind has suffered, yet we have known much of grief and injustice. The wiser among us have profited by the lesson. We have come to see that Sishmindris and Faerlonnishmen share a common enemy—the

Taerleezis. We have all suffered at Taerleezi hands, we all have cause to hate them, and our hatred of the foreigners should unite us."

"Men. Taerleezi. Faerlonnish. All the same." Aazaargh allowed his lower jaw to gape hugely, then shut it with a snap, evidently an expressive gesture among his kind. "All bad."

"In the past, yes. But matters have changed. Now the interests of Sishmindris and Faerlonnishmen have joined. It is for the good of all that we work together to overcome our Taerleezi enemies, to terrify and confuse them. And there is one man among them who is notable both for greatness and wickedness—I speak of their leader, the Governor Uffrigo. When this man dies, his subjects will wonder and tremble. Their fear will weaken them. This Governor Uffrigo must fall. Let your kind and mine join forces to destroy him."

"And then? Faerlonnishmen rule, Sishmindris whipped."

"No longer. Join with Faerlonnishmen to drive the Taerleezis from our land, and your deeds will not be forgotten. The best of Faerlonnishmen know something of honor. We pay our debts."

"Freedom."

"I cannot in all honesty make so great a promise. But I can and do swear to you that humans of conscience will begin working to free you, and we shall never cease until that aim is accomplished. Among us, your freedom will be held as sacred as our own. Now, will you help us?"

There followed a brief, unintelligible colloquy among the Sishmindris, and then Aazaargh addressed the human visitor. "Yes. We join, and the big Taerleezi dies."

TEN

It was midday, and a blanched sun shone directly overhead. The light descended through a fretwork of branches no longer winter-bare, but knobbed with the first growth of early spring. Small green shoots were beginning to appear, and the old, faded mosses were taking on a brighter tinge of color. The world hinted at renewed plenty, but as yet the promise remained unfulfilled.

Along a narrow footpath snaking its way down out of the Alzira Hills advanced a solitary figure. Although he was still young, his steps were halting, and he required the support of a staff. His garments were ragged and filthy, his hair unshorn and tangled. A wide hat, its brim pulled low, partially hid the one-eyed ruin of Onartino Belandor's face.

He must have been hungry, for he paused often to pluck new growth from the low-hanging branches, or from the brambles tangling alongside the trail. These leaves and stems he chewed at some length, but invariably spat forth without swallowing. Several times he paused and knelt laboriously to finger the damp soil in search of edible roots or fungi, but found none. Only once he uncovered a coil of worms beneath a rock, and these he devoured, but his hunger remained unsatisfied.

On along the path he hobbled, lone eye shifting dully to and fro, until the breeze delivered a recognizable scent. He halted. The nostrils in his shattered nose flared and his big chest expanded as he drew a breath to the depths of his lungs. Stepping from the path, he forced his way through thorny undergrowth until, several yards distant, he found the source of the smell.

Beneath a bush lay a trap, evidently forgotten. The metal was red-brown with rust, and the contents—an adult meecher of ordinary size—odorously decomposing. The animal's corpse was riddled with maggots, but this hardly deterred Onartino. Despite their injuries his hands retained considerable strength, and he pried the jaws of the trap apart with ease, then tore the corpse of the meecher limb from limb. His brows contracted as he ate. Presumably the flavor of the meat failed to please him, but the pace of his chewing and swallowing never slackened until the meecher had been consumed down to the last scrap of remotely edible tissue.

He cracked the bones and sucked them dry, then set his staff against the ground and lifted himself to his feet. For a moment he stood as if uncertain, his eye traveling the surrounding wilderness without comprehension, then memory revived and he appeared to remember where he was, and where he wanted to go, and what he wanted to do. He made his slow but unerring way back to the footpath, which he followed downhill for a long time and a long way, until at last he limped from the woods out onto the VitrOrezzi Bond.

He rested for a while at the side of the road—he had no idea how long, for time held no meaning—then resumed his progress toward Vitrisi. The featureless hours passed. He took no notice of his surroundings—the rutted road, the trees, hills and pastures, or even the smoky cloud hovering above the city ahead. He seemed unaware of the occasional vehicle or rider that he encountered, and fellow travelers cultivated a corresponding blindness to his existence. The human eye encountering his face by chance was apt to turn away promptly.

Despite his resistance to physical suffering, he was not immune. As time wore on, his slow pace slackened and his limp worsened, but he did not pause until he came upon a large cart standing at the side of the road. The cart was loaded with burlap sacks of root vegetables. A donkey stood between the shafts. The driver was nowhere in evidence. Presumably he had retired to relieve himself, and would soon return.

Onartino studied the vehicle. His eye blinked. He hobbled forward, tossed his staff in, and then—slowly, with much effort—climbed into the cart. Once ensconced, he bolted a couple of raw potatoes, and burrowed down among the sacks, burying his large bulk as best he could. His refuge was chilly, lumpy, and hard. Various parts of his body ached and protested. The odors of soil and potatoes swamped his senses. There was nothing he could do about any of it. He shut his eye and slept.

The return of the driver failed to wake him, and he slumbered on as the wagon resumed motion. Hours and distance passed. He remained unconscious and hidden from view when the vehicle paused at the city gate and its driver submitted to the obligatory examination. Nobody troubled to investigate the cargo. Cart, driver, and insensible stowaway passed into Vitrisi and now the wooden wheels bumped over cobbled streets.

They halted again at a market square not far from the city gate. The driver dismounted, came around to the rear of the cart, and grabbed the nearest sack. Onartino awoke and sat up slowly. The driver cursed in amazement and backed away. Apparently oblivious, Onartino climbed out of the cart.

Affronted, the driver cursed with increased vigor, and the illicit passenger finally noticed his existence. The single bloodshot eye found him, studied him expressionlessly, and the driver fell silent.

Onartino surveyed his surroundings without apparent comprehension. He spoke two words.

"*Belandor House.*"

Verbal resources exhausted for the nonce, he took his leave.

. . .

The Nor'wilders Way had shrunk to the width of a country lane, and would no doubt soon diminish in status from road to path, destined to dwindle out of existence in the midst of the wild. The Belandor carriage's days of utility were numbered, and even the continuing viability of the supply wagons lay open to question.

The Magnifico Aureste surveyed the prospect without misgiving. The sedan chair riding in pieces atop the carriage could be assembled and readied within minutes to accommodate Innesq. He himself was prepared at any time to transfer to horseback. The contents of the wagons could be shifted swiftly to the backs of the horses and servants. The demise of the Nor'wilders Way presented no insurmountable obstacle.

Of more immediate concern was the threat offered by predatory countryfolk. Presumably refugees from small settlements ravaged by the plague, they roamed the hills in hungry gangs, and they must have been desperate. Nothing short of starvation could account for their suicidal willingness to attack a large, well-armed, well-guarded caravan. But attack they did, and not infrequently.

It seemed to happen most often at sunrise or sunset, when the savory odors drifting from the cookfires must have driven the starving wretches to madness. Had they approached openly and simply requested nourishment, they might not have fared badly. Innesq Belandor would never have ignored the pleas of the hungry, nor would Sonnetia Corvestri. Disinclined to rely upon the generosity of the great, however, they opted for combat, thus idiotically categorizing themselves as legitimate prey to the Magnifico Aureste, whose past experiences qualified him to command the expedition's collective defenses.

Aureste was not particularly interested. The rustic marauders offered no real challenge—or almost none, if one discounted the dawn peppering of ill-made arrows that had claimed the life of a guard some days earlier. The requisite increase in vigilance had been effected, thus rendering repetition of the insult all but impossible. Thereafter, attempted incursions had amounted to little more than occasional insectile dartings too puny and insignificant to hold the magnifico's attention.

His interest revived, however, when the expedition was modestly but decidedly intercepted.

They had paused around midday to rest the horses. The air was clear, and pale sunlight washed an expanse of rolling countryside tinged here and there with traces of springtime color; irregular patches of green groundrambler, groves of fonachia tipped with pinkish silver, the occasional bright burst of goldstar, the first hesitant sigh of dusky sorrows-breath. The scene breathed life and hope, never so much as hinting at the huge hidden presence of the plague.

The Magnifico Aureste was engaged in colloquy with a couple of the guards when some nameless sense of anomaly gripped him, and he glanced back over his shoulder to spy a pair of strangers approaching on foot. Women, both plainly dressed. One tall and strapping; the other much shorter and slighter, unmistakably youthful, with very light, almost white hair.

Females—no threat. Evidently poor and humble—no importance, no interest. Nonentities. Why then did his jaw tighten and the alarm bells peal inside his head? Whence the sense of impending doom?

Turning from the guards, he watched the women, and the source of his uneasiness soon revealed itself. She drew near, and he recognized her. Yvenza Belandor—alive, well, and *here*. Part of his mind marveled. Anger vied with grudging admiration, while some compartment of comprehension told him that he should have expected it. Of course she would pursue him as long as a whisper of strength and life remained in her, for that was her nature. But the thirst for vengeance seemed to have affected her judgment if not her reason. What else could explain a direct and unconcealed advance upon the armed camp of her enemy? Did she expect to bully her way past the sentries?

He saw a guard accost her. There was an exchange of some sort, and Yvenza's brusque gesture encompassed her companion. Unbelievably, the guard inclined his head in apparent respect and permitted them to pass. The women followed his pointing finger straight toward the Belandor carriage, which stood idle at the side of the road.

For a moment Aureste wondered, then comprehended. Of course. The younger woman with the light hair—she must be the gifted girl of whom Innesq had spoken; the so-called kinswoman of questionable pedigree and unquestionable talent, one of the valuable arcanists upon whom the success of the endeavor depended. He studied the slight little figure and searched his memory. When he had taken Ironheart, she must have been there. The resident population of the stronghouse had not been large, and he must have glimpsed her at some time or other, but she had left no imprint upon his customarily reliable memory. Well, if she possessed genuine arcane ability, then she surely knew how to make herself inconspicuous when necessary. She had done so, and succeeded in escaping his notice altogether.

Curious to think of such power and potential inhabiting so frail a vessel. And disquieting to see so priceless a commodity controlled by Yvenza Belandor. No telling what Yvenza would do with it—but she would think of something.

The murder of her archenemy's favorite brother, for example, might strike her as an excellent move. Innesq sat alone and unsuspecting in the carriage, perhaps sunk in one of his trance-like meditations. Despite all his power and intellect, he presented an easy target. Yvenza could slip a knife between his ribs before he noticed her arrival. Quite likely she intended exactly that.

He should have executed her when he had had the chance, should have chained her to an Ironheart wall and blown her sky-high. Perhaps it was not too late to rectify the error.

Then he was running, heedless of dignity, running to interpose himself between Yvenza and his brother. He covered the distance with a speed worthy of youth, but it was not enough; she and her companion were there before him. Her hand was reaching for the carriage door.

"Halt," he commanded.

"Cousin Aureste." The hand retreated. She turned to face him with a smile of apparent pleasure. She looked hale, vigorous, and formidable as ever. "Well met. I hoped I should find you dogging the arcanists."

Her insolence.

"You dare to show your face here." He kept his voice low and controlled, but his eyes expressed many things. "Leave this place, or I will order you whipped hence."

"I'd rather hoped," she returned pleasantly, "that you might offer us the hospitality of your carriage. We've walked such a long way."

Unbelievable. The woman deserved slow flaying. Why did she still exist? Shouldn't she have died of grief and despair weeks ago?

"Do not try my patience, madam. I spared you once. I am not minded to do so a second time."

"Come, coz. Surely it's time to set the grievances of the past behind us. For the benefit of all, don't you know. See, I've conducted my young ward Nissi hither, and now she'll lend her talents to the great arcane endeavor, whatever that marvel is supposed to be. She's a valuable addition to the party, and I trust such an offering purchases my warm welcome among you."

"It does not. The girl may travel with us, but that invitation does not extend to you. Return to whatever hole in the ground you presently call home, and trouble us no more."

"Impossible. Young Nissi here—a sheltered creature, hardly more than a child—relies entirely upon my judgment and guidance. She really can't do without me."

"She'll manage. Rest assured, she'll find no dearth of guidance here."

"Ah, what stranger can replace a foster mother? If I depart, then my ward will insist on accompanying me. Will you not, Nissi? Tell him."

Aureste's attention shifted to Yvenza's companion, who still struck no chord in his memory, and he took her in at a visual gulp; young, small, fragile, confused, scared. And peculiar, he realized. Unlike ordinary girls, with that pallid spindrift hair of hers, that ghostly complexion, those huge, colorless eyes made of moonlight. She wasn't normal, she wasn't comprehensible, and he didn't like her. If she wanted to leave along with her detestable guardian, so be it. *Good riddance.* He held the words in, but glared at the girl, heavy brows lowering, and watched her shrivel beneath his black regard.

Her eyes sought the ground, her shoulders drooped, and she appeared to struggle for breath. At length a tiny, lost whisper emerged.

"*I—I—*"

Aureste waited.

"*I—I—think—*"

She seemed mentally deficient. He grew impatient.

"Well?" he snapped.

Her voice evaporated altogether. Her strange eyes rose to his face, evoking an uneasiness that sharpened his anger. He gave her a look that should have dropped her to her knees, but her eyes remained fixed on his own. It was disconcerting, for he was not certain whether she was highly impudent, or innocently stupid, or something else. Before he could decide, his brother appeared at the carriage window.

"Forgive me, my mind was elsewhere—" Innesq commenced. His eyes found Nissi, and he broke off. For a moment he studied her, then a smile of recognition and great warmth lighted his face. "My dear child," he greeted her.

She was staring, motionless as if dazed, her aspect putting Aureste irritably in mind of some white mouse impaled upon a bodkin. He deemed her incapable of reply, but she surprised him.

"Is it you?" Nissi whispered.

"I am Innesq. We have spoken many times across the spaces that are not."

"You are truly the one?"

"I am."

"But—your face." Her frightened regard shifted from Innesq's visage, to Aureste's, and back again. "And his . . . at Ironheart . . . fire, thunder, and death . . ."

"Ah. I understand. He is my brother, the Magnifico Aureste, and there is a family resemblance between us. He will not harm you, I promise. Come, child—there is nothing here to fear." Innesq extended his hand.

She seized it in both of her own and held on tightly, as if clutching a lifeline.

Innesq had always possessed the ability, Aureste reflected sourly, to win the trust of wild birds, rabbits, field mice, feral cats—all manner of timid creatures. This one seemed to be no exception. But could he train her to perform tricks on command?

"But what a lovely meeting of true minds." Yvenza bobbed a benevolent nod. "Here is genuine family feeling."

Innesq's attention shifted, and he gave her a long, considering glance.

"You are the Magnifica Yvenza?" he hazarded.

"Yes. And you're the clever middle brother?"

"I am Innesq Belandor. I bid you welcome, Magnifica, and I offer my thanks for your care and sacrifice in conveying young Nissi to this meeting."

"It was no sacrifice. Indeed, it was my pleasure."

"Yes. I see that. Yet we are indebted to you, as you must know if you recognize the nature of our mission. Has our objective been clearly presented to you, Magnifica?"

"Oh, I am quite devoid of arcane talent and knowledge. How should I hope to encompass such great ends or plumb such deep mysteries? I'm but an ordinary mortal."

"Scarcely that, so much is apparent. If you will permit me, I should like to tell you—to tell you both—more of our endeavor and its purpose. When you recognize the nature of the peril we confront, there is no doubt in my mind that you will choose to grant us your full support and assistance."

"Gifts without value. My ward Nissi here may be of some use to you, but the same can hardly be said of me."

Just so, thought Aureste. The hag conceded the obvious in order to demonstrate her candor, but she deceived no one. Or did she?

"A woman of intelligence, energy, and determination always has much to offer—if she so wills," Innesq returned. "But forgive me, I neglect all courtesy." Gently freeing his captive hand of Nissi's grip, he opened the carriage door. "Will you not join me? Rest, travel in comfort, and we will talk."

Impossible. His brother could not mean to invite this abominable woman into the Belandor carriage. Even Innesq's trusting good nature could not extend so far.

He would not allow it. He did not wish to humiliate his brother, but he would not allow it.

"The girl may travel with us, if you so desire," Aureste decreed. "As for the old woman, she can have a loaf of bread or two in charity's name, and then she'll be on her way."

"Aureste, I ask you to reconsider." Innesq's grave tone carried a note of reproof.

"Clearly you don't understand. Have you any idea who and what this creature is?"

"Yes—our kinswoman."

"Oh, do not quarrel on my account," Yvenza forestalled Aureste's reply. "I wouldn't sow discord between two loving brothers—indeed, I wouldn't do it for the world. Therefore I will take my leave without further ado. I'll accept those loaves of bread you offered, coz, and thank you for your generosity." She turned to her charge. "Nissi. Come, child. I am not welcome here, so we must leave now."

Nissi shot Innesq an anguished glance.

"They are of House Belandor," Innesq observed. "Will you turn them away?"

"The girl may stay," Aureste returned. "I've already said so."

"But she will not stay without me." Yvenza shook her head with an air of regret.

"I fail to recognize your indispensability, madam." Turning from her to address the odd little white stranger, Aureste consciously softened his voice, but could not quench the wrathful fire in his eyes. "Well—Nissi. Will you travel to the Quivers with us? We should be glad of your company."

The words were civil enough, but they did not produce the desired effect. She scrutinized the ground raptly.

"*Speak up, girl!*" Yvenza commanded. "Tell him."

Wrapping both arms about herself, Nissi raised her head to stare off at an area of sky somewhere beyond Aureste's left shoulder.

"I—must stay with the magnifica," she murmured.

"No need," he snapped. "We shall look after you well, protect you night and day, and provide you with every possible comfort. Listen to me. Don't you see—"

"Stop," Innesq commanded, so quietly and calmly that the interruption seemed almost devoid of offense.

Aureste fell balefully silent, and his brother's attention returned to the otherworldly girl.

"Child, you cannot part from the Magnifica Yvenza?" he inquired.

She shook her head almost invisibly.

"Then we shall not ask it of you. The two of you are of House Belandor, entitled to our regard. Your acceptance of our hospitality honors us. Ladies, will it please you to enter?" Even as Innesq threw wide the carriage door, his eyes sought his brother's.

The message was easily read by Aureste. The peculiar but talented girl was too valuable to lose. She was needed, no matter what the cost. If she wanted to drag a companion along on the trip, then the companion would have to be tolerated. Yvenza could not be killed, cast out, or even openly slighted— at least, not for the moment.

"Oh—" Yvenza affected a certain solicitous distress. "—I am not persuaded that the magnifico will bear it."

He yearned to wring her neck. Instead he replied with such good grace as he could muster, "My brother's goodness schools me. The claims of kinship must not be denied."

"So my late husband believed, and his principles ruled his actions, as you can attest from personal experience, coz. The bounty you bestow upon me and my ward convinces me that you have inherited the Magnifico Onarto's greatness of heart, along with his title, and it is a beautiful thing to witness. Come, then." She gestured expansively. "We shall travel together and pass the hours in conversation. The talented among us, Master Innesq and my little Nissi, will no doubt speak of arcane wonders beyond our understanding. But you and I, Cousin Aureste—why, what should we two speak of but family matters? There is so much that we could share. I could tell you of my son Onartino, and his astonishing recovery—"

Had the woman gone mad?

"—while you," she continued warmly, "will sing the praises of your lovely daughter, who holds such a special place in my heart. What news of the delightful Jianna? I trust she is safe and well at home? Ah, but your face, coz! Forgive me, have I said something I oughtn't? Surely it can't be that she is still missing, after all this time? Oh—oh, I see. Your silence, your expression, confirm my worst fears. But this is quite dreadful. I am desolated. Rest assured, however, that I stand prepared to offer a wealth of comfort and commiseration. I am ready and willing to console you for hours on end—for days, if need be."

He hardly trusted himself to reply. The urge to strike her was almost physical. It was only by dint of stringent self-control that he managed to reply evenly, "The carriage will be crowded. I'll take to horseback." He walked away without a backward glance, and without obliging himself to witness Yvenza's smile of profound gratification.

. . .

Two days later, around sunset, the members of the combined Belandor–Corvestri expedition sat around the communal campfire, finishing the last of a typically rudimentary meal. The fare was mediocre, but bellies were pleasantly full, veins agreeably warmed with wine, tempers comparatively mellow. At such times, a measure of careful socializing was apt to take place among the members of the two households. Most often, Innesq Belandor wheeled himself into the midst of the Corvestris, but variations upon this theme sometimes occurred, and this evening witnessed one of them.

When the last of the meat had been consumed and the last of the tin bowls removed, the Magnifica Yvenza wended an apparently careless way to Vinz Corvestri's side.

He observed her approach with curiosity and some distrust, but no more than he would have reserved for any member of the Belandor tribe, with the exception of Innesq. In fact, this particular Belandor was less objectionable than most, for rumor had it that bad blood existed between her and the Magnifico Aureste. Vinz didn't know the particulars. Apparently some sort of intrafamilial quarrel or trouble had arisen at the time of Aureste's assumption of the title—hardly any surprise in that—but it had all occurred some twenty-five years or more in the past, and he had at that time been young and far too deeply immersed in his own arcane studies to take much notice. Presumably she had settled the worst of her differences with Aureste, else she would not be here now. In which case, what could she possibly want with Vinz Corvestri? But her demeanor was such that he rose to his feet at once.

"Magnifico." Halting before him, she inclined her head with an air of regal courtesy. "We have never met, and it is more than time to correct that error of fortune and circumstance. I am the Dowager Magnifica Yvenza Belandor, widow to the Magnifico Onarto. Our respective Houses, though joined by membership in the famous Six, have stood divided throughout the generations. It is a grievous, senseless rift that I hope the present shared venture may serve to mend—or at least, to commence a repair. Will you favor me with a moment of your time and regard?"

"Magnifica, I am honored to attend you." It was impossible to escape the rhythm of her formality. He found himself shackled, compelled to adopt the uncomfortable high style. Well, he could hold his own, when necessary.

"It is my greatest desire," Yvenza confided, "to promote peace and understanding between our respective Houses. The Belandor–Corvestri enmity has burned on senselessly for too many years. It has devoured wealth, energy, time, even lives. And wherefore? Much has been sacrificed, and to what end? Vengeance? Honor? Tell me, Magnifico—do you know the nature of the quarrel between our two Houses? What was the cause, the original offense, and who was blameworthy? Do you know?"

"I've heard stories. Assorted tales of treachery, broken promises, and betrayal. Differing accounts, all unverifiable, but alike in one respect—the Corvestri kinsmen were always nobly righteous and blameless, the Belandors invariably villains."

"Ah. Just so." She smiled. "And the childhood tales I heard were similar but reversed, populated with virtuous Belandors and wicked Corvestris."

"Childhood tales, Magnifica? But surely you'd have heard little prior to your marriage into the Belandor family?"

"Not so. I was born of House Cheffori, but my mother was a Belandor. The Magnifico Onarto who became my husband was in fact my distant cousin. So you see, the fortunes of House Belandor have always concerned me, and it is the fondest wish of my heart that I may play a role, however minor, in effecting a reconciliation between the two feuding households."

"A laudable ambition, Magnifica." She really wasn't so bad, Vinz decided. True, her aspect of battered stateliness put him in mind of some crumbling monument. Beneath the weathered exterior, however, he detected a nature genial and kindly. "How do you propose to put it into effect?"

"My hopes are supported by our present situation. We Belandors and Corvestris have been thrown together by need, and it's my belief that propinquity will encourage the easy, natural sort of exchange certain to break down barriers. Perhaps we may come to understand and even trust each other. Call me a foolish dreamer if you will."

"I should rather call you an optimist, and the world needs such."

"Well, I will confess that my heart has always ruled my head—a woman's weakness, no doubt."

"By no means, Magnifica."

"You mustn't imagine, though, that I intend to rely upon chance alone. No, I mean to further my purpose by enlisting the aid of such persons of goodwill and good sense as you appear to be, Magnifico Corvestri. Indeed, you are the first that I have approached, for here I am confident of success. Your demeanor reveals your readiness to set all quarrels aside, sentiments clearly shared by your lady wife. I see that the two of you share my longing for reconciliation."

"My lady wife?" Vinz blinked.

"Honors her lord's will, as a dutiful wife must. Her cultivation of the Magnifico Aureste reveals as much."

"Cultivation?" The word tasted bad. Vinz frowned.

"Ah, she is well chosen to serve as the Corvestri ambassadress. I don't believe that the magnifico will find it possible to resist her charm."

"What are you talking about?"

"Come, we share the same hopes. I see her working at your behest. During my short stay among you travelers, I've lost count of the times that I've spied Aureste and the Magnifica Sonnetia engaged in conversation. I've never ventured to intrude upon them at such moments, as the exchanges have appeared so intimate."

"Intimate?"

"By that I mean deeply felt on both sides. Her arguments have impressed him. So much is evident. His stance, his face, and his eyes express all. As for your lady—her gestures and glances overcome all his resistance. Even when they do not directly address one another, his eyes follow her everywhere. Depend upon it, sir—she makes progress, she is certain to succeed."

"Really. Really." Vinz's eyes roved in search of his wife. He did not see her anywhere about, but that meant nothing. He did not see Aureste, either, but there was no cause for concern in that. There was no reason at all for the sudden sick feeling at the pit of his stomach. "Indeed, I believe you mistake the matter. The Magnifica Sonnetia merely displays that gracious courtesy consistent with her breeding. It is bestowed upon all impartially, with none beyond her immediate family singled out for exceptional favor."

"Oh, do not misunderstand me," Yvenza advised. "I spoke nothing of favor. I merely express my admiration of the Magnifica Sonnetia's skilled deployment of beauty, charm, and persuasion in the service of her House. Happy the husband of so clever and gifted a lady!"

Happy? Clever and gifted? Happy? In an instant Vinz's mind boiled with all manner of misgivings. It was absurd—he almost felt ill. The Dowager Magnifica Yvenza couldn't possibly imagine the internal uproar her words had touched off—could she? He darted a covert glance into light grey eyes expressing nothing beyond amiable candor, and immediately repented his own suspicions. He should no more doubt the Magnifica Yvenza than he should doubt the Magnifica Sonnetia.

For one moment he wished them both equally nonexistent. Not that he desired harm or suffering to either; it was just that life would be so much—clearer, straighter, simpler, *easier*—if both were gone.

Sonnetia gone. Sonnetia—beautiful still, and mother of the

best son the universe could possibly offer—no, that was all wrong. Not Sonnetia. Aureste was the one who should go. Aureste encumbered all the world. He should have vanished years ago.

The Dowager Magnifica stood regarding him with an air of kindly encouragement. Evidently a reply was expected, but he had no idea what to say to her. Even as he floundered for words, the faint strains of alien music riding the evening air came to his rescue. An instinctive thrill shot through him. The sound was arcane in origin, beyond question. He drew a deep breath, as if inhaling the fragrance of flowers. His mind tightened and clarified itself at once, while his spirits and confidence rose.

"Hear that? What is it?" Yvenza was watching his face.

"Quiet, please. Let me listen." Vinz strained his senses, mundane and other. The music, slow and indefinably vainglorious, was never the product of material instruments touched by human hands. Resonating grandly through the hollows of the epiatmosphere, it was certainly the work of an accomplished practitioner.

Which one? Every arcane act bore the psychic imprint of its author, individual and distinct as any signature. This music was no exception, but the source was unfamiliar and foreign. *Literally?* It announced itself aggressively; asked for attention—demanded it.

Who?

Whatever and whoever, the music was advancing upon the campsite. Vinz's pulse quickened, not unpleasurably. Unknown talent approached; something new.

"What is it?" the Dowager Magnifica Yvenza repeated sharply.

"An arcanist declares his arrival." He scarcely glanced at her. His eyes traveled in search of Vinzille, who should witness this; and Innesq, and even the odd little Nissi—the people capable of understanding.

"Declaring it rather loudly, isn't he?" she inquired.

She had a point, but what of it? What need of stealth out here on the open road? He cleared his mind to receive the message of the music, whose combination of arcane ethereality and straightforward bumptiousness somehow managed to convey self-congratulation.

His fellow travelers, masters and servants alike, were stirring, staring, listening—all of them caught. Vinz gazed off along the rutted remnant of the Nor'wilders Way to behold a luminous cloud or haze, glowing in shades of crimson, gold, and purple. A conspicuously arcane manifestation, and quite splendid in a gaudy sort of way. On it glided, soft plump billows shifting colors along the rainbow spectrum and beyond, past the comfortable familiar hues and on as far as *vhuun*, only visible to experienced and suitably enhanced eyes. Vinz could not see *vhuun* at present, but a certain corneal itch advised him of its presence.

Closer yet, and now the solid kernel at the heart of the glow distinguished itself—a trio of vehicles: a horse-drawn carriage accompanied by a couple of mule-drawn supply wagons. Bands of green shadow delineated the harnesses, trappings, and decorative escutcheons. Wreaths of pale green flame crowned horses, mules, coachman, servants, and outriders. The carriage windows were curtained in miniature pyrotechnics, starbursting brilliantly and concealing the interior.

The flames were illusory, Vinz perceived at once. No real heat there, no real destructive potential, despite the alarming appearance. He could clear the fiery images from his vision, should he so choose, along with the lambent mists and the glittery starbursts, but he elected to accept the diverting mental intrusion, for now.

The sound swelled as the little convoy drew nigh. Carriage and attendants rolled into the campsite and halted. The music crescendoed triumphantly, then ceased. Flames leaped for the sky, then faded. Luminescence ebbed, and the carriage windows went black. A moment's breathless silence ensued, then the door opened and a passenger emerged in splendor.

His large and stocky frame was clothed in the simply cut garments of an ordinary woodsman. In place of the woodsman's customary homespun and deerskin, however, he sported a jerkin of highly glazed eelskin, deep mulberry in color, oversewn with scores of small medallions winking gold in the firelight. His leggings were of fine wool, his red-heeled boots of black tortoise leather, polished to a sheen. The long-billed cap crowning his well-curled head was rustic in style, but the addition of a lush black plume caught in a jeweled clasp was clearly an urban innovation.

Behind him came a short, bony person with a sad face and dejected demeanor, modestly garbed in brown, and all but lost in the glare of his companion's magnificence.

The newcomer stood tall and still in the firelight, inviting and returning regard. When some internal clock told him that the moment was ripe, he spoke.

"Say, all you Faerlonnish, you Corvestris, Belandors, and such, I expect you already know who I am." A strongly nasal Taerleezi accent flattened every syllable. "But just to be sure, I'll introduce myself. I'm Pridisso—Ojem Pridisso of Iron Hill. You've heard of me, I don't doubt, and now you see me close up and clear. You can look all you like, I don't mind. An arcanist of stature gets used to the attention. Probably you'd like to know if all the tales and legends about me are true. Well, I won't say they're *all* true. The one where I build the mechanical bird that flies me to the summit of Mount Malediction, where I rescue the kidnapped princess single-handed—that's an exaggeration of the facts. But I won't say they're all false, either. You'll have to make up your own minds about that.

"And mind you," Pridisso confided, "there'll be plenty of opportunity to judge, now that I've come among you. I'm not one to crow, but I think it's safe to say that you'll be surprised when you see what we Taerleezis can do. Remember, our experimentation hasn't been shackled by law for the past twenty-five years the way yours has, and that makes a difference. Taerleez has seen progress. I won't go into particulars here and now, but you can rest assured that this venture goes forward to a successful conclusion, now that I've joined, or I might more properly say, now that *we've* joined. My friend and colleague here, Littri Zovaccio of Frinnasi, is a fine arcanist and a valuable addition to our party. He won't say so, because he just doesn't much like talking, but you can take my word for it."

Pridisso's companion acknowledged the introduction with a slight dip of the head. His look of dejection deepened perceptibly.

"Now, the first thing I need," Pridisso continued, "is a word with the man who's been leading this gang so far. We'll want to discuss arrangements. Who's leader here?"

Aureste Belandor was certain to pop up out of nowhere to claim the title. It wasn't just or reasonable, for Aureste possessed not the smallest jot of arcane ability, but he would take it anyway, for that was his way. Then he and this newly arrived Taerleezi boor would join forces to seize command of the expedition and everyone in it. The prospect was so insupportable that Vinz found himself speaking out against it.

"There is no official leader here," he reported clearly. All eyes turned in his direction. Resisting the nervous urge to look down, he kept his own gaze fixed on the newcomers. "We are two distinct parties traveling in tandem. I am the Magnifico Corvestri, and I speak for my own household."

"Oh, yes, I know of you. The shadowscion investigations. I remember your Wide Sending, a couple of years back. Not bad. Considering the state of things over here, really a very decent effort. Good to meet you. Zovaccio here would say the same, if only he wanted to talk."

Littri Zovaccio breathed a sigh.

"I understand what you're saying to me, Corvestri," Pridisso continued, not unkindly. "You've got a democratic outlook and that's good, but I've got to tell you, it's not always practical. I'm not one to criticize, but facts are facts. Any venture needs strong leadership, that's just common sense, as I'm sure you'll agree, once you've thought it over. Now, who's head of the Belandor bunch? That would be Master Innesq Belandor, I expect. Where is he?"

"You are in error, Master Pridisso." The speaker did not raise his voice, but the rich, assured tones were effortlessly audible to all.

Vinz started as if pricked by needles. Just as he had expected, Aureste Belandor had materialized out of thin air, and was moving to take command. Some instinct pushed his glance left, and he spied his wife standing at the edge of the firelight. She had not been there a moment earlier. She seemed to have reappeared along with Aureste, but that was surely a coincidence without meaning. In any case, he could not think about it now, for it seemed that Aureste had more to say.

"I am the Magnifico Aureste Belandor, and I speak for my House."

"The Magnifico Aureste, eh? I've heard of you." Ojem Pridisso took a leisurely survey. "Not an arcanist, are you?"

"No."

"Then what in the name of all that's senseless are you doing out here?"

Vinz's breath caught. He had sometimes pondered this very question, but would never have dared to voice it aloud. An unwelcome reply rose unbidden to his mind: *He's out here sniffing around after my wife.* He pushed the thought away almost before it reached consciousness and focused on pleasanter things. The Taerleezi's manners were deplorable, yet it was deeply satisfying to see someone taking the offensive with Aureste Belandor.

A slight lift of Aureste's brows communicated politely sardonic deprecation of the other's ill breeding. "Am I to assume that you wish to add your party to our group, Master Pridisso?"

"You assume right. We're all going to the same place, aren't we?"

"Then I advise you to set up your camp without delay.

You'll find that we retire early and rise early. Be prepared to set forth at dawn if you expect to keep up with us. We've already dined, so it's too late to invite you to share the evening meal. But the cookfire still burns, and you're free to make use of it. You are both welcome among us, and I trust that your respective contributions will greatly increase our collective wealth of talent and ability."

Vinz's jaw clenched. Just as he had feared, Aureste was taking command—addressing the newcomers as if he were acknowledged leader of the expedition, empowered to speak for all, to grant or withhold favors, to issue instructions and even orders. It wasn't right, but it was happening right before his eyes, and there was nothing he could do about it. Or perhaps there was, perhaps he should speak up, say something to undermine Aureste Belandor and put him in his place.

He could think of nothing to say.

But maybe there was no need after all, for it seemed that Ojem Pridisso did not relish the masterful airs of a Faerlonnishman devoid of arcane ability. With an air of lofty amusement, Pridisso returned, "I thank you for that very kindly welcome. But we won't need to presume upon your hospitality in the matter of the fire. See here, fire's no trouble to us." Bowing his head, he spoke inaudibly and gestured smartly; whereupon the cookfire, hunkered low among the embers, suddenly shot to a height of some ten feet, and deepened in color to an improbable red.

A couple of attendants squealed and drew back, while one of the horses loosed a whinny. Vinz shared their astonishment, but his emotion stemmed from a different source. The manipulation of the fire was a simple feat, well within the reach of a mediocre talent. But he had never expected to see it performed here and now. Since the journey's first day, all arcanists involved had hoarded their power and energy like misers, refusing to spend the smallest scrap without good cause. But this Taerleezi practiced no such economy. He produced showy effects for his own satisfaction, apparently without the least fear of depletion. Were his resources endless—or was he a reckless spendthrift whose extravagance ought to be curbed?

Innesq would probably know. He'd ask Innesq.

Littri Zovaccio gave his head a small, mournful shake.

Pridisso spoke and gestured again. The cookfire resumed its former size and color. He aimed a lazy smile at Aureste.

"I see," observed Aureste, returning the smile in kind, "that you are determined to lighten the tedium of our journey. We shall not lack amusement while you are with us, that's clear. But you have offered lavish entertainment, and we mustn't press for more this evening. You will wish to make camp and dine, and I would not delay you."

Pridisso's look of satisfaction faded. "We'll do that," he returned. "And in the morning, at breakfast, we'll get all the arcanists in this gang together, and we'll sit down and decide how things should be run."

The arcanists. That wouldn't be so bad, Vinz decided. The arcanists *should* be in charge. Not Aureste Belandor, but the people with talent, the people who mattered.

He became aware that the Dowager Magnifica Yvenza, whose existence he had forgotten, was scrutinizing him, and he turned to face her.

"Well." She offered a genial smile. "An interesting development. Is it my imagination, or does it seem that Master Pridisso and our Magnifico Aureste don't quite like each other?"

"I believe that's true, Magnifica."

"Isn't life full of surprises?"

ELEVEN

The ground was moist and yielding, the air was misty and mild. A light drizzle of rain dampened the wiry hair and beard of a figure wending a solitary course across the largely trackless countryside. Raising a steel-jointed hand to a face neatly upholstered in the finest glove leather, the traveler wiped the droplets away.

Pausing at the crest of a rise, the traveler surveyed its surroundings with eyes of amber glass. Directly ahead rose a small structure of sod, surrounded by patches of sketchily cultivated soil. Little more than a glorified hut, the place doubtless belonged to one of those antisocial self-sufficient eccentrics determined to wrest a livelihood from the wilderness. A low beep issued from the automaton. The grumble of internal cogs suggested cogitation. After a moment, it resumed progress.

Advancing straight to the door, it rapped sharply. There was no reply. It rapped again, and still there came no answer. A short succession of irritable clicks preceded the automaton's metallic utterance.

"Denizens of this pathetic, primitive hovel, admit me, if you please. I want information, and it is my intention to question you. Open the door at once. My time is valuable, and I do not like to be kept waiting."

No reply, and the amber glass eyes glinted.

"You inside the hovel, I am not to be deceived. My superior sensory apparatus tells me that you are there within. Admit me. Come, are you afraid? There is no need. I will not harm you, although I easily *could,* with my superior strength. I merely seek truth and knowledge. You will supply both."

Silence reigned, and the automaton lost patience. "I have addressed you with utmost courtesy, and see how I am rewarded. Now I am obliged to assert myself." So saying, it dealt the door a mighty kick. The door flew open, and the automaton entered.

The space within was predictably small, simple, and humble. Less predictable were the filth, the disorder, and the overwhelming stench. The atmosphere was abominably freighted with decay. An ordinary mortal would have gagged on it, but the automaton suffered no inconvenience. And neither, it seemed, did the inhabitants.

There were three people—a man, a woman, and a small boy—all standing still and silent at the center of the dwelling's single room. Their bodies were emaciated, and barely covered in moldering rags. The flesh that showed through the rents in the cloth was greyish in color. Beside the man crouched a large mastiff, as motionless as its master. The clay floor was piled with rotting garbage aswarm with insect life. Spiders had built palaces in the corners. Soot grimed every surface, but the hearth was dark and cold.

The occupants, both human and canine, remained motionless as the automaton came bursting in upon them. Almost they seemed unaware of the alien presence. Only when it addressed them directly did their eyes—milky and curiously fixed—turn slowly toward the doorway.

"Peasants of the reeking hovel," the automaton greeted them, "no doubt you wonder at my presence among you. There is nothing to fear. I am Grix Orlazzu, the true and destined Grix Orlazzu, known as GrixPerfect to distinguish me from certain shoddily constructed, defective early drafts of the Grix design. As it happens, however, it is just such a defective draft that I now seek. Inferior though he is, yet he is my predecessor, possessed of information that must be transferred to my memory. But he has vanished prior to completion of this task, and I do not know what has become of him. Perhaps he has wandered off into the hills and lost his way. Perhaps he has received a blow to his fragile skull and lost his fragile wits. Perhaps he has fallen into a pit or ravine, and cannot escape. Something prevents him from fulfilling his obligation to me, but I will find him and set matters right. Therefore, you organics of low estate, I ask you now—have you recently seen a human, distinctly similar to me in appearance, though less well made and durable? Speak."

Silence.

"He calls himself Grix Orlazzu," GrixPerfect expanded. "He claims glory as my creator. This can hardly be, for how can a being of water and mud make something stronger and better than itself? There can be no question, however, that this organic Grix existed *before* me. His experience grants him knowledge that must be passed on to me. It is his duty, and he will fulfill it. He will *talk* to me. Have you seen him?"

His listeners were silent. Their filmy eyes communicated nothing, and the automaton's forbearance began to fail.

"Come, what is this? Are you haughty? Are you insolent? Are you mentally deficient? Or can it be that you are deaf and mute?"

No answer, so sign of comprehension, and GrixPerfect surveyed its hosts closely.

"Ah. Yes. I perceive the difficulty here." Its look of affront faded. "My finely calibrated sensory apparatus detects no evidence of respiration, heartbeat, or flowing currents. Moreover, the temperature of your bodies does not differ from that of the atmosphere, a deviation from the normal state of humans and canines. I note too that certain portions of your anatomy have commenced decomposition. The essential processes of life do not take place, and therefore all of you must be regarded as not alive, or—as it is often termed—dead. Yes, you four organics are unquestionably dead. This accounts for your dullness and discourtesy. You should not be stirring, however—not so much as a blink of your filmy and peculiar eyes. It is incorrect and unbecoming. I advise you to desist."

The advice was sound, but the dead organics ignored it. Moving as one, as if in response to silent commands, the four of them advanced upon GrixPerfect. The automaton stood its ground as they drew near, their slow footsteps scraping over the clay floor. It did not object as the four of them clustered closely about it, in the manner giving rise to the popular belief that the Wanderers deliberately sought to spread contagion. Only when they ventured to touch did GrixPerfect voice an objection.

"Remove your filthy, decaying, rat-nibbled hands, if you please. And command your dog to cease tonguing my ankle. I do not like to be touched. I will not endure familiarity."

The groping hands did not withdraw. Their touch was soft and limp, but persistent. A cold arm twined about the automaton's shoulders. GrixPerfect shrugged it off.

Evidently taking her cue from the dog, the woman leaned forward to lick the automaton's leathern cheek with an oozing tongue. GrixPerfect shoved her away.

"Dead peasant people, I do not wish to quarrel, but I must observe that your presumption is offensive. I have informed you once, with perfect civility, that I do not like to be touched. And yet you continue—but stop, what is this?" GrixPerfect paused a moment to survey its surroundings. "What is happening? I observe an alteration in the environment. It is sudden and extreme. There is a change in the properties of the light, and the norms of reflectivity have shifted. The pressure and composition of the atmosphere have changed. The attractive force of the world, or at least this portion of it, has transformed. Tremors rock the ground. And the solidity—or, if you would, the reality—of the material objects around us has been severely compromised. Dead people, are you responsible for this?"

No answer.

"If you are responsible, I must insist that you cease. It is not your place to change the world in ways whose consequences cannot be measured or predicted. You know not what you do—perhaps because you are organic, or perhaps because you are dead. Either way, it must end. Answer, if you please."

Silence.

"This is intolerable." Shaking itself free of all encumbrances, the automaton made for the exit. Decomposing creatures both human and canine shuffled in its wake, but it reached the door well ahead of them all. There it turned to address them.

"You all should know that the treatment I have received here has been objectionable. Your manipulation of natural law has been impertinent and inconsiderate. You have not made me feel welcome or valued as a guest. In that, I judge you typical of humankind.

"Understand that I will not endure it. I wish nothing more to do with you, and thus I take my leave, but not before I have offered you a word of sound counsel. Attend, if you please. These changes that you have worked upon the pattern of the world—they are not improvements. The dwindling solidity, in particular, must be regarded as an error. Perhaps you will reply that it is entirely a matter of taste, but if you are wise, you will trust my judgment and restore all to its former state. Dead peasants, I bid you good day."

So saying, the automaton exited the building and strode off into the mists, intent on resuming the quest for its missing creator.

· · ·

In the study of the private apartment situated on the second story of the Cityheart, the Governor Anzi Uffrigo sat at his desk. A spread of papers covered the surface before him, but one document among them monopolized his attention. It was a personal letter intended for his eyes alone. The arrival of pleading petitions was no uncommon occurrence, but this one was noteworthy in at least two respects. It had been written by a woman, and it offered exceptional reward in exchange for a large favor.

For at least the twentieth time Uffrigo examined the missive, with its clear, decisive handwriting on plain stationery of good quality. No ornamentation, no perfume, no feminine witchery, but still—her gender and her circumstances caught his interest. The Maidenlady Strinnza Coranna, daughter of the late Recognized Voro Coranna, executed twenty years ago for crimes against the Taerleezi state. He remembered the case well enough; he himself had signed the Faerlonnish loyalist's death warrant. He had witnessed the Recognized Coranna's decapitation, and clearly recalled deploring the headsman's dearth of skill.

There had been a widow and some children who—owing to the promptness with which Coranna had volunteered a full confession—had gone unmolested. They had even been permitted to retain a measure of their wealth; although, to be sure, House Coranna had been stripped of its noble rank, and surviving members had been exiled from Vitrisi.

Now one of them was back in evidence, requesting full reinstatement of the Coranna name, estate, and privileges. And she was willing to pay handsomely for these things. In token of her regard, she had written, she begged leave to present His Excellency the Governor with a brace of fully mature, well-grown male Sishmindris. Such a gift was remarkable in itself, but incredibly, there was more—and better. The maidenlady offered a collection of documents, property of her disgraced father and secretly guarded by members of the Coranna family for the past two decades. Personal messages for the most part, they revealed the names of many of the Recognized Voro's co-conspirators and fellow criminals of the Faerlonnish resistance.

Numerous Faerlonnish of high Houses had come under suspicion at the time of Voro Coranna's downfall, but no evidence against any of them had been discovered, and their crimes had gone unpunished, to the Governor Uffrigo's lasting dissatisfaction. For twenty years the guilty parties had lived free, comfortable, and insolent. Several of them enjoyed wealth and ease unusual among the conquered. But now at last the truth was coming to light; late, but not too late to take action against the enemies of Taerleez.

The chimes in the clock tower above the Cityheart struck the hour, and there came a knock at the door. The governor looked up.

"Come," he said.

The door opened, a guard's face appeared, and then the announcement, "The Maidenlady Strinnza Coranna."

"Admit her."

The guard withdrew, and a woman entered. She was young—she must have been a small child at the time of her father's death—and simply dressed. She could not have been described as a great beauty, but she was decidedly pretty, with a pale, fine-featured face framed in dark hair drawn back in a knot. Her eyes were quite exceptional—large, grey-blue, and intense in expression. As for her figure, it was completely concealed beneath a long, plain cloak colored the grey of winter tree trunks. Should her form prove as pleasing as her face, then it might be worthwhile to determine just how high a price she was willing to pay for the reinstatement of her House.

In the matter of the Sishmindris, she had kept her word, bringing two of them with her. They were neither fashionably svelte and supple, nor fashionably garbed. Quite the contrary, they were broad and bulky with muscle—probably the largest and most powerfully built Sishmindris that he had ever seen. Their livery, if it merited such a title, was modest to the point of shabbiness. They could lay no claim to smartness or style, but were doubtless capable of tireless labor. By any and all standards, the offering was impressive.

"Maidenlady." Uffrigo inclined his head with an air of gracious warmth, but did not rise from his seat. She was Faerlonnish, and the daughter of a criminal, after all.

"Excellency. I thank you for receiving me, and I ask permission to present you with a gift in token of my gratitude and appreciation. Will it please you to accept the Sishmindri brothers, Zayzi and Frayz? You will find them strong, willing workers, and highly serviceable."

Her voice was low and melodic, yet possessed of an odd quality, something brittle and crystalline as winter's delicate flowers of frost on glass.

Nonsense. She was young, attractive, and in need of his favor. The best of all possible petitioners.

"Brothers, eh?" He smiled, using his own mournful poet's eyes to beam encouraging susceptibility. "There's a pretty touch. They are certainly fine, well-grown specimens, and I thank you for the gift. But come, maidenlady. Will you not approach and seat yourself? I'll order refreshment, and we shall chat at leisure."

"Your Excellency is most gracious." Approaching, she took the chair he had indicated, directly opposite him. The Sishmindri brothers flanked her closely, in the manner of trained bodyguards. Evidently the amphibians had failed as yet to comprehend the transfer of ownership.

Examined at closer range, her eyes were handsome as ever in size and color, but Uffrigo noted something displeasing in their expression, or rather their lack of expression. A rime of blue-grey ice seemed to conceal every trace of thought and emotion. Her pretty young face was mask-like, altogether unreadable. His initial impression had been favorable, but now he was beginning to decide that he did not quite like her. His air of cordiality, however, remained intact.

"Shall I ring for some wine, maidenlady?" he offered mellifluously.

"I would not abuse Your Excellency's hospitality by too free an encroachment upon your time and patience. You have granted me this audience, and I in turn have offered up promises, one of which involves the delivery of certain documents. Here they are." From somewhere beneath her enveloping cloak she brought forth a small paper packet. Leaning forward in her chair, she placed it on the desk before him.

Well. No pretty hesitation, no trace of shyness or uncertainty. Utterance direct, economical, to the point. The young lady was all business. Her almost masculine bluntness was not particularly attractive, but perhaps there was something to be said for clarity. He picked up the packet and saw that it was elaborately sealed with wax and bound with string. It would have been easy to break the seals and cut the string, but Uffrigo did neither. Taking up a letter opener as sharp as any dagger, he carefully shaved the waxen seals off one by one, preserving each whole. This done, he inserted the point into one of the many knots in the string, and gently, lovingly began to worry it loose.

A stranger observing him might have thought that the governor took extraordinary pains to avoid damaging the packet's contents. Some other stranger, fancifully analytical, might even have concluded that the unnecessary delay reflected some sort of unacknowledged reluctance or fear. Neither observer would have been correct. A connoisseur in all his pleasures, Anzi Uffrigo appreciated the flavor of anticipation, prolonged and reduced to an exquisite concentrate. He knew how to savor it in full.

So absorbed in his delicate task was he that the governor did not immediately note the advance of the two Sishmindri brothers, Zayzi and Frayz. A subtle shifting shadow alerted him, and natural instinct warned him. With speed worthy of a viper, he dropped the packet, rose to his feet, and expertly thrust his dagger-pointed letter opener under the ribs of the nearest Sishmindri. Blue-green fluid gushed, and Zayzi or Frayz fell. Almost simultaneously, Uffrigo's left hand stretched forth, found the bellpull beside the desk, and yanked.

A large, web-fingered hand closed on the outstretched wrist. The captive arm was twisted behind its owner's back. A second powerful greenish hand clamped over the governor's mouth.

Uffrigo could neither move nor speak, and he could hardly breathe, but he could see well enough. His visitor, Voro

Coranna's daughter, as she claimed to be, was on her feet, coming around the desk, and now she had a knife in her fist. She would never dare to use it; she was nothing more than a girl.

She halted before him, and he saw no rage or hatred in her eyes, but only a cold purpose.

Still he did not believe it.

"Anzi Uffrigo, Taerleezi despot and murderer, thus my country frees itself of your tyranny." She spoke as dispassionately as a judge pronouncing sentence, but her pretty face reflected stern exultation.

The remark seemed melodramatic and artificial, like something from a bad play. He could imagine her standing before a glass, rehearsing intonation and expression. Ridiculous, really. But there was no time to consider such matters, for her hand, clasping the poniard, flashed toward him, and the blade sank into his throat.

He saw the arterial spurt of his own blood, and felt little beyond shocked incredulity. She was still standing there, apparently calm and unmoved, but behind her the door was opening, and into the study stepped one of the servants, in obedience to the summoning bell. Uffrigo was unable to draw breath, much less call for aid. He knew that assistance had arrived too late to save his life, and it was the last thing he knew.

• • •

Taking in the situation at a glance, the servant—evidently trained to double as impromptu bodyguard, as required—drew a dagger from his belt while lifting his voice in a great cry for help. The surviving Sishmindri, Frayz, released the governor's body, which collapsed like disappointed expectation. Launching himself across the desk, the amphibian collided with the servant, his momentum sending the two of them crashing against the wall. As if wordlessly expressing the pent hatred of years, Frayz locked powerful hands about the human neck and squeezed.

The servant plunged his blade once, twice, three times into the Sishmindri's side. Frayz staggered, and his grip loosened perceptibly, but he did not let go. Springing to her ally's aid, Celisse drove her poniard underhanded at the servant's midsection. Twisting desperately, he managed to knock her arm aside. When she came at him again, he slashed, his blade opening a long, deep gash along her forearm. The weapon dropped from her grasp. Her arm was instantly soaked with blood.

The wounds that the Sishmindri had received were mortal. Frayz sank to his knees, clearly in extremis, yet somehow maintaining a grip on his enemy's throat. Seeing this, Celisse straightened. There was nothing she could do for him. Pausing briefly to survey herself, she found that her cloak was sprayed with blood and blotched with two or three spots, inconspicuous against the dark fabric. With any luck, the marks would go unnoticed. She drew her wounded arm back out of sight beneath the woolen folds, then cast a final deliberate glance about her and walked out of the room.

She had noted the route from the Cityheart entrance to the governor's apartment with care upon arrival, and she remembered it perfectly now. Walking briskly but without the least appearance of haste, she retraced the path that she had followed with her Sishmindri companions scant minutes earlier. As she went down the corridor, she encountered a trio of armed guards hurrying in the opposite direction, toward Uffrigo's study. As they passed, she contrived to throw them a glance of mild curiosity, as if wondering at their air of urgent purpose. They, for their part, scarcely noted the existence of the plainly clad, quietly respectable-looking young woman.

She passed them, and continued along the hall; down a curving stairway to the ground floor, then on along an endless mirror-lined gallery to the grandly columned entrance hall, teeming with servants, guards, sentries, messengers, liveried Sishmindris, tradesmen, petitioners, and even the occasional person of quality. She crossed the endless expanse of marble floor to the tall doorway, and always she listened for the shouting voices and the pounding of pursuit behind her, but there was none.

Through the door and out into cool springtime air clouded and scratchy with smoke. Down the broad marble stairs to the paved drive, and still no commotion behind her.

At the end of the drive, the great gate stood open. The sentries on guard nodded affably to her as she went through, passing from the Cityheart grounds out into the Plaza of Proclamation.

The plaza was alive with citizens, many of them masked against contagion. She had considered this beforehand, and a full-face black velvet vizard reposed in the pocket of her grey gown. She could not put it on, however. The right arm hidden beneath her cloak was bathed in spreading wet warmth. An experimental flex informed her that her right hand was useless. She was bleeding profusely, in pain, and in need of a physician's care.

She knew where to find a doctor—the most able and trustworthy doctor in all the world. He was here in Vitrisi looking for her, and the name of his inn had been dropped in her ear several times during the last few days. She had seen fit to ignore it, but no longer.

And now came the sound she had been waiting for from the moment she had exited Governor Uffrigo's study: the shouts, the public alarm. She cast a glance behind her to behold a party of Taerleezi guards charging from the Cityheart.

Picking up her skirts with her one good hand, Celisse Rione fled for the Lancet Inn.

· · ·

"Are you telling me," Jianna demanded, wide-eyed and awestruck, "that you've found a cure for the *plague*?"

"Oh, if only life were that easy. No, it isn't a cure," Rione replied.

"But I thought you just said—"

"I said that I've been developing a treatment that shows promise."

"Cure—treatment—there's a difference?"

"Much, I'm sorry to say."

The two of them sat at a small table in the Lancet Inn's pleasantly old-fashioned common room. It was midafternoon, too early for dinner, and the place was relatively empty. Therefore the fire had been allowed to dwindle to embers, and the lamps remained unlit, despite the gloom of the smoke-suppressed daylight. Jianna did not mind. To her, this chamber with its age-darkened beams overhead, its narrow windows with tiny leaded-glass panes, its massive stone mantel, was purely beautiful. She sat here drinking cups of warm herbal infusion with Falaste Rione, who was enjoying a brief respite from his labors at the neighboring Avorno Hospital. She could listen to his voice and watch his face. There was nowhere she would rather have been.

And now he had dropped a conversational bombshell.

"Well—what is it, then?" she prodded. "Tell me."

"It's difficult to explain. It starts with the observation that the plague is singular in its manifestation. Its victims display the symptoms that we all know, but there's something more that I've never before encountered. The only way I can express it is to say that the malady seems less conventional disease than demonic possession."

"I thought you didn't believe in such things."

"I don't. I wasn't speaking literally, although there *is* something uncanny about it. What I mean is that the plague patients seem almost—transformed, lost to themselves."

"Delirious?"

"Often, but not in the usual sense. It's as if their bodies and minds have been invaded and occupied by some alien entity."

"If your patients are strangers to you, and you didn't know them before they fell ill, how can you be certain that they've changed so greatly?"

"Because the invading entity that I speak of isn't human."

"They turn into wild animals? Werewolves?"

"No, they don't resemble anything known or recognizable. It's like nothing I've ever seen. And yet I'd swear there's intelligence there, but of a sort that I can't fathom."

"I can't imagine it. What do they do or say that seems so inhuman?"

"Hard to define it. It's in their eyes, their voices, their inexplicable words, the way they use their bodies. I've a host of impressions, but nothing tangible to offer."

"The only way I could really understand would be to see for myself. And that's exactly what I *should* do. Come, Falaste. I'm a good and useful assistant. You accomplish more when I'm there to help, and you know it. Take me with you next time you treat the plague patients. Don't you owe it to them to make use of my abilities?"

"No. I don't owe my patients your life."

"Only your own?"

"I take steps to protect myself. I wear the oilcloth coverings, the beaked mask, lenses, and gloves. I breathe medicinals and swallow decoctions before leaving the hospital."

"I could do the same."

"No. We've already spoken of this. I won't bring you into contact with the plague. You'll stay away from it, if I have to order you barred from the Hospital Avorno."

"That's rather dictatorial." Her frown was halfhearted at best. In reality, his protectiveness pleased her.

"Humor me. It's for the best."

"Oh, all right. Then at least be so good as to tell me how you battle this alien invader that you won't allow me to see."

" 'Battle' isn't quite right. 'Influence' would be more accurate. Or perhaps 'persuade.' "

"You *talk* with it? Engage in debate?"

"Nothing nearly that civilized. Essentially I try to render the occupied territory so inhospitable that the invader will sometimes abandon it."

"You can't mean that you torture the sick and dying!"

"Nothing nearly that *un*civilized. I wrap the patients in heavy canvas that restricts all movement, in the manner of swaddling clothes. I bandage their eyes and plug their ears. I set up barriers of screens or hanging blankets designed to keep the air about them as still as possible. Those capable of taking nourishment receive the blandest gruel, as nearly devoid of taste or texture as I can concoct."

"You wouldn't call all that torturous?"

"Perhaps it would seem so to a normal, healthy individual. But these patients—I believe that their human perceptions are largely suppressed. They're absent or unconscious."

"And the other—thing?"

"I can't know its mind. But I suspect—thwarted, wearied, dissatisfied with inactivity."

"Bored?"

"In human terms. And sometimes, so much so that it withdraws, granting the victim a chance of survival."

"As simple as that?"

"No, there's more. The bathing and cooling of fevered bodies, the administration of fluid, the cleansing vapors, the powdered medicinals, the liquid decoctions—all that you might expect. But none of it offers the slightest hope unless the invader has first been expelled—or rather, motivated to depart."

"Which you've actually succeeded in doing?"

"A few times, yes. My success rate has improved since I started using shernivus."

"I want to see."

"I thought we just agreed—" Rione broke off. His eyes locked on something behind her.

"What is it?" Jianna turned in her seat to follow his gaze. She saw a cloaked figure standing in the doorway.

"My sister." He was already on his feet and hurrying toward her.

Jianna stood up and followed. A few steps carried them to Celisse.

She looked dreadful; grey-faced, tight-lipped, glass-eyed. She leaned against the doorjamb as if for support, and her breathing was labored.

"I've been hurt," she informed her brother, breathless but calm as always.

"Come with me." Drawing her from the doorway, he led her across the foyer and up the stairs.

Jianna trailed close behind. She had noted spots of blood on Celisse's cloak.

What's happened? And the question arose unbidden, *What has she done?*

Up the stairs to the landing, and through the arched door on the left into Rione's room. At once he undid the fastenings of his sister's cloak, slipped the garment from her shoulders, and tossed it aside.

Jianna's breath caught. Celisse's right hand and forearm were drenched in blood. Her bodice and skirt were liberally splotched. Her sleeve was torn, the gashed flesh beneath bleeding plentifully.

"Any wounds other than the arm?" Rione was already busy rolling her sleeve back.

She shook her head.

"Good. Nasty cut, but it will heal, if treated properly. Here, sit down." He placed her in a chair, then turned to Jianna. "Noro, please bring a basin of water, soap, and my bag."

Jianna obeyed. She returned in time to hear his next question.

"How did you get this? What happened?"

"I think you already know."

"Were you followed here?"

Celisse's eyes, iced with animosity, rose to Jianna's face, then turned away. "Get rid of her," she commanded. "I'll tell you everything, but I won't have that wide-eyed little honeykitty of yours hanging about."

Little honeykitty? Jianna clamped down on her outrage. She was an experienced and skilled assistant. And more.

Rione would surely spring to her defense. Confidently, she looked to him.

"Noro." His expression conveyed mild regret. "Set those things down, and then you may go."

"But—"

"Please. My sister and I want a moment alone. Step outside and take a breath of fresh air."

"I see. Certainly. Just as you wish." Depositing her burden on the table beside him with exaggerated care, Jianna turned and stalked to the door. Her spine was very straight, her demeanor very dignified, and inside she boiled with fury. *You may go*. He might have been speaking to some serving wench. At a word from his sister he'd *dismissed* her, even told her to leave the building, as if simply leaving the room weren't enough. He should have supported her, informed Celisse that his assistant's presence was essential, and so he would have done if he truly valued her, as he had so often claimed.

Obviously she was altogether dispensable.

The tears rose to her eyes, and she blinked them away. Celisse Rione would not see her tears. Although, just possibly, Celisse's attention was otherwise engaged at the moment. As she exited Rione's room, she shut the door behind her, resisting the impulse to slam it, then hurried down the stairs at an angry clip. At the bottom, she hesitated. She could go back into the common room, order another mug of herbal infusion, and sit there drinking it. Alone. No. Better to take his suggestion, go outside, and come back—whenever she felt like it. If she felt like it. Let him knock on her door when he wanted her help, and find her absent. Let him not know where she was or when she would return, if ever. Let him see how he liked *that*.

She walked out through the front door, and the chill struck her at once. She had not thought to bring her cloak or vizard, but the thought of going back inside and up those stairs to collect them was insupportable. She would do without; the air was not that cold.

The streets were smoke-veiled, as usual. The sky was lost, as usual. The pedestrians were muffled and masked, as usual. But the arrangement and activity of the citizens out on the street were unusual.

Numbers of them stood about in clumps, conversing with exceptional animation. Her curiosity ignited. She drifted near a group of three masks, hoping to catch an informative word.

"Dead," proclaimed a mask.

"No. Wounded. Nothing serious," returned another.

"I heard dead." The third hooded head nodded.

"Twaddle," opined the first. "It's just not that easy to kill a—Taerleezi governor."

Jianna fancied that he verged on the use of some other, choicer descriptive term, but reined himself in, and with good reason. In this time of masks and anonymity, no one could know who might overhear an unguarded word on the street, and free expression could cost dearly indeed. But she scarcely noted the near indiscretion, for she finally understood.

She had been almost willfully blind. She had never allowed herself to entertain the remotest possibility that Celisse Rione would accomplish her self-appointed mission. Celisse might succeed in stirring up all sorts of unnecessary trouble, but— assassinate the Governor Uffrigo? Nonsense.

She had seriously underestimated Falaste's little sister.

She's actually done it. She's killed him. That fanatical lunatic!

"A woman, I've heard," one of the masks announced.

"No. Rogue Sishmindri."

"Woman *and* Sishmindri."

"Twaddle. Do you believe that?"

Jianna believed it completely. Her first thought was to warn Rione, and she even took a step back toward the Lancet Inn, then halted. Rione already knew. By this time, his sister would have confessed all. *I'll tell you everything, but I won't have that wide-eyed little honeykitty of yours hanging about.* Almost certainly he had known before she had spoken a word, perhaps from the moment he had spied her there in the door-way. *Were you followed here?* He knew exactly the risk he undertook in assisting the governor's assassin. No wonder he had proved so ready and willing to send Noro Penzia away. No wonder he had urged Noro Penzia to get out of the building. No wonder.

And petulant Noro Penzia hadn't understood anything.

She wanted to run back inside; but he didn't want her there. Or perhaps he really did.

While she stood vacillating, a party of Taerleezi guards sporting the purple-and-gold cockades of the governor's household came rushing into Cistern Street. They paused briefly to accost the first group of civilians they encountered, and words were exchanged, inaudible to Jianna. A masked individual pointed at the Lancet Inn. The guards made for the inn at a run. They reached it within seconds and went in.

The clots of citizens scattered about Cistern Street were swiftly coalescing into a crowd gathered before the Lancet Inn. Jianna stood frozen in body and mind. There were no thoughts in her head, no room for anything beyond terrible fear.

There was little commotion or conversation. The crowd, sensing significant events, simply waited, and the minutes passed like silent centuries.

The door was closed. Whatever passed on the other side wasn't real so long as it stayed closed.

But the eons expired at last, and the door opened. The guards emerged, and with them came Celisse and Falaste Rione, both in manacles. There was a collective intake of breath at sight of Celisse, with her youthful face, her bandaged arm, and her bloodstained dress.

"Good work, lass!" someone called out.

Glaring Taerleezi regard raked the crowd. But the audacious speaker, a masked man standing in the ranks of the masked, remained forever unidentifiable.

Celisse's head came up. A faint, fulfilled smile touched her lips.

Jianna did not notice. Her eyes were fixed on Falaste Rione's face. *It's not fair, he didn't do anything wrong, he wasn't part of his crazy sister's plans, he was trying to stop her, he's completely innocent, leave him alone, it's not FAIR!*

Rione's eyes ranged, and quickly found her. For a moment he stared hard, as if trying to imprint her image upon his memory for all time to come.

I love you, she told him with her eyes. *Now and always, I love you.*

Perhaps he read the message. She wanted beyond all things to believe that he did. His face turned away from her. Had the visual connection persisted, the guards would have noticed.

Taerleezis and prisoners advanced, and the crowd parted before them. Falaste and Celisse passed within a few feet of Jianna, but neither glanced in her direction. Along Cistern Street they marched, around the corner, out of sight, and they were gone.

They were gone.

TWELVE

For a long time Jianna stood frozen, blind stare fixed on the Lancet Inn. The crowd clustering about the place remained for a while to watch and speculate, but nothing more happened, and interest began to wane. The occurrence itself was obviously red-hot. An attempt upon the governor's life—or perhaps his murder, nobody actually knew yet—followed by the arrest of an attractive, bloodstained young woman and her male accomplice, who looked remarkably like her, was certain to hold public attention for some time to come. For the moment, however, there was nothing more to see. A few resolute spectators loitered on in hope of new developments, but the majority of citizens gave up for the present and drifted away.

Jianna was only marginally aware of the human mass thinning out around her. Her mind continued to malfunction, refusing to form coherent thoughts. Falaste had been taken away. He was a dead man, doomed beyond hope, and it was all his lunatic sister's fault. That was all she knew.

At last, however, she became aware that she stood alone in a public street, with the spring air raw on her skin, and the curiosity or impatience of passersby sharp on her perceptions. She needed to go somewhere, find something, do something to help Falaste.

Absurd. There was nothing she could do, nothing anyone could do. Even the Magnifico Aureste, with all his wealth and influence, would be powerless to intervene in such a case as this.

She became aware that tears were streaming down her cheeks. It seemed futile to wipe them away. Her feet were carrying her, apparently of their own accord, back into the Lancet Inn.

Widow Meegri, seated as usual at her desk near the front door, looked up as Jianna entered. Her face clenched like a fist.

"You," she accused.

Jianna jerked a wordless nod and headed for the stairs.

"Stop there."

Jianna obeyed.

"Yours." From under the desk, Widow Meegri produced a familiar pillowcase, stuffed to bulging. "Everything you brought. Take it and clear out."

"I am no longer welcome here?"

"Don't look at me like that. You silly hussy, don't you know when somebody's trying to help you?"

Jianna's silent stare communicated incomprehension.

"Do you think that all the Taers have vanished into thin air? Two of them are upstairs right now, ransacking your fine Dr. Rione's room for anything they can use. And when they've done pillaging the place, what do you suppose comes next? Questioning the staff and guests, you may be certain. Mind you, I'm not one to blab, but there's plenty hereabout with great, big, flappy mouths. And everybody from the ostler down to the spitboy knows about your . . . friendship with the doctor. How long exactly do you think it will be before the Taers hear all about it and come after you?"

"I'm his assistant. I've done nothing wrong."

"Assistant. Hmmph. That's a new name for it. Listen, missy. I don't approve of your carryings-on, I never have. Still, you're Faerlonnish, and I'm not about to throw one of our own to the Taers, not even one of our worst. So be glad I'm a patriot, and be off with you. Quick, now."

Sound advice. Shouldering her sack, Jianna departed.

Back out again on the smoky street. Alone, now; quite alone, as she had never been in her entire life. The totality of her new isolation struck her all at once, and suddenly she was very cold. Digging into the sack for her cloak, she wrapped herself in the woolen folds, but the internal chill persisted. She thought then of going home to Belandor House. Damages notwithstanding, it was still familiar and dear.

No. No peace, no comfort, no home at Belandor House. Until such time as her father returned, there was nothing for her there.

Where? What?

Another inn, somewhere. Another room to sleep in, a hole to hide in. Yes, she must find one. And perhaps the search would occupy her mind, prying at least a few of her thoughts away from Falaste, and all that was happening to him now, and all that doubtless lay in store for him. She would lose all self-command if she let herself imagine it; she would go mad.

That last look he had given her as they had taken him away was more immediate and vivid than the meaningless reality of Cistern Street. She carried it with her from the Lancet Inn.

• • •

They had come to a dank and melancholy region, where the remnant of the road wound among mud-rimmed pools of black water shaded by countless low-hanging branches festooned with loops of trailing grey moss. Here the dark water offered the sky's reflection in tones of lead and steel. Here the embrace of the moss slowly choked the life out of the trees. And here the character of the world began to alter.

It had been going on for some time before Aureste really noticed the change in his brother. Innesq had always been eccentric, given to sudden silences and unpredictable abstractions. His demeanor throughout such interludes remained calm and benevolent, but markedly distant. The episodes were unsettling but familiar, and Aureste had long since learned to ignore them. This time, however, the symptoms were extreme.

Never had the abstractions seemed so profound. At certain moments Innesq appeared lost to the world; lost beyond recovery, though still physically present. The first time that he had confronted the white face and stony dead eyes, Aureste had paid little heed. His brother's peculiar arcanisms were unsettling but generally of brief duration. And sure enough, the fit or whatever it was had passed quickly, and Innesq had returned, composed and good-humored as always, but reluctant to discuss the matter.

Aureste had dismissed the incident as a fluke, unlikely to recur.

But it had recurred, within hours. This time Aureste had pressed for an explanation, only to receive a mild and maddening reply.

"I shall explain as best I can, when the time is right."

Innesq was unbendable, further questioning useless, and Aureste had been forced to content himself with observation alone. Over the course of the next forty-eight hours he kept close watch, and thrice more witnessed his brother's brief descent into staring insensibility. Eventually it dawned on him that Innesq was anything but insensible. His faculties were concentrated to the utmost and directed—elsewhere.

Somehow, Aureste fancied the object of attention unappetizing. He could hardly have said why. But once or twice, while observing his brother's colorless lips framing silent syllables, a shuddery qualm took him; a stab of horror that he suppressed instantly and without analysis.

It was no longer possible to ignore or dismiss Innesq's symptoms. Aureste waxed unwillingly attentive, and soon noted similar manifestations on the part of every arcanist in the group. All of them, from flamboyant Ojem Pridisso down to odd little Nissi, were periodically . . . absent. Even the boy, Sonnetia's son Vinzille, could sometimes be seen, blank gaze fixed on nothingness, inner ear attuned to—what?

He watched and he listened. He glimpsed fear in the eyes of Vinz Corvestri. He saw inexplicable, inappropriate smiles curving the silent lips of Littri Zovaccio. He saw the girl Nissi periodically alter in expression; her eyes, gait, and gestures all assuming an indefinably alien aspect. And once he caught a snatch of conversation between Pridisso and young Vinzille Corvestri.

I say we get together and send It a real burn, something to teach It that we don't like trespassers. Vinzille's voice, youthfully defiant.

And then Pridisso, mildly amused, *Going a little too fast there, my lad. We ignore It. We exclude It. That's all for now.*

He had seen and heard enough. Aureste returned to his brother.

"It's here among us—the thing you call the Overmind," he accused. "Don't trouble to deny it."

"I do not intend to," Innesq returned equably.

They sat in the stationary carriage. The servants were setting up camp for the night. Yvenza and Nissi had wandered off somewhere, affording Aureste the rare opportunity to speak to his brother in privacy and comfort.

"Why the secrecy, then?"

"No secrecy. I did not wish to speak without understanding, that is all."

"And now?"

"And now I begin to fear that true understanding will always elude us. Its intelligence is too unlike our own; we may never bridge the gap. My efforts to communicate have failed. Either It does not hear me, else ignores me, or perhaps I myself am at fault and cannot hear It. Nonetheless, I have acquired shreds of knowledge, enough to see that peace between us is impracticable, for the universe that supports and sustains either one of our races ruins the other."

"Races?"

"Yes, those ancient Inhabitants were and are a race—not like our own, of course, for they are not composed of flesh or even of solid substance as we know it. Yet they are individual sentient entities capable of joining with others of their own kind to form a whole being. That is, what we humans strive for by any and all means, but never successfully achieve for more than moments."

"Cozy."

"Indeed. Their accomplishment is astonishing. To savor it in full, however—to live and function freely—they must restore their own world. That is another way of saying that they wish to take back their home."

"You're telling me that this regiment of monsters means to exterminate us."

"I do not think so, although their victory will produce that effect. My general impression is rather of an ambition to absorb and encompass all into the living whole. I could be mistaken, but I believe that there is no malice, no anger, no desire to destroy, but rather, to build. They—or rather It, the collective Overmind—seeks to inhabit all living matter."

"All? Plants, too?"

"I believe so. Eventually."

"They—It—has a disappointment in store. I presume that you and the other arcanists are the only people here able to hear It."

"So far."

"You sound as if you expect a change."

"I fear that it is inevitable."

"I hope you're right. It's best to know the enemy. I look forward to hearing Its voice."

"You may come to change your mind. You see, when you hear—or rather, experience—the voice of the Overmind, it will seem to come from within yourself. That is to say, It will communicate to the extent that It has successfully gained entry. You will sense clearly, quite insistently in fact, that It wants more. It wishes to permeate your entire being, to fill you with Itself. In short, to more than own you—to *be* you, to make you a functioning part of Itself. Do you understand me?"

"Certainly. It wants to invade, conquer, occupy, and own. What could be simpler or plainer?"

"It is neither simple nor plain. You express yourself in

purely human terms, but we confront an inhuman intelligence. Stop and consider. This being is ancient beyond measure, gigantic beyond imagining, and native to this world as we are—here before us, in fact. The depth of Its huge mind— the breadth of its experience—the very nature of Its incorporeal existence—"

"Innesq, must you always complicate matters?" Aureste drew an impatient breath. "We've an enemy that threatens us. We join forces, destroy it, and there's an end."

"Scarcely. I doubt that all the combined human force in our world could destroy the Overmind. And I cannot say that I am altogether sorry for that, for It is truly a most extraordinary—"

"Defeat It, then. Diminish It. Contain It. Will that do?"

Innesq's silent nod conveyed reluctance.

"How long before I'll be able to hear It for myself?"

"I do not know. Probably not long. I should not be so eager, if I were you. Enjoy your freedom while you can. Once the Other manifests Itself, there is no complete escape, except perhaps in unconsciousness deeper than sleep. The weight of Its presence grows burdensome, and those without the strength of will or the arcane technique to exclude It are apt to suffer."

"Oh, I'll manage well enough."

"I daresay you will, but others may not fare so well."

"The guards and servants, you mean."

"They are the most likely to suffer, but they are not the only ones."

"Yvenza's girl—that Nissi. She strikes me as possibly weak-minded."

"Think again. She has spent a lifetime learning how to conceal and protect herself. She is well prepared to resist the Overmind, provided she truly desires to do so. No, there are others for whom I fear more."

Aureste continued to watch, and soon identified the object of his brother's most immediate concern. The youngster Vinzille Corvestri was visibly failing. From day to day, the lad was wasting away; weedy frame losing substance, flesh losing all color, greenish eyes dulling. He looked drained and sick, far older than his years.

Vinz Corvestri's son might shrivel like a raisin, and welcome. The youth was arrogant and hostile. While technically correct in utterance, he nevertheless managed to convey his dislike of and contempt for the Magnifico Belandor.

Which was returned. What reason to suffer the thinly veiled insolence of an impertinent adolescent? As far as Aureste was concerned, young Vinzille Corvestri would have been altogether expendable, but for one consideration: The brat's loss would surely trouble his mother.

. . .

Sonnetia Corvestri looked down at her son. Vinzille sat on the ground, back pressing a large rock, head sunk on his breast, fast asleep. The ground was damp and the rock was hard. It was late afternoon, and the sun hovered just above the horizon. There was no good reason for an active boy to sit there sleeping in such a place and at such a time.

The servants were busy setting up camp. Their voices rang, and the knock of mallets on tent pegs punctuated their activity, but Vinzille slept through it all. His slumber appeared deep, but not peaceful. Stirring continually, he frowned and muttered in his sleep. Sonnetia bent close to listen, noting his greyish pallor. His words were largely unintelligible, but she caught a few of them.

"Keep It out . . . send It a burn . . . a real burn . . ."

Her own brows contracted. She touched his forehead lightly, then his shoulder, but he did not wake. Shaking him a little, she urged, "Wake up, son." There was no response, and she repeated the command.

Vinzille's eyes opened and he stared into his mother's face without recognition.

"You're ill," she told him. "You're running a fever, and you shouldn't be sitting on the wet ground. I want you in bed as

soon as your tent's up. Until then, better go back to the carriage and—"

He mumbled something unintelligible, and then spoke
clearly. "Back off. Keep out."

"Please just do as I ask. Believe me, it's for your own good."

"Stay out."

He dragged himself to his feet, glassy eyes fixed on the
empty air, and she saw that he was not speaking to her. In fact
he appeared unconscious of her presence. Ignoring her outstretched hand, he turned wavering footsteps away from the
campsite.

Sonnetia issued a quiet command to the nearest Corvestri
servant. Vinzille was promptly seized and bundled off to the
carriage. The boy offered no resistance; indeed, seemed
largely unaware. She followed to see him comfortably installed upon the cushioned seat, assigned watch duty to the
servant, then hurried off in search of her husband.

. . .

Vinz Corvestri whipped his will as best he could. He stood
alone in a small grove at some slight remove from the camp.
He was perfectly still, face expressionless, and nothing in his
outward aspect suggested mental turmoil. Inwardly, he struggled for control; or rather, he struggled for the courage to re-
linquish some control and admit entry of the Overmind. Only
a very little, to be sure; just enough to permit the possibility of
communication. It was the reasonable and necessary course,
but difficult.

Instinct reinforced by years of training and experience bade
him resist the invader. He had successfully done so for days on
end, and might continue indefinitely. Harder by far to open
the gates and bid the enemy welcome. That It was his enemy
he did not doubt, despite Innesq Belandor's belief in Its essential lack of malice. His own perceptions told him that gigantic purpose composed Its very essence. Nothing would turn It
from Its goal while awareness existed. Still, It was doubtless

an intelligent entity, and the possibility of communication, however remote, demanded investigation.

Accordingly Vinz lowered his mental defenses to a very small degree, as much as he could bring himself to sacrifice, and the results were immediate.

It was there with him and in him. He could feel the exploratory pressure of Its huge presence, and he sensed Its interest and Its sense of purpose.

Push It out. Shut the gate and lock it. Vinz fought the natural impulse. Marshaling his will, he compelled himself to yield a little more, a very little, and his sense of Its vastness intensified at once. It was as great and as old as the world. In effect, It *was* the world, the living awareness of the totality.

This last impression he recognized as an echo of the Other's sense of Itself. Excitement sparked across his mind. For the first time, he had glimpsed something more or less recognizable. Perhaps by dint of combined patience and courage, he might see more. Perhaps he might even initiate a conversation, thus revealing himself to the Other as something more than empty vitality awaiting occupation by Itself. He might glean insight exceeding anything so far discovered by any of the others, even Innesq.

He dared to relax his mental resistance a very little further, and even as the Other's power pressed upon the apparent weakness, he advanced his mind to meet It. For a moment he believed that his overture had caught Its notice, but then the potential connection snapped, and he became aware of motion and noise—a voice, a summons, a demand.

Vinz blinked, and the world refocused. He felt a little sick and dizzy. His head hurt. The Other had withdrawn, leaving him free but disoriented. His wife stood beside him. She was shaking his arm and calling his name. She did not know what she had interrupted, she had no idea what had been lost. Typical. She did not understand, and more to the point, she did not care. She never had.

"Stop. Enough." The words were indistinct. His tongue seemed thick and stiff.

"Magnifico, a word. A moment of your time."

He winced. Her voice, while low and beautifully modulated as ever, somehow clanged like a bell.

"Not now."

"Please. It's about Vinzille. He's ill."

"What's the matter with him?" Confusion receded. She had caught his attention.

"He's running a fever. He seems delirious. When I told him to go to the carriage, he started to wander off in the opposite direction, as if he didn't know where he was going."

"He was on his feet and walking? Then he isn't as sick as all that."

She paused a moment as if to control a spontaneous response, then replied evenly, "I've never before seen him in such a state. I am troubled."

"How long has he been ailing?"

"He's not been himself for days. This afternoon is the first I've seen of definite illness, though." No immediate reply was forthcoming, and she prompted, "Surely your skills will serve to restore him."

Irritation popped, and it took Vinz a moment to identify the cause. His wife spoke with her customary courtesy and decorum. She addressed him with every outward sign of respect, yet something in her manner, her stance, her eyes, subtly suggested reproach—as if it were *his* fault that Vinzille had taken a chill or a minor ague. *His* fault, she silently seemed to accuse, for dragging an adolescent just barely past childhood off into the wilderness on a mission rightfully the province of seasoned arcanists; for exposing the boy to danger both mundane and supranormal, for failing in his duty to protect his son. Or perhaps she implied none of these things, perhaps it was his own conscience that chafed him. Either way, self-respect dictated self-justification. Vinz drew himself up.

"My skills, Magnifica, are a commodity to be carefully conserved at present," he reminded her. "The success of our endeavor depends upon it."

"Yes, I know that. But surely the protection of your son's health represents a legitimate and necessary expenditure."

"Necessary? That is the question. There's little sense in taking alarm and resorting to extreme measures every time Vinzille sniffles. He's a strong and healthy lad. He'll be well again within hours without benefit of arcane intervention. It's better that way."

"I should like to believe that, but I can't—and neither will you, once you see him. Trust me when I tell you that this is no ordinary malady. In fact, I think it must be arcane in origin."

"And what makes you think so, exactly?"

"It isn't easy to explain. The way he looks, the sound of his voice, his expressions, the way that he moves—all seem foreign and unnatural. But you must see for yourself. Will you come to him?"

Her manner was perfectly correct as ever, but Vinz's sense of guilt and uneasiness sharpened. What right had she to blame him? He was not accountable to her; it was supposed to be the other way around. She should be made to understand that, here and now.

Crafting a tolerant smile, he spoke in kindly reassuring tones. "Magnifica, it's only natural for a mother to fear for her son, and nobody can blame you for it. In this case, however, your maternal instincts have overridden reason. You perceive arcane influence, or you think you do, when in fact you are hardly qualified to judge. Come, now. You speak of 'foreign and unnatural' appearances, and it's all very vague, very emotional, very imaginative. There's no real evidence here of anything beyond ordinary physical affliction viewed through the lens of your fears. You see that for yourself, don't you?"

He paused. She said nothing, and her expression came close to curdling his smile, but he soldiered on. "I hope that your own good sense will teach you the absurdity of your terrors. But I truly wish to offer you all the support that a constant wife and mother deserves, and therefore I tender my promise—if our son's hot humor fails to correct itself naturally within the next four and twenty hours, then I shall examine him and administer such arcane assistance as circumstance warrants. There, will that content you?"

At this point she should have assented, but she was silent. She was staring at him as if he were some sort of insect caught clinging to her skirts. At last she inquired simply, "You won't use your powers to help our son?"

"When I'm certain that he needs my help, but not before. Consider the task at hand and try to think of the greater good. Forget personal concerns if you can—"

"Enough. Stop there."

She had not raised her voice, but he muted himself at once, without thought. He had never seen such a look on her face before—eyes narrowed, jaw hard—and it was as if he faced a stranger.

"Listen to me, and listen well." Her voice was still low and quiet, but cold as the end of time and space. "Some arcane force has taken hold of Vinzille. I feel it, I see it, and it is entirely real. He needs your help and he needs it now. Don't speak to me of conservation, don't prate of the greater good. Just do what you must to shield him. If you are his father, you'll protect him. Now, will you go to him?"

He controlled his own impulse to yield. He had yielded to her too often—it was downright unmanly. Moreover, she was wrong about Vinzille; the boy was in no real danger. Affecting an air of patience, he replied, "I've already promised to examine him twenty-four hours hence, but I doubt that it will be necessary—he'll have recovered before then. In the meantime, madam, try to control your hysteria."

"I am far from hysterical, but you are making me very angry." She took a deep breath. "Listen. I know next to nothing of arcane matters, but it doesn't take a trained adept to see that this Overmind you seek to thwart has become a real presence in our midst. I know that Vinzille is under Its influence now."

"You know nothing of the sort. In one breath you rightly concede your own ignorance, then you turn around and—"

"I also know that you can shield him against that influence, should you so choose."

"Even if that were true, I'm not certain it would be the wisest course."

"Protecting your son would be unwise?"

"There is such a thing as overprotection. Would you lock the boy in a box, for his own good? Vinzille is destined for great things, but he'll never reach his full potential unless he's given a chance to confront and experience arcane force in the real world. Reading the scrolls and chronicles, memorizing and performing exercises, practicing in his father's workroom— these activities teach and prepare him, but they're not sufficient. You ask me to shield our son from the force of the Overmind? If anything, I'd increase his exposure—it will serve to strengthen him. He'll be the better arcanist for it."

Vinz was starting to feel better. With a few well-chosen words, he had simultaneously asserted and justified himself. He was no erring father, careless of his son's safety. Rather, he was a wise guardian and instructor, guiding his talented boy to brilliant maturity. His aims were high and his judgment sound. He would have been downright pleased with himself, but for the look on his wife's face. It was an expression he had often almost unconsciously looked for, even expected to find there—a glaze of chill contempt.

"No," said Sonnetia.

Vinz felt the color flood his own face, and sought relief in anger. How dare she look at him and speak to him like that? Forcing himself to meet her eyes, he replied steadily enough, "Magnifica, you will accept my decision."

"No," she repeated. "Vinzille needs help. I intend to get it for him. If you won't oblige, then I must seek elsewhere."

"What do you mean?"

"I should think it's clear enough. There are other arcanists here, with skills to equal yours. I'll go to one of them. Innesq Belandor seems fond of Vinzille. He'll not refuse me."

"You stay away from Innesq!"

"The Taerleezis then. Pridisso and Zovaccio. Or even that odd girl Nissi. One or another of them will help."

"You deceive yourself. They are my colleagues—my allies and peers, not yours. Do you seriously believe that any one of them would cross me in order to oblige you?"

"Yes, Magnifico. That is exactly what I believe. But we'll soon know. I'm about to put it to the test."

"I absolutely forbid it. You will not humiliate me, madam!"

"I've no desire to humiliate you. I only mean to help my son."

Incredible. She was openly and brazenly defying him. She was turning her back on him and walking away.

"Stay where you are," he commanded.

She ignored him.

Vinz's dismay was tinged with desperation. He did not know what to do, but one thing was clear—he could not countenance flagrant disobedience. She would never respect him if he allowed it; he had to act. His desperation boiled. Grasping her arm, he spun her around to face him. He did not hurt her, but certainly he had never in all their years together handled her so peremptorily, and he experienced a thrill of mixed trepidation and exhilaration.

"I told you to stay where you are," he repeated, and his voice was excellent, convincingly assured and masterful.

"Take your hand off me." Sonnetia's voice remained quiet and well controlled. But her eyes—green speckled with brown like a forest brook, ordinarily cool and gracious as a forest brook—had caught fire.

It was astonishing. He had never seen her look like that, never dreamed that the calmly unreadable eyes could blaze with such unequivocal anger, and he checked the impulse to take a step backward. For a moment he wondered, almost fearfully, what she might do. Some part of him had always wondered what would happen should her habitual self-control flag. But then, in truth, what *could* she do? He was not a large man, but he was certainly heavier and stronger than she. Moreover, as her husband, he had every legal and moral right to rule her. No, more than the right, it was his duty. Timidity and self-doubt had caused him to neglect his duty for years, but the time had come to correct that error.

"Silence," Vinz Corvestri commanded. "You'll listen and obey, else know my displeasure. You will curb your tongue and spare my colleagues your complaints. They've serious concerns to occupy their minds, they've no time for your vapors. As for my son, he's well enough. He suffers from nothing more than a passing arcane incursion, too minor to address. I understand your fears, but you've reached the limit of my indulgence, and it's time for you to accept reality. No more of tantrums and troubles. Hold your tongue, bide your time, and all will be well. Do you understand me?"

"I told you to take your hand off me." Sonnetia's voice was very quiet, but easily heard. "I also told you, not long ago, that I won't tolerate abuse. If you've forgotten, I take the opportunity to remind you."

Alarm shot through Vinz. He had seriously overstepped his bounds, and he should apologize at once. She was always magnanimous, and a display of sincere contrition was certain to purchase her forgiveness. But then, he had treated her with regard bordering upon reverence throughout the course of their marriage, and where was the good of it? Did she love him, admire him, or even respect him? She respected strength, and he had plenty. He would show her.

"Abuse?" His hand stayed where it was. "Woman, you don't know the meaning of the word."

"Do you propose to teach me?"

It was a direct challenge, the first he had ever received from her. Her tone was perceptibly scornful, and his alarm grew. This exchange with his wife, which had begun with her simple request for his help, had swiftly swollen into something larger and uglier than he had ever expected or intended. All he really wanted was to go back, start over, and do it differently, turn it into something controllable. But there was no going back, not without major self-abasement. If he backed down now, he was granting her the upper hand for all time to come, and she would despise him for it. The whole world would look down on him.

"Don't provoke me." Vinz took a deep breath, and the answer was clear before him. It had been there all along, had he only allowed himself to see it. "You will behave as a dutiful wife, discreet and sedate. You'll not go pestering my colleagues. You'll keep your idle imaginings to yourself."

"If you wish to conduct a civilized discussion, you'll release my arm. I won't ask again."

"Disobey me—spread rumor, sow doubt and fear—and you will be confined to the carriage. Moreover, you are apt to find your powers of speech suddenly curtailed, along with your ability to write. Do you hear me, madam?"

"I hear, but surely I mistake your meaning. You are not threatening to stop my voice with an arcane gag?"

The objectionable hand seemed to have been forgotten for the moment. She was still staring at him, but her expression had altered, disdain yielding to shocked incredulity. It was almost as if she were seeing him for the first time, and some sort of guilty compunction stirred inside him, but Vinz pushed it away, for this was exactly the desired effect. More than time for her to see him at last for what he truly was—a personage of consequence, a magnifico of the Six, an arcanist of power and skill, and, above all, her rightful lord.

"I am telling you that I won't tolerate defiance," Vinz returned.

"Do you know what you are doing, Magnifico? Do you realize that you are contemplating a form of betrayal that I would never forgive?"

There it was, the threat that he most dreaded, spoken aloud

and out in the open. There was still time to apologize, but Vinz managed to conquer his weakness.

"Nobody is asking your forgiveness. There is nothing to forgive." He released her arm. "I assume that you comprehend and will respect my wishes. Now leave me."

For a moment she stood surveying him, then her jaw set and she retired without another word.

He had emerged as clear victor. Indeed, within the confines of their marriage all genuine power belonged to him, and always had. He had simply lacked the courage to use it, until now. Self-assertion, however, seemed to exact a curious price in depletion, much like the exercise of arcane skill. He found himself drained and oddly depressed. No matter. The unpleasant sensation was certain to pass quickly, and would no doubt lessen as he grew more accustomed to ruling his household.

But time passed, and his discomfort persisted. He saw nothing more of his wife. She did not share the evening meal with him, and he did not know where she was. Off somewhere sulking, probably. Trying to make him feel guilty, trying to make him feel small. She wouldn't succeed.

The darkness deepened as the campfires sank. The travelers took themselves to their respective places of rest; well-appointed tents for the quality, bedrolls spread on the ground for the servants. Sonnetia was nowhere in evidence. Probably she had repaired to the Corvestri carriage to sleep, her refusal to share her husband's tent a deliberate communication of her discontent. Well, she could nurse her ill humor for as long as she liked, and welcome.

Vinz stretched himself out upon a pallet furnished with clean linen, thick blankets, and a feather pillow. It was nearly as comfortable as his own much larger bed in the master suite of Corvestri Mansion, but sleep eluded him. The tent's second pallet remained empty, and his mind roamed in search of its rightful tenant. Sleeping in the carriage, almost certainly, but what if she had sought warmth and refuge elsewhere? Beneath some other canvas roof? *Aureste's?*

She had gone to him for help, not long ago. She had not turned to kin or to friends for assistance in securing her husband's release from prison. She had run straight to Aureste Belandor.

And it had been a sound choice. The Magnifico Belandor had exerted his influence, receiving ample recompense in the form of the Magnifico Corvestri's arcane services. It had been a simple, straightforward exchange of favors.

There were other men of wealth and power that she might have approached. But she had chosen Aureste Belandor.

Nonsense. Unjust suspicions of a faithful wife. She was in the carriage, or perhaps she was watching over Vinzille's sickbed. No, probably not the latter, for Vinzille—granted a small tent to himself for the first time, and glorying in the novelty of private territory—would brook no maternal cosseting. He would not want her hovering over him, and Sonnetia would respect his wishes.

The night chilled around him, despite the good blankets, and Vinz remained wakeful, restless thoughts divided between wife and son. Sonnetia had exaggerated, of course. The boy could not be as sick as all that. It was some commonplace disorder, nothing more. But sleep did not come, and the ugly fancies cavorted in his head.

Around midnight, he rose from his pallet. Wrapping himself in a heavy cloak, he stepped out of the tent into an exceptionally clear night. For once, the mists were nearly absent. The moon, approaching fullness, was circular but for a slightly flattened section of its rim. The stars all but shouted.

A few yards apart from his parents' spacious shelter stood Vinzille's tent. Small, hardly enough space to accommodate anything more than an adolescent boy's bedding, with a low entrance designed for crawling, or at least stooping. He went in, letting the canvas flap fall shut behind him.

A small compartment sewn into the lining of the cloak contained an ovoid tablet, which he drew forth and swallowed. The effects were almost immediate, and his mind opened like a rose in the sun that was the Source. There was no light within the cramped enclosure, but his surroundings were perfectly visible, down to the fine detail of loose thread at the edge of a patch in the canvas ceiling.

Vinzille lay sleeping, his slumber restless and uneasy, but profound. His father's entrance had failed to wake him. Vinz knelt to examine the boy. For a few moments he simply observed with his enhanced vision, then laid a careful hand across his son's brow. Vinzille stirred and mumbled, but slept on. His flesh was dry and hot; feverish, beyond doubt. Mundane or arcane?

Vinz directed his perceptions through the point of dermal contact deep into the boy's sleeping consciousness and beyond, into the realm of dream, emotion, instinct, reflex. He looked, and comprehended at a glance. Sonnetia had been right—by sheer chance, no doubt, as she was no qualified judge, but her guess had been a good one. Vinzille's first defenses had been breached, probably in some unguarded moment; he was still too young to avoid all such lapses. The penetration was superficial as yet, but would deepen if left unattended.

For now, treatment remained sure and simple. Vinz exerted his arcane self for the first time in days, with enjoyment and without remorse. It was, as Sonnetia had justly observed, a legitimate and necessary expenditure of power. When all was done, his sense of satisfaction easily outweighed the inevitable exhaustion. He looked down at his son, sunk in peaceful and healing sleep. Vinzille's color was good, his breathing easy and even, his fever gone. A light arcane shield guarded the integrity of his being, and he would shortly receive additional instruction in the essentials of self-protection. For the moment, all was well.

Retiring in silence, Vinz returned to his own tent, where he sought and found peaceful and healing sleep of his own.

In the morning he emerged to discover Vinzille already up, dressed, in high spirits, and busy devouring a breakfast whose vastness suited the appetite of a healthy thirteen-year-old boy. The Magnifica Sonnetia was there as well, collected and perfectly groomed as always, despite a night's doubtless uncomfortable repose in the Corvestri carriage.

Vinz drew his wife aside. Yesterday evening's anger had vanished, he noted. The dappled greenish eyes were cool and gracious again, bolstering his general pleasant sense of restored order. He thought her expression somewhat uncharacteristic—he might best have described it as impersonal—but that could have been his imagination.

"You see, Magnifica," he invited. "Our son is quite well again."

She acknowledged the apparent truth of this observation.

"He recovered naturally and swiftly, just as I predicted."

She inclined her head.

"And I trust this lesson will teach you at last to place full trust in your husband's wisdom."

THIRTEEN

A new lodging house, a different neighborhood. This one was called The Bellflower, and it was decent enough, with its well-swept entry, its polished brass lanterns, and its steep roof of grey-pink slate. The room Jianna took was likewise decent, situated at the quiet rear of the building, with an incongruously cheerful patchwork quilt on the bed and a generous washstand. All appeared reasonably clean, with the exception of the windows, which were grimed with soot. These days, this last reflected no discredit upon the management.

She scarcely noted her surroundings. Her fellow residents did not exist. A single need filled her; she thirsted feverishly for news of Falaste. In order to get it, she was obliged to assume an appearance of sociability quite at odds with her natural inclination at this time. Right now every instinct bade her seek the privacy and comparative safety of her newly rented room. She wanted to shut the door and hide in there, in the bed or under it, seeing and communicating with nobody. Instead she ventured forth every day in hooded cloak and vizard, walking the smoke-smudged, plague-smitten avenues in search of information; fact, theory, rumor, gossip—anything. She became the instant friend of the shopkeepers, the push-cart vendors, the local marketwomen, the runners, and the cripples. She soon came to know the apprentices, the beggars, a few Deadpickers, and even one Taerleezi guard, who offered smiling tidbits and flattery in clear hope of a sweet return.

For a while there was little to glean. The Governor Anzi Uffrigo had been assassinated by a knife-wielding young woman, supported by a brace of big Sishmindris. Both Sishmindris had died on the spot. One of the governor's servants had wounded the human killer, who had fled to the Lancet Inn, where she had been tracked and captured along with an accomplice. So much was known by all. But who was she? Had the two acted on their own, or were they part of a larger conspiracy? Were there to be further arrests? Would the two be tried separately, or jointly? Would they be tried at all, or simply executed out of hand? And most important, what sort of reprisals would be visited upon the city by Uffrigo's acting successor, the Deputy Governor Hecti Gorza, a Taerleezi official of dingy reputation?

There was much conjecture, but little by way of solid fact. As the days passed, however, certain statements were repeated with a frequency and consistency suggestive of truth. The name of the murderess was Celisse Rione, but little was known of her life. Apparently she was not a resident of Vitrisi. Her accomplice was her own brother Falaste Rione, a young physician of growing repute, known to the denizens of the Avorno Hospital. The siblings were currently held in the Witch, each in solitary confinement. Although they were to be tried jointly, no communication between the two was permitted. The content of Falaste Rione's statement remained unknown, but it was generally believed that his sister Celisse had already confessed to the crime. Confessed willingly—indeed, proudly. It was said, however, that she refused to incriminate her brother—or perhaps, to share credit with him—steadfastly maintaining his complete innocence.

This particular rumor offered a certain measure of hope. Celisse Rione was a rabid Faerlonnish patriot, eager to boast of her exploits. If her brother shared her fanaticism, he would proclaim his own involvement to the skies. Evidently he did no such thing, and his sister, the known murderess, absolved him of all complicity. Perhaps her statement would carry some weight with the Taerleezi judge—or judges—or whoever would actually preside over this case. Who *would* preside?

Nobody knew, as yet. More to the point, nobody seemed to think that it mattered much. Public interest and speculation seemed to center upon the probable forms of torture employed in the interrogation of the two prisoners; the specific method of their (possibly public) execution; and the larger issue of Taerleezi reprisals.

Jianna could scarcely bear to listen. When the merchants or the beggars spoke of torture, sickening images glowed in her mind. Worse than terror, however, was ignorance. Above all things, she needed to know what was happening to him. Perhaps, after all, the world was not altogether devoid of miracles. Perhaps a Faerlonnishman might receive a fair trial. An innocent man might even prevail. It was not impossible. He would have his sister's testimony to support him. Maybe a few of those numberless patients owing him their lives would step up to vouch for him. And then—the thought was roseate as the dawn—she herself might even testify for him. Stand before the Taerleezi tribunal, tell them that Falaste Rione had come to Vitrisi in order to save the governor's life, and make them believe it.

No. The dry and dismal voice of reason intervened. Worse than useless, she would do more harm than good. Everyone took her for the doctor's harlot. They would dismiss her testimony, and simply arrest her as another member of some imaginary conspiracy.

But then, perhaps he didn't really need her help or anyone else's. He had his own resources—his intelligence, his calm and forthright manner, his exceptional voice, his face, his eyes. No judge could listen to him speak, and fail to believe. Or so Jianna strove to convince herself.

Too soon it became clear that her local inquiries were yielding little of reliable worth. Her neighbors were no better informed than she, but perhaps another section of town might offer richer gleanings. The trial, whenever it was held, was certain to take place somewhere within the Cityheart. The servants, guards, attendants, functionaries, and officials living and working within the old palace complex might have seen or overheard things, picked up scraps here and there. Yes, the

Cityheart was surely the font of knowledge, and there she must go.

The Bellflower stood in what had once been a fairly prosperous section of Vitrisi, not more than half an hour's walk from her destination. She set forth in the early morning, before the sun had cleared the rooftops. The winding streets still lay drowned in shadow, and the smoke scratched at her eyes, but nevertheless the atmosphere was perceptibly vernal. As she walked, the air lightened, while the city woke and came to life around her. The masked citizens emerged from their shelters to resume their masked business. Hooded and gloved vendors hawked their wares, cocooned pedestrians hurried upon their nameless errands, rag-shrouded beggars importuned from the shelter of deep doorways and alleys. The Scarlet Gluttons foraged voraciously, and the Deadpickers did likewise. Once, Jianna came upon a trio of the faceless workers methodically toting the previous night's yield of corpses from the depths of some private dwelling marked with the familiar red X. As she watched, they tossed two stiff bodies into their cart, went back inside, came out with one more, then took their unhurried leave.

She never so much as flinched. Such sights had become commonplace. Of course, it might have been different had any of the corpses displayed a desire to climb out of the cart. Even now, she could not look upon the Wanderers unmoved.

This morning she was not obliged to do so. On she trudged at the steady pace that she could maintain for hours if necessary, and never once encountered a walking corpse, although she glimpsed a couple of reasonable facsimiles. For it was regarded as a gesture of stylish bravado among a certain perverse element of Vitrisi's youth to coat face and hands with grey-white chalk powder, to smudge charcoal shadows about the eyes, and to assume the stiff-jointed, lurching gait of a newly risen corpse. "Perambulationists," these wags called themselves. Their shambling jaunts were known as "promenades," and nothing gave them greater pleasure than to pass themselves off as genuine Wanderers. Their sense of fun quite eluded Jianna's understanding.

This morning, the streets she traveled were blessedly free of Wanderers and Perambulationists alike. The swirl of activity appeared ordinary by recent standards, but the sting in her nostrils and eyes told her that the concentration of smoke in the atmosphere was more than ordinary. The flavor of this particular smoke seemed anomalous, and there was something peculiar in the motion of the air. Then, quite abruptly, she found her way blocked by a tall, new-looking wooden barrier extending across the entire width of the street. Armed Taerleezi guards flanked the gate in the wall. She passed through without difficulty. On the other side, the city streets ceased to exist.

She halted. Her amazed glance swept a charred and tumbled wilderness, and it was as if she were coming home to a fire-blasted Belandor House all over again. Every building between the wooden barricade behind her and the Cityheart complex before her had been leveled—torn down, burned down, or blown up. The small avenues and byways winding about the Plaza of Proclamation had vanished, along with scores of wooden, stone, and brick structures; houses and tenements, inns and taverns, merchants' stalls, workshops and warehouses—everything. All that remained were countless mounds of rubble and ash. Some of the blackened heaps bulked wide and tall, yet the entire area seemed startlingly open and exposed, almost naked, compared with what it had been but days earlier.

For a moment or two she did not understand, and stood puzzling over the cause. Seismic quakes? Arcane mishap? Accidental fire? Intentional fire, kindled to control the spread of the plague? Then comprehension dawned, and it was only a matter of seeking confirmation.

There was no dearth of potential informants. Everywhere she looked, the laborers were burying ash in trenches, chopping or sawing burned joists and rafters into fragments of manageable size, sorting salvageable masonry, and hauling rubbish away in carts and wheelbarrows. It was just the same work carried out by Sishmindris among the ruins of Belandor House, but here the toilers were uniformly human; even the carts were drawn by men, women, and children. Taerleezi troops supervised the project, and Jianna noted without surprise that sluggish or ineffectual workers were disciplined smartly.

There were plenty of citizens observing the scene, and she turned to the nearest, a being whose shape, features, age, and gender vanished beneath a hooded cloak, gloves, and full-face mask with mesh eye-guards.

"What?" asked Jianna concisely.

"What d'you think, twit?" came the counter query, in a woman's voice laced with the Vitrisi street accent.

"Revenge for Uffrigo?"

"Never. Perish the thought. This here is all pure city improvement. It's for the good of everyone, you see."

"No. I don't see."

"Well, it's like this. Following the good Governor Uffrigo's murder—may his spirit enjoy the peace that it deserves—our Taerleezi shepherds decided to establish a Clean Zone surrounding their Cityheart. For everyone's protection, this Zone had to be spanking clean as a boiled skull. Naturally this meant doing away with every single building within the sacred precinct—those building just weren't *clean*. Now, you might want to ask what all this would mean to the folk living or working in those condemned houses, but that would be a silly question. You don't imagine that our Taerleezis haven't given this matter plenty of thought, do you? Well, they *have* thought about it, and their solution shows off all their wisdom and benevolence. They've offered any and all able-bodied homeless citizens gainful employment, cleaning up the mess left here after the fires—clearing the land, dragging the rubble away, scraping up all those burned bodies, and so forth. Anyone willing to work gets food—crusts and grease soup once a day—and shelter. Right over there." The flick of a gloved finger directed her listener's attention to a nearby stand of large dust-colored tents, suggestive of canvas barracks. "Who could ask for anything more?"

"And what happens when the work here is finished?"

"Well, then they starve, I guess. Unless the Taerleezis take pity, and start up a new work program. Maybe another Clean Zone, in another part of town. That should do the trick."

Jianna had no answer. For a little while she stood watching the destitute Faerlonnish workers, many of them inadequately clothed against the cold. The majority lacked protective masks, and the faces she glimpsed were uniformly grey with ash and exhaustion, pinched, drained, and hopeless. The Taerleezi overseers were not above bullying and beating the conspicuously underproductive, without regard for age or sex. Not far away, one of them was kicking the ribs of a prostrate malingerer who could not have been above ten or eleven years of age.

As she looked on, she grew conscious of new emotions— disgust, indignation, helpless rage, together with a current of poisonous, oddly delicious nectar that she identified as hatred. Curious. She had lived among the Ghosts of the resistance, tended their wounded, listened to their conversation, and gradually absorbed some of their convictions. She had come to resent the foreign occupation of Faerlonne, as she had never resented it while living beneath her father's roof. But she had never actually hated the Taerleezis until now.

Then she thought of the tales she had so often heard of Aureste Belandor's support of and cooperation with Faerlonne's conquerors, and for the first time in her life, she felt the force of those accusations. Her father, people claimed, was party to outrageous crimes against his own country and compatriots. He was a traitor and an outcast. So many tongues had repeated these stories, with such certainty and anger, that it was becoming all but impossible to dismiss them. Even Falaste believed the worst of Aureste. He never came right out and said so, but she knew.

Falaste was unlikely to be thinking anything at all about Aureste Belandor, just now.

"Have you heard any news about the Rione trial?" Jianna turned her head to discover her companion already gone, anonymity forever intact.

She walked on toward the Cityheart, and presently her way was blocked again by a second barrier of recent construction, this time a fence of iron bars surrounding the building. Beyond this fence neither she nor any other member of the general public was permitted to set foot. Evidently the Deputy Governor Gorza did not intend to repeat the errors of his predecessor.

A group of masked idlers loitered at the barrier, and she took a place among them. A few seemed to wait there for want of anything better to do, but most shared her interest in the trial of the Governor Uffrigo's assassin. Despite their curiosity, they knew next to nothing. It was a sure thing, they unanimously insisted, that the trial had not yet actually begun. It would begin shortly, perhaps even upon this very day, but was likely to prove a brief, perfunctory affair. Apart from this they had little to offer beyond speculation. The gloomiest among them prophesied prolonged and torturous interrogation sessions for each defendant, culminating in a double public execution of spectacular and inventive savagery. The most optimistic ventured to hope for a short trial followed by a mercifully quick death for the siblings. Grim or sanguine, however, all seemed to express a certain discreet affection and respect for "the Little Faerlonnish Lioness," as they dubbed Celisse Rione.

Jianna was far from sharing their admiration. "The Little Faerlonnish Lioness" had brought Taerleezi wrath crashing upon hundreds or thousands of helpless Vitrisian heads, destroying herself and her wholly innocent brother in the process. The Little Faerlonnish Lioness had killed Falaste. Did she suffer an instant's guilt and remorse, or did she deem his life an acceptable sacrifice? The Little Faerlonnish Lioness could twist on the torsion tower, and welcome.

But no, that was bad thinking. Her mind was working as if Falaste had already been tried, condemned, and executed. In truth, the trial had not even begun, and he still had a chance. A good chance, she told herself stoutly. No matter what these doomsayers all around her might think about it. And she wouldn't really want to see anyone die by torsion—certainly not Celisse Rione, who always said and did what she truly believed to be right.

Time passed. Around midmorning some nameless drone emerging from the Cityheart passed through a gate in the fence into the Clean Zone, where he was surrounded at once by the curious and importunate. The drone—a clerk in the Office of Public Records—had little news to offer. The Rione trial had not yet commenced. He had heard that it should start very shortly, but he couldn't say exactly when. Having nothing more to offer, he was permitted to depart.

More time. Some of the loiterers drifted away, their place taken by others, equally devoid of identity. Jianna waited. When at last she grew hungry, she bought some cheese and apples from a nearby vendor, then resumed her place at the fence. Lowering her vizard, she began to eat.

"Are you mad, woman?" a neighbor inquired.

Confused, she regarded his black oilcloth visage and membranous eyepieces in silence.

"You're not going to *eat* that?" A male voice, indeterminate age, high-pitched. "Please don't tell me that you're going to *eat* that."

"Very well. I won't tell you."

"Listen to me. You must never, *never* eat food sold on the street. You don't know where it's been, who's been touching it, *what's* been touching it. It could be riddled with plague, *permeated* with plague! You must only eat food purchased from good, sound farmers, fresh from the country, in the morning markets. That's the only way to know that it's wholesome."

"How am I supposed to know who's a good, sound farmer? Anybody could sit around the market selling infectious produce."

"Is the woman stupid? Has she never heard of a Troxius medal? You touch the medal to your food. If it's poisonous, or plaguey, the gold turns black. Try it now on that apple. It'll be the Black Trox, you mark my words."

"I don't have a Troxius medal."

"Are you in earnest? Are you insane? Are you *trying* to kill yourself?"

"Not at all. I just don't really believe that all those medals, and charms, and amulets, and so forth actually do any good. Washing, now—that really helps. I don't know why, but it does."

"You are a reckless and sadly misguided person. Another few days and you'll find yourself dead and Wandering, see if you don't. In the meantime, I don't want to stand anywhere near you. With an attitude like yours, you're probably *radiating* morbid humors." Turning pointedly from her, he marched away.

Jianna's frown shifted from his back to her provisions. Was he right? Not about the Troxius medal, that was nonsense, but the food? Perhaps she should proceed with caution. Drawing forth the tiny bodkin that served a variety of purposes ranging from self-defense to cleaning fingernails, she pared the apples, sliced a thin outer film from the cheese, and continued the interrupted meal. But now she could not help but wonder. She had removed the possibly contaminated outer layers, but what if the tree whose fruit she now ate had sunk its roots into soil rich and rotten with the buried bodies of plague victims? What if the cheese came from goats fed and milked by diseased hands? Nothing in the world was altogether trustworthy. If she let herself think about it, she would soon find herself unable to eat anything at all.

More time, indescribably slow and weary. The empty hours limped by like cripples. When Jianna grew tired of standing, she sat down on the ground, heedless of the filth and ash of the Clean Zone. When she could no longer bear standing or sitting, she walked about a little, then returned to her place at the fence. Thrice more, servants or messengers emerging from the Cityheart were waylaid and questioned, but there was nothing to be had from them.

And then it was past midafternoon, too late in the day for a new trial to begin, too late even for a travesty of a trial to begin. The idlers at the fence gradually dispersed. Jianna was the last to depart. Torn between disappointment and relief, she returned to The Bellflower.

She was back in the Clean Zone the next morning, and her second day of waiting repeated the first. The same endless hours, the same collection of idlers and stragglers barren of knowledge, the same tedium, the same suspense.

It would start very soon. They all said so.

It did not start that day.

The third morning, shortly before noon, a masked nonentity emerged from the Cityheart to inform the faithful at the fence that the trial of the Rione siblings had commenced. Instantly the atmosphere was charged. The nonentity—personal lackey to one of the three judges presiding over the Taerleezi tribunal—was surrounded, besieged, and hammered with pleas for news reports. Evidently flattered by the attention, the young man—the voice emanating from the mask sounded young—promised to oblige, and kept his word.

Repeatedly throughout the ensuing hours he returned to relate events of the trial. The two defendants, he reported early on, appeared healthy and adequately nourished. Evidently neither had suffered physical abuse; at least, nothing to speak of. The doctor fellow, Falaste Rione, was bruised a bit about the face, but that was trifling. His sister was unmarked, respectably attired, and quite handsome, for a murderess.

Bruised about the face?

Not long thereafter, he returned to announce that the public prosecutor was now presenting his case, and doing so magnificently, with thundering grand oration and splendid, majestic attitudes. Anyone hearing him speak was certain to perceive the accused as a pair of the lowest, filthiest, vilest criminals ever to pollute the suffering world. No defense attorney in the world stood much of a chance against such a prosecutor, in the reporter's opinion. But that question was academic, for the Faerlonnish Riones, unlike Taerleezi nationals, were not entitled to legal representation. They would eventually be given the chance to speak up for themselves, if they could think of anything to say.

Then came the prosecutor's heartrending description of the martyred governor's manifest virtues—his integrity, industry, and high courage, his unswerving sense of duty, his generosity, tender heart, and general benevolence. Truly, his murder had robbed the world of a noble ornament.

The response of the largely Faerlonnish audience to this interpretation was tepid.

A couple of hours later came the news that various witnesses to the crime's immediate aftermath had been testifying, with a particularly thrilling account offered by the servant who had actually confronted the bloodstained murderess above the body of the slain governor, survived her knife-wielding attack upon himself, and succeeded in wounding her prior to her flight from the Cityheart. Likewise gripping proved the testimony of the guards who had pursued the killer through the streets of Vitrisi, finally overtaking her at the Lancet Inn.

Celisse Rione and her brother had surrendered without a struggle—the two of them paralyzed with despair, overwhelmed by the might and fearful grandeur of the Law, opined the prosecutor. Thus they had survived to stand trial, and to pay their debt to the society they had so grievously wronged.

The afternoon was well advanced before the lackey reappeared to inform his listeners that the testimony seemed to be drawing to a close, and that the two defendants had been granted the privilege of speaking in their own defense. Both had availed themselves of the opportunity.

Jianna, sunk in a daze of misery throughout the last two hours or more, was suddenly alert again, for this was the news she had been waiting for. Finally Falaste was to be given his chance and, being Falaste, he would make good use of it. He would speak, and he would persuade them of his innocence. For who could look into his clear, grave eyes, and listen to the music of his wonderful voice, and fail to believe?

They had done surprisingly well, the lackey reported, all things considered. It had been ladies first, of course. That was only manners, and besides, everybody was most interested in hearing what the actual killer had to say for herself. And she had not disappointed.

Listening to Celisse Rione in that courtroom was sort of like watching fireworks on a very cold night. She'd had plenty to say, and it was all completely incendiary, but delivered in the coolest, calmest, most deliberate-sounding tone imaginable. First off, she'd confessed freely to the killing of Governor Uffrigo, but she refused to regard it as a murder. "Execution," she had called it. Anzi Uffrigo had been executed for his crimes against the nation of Faerlonne and the city of Vitrisi. She harbored no personal animosity. The governor was a stranger whom she had never met prior to their confrontation in the "Palace Avorno," as she insisted on calling the City-heart. She had acted in defense of her country, she had done her duty as any decent Faerlonnishwoman would. She did not repent her actions or wish them undone, nor did she begrudge the price she knew she must pay.

Only one thing would she desire to change—her brother's wrongful involvement in this affair. She had acted on her own, with assistance from nobody other than a pair of rogue Sish-mindris. Falaste Rione had not been party to the plan, he had known nothing of it. He had simply performed his function as a physician and bandaged his sister's wound, nothing more. For that he deserved neither blame nor punishment. She herself, on the other hand, gladly embraced punishment. She would die quite content in the knowledge that she had made herself useful.

Yes, it had been quite a speech. She had held her audience spellbound while she spoke, and at the end of it there wasn't a single listener who didn't recognize the young woman as a dangerous criminal, and probably not one who didn't entertain an odd sort of respect for her.

After that it had seemed almost anticlimactic to allow the brother his say, but Falaste Rione had surprised them all by holding collective attention almost as effectively as his sister. His style was very different, of course.

Very, thought Jianna.

Celisse spoke as if delivering messages penned by some higher power. With Falaste Rione, it seemed more as if he were a friend sitting at your fireside, talking just to you. There was something about him that came across as decent and honorable, and it was easy to believe him.

That's it exactly.

His statement had been brief and, unlike Celisse, he had maintained his complete innocence. He had not been in any way involved in the governor's assassination. From the day of his arrival in Vitrisi he had actively sought his sister, but he'd not seen or spoken to her prior to the afternoon of the murder, at which time he had offered her medical treatment. He very much respected his sister's Faerlonnish patriotism, her courage and resolve, but he did not condone her methods, and he had never been party to her plan.

Just about what Celisse herself had said. It would be easy to believe and tempting to exonerate the attractive young physician. Almost a pity that it couldn't happen.

You don't know that. You can't know that!

Under Taerleezi law, the Faerlonnish defendant's offer of help to the fugitive murderess established him as an accessory to her crime. His claim of innocent ignorance, even if true, changed nothing. The prosecutor had been quick to point this out, lest it be forgotten.

And now all testimony and oratory were done. It was time for the judges to rule. Deeming their task difficult, Jianna expected lengthy deliberation. She was unprepared for the promptness with which the lackey returned to announce the conviction and condemnation of both defendants. Celisse Rione and her brother Falaste were to die by simple torsion. No additional tortures had been decreed.

A murmur of confirmed expectation arose about her, but Jianna did not hear it. For a time she heard and saw nothing, although she remained upright, open-eyed, and more or less conscious. A curious numbness seemed to have dulled all thought and feeling. She had a vague sense that this natural anesthesia would prove temporary in nature, and should be prolonged to its uttermost limit.

Eventually she became aware that she was standing alone, fists clenched on the iron bars of the fence surrounding the Cityheart. The loiterers had gone, their curiosity satisfied for the moment. The light was failing; evening was drawing on.

Her feet carried her back to The Bellflower, apparently without instructions from her mind. They carried her up the stairs, along the hall, and through the door into her own room; her expensive private room. It was a worthwhile expense. A place to herself, a solitary refuge right now, was worth any amount of money.

There was a bed in front of her. She went to it, kicked off her shoes, crawled in, and drew the covers up over her head. For an indeterminate period of time she lay there, eyes shut, neither asleep nor truly awake.

. . .

Pleth Chenno, on duty at Belandor House's front gate throughout the morning, did not immediately notice the stranger. Time passed, however, and eventually he became aware that the large figure hulking on the far side of Summit Street seemed disinclined to depart, whereupon he took a closer look.

It was not possible to see much through the smoky mists. The stranger was tall, broad, and ragged. A wide-brimmed hat shadowed his face and hid his hair. He wore no mask. Somehow he did not give the impression of advanced age, but he leaned for support on a staff.

Chenno did not like the look of him, but so long as the stranger maintained a properly respectful distance, there was no cause for concern.

The stranger, however, appeared blind to the dictates of propriety. Presently he crossed the street. As he approached, Chenno got a better look, and his initial sense of uneasiness sharpened to revulsion. Of all the pedestrians roaming the city, this one above all *should* have made use of a mask. The face visible beneath the hat brim was a ghastly ruin—broken and destroyed, the right eye gone, its empty socket surrounded by swollen, livid flesh. Chenno resisted the impulse to back away.

Closer yet, and Chenno found himself staring into a single eye the color of slush laced with blood. The eye was inanimate, and he could barely bring himself to meet its lifeless regard. Clearly, however, this was no Wanderer.

It would not do to appear timid. His grip tightened on his halberd, and he commanded harshly, "Clear off, you."

There was no sign that the other understood. The dead eye never blinked. Its owner was a madman or an idiot. A couple of blows should send him limping on his way.

Before the strokes had been dealt, however, the mouth in the ruined face worked hard, and a couple of words fought their way free.

"*Belandor House.*"

"No beggars allowed here."

"*Belandor House.*"

"Looking for a drubbing, you crack-brained gargoyle?"

"*Girl.*"

"What?"

"*Girl. Mine.*"

"Yours, eh? She must be a real beauty. But you won't find her here."

"*Jianna Belandor. Mine.*"

The name of a Belandor lady upon the lips of this gutter wreck—it was insupportable. Chenno was outraged on behalf of his employer.

The abrupt disappearance of his niece days earlier had thrown Master Nalio Belandor into fits of quivering wrath. He had harangued the household staff at passionate length, refused nourishment for the space of an entire day, shut himself in his chamber for hours, and finally emerged to stalk the north wing corridors, muttering to himself. The servants privileged to overhear brief snatches of his monologue had caught the words "Magnifico Tribari," repeated in tones of scandalized grief. At last, Master Nalio had recovered himself so far as to forbid the name of the runaway to be spoken aloud in his presence.

"*Jianna Belandor.*"

"That's it. Now you lose the rest of your teeth." Chenno swung the haft of his halberd at the impertinent maimed mouth. To his astonishment, the weapon was arrested in mid-arc and wrenched almost effortlessly from his grasp. He would never have dreamed that the limping ruin before him possessed such strength. He had scarcely begun to marvel before the halberd swung again, its ax blade sinking deep into his skull.

• • •

For some time Onartino Belandor stood quite still, regarding the dead man at his feet. Eventually his eye rose from the sentry to the gate, which remained closed and locked. Beyond the gate rose the partially reconstructed house, presently out of reach. The atmosphere about him vibrated with a kind of squawking yammer, reminiscent of the call of the Scarlet Gluttons, but more annoying. He let his bloodshot gaze travel, and discovered himself surrounded by excited citizens, all observing from a safe distance. Some internal voice must have advised him to depart. Turning his back on Belandor House, he hobbled away along Summit Street, and all in his path hastily drew aside to let him pass. Moments later, the smoky mists swallowed him whole.

Nobody presumed to follow.

FOURTEEN

Early morning, and the camp was awake and astir, cookfires jumping, pots bubbling, voices babbling. As the Magnifico Aureste emerged from his tent to greet the new day, he discovered a scrap of paper pinned to the canvas flap masking the entrance. How it had come there, placed by what hand, he did not know. His lips tightened. His past experience of anonymous notes was consistently unpleasant. He did not welcome additional unpleasantness now. Nevertheless, he plucked the paper from its place, unfolded it, and beheld handwriting almost familiar as his own, even after all these years.

Meet me at the fallen tree.

That was all she had written. No signature, no time specified, no clear identification of the fallen tree. She had known that none would be needed.

He did not bother with breakfast, but lost no time in making his way back a few hundred yards along the faint dirt track that was all that remained of the Nor'wilders Way. His step was brisk, his mind aflame with curiosity tinged with uneasiness; for she would not have summoned him lightly.

The fallen tree lay several feet from the roadway, its presence partially obscured by weedy undergrowth. Nevertheless, he had noticed it in passing, the previous day's late afternoon. Indeed, it would have been hard to overlook, for the long prostrate carcass was charred and blasted, presumably by lightning, while the blackened stump still stood upright, dramatically crowned with sharp spars and fragments.

She was standing beside the stump, her back toward him. She was wrapped in her long, dark green cloak, but the hood was down and the chestnut glint of her hair offered the one touch of warm color in the muted landscape.

"Magnifica." He halted at a courteous distance.

She turned to face him. She was beautiful as ever, but pale and—to him—visibly unhappy.

"Magnifico. Thank you for coming."

"Madam, I am honored to attend you." *What's wrong, Sonnetia?*

"I've requested a meeting at this time because I find that I must ask a favor of you."

She would hate to ask anything of him. Nothing less than dire need would drive her to it. He produced the correct words. "Madam, it is my privilege to serve you. All my powers and resources, such as they may be, are yours to command." *Now, what is this?*

"You are most generous. Briefly, then—I desire you to speak to your brother Innesq Belandor upon my behalf."

"I'll speak willingly, of course. But you must name a topic."

"The topic is my son Vinzille."

"A little more specific, please."

"I would entreat you to ask your brother Innesq to watch over Vinzille. To guard his health and safety. Your brother's talents are exceptional. I know he could do this."

"I daresay. But—forgive me, madam—are the talents of the lad's own father not likewise exceptional? The Magnifico Corvestri appears to have forged a certain bond of friendship with my brother Innesq. Even so, I can hardly suppose that he would relish Belandor interference in the private affairs of House Corvestri."

"Perhaps he wouldn't. But my son's welfare is far more important than the Magnifico Corvestri's approval."

She spoke with her habitual composure, but Aureste, still attuned to every inflection of her voice, caught a note of resentment or defiance that piqued his curiosity.

"You've reason to fear for your son?" he probed cautiously.

"I'm certain of it. Have you not noticed how ill he's been lately?"

"I thought the lad looked peaked for a few days. He's well now, isn't he?"

"Yes—now. He's improved remarkably overnight. But how long will he remain well? His malady is arcane in nature. Even the Magnifico Corvestri admits as much. But for reasons of his own, my husband is unwilling to protect our son. He and I are very much at odds on this."

"I see. A most difficult situation," Aureste sympathized gravely, careful to conceal every outward sign of satisfaction. *He and I are very much at odds* . . . The words were music.

"Your brother will understand the nature of the problem. He has the skill and power to combat it. Beyond that, he's generous in nature, and seems fond of Vinzille. I believe he will help."

"All of that is true, but one point puzzles me. Why do you need or want my intercession? Why do you not approach Innesq directly? Permit me to observe that your powers of persuasion are formidable, far exceeding my own. Moreover, the fears of a mother for her child are compelling, and certain to engage the sympathies of listeners far harder of heart than my brother. Speak to him yourself, Magnifica—he'll not refuse you."

"I can't speak to him."

"Once upon a time, you were less timid."

"I'm not timid now."

He studied her. Her eyes were downcast, her face colorless. She appeared agitated, unhappy, and even, he fancied, embarrassed or ashamed.

"Then what is the difficulty?" he asked, as gently as he knew how.

"My husband has forbidden it."

"Is that all? Surely you don't trouble yourself over such a trifle?"

"A husband's legal authority is no trifle. Ask any magistrate."

"True enough, but in this case a technicality, surely? The magnifico would scarcely presume to enforce it." *The little pipsqueak wouldn't dare.* "It's my understanding that he's always afforded you the greatest respect, as indeed he should—House Steffa stands behind you."

"House Steffa has declined, and I doubt that its present master would concern himself overmuch with the complaints of a kinswoman who married into House Corvestri so many years ago. As for the Magnifico Corvestri, your understanding is correct—he has always afforded me respect. Until lately, that is. Lately he has altered."

"How and why?"

"He displays a peculiar determination to assert mastery within his household. I say 'peculiar' because it's redundant. His position as head of the family has never been challenged or questioned. Certainly not by me. I've always taken care to address the Magnifico Corvestri with the courtesy and deference that his position demands."

That can't always have been easy. He had a sudden sense of her courteous, deferential life, and unwonted sympathy touched him.

"But it hasn't been enough. In recent weeks, he's been treating me like some sort of unruly Sishmindri in want of discipline," Sonnetia continued. A flush of color had crept into her cheeks. As she spoke, the rigid formality of her speech insensibly relaxed. The words hurried out as if released from prison. She looked and sounded years younger. "He's turned into a bullying tyrant, and I don't know why. I've an idea, but I don't know for sure. I keep telling myself that it's all temporary—that the troubles will end and he'll be himself again—but time passes, and it doesn't happen."

"Has that creature dared to raise a hand against you?"

"No, no, he hasn't, so far."

"So far?"

"Sometimes I think—but no, he's never struck me. Probably he never will. I've told him I won't endure it." She paused and frowned, as if wondering at herself. "I can hardly believe that I'm speaking aloud of such things—and to you, of all people."

"Once in a quarter century or so can't hurt."

"Probably it would have been best if I hadn't insisted on coming along on this trip. I could have stayed at home, had some time without him, and it would have been so sweet, so free. But I was worried about Vinzille, you see. I wanted to watch over him, and it turns out that I had cause to fear. He's been attacked in some arcane sort of way. His father won't protect him, and when I told Corvestri that I meant to seek assistance elsewhere, that's when things got worse than I ever expected."

"What did he do?"

"He was furious. Told me he wouldn't allow me to humiliate him. Told me that he'd confine me to our carriage if I disobeyed. And finally, suggested that I'm likely to find my powers of speech suddenly curtailed, along with my ability to write."

"*What?*"

"You heard me. So you see, I really can't approach Innesq. But nobody's forbidden me to speak to you."

"But this is unbelievable. Are you telling me that the little scorpion is actually threatening to turn his arcane power against his own wife?"

She nodded.

"Arcanists don't do that, at least not openly. There are civil and criminal laws in Vitrisi, not to mention generally accepted codes of conduct. Ethical standards. Quite stringent, I'm told."

"Perhaps a little less stringent, out here in the middle of nowhere."

"We'll see about that. We'll learn the verdict of his peers

when I tell every single one of them, including the Taerleezis, exactly how he's abused you."

"You'll do nothing of the sort. Do you think I want to cause discord among the arcanists? They need to work together, 'as one,' as your brother puts it. That's difficult enough under the best of circumstances. You mustn't do or say anything to make it harder. Think of our purpose, and hold your peace."

"Very well, I'll say nothing to the arcanists. I'll simply go to the Magnifico Corvestri and inform him quietly that he will honor you as you deserve, else I'll personally thrash him to within an inch of his life."

"You will not. Don't make me sorry that I've confided in you."

"Why confide in me at all if you don't expect me to act? Shall I hear you describe your ill treatment at the hands of an unworthy man and do nothing? What do you want of me?"

"I've already told you. I want you to ask your brother Innesq to watch over Vinzille. That's all I ask."

"Not enough."

"More than enough. You'll have to content yourself with granting small favors." She offered him a smile at once ironic and forlorn.

He had, without conscious intention, drawn near her as they spoke. Now he stood close enough to catch her faint, clean fragrance. For a moment the urge to touch her was almost overpowering. He mastered it with an effort and stood very still, looking down into her eyes.

. . .

"They are together," Nissi whispered.

"You're certain?" Yvenza demanded.

The white head bobbed. The moonbeam eyes remained shut.

"What do you see?"

"Nothing."

"Don't quibble. What do you perceive, then?"

"Their tracks upon the epiatmosphere have come together."

"Epiatmosphere? Never mind, it doesn't matter. Where are they?"

"They have gone back the way we came. Not far."

"What are they doing?"

"I do not know."

"Do not know, or will not say?"

No answer.

"Look deeper," Yvenza commanded. "Try harder. Put some effort into it."

"That . . . will not help."

"I insist."

Nissi's brow creased. Her hands began to shake. Her eyes opened and sought the ground.

"It is gone, now," she confessed, almost inaudibly.

Yvenza regarded her trembling protégée narrowly. "So I see. You're too easily distracted. Your concentration's weak. You must improve."

Without raising her eyes, Nissi nodded almost imperceptibly.

"Work on it every day. That's what your friend Innesq Belandor would tell you, isn't it?"

No audible or visible response.

"In the meantime you've given me enough, assuming that you're right. I'm relying on your accuracy. If you misinform me, I'll look foolish—something I don't enjoy. You, with your talents, can surely foresee the consequences."

Nissi wrapped both arms tightly about herself.

"But come, girl. Behave properly, and we'll do well enough. For now, your first concern is self-improvement. I want you to practice long and hard. You understand me? Practice." Without awaiting confirmation, Yvenza turned and walked away. Her quick paces soon carried her across the campsite into Corvestri territory, where the servants were engaged in dismantling the tents and harnessing the horses. The morning cookfires still burned, and beside one sat the Magnifico Corvestri, balanced upon a collapsible stool and peacefully consuming his breakfast.

She went straight to him and halted.

"Magnifico, I bid you good morning." An amiable, courteous inclination of the head accompanied the greeting.

Vinz glanced up with a look of surprise and rose to his feet at once. "Magnifica Yvenza. I am honored, madam. Good morning to you. Pray be seated. Will it please you to share the morning meal with me?"

"I thank you, sir, but no. I would not presume so far upon your good nature. In fact, I do not mean to trouble you at all, but come only in search of your lady wife. I am here to beg a favor of her, but it seems she hasn't yet returned to hear my suit."

"A favor? Perhaps I can assist you, madam?"

"Oh, I doubt it, sir. Unless, perhaps, you've spent a considerable span of time toiling in a stillroom. I'm told that the Magnifica Corvestri has devised or possesses a sovereign remedy for the grinding joints, and I would beg the recipe of her. But it seems that she hasn't yet returned."

"Returned?"

"One of your fellows told me an hour or more ago that the Magnifica Sonnetia had walked off. No doubt she'll be back soon enough. I'll catch her up sometime today. There's no call for haste."

"Walked off? Walked off?" Vinz Corvestri's affability congealed. "I don't know what you mean. She hasn't gone anywhere. What fellow of mine told you this? Who spoke of her? Point him out."

"Magnifico, you appear displeased."

"Indeed I am displeased, and with reason. The Magnifica Corvestri should not risk her safety wandering about on her own, out here in the wild. If one of the guards saw her walking away, he should have followed and protected her, whether she would or no. The guard was remiss. Which of them was it?"

"Oh, I couldn't say, I hardly marked. But truly, you've no cause for concern. The lady never wandered off on her own. She was, I'm told, accompanied by the Magnifico Aureste Belandor, who's doubtless capable of furnishing all the protection that any frail female could possibly need or desire. Your wife is safe in the hands of a great nobleman. Therefore, sir, be at ease." Smiling, she bobbed a reassuring nod.

Vinz Corvestri failed to take her advice. His face appeared to crack in places and resettle. For a moment he stood staring through her, then collected himself so far as to mutter a nearly incoherent promise to send his wife to the Magnifica Yvenza at the first opportunity. With that, he turned and hurried away.

• • •

Had his tent remained standing, Vinz would have sought that refuge. As it was, he made do with the shelter and comparative privacy of the Corvestri carriage. Once inside, he pulled all the shades down, excluding the eyes of the world and throwing the small space into deep gloom. For a few moments he sat there, jaw tight, belly aflutter with apprehension and nauseating suspicion. Very soon, however, the expertise born of endless practice enabled him to compose himself. He sat, breathing deeply and slowly. Presently he swallowed a small white lozenge that further cleared and expanded his mind, permitting suppression of all guilt over the personal use of precious arcane power. It was, as his wife would have it, a legitimate and necessary expenditure.

A small satchel stocked with an assortment of carefully chosen items reposed beneath the seat. Vinz retrieved the satchel, drawing therefrom a flask of clear, colorless liquid that was not water, and a shallow bowl. He set the bowl upon his knees, poured a quantity of fluid into it, laid the flask aside, and went to work.

So deeply satisfying, to drink strength at the Source once again after much deprivation, but he was in no fit state to enjoy it. His technique was far more sophisticated than Nissi's, granting him visual access to subjects sufficiently close at hand. He flexed his mind, and the sharp, clear images formed themselves in the bowl.

At the moment he could see the little pictures easily, despite the dimness of the atmosphere. And it was as she had said, as he had known it would be—

His wife and Aureste Belandor, off somewhere out of sight, together. At least the two of them weren't touching. Both were fully clothed, standing up, and not touching. They were talking, though. Their mutual attention appeared intensely focused, their conversation meaningful to both, and *he couldn't hear a word of it.* No arcane procedure or sequence presently at his command would allow him to listen in.

Vinz's ravenous gaze shifted from face to miniature face. He soon discovered that he lacked the ability to read lips. He could distinguish a word here and there, nothing more; not enough to tell him anything. But the faces—he could not look away from them. Both were so animated, so expressive—although of what, exactly, he did not know. Especially hers. She was standing close to Aureste Belandor, looking up at him, and her face was mobile, changeable, while her eyes were filled with something atypical. Tears? No—light. Her eyes were brilliant, remarkably alive. He had never seen her look quite like that before. He had not even known that she could. He had some vague sense then that in all the long years of their marriage, he had never really beheld her full beauty. She had always managed to withhold something, and he had deemed her cool or remote by nature—a creature lovely, graceful, and essentially unreachable as some exquisite fish glistening in a garden pool.

Wrong. She was not cool, far from it. And she was not unreachable.

Aureste Belandor could reach her. Now and always.

He had known it all along. Pain stabbed him.

The images in the bowl were shaking and fuzzing oddly. The faces were blurring, loosening, fading, vanishing.

Gone.

Vinz Corvestri blinked. He sat alone in a darkened carriage, with a bowl of clear fluid balanced on his knees. His pulse raced, his face burned, his breath came in gasps. There were no faces, no pictures, nothing to see. For a moment he was bewildered, and then he understood. He had let it slip. For the first time in many years, he had allowed emotion to shatter his concentration, and his connection to the Source had broken. He had thought himself far beyond such juvenile lapses, but he had been wrong.

He was too old and too accomplished to fall prey to such weakness.

It was chilly and secret inside the carriage. His hands were unsteady and the fluid in the bowl was sloshing. The pictures were gone, and for now he could not call them back. He was alone and essentially blind. The tears were scalding his nearly useless eyes.

He hurled the bowl away and heard it smash against the opposing wall. Moisture sprayed, and there was a tiny hiss as the leather upholstery yielded to the onslaught. He heard and smelled, but scarcely noticed. Fiery images burned in his brain. It was only the confirmation of ancient fears, but the certainty possessed hideous novelty.

She had not as yet betrayed him—not in the obvious sense. So much he was willing to believe. But her mind and heart had turned elsewhere.

No. They had always been elsewhere.

Vinz became aware that the tears were streaming down his cheeks. Thank Fortune for the lowered shades, thank all good luck that nobody could see. For this one moment, he was less than a man.

And if so, whose fault was it? Certainly not his own. He had followed the rules, always tried to do all that was right. Others could not claim as much. Aureste Belandor could not.

It was unfair and unjust. The good man—the faithful husband and provider—deserved reward. The interloper deserved the reverse.

The world would only laugh, but there was no point in blaming the world. There was a better target.

Aureste Belandor. Everything had been well, up until the time that despicable kneeser had intruded. Without him, all might be well again.

Without him. It was a beautiful thought, a precious thought. Vinz hugged it close, and a kind of peace descended upon him.

. . .

Throughout the day, the Nor'wilders Way seemed to fade in and out of being. For a few hundred yards at a stretch, the faint track barely marking the hills would be visible. Then it would disappear, only to resume its marginal existence somewhere farther on. In the midafternoon the road vanished once and for all.

From his vantage point on horseback near the front of the party, the Magnifico Aureste surveyed the prospect. Before him rolled a stretch of small but emphatic hills, the sharp descents and ascents littered with rock and prickled with the knee-high, stout wooden stalks of slumbering meecherhaven, mingled with bushy querria poised upon the brink of spring's explosive awakening. The road was gone, and he sensed finality in its departure. There was no possibility of drawing the carriages and larger wagons over such terrain. He himself had made provisions for this inevitability. Had the others the wit to do the same?

He ordered a halt and was obeyed by all. Without pausing to answer questions or to quash arguments, he rode back to the Belandor carriage, to find Innesq's pale face framed in the window.

"The road has ended," Aureste announced. "The carriages and larger wagons are henceforth useless. You'll proceed in the sedan chair, as soon as the lads get it assembled. Our supplies will be transferred to pack animals, which means that some of the servants will be walking. We'll slow somewhat, but we'll do well enough. But I wonder if the Corvestri group and the Taerleezis are adequately prepared. If they've dragged along more than their horses and mules can carry, then we'll be bogged down here for hours while they argue over what's to be left behind. I haven't the patience."

"You never did," Innesq agreed. "Take heart, the trouble may be less vexing than you imagine. Allow me a moment." Turning from the window, he conferred in low tones with the passenger seated beside him.

In the dimness of the carriage interior, Aureste descried a pale patch that had to be the girl Nissi. In the opposite seat, a coalescence of shadows marked the presence of the Magnifica Yvenza, who was about to lose the comfort of wheeled transportation. Innesq would insist on furnishing the hag with a mount, though. Well, the meanest donkey available was what she would receive; Aureste would enjoy that small satisfaction at least.

"So be it, then." Innesq turned back to the window. "Brother, the arcanists among us must address this situation. We shall do what we can to preserve the utility of the wheeled vehicles."

"You surprise me. I had thought your talents too valuable to waste upon such mundane matters as the smoothing of roads, kindling of fires upon damp wood, and so forth. Or so I've been given to understand."

"Conservation of arcane resources is important, but so, too, is the wise use of time. The changes all about us go forward apace—surely you have sensed them. We had best proceed to our destination as quickly as may be, and necessity justifies the use of power. Perhaps it is not such a bad thing— this will be our first real attempt to join our powers and work as one. We shall learn how we six fare together."

Six. So Innesq regarded Corvestri's half-grown whelp as an arcanist worthy of inclusion. Interesting.

A servant transferred Innesq to the wheeled chair. Nissi slipped like trickling water from the carriage. She wrapped her small hand in a twist of Innesq's loose cloak. Together the two of them made their way over the rocky ground to a clear, flat space where the arcanists were gathering.

Aureste followed, staying close enough to see everything, yet maintaining a considerate distance. Others were doing the same. Not far away he saw the Magnifica Sonnetia, her fine brows bent in a thoughtful frown, but he couldn't let his gaze rest on her lest he lose all track of the matter at hand. The Dowager Magnifica Yvenza was likewise present and attentive; best by far to ignore her presence. She was, after all, nothing more than a pathetic remnant, ruined and powerless. Save for her hold upon the girl Nissi, the old woman was dust.

Why could he not quite believe that?

All six of them were converging, without obvious benefit of verbal or written exchange. Either instinct or else some silent summons had drawn them. When the group was complete, Ojem Pridisso spoke with authority.

"All of us here already know what has to be done, so there's no need to waste time in talking. Now I want you to form a circle, and be sure that the youngsters alternate with seasoned hands. Corvestri, you keep your son beside you. Belandor, you'll stay next to Miss Nissi."

His colleagues meekly obeyed.

The vertical crease between Aureste's brows deepened. Pridisso's lordly tone was galling, and the coarse Taerleezi accent underscored the offense. He was taking charge as if he fancied himself commander-in-chief of the expedition. He was actually issuing orders to an adult male member of House Belandor.

Aureste took a deep breath, preparatory to loosing verbal acid, met his brother's eyes, and held his tongue. Innesq's expression was serene and subtly amused, his message clear. He neither needed nor wanted a defender.

They formed the circle, as instructed. Aureste scanned the sextet; six highly individual members, bearing little resemblance to one another in form, feature, personality, manner, or any other readily observable attribute. Could such disparate beings truly merge their minds and talents? Could they, in fact, perform at all out here in the wild, with the chill breeze sweeping through to rattle the woody stalks of meecherhaven, and an audience of the curious looking on? Why, Innesq liked to shut himself away in his workroom for days at a time, just to avoid observation and distraction. On the other hand, Innesq could exclude the world and everything in it from his consciousness, when necessary. Such intense focus of concentration was an essential skill of the arcanist, and all six of them would possess it to varying degrees.

Pridisso's voice was hammering again.

"Now, this is by way of being a trial go, an experiment, so we'll proceed without benefit of artificial enhancement or stimulation, if you please. And friends, let's have no complaints about that. Without the powders and pills to cloud the issue, we'll all get a clearer sense of one another, and I'll see a truer picture of the raw material I have to work with here. Our task is an easy one, so let's to it. Upon my signal."

Aureste contained his disgust.

The arcanists fell silent. Very quickly, their faces emptied and their bodies stilled. Presumably they continued to breathe, but that small motion was invisible. To all appearances, they had petrified. Aureste studied his brother's face, and uneasiness snaked through him. Innesq resembled a corpse. That marble visage, those eyes so wide and unseeing, did not belong to the living world.

The cold seconds ticked by, and his uneasiness deepened. He had never seen Innesq look like that, and he knew to his marrow that it was wrong. Did others share his conviction?

He chanced a glance at Sonnetia, who stood a few yards from him, attention wholly fixed on her son's immobile face. He saw anxiety in her eyes.

No movement. No sound other than the wind chattering the meecherhaven. No visible sign of life among the arcanists. And nothing at all happening, so far as he could see, but he knew better than to trust in appearances.

He let his eyes travel from living statue to statue, and saw then that a change of sorts had occurred. In some manner that defied definition, the six faces had assumed a look of kinship. The similarity certainly did not reside in form or feature, nor in expression, for expression was absent. Yet somehow the six resembled one another as unmistakably as he and Innesq shared a family likeness. He could hardly account for it.

They began to speak—or sing—or chant; he could not decide upon the appropriate verb. The voices rose and fell in perfect unison, merging almost indistinguishably, save for one anomaly that his ear caught from time to time—variation in the pitch of young Vinzille Corvestri's voice, which was in the process of change. Would that uncontrollable element disrupt the whole endeavor? The question floating about the periphery of his mind was answered almost at once, for the six voices reached a crescendo, and the world began to alter.

The nature of the transformation was not immediately apparent to the waking mind or senses, but something was happening to the land. It seemed to be rearranging itself in some inexplicable way. Even as he strained intellect and senses in an effort to understand, another change occurred.

He felt it first as a kind of pressure upon his mind—the touch of something incorporeal, yet identifiable as an entity; something vast and ancient. It was intelligent, and Its will was limitless.

Aureste drew in his breath sharply. His hands flew to his temples as if to contain or capture the intruder, but It was inside him and unreachable. An uncharacteristic sense of powerlessness filled him, coupled with terror sharper than any he had known since childhood. For an instant he actually sensed himself teetering on the verge of panic.

He would not suffer it. He was Aureste Belandor, and it was not for him to give way. He took a moment to compose himself, and then, again master of himself, he could fix his attention upon the invader, survey It and discover Its weaknesses.

There were no obvious points of vulnerability. Closer study was indicated.

He willed himself to serenity, much as he imagined that his brother might have done. Once thoroughly calm, he was free to observe.

The hands at his temples were shaking. He steadied them, but the flesh inside the leather gloves was freezing cold. Perhaps he was not quite as calm as he had imagined, yet he succeeded in catching another hint of Its nature.

Purposeful. Inexorable. Profoundly alien. Its passions—if any—were unfathomable; although he caught an echo of something like curiosity. He suspected that the joint arcane endeavor had drawn Its attention, but this was uncertain. One intention reached him clearly, however. It wished to absorb him utterly unto Itself, to annihilate his individual identity while sparing him physical death.

The concept was deeply repugnant, and he rejected it violently. In so doing, he expelled the intruder, reclaiming full ownership of his mind.

The Magnifico Aureste was himself again. He was breathing hard and drenched in sweat, despite the coolness of the air. He had no idea how much time had passed. The horse beneath him was grazing the first small shoots of new vegetation. The circle of arcanists had broken. Its members, pale and drained, were drifting off, their task presumably completed. Before them lay an expanse of clear and navigable dirt roadway, extending some twenty feet or so.

Twenty feet? Aureste blinked. What was the good of that? But then, Innesq had participated in the project, and he knew his brother. If Innesq had chosen to invest time and precious energy in the creation of the twenty viable feet, then there had to be good reason.

He could not puzzle it out now. He was a little dizzy, his thoughts unusually blurred and slow. He would consider the matter later, when he had recovered from the effects of his first confrontation with the Overmind.

FIFTEEN

The view from the tower window, ordinarily drab, had lately taken on a morbid fascination. Hands hard on the iron bars, Falaste Rione gazed down at the prison courtyard, where the workmen were busy assembling the torsion tower. The wooden scaffold had been completed early in the day. For hours since then, the workers under the supervision of the executioner had been struggling with the big wooden uprights that supported the famous twin wheels, studded with wrist and ankle fetters, and geared to rotate in opposite directions. They must have been strangers to the task, for they were slow and uncertain. But they would surely succeed in the end.

It would have been better not to watch, but he found it impossible to look away. In any case, there was little else to see. His tiny cell contained a straw pallet, a bucket, and nothing more. Grim though his lodgings were, he qualified as one of the favored among the Witch's inmates. His window admitted daylight and fresh air. The fresh air was often bitterly cold, but it swept away the worst of the stench. The window was an exceptional luxury.

Down below in the courtyard, the workmen were complaining, and the executioner was yelling at them. Rione studied the man preparing to kill him—an ordinary individual of substantial build, bald patch on top, plainly dressed. Nothing about him to suggest the nature of his profession.

A noise behind him pulled his attention from the courtyard. He turned to face the door, and his muscles tensed, for he knew what was coming. The wooden panel masking the square of iron grillwork in the door was about to slide away, and the faces were about to reappear at the little window. Even in these grim times, there were countless inquisitive idlers glad to pay the Witch turnkeys for the privilege of viewing the governor's assassins at close range. Such commerce was officially prohibited, but the trade was far too lucrative to refuse. Thus Falaste Rione often found himself on display, not unlike a rump-faced hibiluk at the public zoo, before the zoo had closed.

The unabashed openness with which the visitors simply gawked never failed to astonish him. Likewise remarkable—the commentary upon his appearance, manner, demeanor, intellect, and character, all uttered freely, as if the observers imagined him deaf, or bereft of understanding. Even more amazing was the impertinence of the questions directed to him through the grille. There was nothing in the world they hesitated to demand of him, from a personal account of the crime, to revelations of intimate habits and preferences, to a description of his reflections upon impending execution. Did he fear the proverbial pain of torsion? Would he walk to the tower tamely, or did he mean to struggle? Was he at all worried about soiling himself? His only recourse at such times was to turn away and gaze out the window. When he did so, some of his visitors waxed resentful, while others whined reproaches.

No doubt his sister, Celisse, an object of far greater interest than himself, received similar attention on a larger scale. Being Celisse, she might enjoy it.

The square panel remained shut, but the whole door opened. A brace of large guards bulked on the threshold. He knew them both by name: Ori and Chesubbo. Both tough and professionally callous, but not such bad fellows. Why here now, though? It shot through his mind that his execution had been advanced by a couple of days, and they had come to take him to his death. But no, impossible, the tower wasn't ready yet. Another interrogation—some sort of confession to sign? To what purpose?

"Come on, then," Ori commanded.

"Move it, Doc." Chesubbo clapped his hands sharply.

"Where?"

"You'll see. Nothing to worry about."

He did worry, but there was no point in further query. Conducting him from his cell, they led him down a narrow staircase, along vaulted stone corridors into a section of the prison he had never seen before. His wrists were free of manacles. As they walked, the guards flanked him closely, but did not touch him; a favor that might almost have been interpreted as a mark of something like respect.

Instinct told him that they were leading him toward the south face of the building. Presently they came to a heavy portal whose guard stepped aside at a word from Ori. They went through and Rione found himself in a narrow, covered walkway, with windows on both sides affording a view of walled gardens. Still bare and almost colorless at this time of year, but unquestionably real gardens, with a flagged path winding among sculpted flower beds, thoughtfully placed shrubs, trellises, and a few of the earliest phileefis glowing purple against the dark soil. *Here?* He had never expected to glimpse another garden in this lifetime. But there was no time to wonder or admire, for they were hurrying him along the walkway and through another door at its far end.

The world changed again, and he found himself in some sort of chamber furnished with wall hangings, mossy velvet window draperies, a few small tables, chairs and benches plumped with cushions. The function of the room, with its ordinary décor, was not quite apparent, but function was not the point. What struck Rione forcibly was the realization that he now stood in a private dwelling. This room was not part of the Witch prison; it was part of somebody's home.

Whose? Scarcely a mystery. The residence of the prison's governor adjoined the Witch at the south side of the building. They had brought him to the governor's own house. Surely not for interrogation. The facilities within the prison itself were well designed to effect efficient extraction of information. They would not have brought him here for official questioning. Unofficial, then? The prison's Governor Sfirriu, like so many others, wished to plumb the brain of a famous criminal? Possible, but why take the criminal out of the prison for it?

Alternative possibilities?

The famous criminal was also a physician of growing repute. That might have something to do with it.

A young man entered—a skinny, slightly green-faced creature clad in the unassuming garments of a servant in a moderately affluent household.

"This the one?" he demanded in a voice that matched his person.

Ori replied affirmatively.

"This way, then." He marched out again. Guards and prisoner followed.

The house was comfortable and solidly respectable-looking, but not large. Within seconds they came to a closed door upon which the servant rapped sharply. A man's voice from within bade them enter.

They walked into a small office or study, with a good coal fire blazing on the grate. And there behind a plain wooden desk sat the prison's Governor Sfirriu—a middle-aged Taerleezi, running to fat, grey of hair, lined of face, tired and harried-looking. He gave the impression of having sat behind that desk for many unfulfilling years. The two guards saluted. Rione waited.

"You are the physician Falaste Rione?" Sfirriu demanded.

"Yes, Governor." Rione inclined his head politely, but without servility.

"You have been convicted of complicity in the assassination of the Governor Anzi Uffrigo, and accordingly condemned."

"Yes, Governor."

"You will no doubt wish to profess your innocence."

"I've done so at length and to no avail, Governor. There

seems little point in repetition." This bordered on insolence, but one of the few consolations of his present situation lay in the irrelevance of consequences.

"You are correct," Sfirriu agreed. Addressing the two guards, he commanded, "Wait outside."

Ori and Chesubbo traded surprised glances, but obeyed mutely. The door closed behind them.

Rione's sense of wonder deepened.

Prison governor and prisoner surveyed one another. The governor broke the silence.

"It's said that you're a man of parts," Sfirriu observed at last. "They speak well of you at the Avorno Hospital."

Rione waited.

"They describe you as a physician of exceptional gifts."

"I am a physician, Governor. I try to make best use of my abilities, such as they are."

"Certainly, certainly." Sfirriu frowned upon the documents cluttering his desktop. "They say *exceptional* gifts. New ideas. New methods. Remarkable results. Almost magical."

"If I possessed magical power, Governor, then I would not be here now."

"I'm told that you've treated cases of the plague. Is this true?"

"Yes."

"And they've recovered?"

"Some of them."

"You claim power to cure the plague?"

"I've a treatment that's proven effective in some cases."

"How many?"

"Ten or twelve, I believe."

"That's all? Out of how many that have received this treatment?"

"Perhaps a couple of dozen."

"Not good enough."

"I agree, Governor."

There was a comfortless pause, during which the governor

appeared preoccupied with one of the papers on the desk. At last he looked up, met the prisoner's eyes, and remarked abruptly, "What I say to you now is to be held in confidence. Repeat a word of it, and things will go far harder than need be for you and your sister alike. I leave it to your imagination to supply possibilities. You understand me?"

Rione inclined his head.

"Very well. I have decided to grant you the opportunity of employing your physician's skills. Your patients are afflicted with the plague."

"My patients?"

"Two of them. Members of this household. There's the need for discretion explained."

Well explained. The governor did not wish to find his home placed under quarantine.

"Both female," Sfirriu continued. "Thirty-eight and seventeen years of age, respectively. Ailing since last night. As of today, their malady had been identified as plague. You are the first physician to be consulted."

Indeed. A conveniently captive physician, unable to carry his knowledge beyond the prison walls.

"Servants?" Rione queried.

"My wife and oldest daughter. Note that your patients are persons of consequence. You will call upon your best abilities and exert yourself to the utmost."

"Will I? You overlook one detail. My exertions, if any, are scheduled to be cut short in a day or less. Not enough time to effect a cure."

"Time. Ah. Well. As far as that goes, there is perhaps some room for maneuvering."

"How much room, would you say?"

"Difficult to judge. Within these walls, I wield considerable power, but I can't offer miracles. I can't, let it be clearly understood, offer you a pardon or a commutation of sentence. I can, however, order a stay of execution."

"How long a stay?"

"That would depend on you."

"To borrow your own phrase, Governor—not good enough."

"Take care. You're in no position to state terms."

"I've nothing to lose. What better position?"

"Think again. As a doctor, you understand better than most the mechanics of execution. You know that death by torsion can take place in an instant, or it can be prolonged for hours, according to the whim of the executioner—or the instructions that the executioner has received. The agony of the experience may be intense and immediate—or it may be dulled and distanced by the administration of merciful draughts. No doubt you're familiar with such draughts."

"I am. They've numbered among the most precious of the medications I once carried."

"In this?" From beneath his desk Governor Sfirriu produced a familiar leather bag. "Come, no need to hang back, you may take it. The sharp-edged and pointed metal instruments have been removed, but most of your supplies remain. I trust you'll make good use of them."

His bag, his beloved paraphernalia, largely intact. His hand itched to grasp it, but he did not move.

"Governor, let us understand each other. I can't be constrained to serve you, I don't fear threats. Rewards are the more effective incentive. What can you do for my sister and for me?"

"I can promise your sister a quick and merciful death. Nothing more can be done—she's too notorious, too conspicuous. In your own case, as I mentioned, there is some room to maneuver. I'll do as much for you as I can, for as long as I can. That's all I can pledge in good faith."

Rione believed him. His hand yearned for the bag. *To be a doctor again, if only for a little while.*

"I want to see my sister," he said.

"Tend your two patients diligently through the day, and you may visit your sister tonight."

It was a remarkable privilege. More than he had ever really expected. He nodded and took up his bag.

"My lad Tuza, who admitted you, is the only servant in the house aware of the real situation. If the others knew, they'd run. Tuza will conduct you to the sickroom, and he'll be there to carry your reports to me, or to fetch the items that your plan of treatment requires." Sfirriu tugged the bellpull. "And one more thing—should either or both of your patients die, the news is to be carried to me alone. You understand? Only to me."

Rione nodded. The door opened and Tuza stuck his head in.

"Take him to them," the governor commanded.

Rione followed Tuza from the study, and the two guards waiting outside the door fell into step behind them. A few paces along the hall, then up the nicely polished wooden stairway to the second-story hallway and an assortment of doors, most of them ajar, one firmly closed. Tuza arrowed for the closed door.

"Here," he said, and shot the physician a speculative side-long glance.

Rione went in alone, shutting the door behind him. The window curtains were drawn, and he allowed his eyes a moment to adjust to the low light. He stood in an ordinary bed-chamber furnished with two cots, both occupied. Drawing a beak-nosed mask and impermeable gloves from his bag, he donned the protective garments before approaching his patients. A mature woman lay tossing and moaning in one bed. In the other was a similarly restless young girl who might, under happier circumstances, have been rather pretty. A cursory examination confirmed the accuracy of the governor's diagnosis. His wife and daughter both displayed the tri-lobed carbuncles of the plague.

Both were feverish and only semiconscious, but their hearts still beat strongly and their lungs seemed sound. The disease had taken firm hold, but had not yet conquered. The sufferers might perhaps still be saved.

He opened the bedroom door, and the two guards waiting in the hall instantly stepped forward to block his exit.

"Tuza," Rione requested.

"Here." The servant edged past the human barrier.

"Here's what I need." Rione rattled off a list of items, all easily obtainable. As he spoke, his memory sped back to other days, other instructions issued to another listener. Into his mind flashed the image of her face; a pale, pure oval dominated by a pair of great dark eyes and startlingly strong black brows.

Not the time to be dreaming of her. She was safe and free. With any luck, her sense of self-preservation would carry her back to her family home, obnoxious uncle notwithstanding. The fragrance of her hair filled his mind for an instant.

"I'll get them." Tuza was gone.

Crossing to the window, he pushed the curtain aside and looked down upon a flagstone terrace adjoining the garden that he had glimpsed earlier. A leap from the second story would land him in an enclosed private enclave that was itself embedded within the prison property surrounded by the high outer wall. No escape through the window.

Muted whimpers drew his attention back to the task at hand. His patients suffered, but he could and would furnish relief within minutes. The procedures that he now contemplated— designed to suppress the physical senses, in hopes of wearying the invasive entity—were best performed upon unconscious subjects.

A small writing desk and chair occupied one corner of the room. Rione seated himself. From his bag he withdrew a selection of vials, bottles, flasks, a measuring cylinder, and a miniature balance, all of which he placed on the desk before him. For a moment he eyed the items consideringly, then set to work.

· · ·

By early evening, much had been accomplished. The eyes of the patients had been blindfolded, their ears stopped with waxen plugs, their bodies wrapped in the dampened sheets that both restricted movement and cooled the heat of fever. For hours they had slumbered deeply, thanks to the power of narcotic potions. At twilight they began to stir, heads turning from side to side, bodies weakly twisting within the confines of their damp wrappings, whereupon Rione administered draughts created to kill pain and dull all sensation. Movement ceased.

So far, both patients were responding in accordance with his experience of such cases. There was cause for guarded optimism, but the outcome remained very much in doubt. As he stood atomizing fresh, cool water over the linen bundle containing the governor's wife, there came a cautious scratching at the door. He opened it to confront Tuza, who informed him that his meal was ready.

Rione was mildly startled. Absorbed in his work, he had forgotten about food. Stripping off his mask and gloves, he set them aside on the tiny candle stand beside the door and stepped out into the hall. Ori and Chesubbo were immediately beside him. Their vigilant proximity suggested ignorance of the plague's presence in the governor's house. Tuza, on the other hand, maintained a careful distance.

At the end of the hall, a door opened on a very narrow stairway leading up to an unfinished attic. The slanting ceiling with its bare rafters was high enough at the center for a man of moderate height to stand upright. Crates, barrels, and bulging sacks lay everywhere, but the place was bare of furniture other than a small table of unfinished wood and a three-legged stool. A lighted candle in a tin dish stood on the table, together with a pitcher, a cup, spoon, and a covered dish.

"Yours." Tuza gestured.

Rione sat down.

"Anything else you need?"

Rione shook his head, and Tuza exited hurriedly. Ori and Chesubbo followed at a more leisurely pace. Their heavy footsteps clumped to the foot of the attic stairs, where the sound halted. He could imagine them standing there, waiting for the physician-prisoner to finish eating, and wondering at the extreme peculiarity of the situation.

He poured himself a drink and swallowed a mouthful—cider, fresh and hinting of cinnamon. He took the cover off the dish to reveal a bowl of stew, still warm, with nuggets of meat and assorted root vegetables; a quantity of brown bread; two apples and a pear, the fruit worm-free. It was better food, more plentiful and nourishing, than he had tasted since the day of his arrest. Not that he had suffered much from hunger; trial and condemnation had done little to stimulate his appetite. It was clear, however, that Governor Sfirriu wished to keep him healthy and active so long as his usefulness continued.

He ate his dinner and departed the attic. Tuza was nowhere in evidence, but Ori and Chesubbo still waited in the second-story hallway.

"This way," Ori commanded.

They hustled him along the hallway, past the closed sickroom door, down the stairs, and back the way they had come hours earlier. He assumed at first that they were returning him to his cell for the night, but soon found himself mistaken.

Back along the walkway, back into the stone heart of the Witch, but not back to the spiral staircase leading to his tower cage. They took him by a different route to a low, sad gallery lined with iron-strapped oaken doors; all closed, all blind, all anonymous. They came to the door, indistinguishable from its fellow doors, at the far end of the gallery, and there they stopped.

"You've got fifteen minutes," Chesubbo announced. "Make the most of it. She's for it tomorrow morning."

"Your sister." Ori answered the prisoner's look of silent inquiry. "Your knife-slinging, Sishmindri-corrupting, sedition-spouting little sister."

"She's a one," Chesubbo conceded, not without admiration. He slid the heavy bolt and opened the door.

Rione walked in. The door thudded shut.

Her cell was considerably larger than his own. She had a cot, a plain table and chair, a bucket tactfully equipped with a lid, and a tiny grease lamp, by whose smoky yellow light the scene was visible.

Celisse was seated at the table, an untouched meal before her. As the door opened, she turned to face it. Her eyes widened at sight of her brother, and she rose to her feet.

Rione was conscious, for the first time in days, of his unshaven face, his unwashed and doubtless malodorous person and clothing. Celisse had somehow contrived to keep herself clean, or at least to maintain the appearance of cleanliness. Her dark hair was neatly ordered, her dress unspotted, her fingernails surprisingly free of grime. Her face, always light of complexion, was a shade paler than usual, her sole outward manifestation of unease. So she appeared on the last evening of her life.

Across his mind wheeled a hundred recollections of the past that they shared. Celisse, as an infant and then a toddler, growing and learning in the halls of Ironheart. Celisse, an orphan, turning to the Magnifica Yvenza for guidance, instruction, and adult affection. Celisse, sitting at the feet of Yvenza, absorbing the magnifica's attitudes and convictions. Celisse, trained and indoctrinated from earliest childhood, methodically forged and shaped. When he himself had come to Ironheart, he had been old enough to recall the face and words of his father. Celisse had known only Yvenza.

"You've come to say good-bye," she observed, voice clear and manner composed as always.

Something inside him seemed to be breaking. For a moment he doubted his own ability to frame a reply, then managed to utter a few unsteady words. "Oh, my dear. We've only a very little time."

"It's more than I ever expected. Come, Falaste, take heart. I am not afraid, nor should you be. Remember, we die for Faerlonne."

"That comforts you?"

"More than comforts. It fills me with joy and gratitude. I only wish that I might share this sense with you. Tomorrow, if we go together, then I'll hold your hand if I can. If that isn't permitted, then you must keep your eyes fixed on mine, and what you see there will ease your way."

"Celisse, I'll not be with you. I don't go tomorrow."

"No? What has happened?"

"I've been granted a stay. I don't know how long."

"But how? Why? Instinct bids me rejoice for you." She curved a faint smile belied by frowning brows. "Reason dictates otherwise. What we both face is best concluded quickly."

"Yes, you're right. That's one reason why this meeting between us now is so important. Listen—the thought of you suffering pain is more than I can bear. I've chosen accordingly, and therefore I *can* help you. See here." From the depths of his pocket Rione drew two small packets of heavy paper, sealed with wax. "These are gifts of value. Swallow the powder in the packet sealed in blue tomorrow at dawn, and all that follows will be distant and unreal as a half-remembered dream. There will be no pain, no fear, no anguish. Or, if it seems better, swallow the entire contents of the packet sealed in black tonight—and there will be no tomorrow. You understand me?"

"No. I do not understand you." She made no move to accept the proffered packets. Her eyes drilled into him. "How did you obtain these 'gifts of value,' brother? Where did they come from?"

"From my bag. I've always carried them."

"You and your bag parted company at the Lancet Inn."

"They've allowed me use of it. For a little while, I'm a doctor again."

"That's surprising. Our Taerleezi despots aren't wont to display such generosity. Who are your patients?"

"People in need."

"Speak plainly. Surely we must have nothing but honesty between us now. Who are your patients?"

"Governor Sfirriu's wife and daughter. Both have fallen dangerously ill."

"By that I suppose you mean they've taken the plague. Nothing else would account for the use of your services."

"Yes. I've been warned against speaking of it, but I won't lie to you. Plague has penetrated the Witch. Sfirriu has heard of my work, and requested my services."

"Which you gladly supplied. Here is what it is, then. In return for a stay of execution, and perhaps a few small favors—better food, maybe extra blankets and candles—you've sold yourself to the enemies of Faerlonne. You are the servant of the Taerleezis."

"Celisse. They are two women—one of them only a young girl—both desperately ill, both in pain. Certainly I'll help them all I can. Their nationality means nothing."

"It means everything. Among the Taerleezis, there are no innocents. So long as they infest our land, they are all equally guilty. You know this is true, but lack the resolve to admit it to yourself. Whatever privileges you've secured by this bargain of yours aren't worth the price. You must make amends. Listen. We two now share a secret valuable to the Faerlonnish cause. When the word goes out that this prison, its governor, and all his minions have taken contagion, then the Witch is thrown into disarray and placed under quarantine, its usefulness to our oppressors diminished or even destroyed. You must spread the news to all within hearing—to guards, fellow prisoners, visitors—everyone. And I shall do the same. Tomorrow, when I am given leave to speak, I shall step to the edge of the scaffold and proclaim the truth to all Vitrisi."

"And then? Have you considered the consequences? The fear and rage your words ignite will turn themselves upon—

whom? The scapegoat is neatly tethered in place. There will follow a wholesale massacre of prisoners. They'll be slaughtered by the hundreds, and nearly all of them are Faerlonnish. The Taerleezi authorities will doubtless welcome the purge."

The cold glint in Celisse's eyes extinguished itself. She jerked a grudging nod. "Very well. It is not the moment. At the very least, though, you must change your own course. You must cease treating these Taerleezis at once. No doubt you'll be punished, but you can bear it, and your honor will be whole again. I want your promise that you will do this."

"It would seem that our views of honor differ. To me, there's no honor in refusing medical care to sick and suffering women. But let's not speak of that."

"What would you rather speak of, then? Your 'gifts of value,' perhaps? I thank you for your eagerness to smooth my path, but you must understand that I accept no gifts from a creature of the Taerleezis."

"We can't quarrel. Not now."

"You'd like it better if I trembled and wept. Then you might comfort me, while imagining yourself wise and strong. I regret to inform you that a traitor and kneeser has lost the right to think so well of himself."

"You don't actually believe—"

"I don't flinch away from the truth. I call you a kneeser, because that's what you've made of yourself. You're a traitor serving the Taerleezis, as low as the worst of the kneesers, as contemptible as Aureste Belandor himself. I wish you'd adopt a new identity and give up the name Rione. You bring shame upon it."

"I won't fight with you. Sister, we meet for the last time in this world."

"Or in any world. If there are worlds or lives beyond death, then you and I will inhabit different spheres, for our souls are surely made of different stuff. Here and now, I don't choose to share my time with a servant of Faerlonne's enemies. Take yourself from my sight, and take your gifts with you."

"I'll leave them. There's a long night ahead. You might be glad of them, before morning."

"I'll accept nothing. Best keep them for yourself, you've more need of such artificial support than I. Take them away, or I'll turn them over to the guards and explain how they came to me. You might lose a few of your privileges."

"Please. Be just to yourself. Only allow yourself a little time to think."

"Not when I see what thinking has made of you. Time for you to go now, Falaste."

"We've another few minutes."

"I don't want them. We've nothing left to say to each other, and my eyes are tired of looking at you. You aren't the person I thought I knew. You're no true Faerlonnishman, no patriot, and I'm glad now that I'll not be sharing my death with you. So take your 'gifts of value,' and get out. You are not my brother."

She turned her back on him. For a moment Rione studied the infinitely unyielding set of her shoulders, then dropped the sealed packets back into his pocket, and rapped hard on the cell door. Chesubbo opened it, and he walked out.

SIXTEEN

Jianna lay in bed, the quilt pulled up to her chin. She was motionless, eyes closed, and anyone seeing her there would have thought that she slept. In fact she was wide awake, the thoughts boiling in her head.

For a long time—or at least it seemed very long—she had lain there wrestling with a single, dreadful question:

Should she attend Falaste Rione's execution?

On the face of it, the idea seemed to spring from the realm of nightmare. To voluntarily witness the unhurried destruction of the man she loved—it was almost unimaginable. To stand there watching, doing nothing, while he suffered and died before her eyes—she wasn't certain that she possessed the strength. If she endured it and came through with reason intact, then the memories and images would haunt her for the rest of her life.

She didn't want to go, and she didn't have to go. She need only remain where she was, safe in bed in a locked room with the window curtains drawn. The event would take place, and she would hear about it, hear too much, but there would be no sights and sounds to poison her mind forever. She had the right to spare herself all of that.

But another thought *would* recur: Her presence among the spectators might serve Falaste. Provided he spied her, he would know that he was not alone. He would sense her love and support, surely deriving some comfort therefrom. Also he would see that she was safe and well, and that, too, would comfort him.

It was little enough, but it was the only thing in the world that she could do for him.

And now there was no time left for internal debate. Time

had all but run out. The execution would take place in the morning, only a few hours away.

She hardly knew when she reached a decision. Somehow her eyes were open and she was on her feet. It was dark in her room. She groped her way to the window and pushed the curtain aside, admitting a faint trickle of light. The low-hanging moon proclaimed the dead of night.

Ingrained habit wrapped her in her woolen cloak. Her mind was set on other things, and she probably would not have felt the cold. A pocket in the cloak contained her mask, but she did not remember to put it on.

It was not too soon to set off for the Witch. It was not a long walk, but she needed to be among the first on the scene. The execution of the governor's assassin—who happened to be a young and attractive woman—together with her brother-accomplice was certain to draw a big crowd. Only the determined and devoted willing to arrive at dawn or earlier and to wait for hours in the prison courtyard would enjoy the choice positions at the foot of the scaffold. She needed to secure such a position. She must stand where he could see her and read the message in her eyes.

Leaving The Bellflower behind, she made her way through the sleeping streets. The way was dark and the moonlight feeble. Another night, another occasion, and she would have worried about losing her way. Now she thought nothing of it, but simply trusted her feet to carry her. Her trust was not misplaced. She navigated the tortuous route without thought or hesitation, and without a misstep.

Another night, another occasion, and she would have worried about wandering the streets of Vitrisi alone in the dark, without a guide or protector, without the smallest weapon. Every darkened alleyway that she passed might harbor footpads, rogue Sishmindris, or worse. But such thoughts never entered her mind now, and her luck held. She walked unknowingly through regions of sinister repute, and nobody troubled her.

The streets, in fact, were nearly deserted. Once she came upon a trio of masked men engaged in quiet conference. They fell silent as she approached; six eyes fastened glitteringly upon her. Jianna scarcely noted their existence. Wholly absorbed in her thoughts, she drifted by unseeing. The eyes followed her every move. Miraculously, nobody laid a hand on her, or even ventured a word.

On she went, until her path crossed another's, this time impossible to overlook. At the Y-shaped intersection of three narrow lanes, she came upon a solitary Wanderer. The undead, lately a man, was singular in appearance even by the eccentric standards of his kind. At some point in the recent past, a piece of crude surgery or cruder arcanism had amputated both of his legs at the knee. Immobilization of the corpse had presumably been the goal, but in this the anonymous experimentalist had failed. The Wanderer had simply inverted himself, and was now walking Vitrisi on the deteriorating remains of his hands.

Jianna halted, transfixed. The Wanderer advanced upon her, upended rags fluttering like moth wings in the moonlight. His progress was lurching and irregular, but quite swift; his sense of balance admirably intact beyond death. Jianna recalled then that the undead were known to seek contact with the living. There were gruesome stories, in fact, of women set upon and subjected to contact of the most revolting intimacy. Perhaps true, perhaps not, but certainly true that she should remove herself from the Wanderer's path. Yet somehow it seemed that her limbs had frozen—that she was deader than he was.

He was near enough now to waft a faint stench of putrescence that disgusted her but failed to break her paralysis. As he drew level, he turned his head and she caught a brief glimpse of milky eyes, empty behind dragging locks of filthy hair. An odd sense of pity touched her.

"It's all right," she whispered, startling herself with the sound of her own voice. "I don't care, it's all right."

No sign that he had heard much less understood her. The whitish eyes turned away. The inverted figure, back arched and stumpy legs widespread for balance, lurched away on its hands. Passing beyond the borders of the moonlight, it vanished into the dark.

Jianna released her breath in a sigh. Some part of her had wanted the Wanderer to accost her, to infect and destroy her. That done, all personal control and responsibility ended. She could not then proceed to the Witch to watch Falaste Rione die.

She willed herself to resume progress. There were no more encounters or delays, and too soon she found herself at the front gate of the prison. This gate was customarily left open, for the courtyard beyond was open to the public. Most days the place was alive with visitors, guards, beggars, pickpockets, and hawkers. On execution days, the crowds were particularly large and lively. Of late, execution days had become increasingly commonplace. Following the establishment of the Clean Zone, many hangings and mutilations formerly performed in the Plaza of Proclamation now took place at the foot of the Witch.

The coming day was exceptional, however. Nothing could have attested to this more clearly than the presence of the torsion tower in the courtyard. There would be no commonplace hanging for the Governor Uffrigo's assassins. A more exotic form of destruction awaited them.

Jianna studied the tower—a sturdy, crude construction of raw beams, supporting a central post that carried two wheels. Had she not already known, she would scarcely have guessed its function. As it was, every cog, gear, and lever of the mechanism possessed a deadly significance. At the rear of the scaffold waited a long wooden box whose purpose was likewise apparent. She tore her eyes away, and only then realized that she was not the first to arrive.

At the foot of the scaffold, occupying the very best position directly in front of the torsion tower, a cloaked and masked figure sat upon a small blanket. A portable brazier glowed beside him or her, and there was a wicker basket presumably containing refreshments. Jianna advanced to claim the second-best position in the courtyard. Having brought no blanket or cushion, she seated herself cross-legged on the ground, indifferent to the cold and moisture. As she settled into position, her neighbor's hooded head turned a trifle, and she caught the quick glint of sharp eyes. She remembered then that she had come to this place bare-faced; an unusual condition in these unwholesome days. Drawing the mask from her pocket, she put it on. She would remove it again when the time came.

She waited, and a welcome blankness descended upon her mind. She thought nothing, felt next to nothing, saw and heard almost nothing. Only vaguely was she aware of the hours passing, the moon setting, the night dwindling to its conclusion. At some point, the chill of the ground working its way into her bones broke through her stupor, and she stretched forth her hands toward her neighbor's glowing brazier. A hostile grunt warned her off. The warmth of the coals was to be enjoyed by the owner alone.

Time passed. Some peripheral area of consciousness registered the arrival of a few more people. A trio of boisterous youths took possession of the space to her left. A woman with a baby settled down behind her. A couple more masked and unqualifiable individuals came in with large quantities of food, whose aroma only stirred her revulsion.

As morning dawned and the skies began to lighten, activity picked up noticeably, with interested citizens arriving in pairs and groups. The area immediately surrounding the scaffold was now packed with humanity, and the luxury of a blanket spread out on the ground had become impractical; the spectators stood elbow-to-elbow. The sun rose to touch dull glints off the Witch's leaden roof, and still they came. Presently the dense living mass filled the courtyard from scaffold all the way to the gate.

The close press of the crowd jolted Jianna from her merciful lethargy. Somebody's elbow jabbed her ribs; somebody's breath stirred her hair. She tried to step away, but there was nowhere to go. Just as well. Had she retreated, she would have lost her enviable position at once. As it was, nobody stood between herself and the scaffold. She could see clearly and, more important, be seen. Once she unmasked, he could not miss her.

The morning sun climbed, and a lone man mounted the platform to perform a quick final inspection of the tower mechanism. His air of proprietary expertise marked him as the executioner, but he did not conform to the popular stereotype. He was not huge and brawny, nor did he sport a black hood. He was just an ordinary-looking man. Evidently satisfied, he signaled, and the prison door opened.

The crowd went silent as a small party emerged. At its forefront walked a greying man with Taerleezi features, attired in a quasi-military uniform of some sort. Presumably this was the governor of the prison, obliged to preside over so significant an execution taking place within his domain. Behind the governor scurried some nameless attendant bearing a ledger and documents. Then came a pair of guards. Between them walked Celisse Rione.

Jianna stared, almost incredulously.

It was strange, even eerie seeing her thus, for she looked impossibly normal and familiar. She seemed, in fact, very much her everyday self—dark hair neatly coiled, garments sober and practical, just as she had appeared in the camp of the Ghosts. She was pale, but little more so than usual. Her spine was straight, head high. No trace of fear touched her face; quite the contrary, in fact. Her expression conveyed a serene exaltation suggesting beatification.

There was no sign of Falaste Rione.

For a moment Jianna was confused, and then two possible explanations suggested themselves. They meant to execute Celisse, and when it was done, they would bring out her brother. Or else he was already dead, perhaps at the hands of brutal guards or interrogators. A shudder shook her. She clasped her gloved hands tightly together to still their trembling. Perhaps it would have been better to look away or to shut her eyes, but the scene playing out on the scaffold gripped her inescapably.

The governor nodded, and his flunky read forth the list of Celisse Rione's crimes, specified the date of her conviction and condemnation, then sped through the brief text of her death warrant.

Celisse listened without apparent emotion. Only the reference to "the sovereign authority of the state of Taerleez" brought a faint, pitying smile to her lips.

The reading concluded, and the condemned was offered an opportunity to speak a few words, of which she predictably availed herself.

Celisse stepped to the front of the scaffold. The two guards flanked her closely, their hold on her arms forestalling all possible leaps and excursions.

"Good citizens, I speak to those among you who love our country." Her voice, although not loud, was clear, steady, and audible throughout the courtyard. Her listeners strained hungrily for every syllable. "The true patriots among you are more than my friends—you are my brothers and sisters. To you, I say that I die today in earnest hope that I have furthered the cause of Faerlonnish freedom. If I have succeeded in performing a service of value, then life has been good to me, and I am content. Only one last favor do I ask, one last hope to carry to the grave—that the brave and true will carry on the fight, that you will never cease and never rest until our land is whole and free."

The potent combination of her words, her youth and good looks, her musical voice, and a certain studied simplicity of manner affected many listeners. Jianna heard a couple of muted sobs nearby, while a restless rustling swept the crowd.

Perhaps fearing an outbreak of popular protest or demonstration, the guards hurried the prisoner to the tower. There her wrists were attached to the top wheel, her ankles to the bottom. A blindfold was offered and politely refused. Her face remained exposed to general view. Her expression of calm certitude never altered. The executioner plied his levers. The wheels of the torsion tower turned, and Anzi Uffrigo's assassin died.

It was done. Celisse Rione was gone. Jianna stood motionless, stunned by the speed and finality of it. The prolonged agony of death by torsion was proverbial. It was a known fact that a skilled executioner could draw it out for hours. But Celisse's slender body had broken within seconds and her sufferings had been of the briefest duration. The authorities had clearly neglected an opportunity to exact vengeance upon the murderess of the Taerleezi governor and self-proclaimed enemy of Taerleezi authority. Strange. Whose decision, and what was the reason?

Her mind was in no fit state to address such issues.

They took Celisse's body down from the tower, deposited it in the waiting wooden box, and carried the box from the scaffold. The governor of the Witch, his attendant, and the guards with their burden vanished back into the prison, and the heavy door closed with a conclusive thunk.

The crowd was quiet, its mood somber and unsure. Jianna waited, eyes closed behind her mask, ears attuned to the sounds she expected—the door opening again, a responsive stirring among the spectators as the guards and officials reemerged with a second condemned prisoner in hand.

The seconds passed. All that reached her ears was the neutral buzz of low-voiced conversation. Nothing happened. At last she opened her eyes again to direct an inquiry to her nearest neighbor.

"What about the other one—her brother? What about Falaste Rione?"

A wordless shrug was the sole reply.

Confusion possessed her, but there was also the slightest brightening of hope for a miracle, hope tenuous as the first

glow along the edge of tinder fragments kindled in a down-
pour.

"The brother?" she whispered.

No reply. No information. No further activity. Jianna
pressed her hands to her temples.

Another indeterminate passage of time, and she became
aware that the crowd was thinning around her. The immediate
pressure diminished, the sense of personal space increased,
the air seemed to clear—and the prison door remained shut.
She drew a deep breath and strove for mental clarity.

They were not executing Falaste Rione today. Of course, he
might already be dead.

There was room to breathe, room to move. The citizens
were flowing from the courtyard. She allowed herself to drift
on the human current, and she was back out on the street
again. She let her feet carry her where they would. Her mind
gradually thawed. Thoughts began to form.

The thoughts touching upon Celisse Rione's last moments,
she pushed away. *So young. So dead.* Celisse had chosen her
own path, destroying her brother along with herself. She did
not want to think about Celisse.

But Falaste—alive or dead? Sick or well? Scheduled for execution another day?

Nobody knew. Oh, not literally. The governor of the Witch
knew. So did a few officials, some guards, a turnkey or two.
But for all practical purposes, from her immediate perspective, nobody knew.

Not entirely true.

Her mind seemed to be coming back to life. Almost she felt
it tingling inside her skull.

The Ghosts always know everything about everything.

What of it? She knew nothing of the city Ghosts, nor they
of her.

Think again.

She had met a Vitrisian Ghost once, not so very long ago.
With any luck, he would remember her face.

In an instant it was whole in her mind, as vivid as if it had happened yesterday. The incongruously happy afternoon that she had spent with Falaste, combing the city for his homicidal sister. His decision to enlist the aid of the Ghosts. The cloak-and-dagger method of communication. "... *Last night I placed a copper inside the crack in the base of Duke Dalbo Strenvivi's statue in the Strenvivi Gardens. That copper signifies my request for an afternoon meeting* ..." She remembered it all.

She stopped dead, fully aware of her surroundings for the first time since she had wandered out of the prison courtyard. She stood in Biso's Gate, a quiet little lane not far from her lodgings. She had unconsciously been making her way back to The Bellflower, the only refuge she knew. She looked about her. To the left rose an old livery stable, closed and boarded long ago. Several dwellings were similarly boarded at door and window, and one of them flaunted the red X. The denizens went about their business, identities lost behind full-face masks equipped with herb-stuffed nasal projections. Not long ago, such a scene would have struck her as fantastic. Now it was commonplace.

Her own mask featured no beak, but offered a pair of gauze eyepieces that she now tweaked into position. Thus fortified, she turned her newly purposeful steps north, toward the Strenvivi Gardens.

· · ·

She had not seen the Strenvivi Gardens in nearly a year. She had last visited in late spring, when the flowering trees had shone at the height of their glory. She had come there with her father, and together they had admired the blossoms, fed seeds to the swans, and wandered the white gravel paths, chatting and laughing together. And the presence of four Belandor bodyguards assigned to block the approach of hostile, critical, importunate, or murderous strangers had not struck her as strange at that time. It was all that she had ever known.

The recollection of her father did not stab with the force of earlier days; her mind and heart were filled with Falaste and his plight. One thing had not changed, however. She still tried to imagine what Aureste Belandor would advise, what Aureste would choose in similar circumstances. She could guess what he would say, what he might do now, and she was doing it.

The Strenvivi Gardens had changed considerably since her last visit. The once beautifully manicured grounds were unkempt and almost colorless. The white gravel formerly lining the paths had sunk into the mud. The pond had been drained, and there was not a swan in sight.

But Duke Dalbo Strenvivi's equestrian statue had not altered. There was Dalbo in his usual place, he and his horse caught in cast bronze forever. There sat Dalbo in all his conquering magnificence; his incomparably arrogant pose, his wrinkled lip and sneer of cold command a testament to the genius of the sculptor.

The statue was perfect, but its dark green marble base had not fared so well. The stone was webbed with cracks, most of them hairline, a few larger, and one gaping a fingerwidth.

That had to be the one. She cast a quick glance around her. Nobody was watching. In fact, there was hardly a soul in sight. Evidently the gardens had declined in popularity. She slipped a copper coin into the crack, then stood up and took her leave of melancholy, neglected Strenvivi Gardens.

And after that there was nothing left but to wait for the time to pass. The coin she had left communicated a request for an afternoon meeting, and it was already nearly midday. There could be no response before tomorrow afternoon at the earliest, and it might take considerably longer than that. Or the request might be ignored altogether.

No. Aureste's daughter would not let them ignore her.

She forced herself to enter the first cookshop that she saw. Food was the last thing in the world that she wanted, but information was another matter, and perhaps there was some to be had.

The place was small and lively, well patronized at this time of the day. She seated herself at the long common board and ordered a mug of warm orange-water. The faces around her were bare, so she removed her own mask. Her orange-water arrived. She sipped without tasting, and listened.

The Rione execution was unquestionably the topic of the hour, and there was no dearth of talk. A couple of individuals present had actually witnessed the event, and they furnished detailed descriptions sugared with praise of the Little Faerlonnish Lioness. Her courage had been sublime, her last words a clarion call to her countrymen. Her youth, her beauty, her patriotism, her greatness of heart . . . inspirational.

Jianna waited, but no one spoke of Falaste Rione, and at last she ventured a question:

"But what of her brother—was he not condemned as well?"

The brother hadn't been there, the experts informed her. His name hadn't been mentioned, there was no death warrant. He seemed to have been overlooked.

But how? Why? Had his sentence been commuted, or his execution simply postponed?

Nobody had the faintest idea.

Jianna paid her reckoning and left. Returning to The Bellflower, she immured herself within her room and waited for the hours to pass. They did so at their own unhurried pace. Around twilight, she forced herself to consume a light meal of cold items from the basket of provisions that hung on the hook in the low ceiling, safely out of reach of the mice. She wanted nothing, but needed to maintain her strength, for tomorrow she would walk some distance.

Darkness fell and she sought her bed, but sleep eluded her. The image of Celisse Rione upon the torsion tower burned behind her closed lids. There was no quenching it. She sat up in bed, hugging her bent knees. Sleep was out of the question. She was wide awake and certain to remain so.

Rising from bed, she slid her bare feet into a pair of soft

leather slippers, part of her expensive cannibalized trousseau, and draped her cloak over her shift. She stepped to the fireplace, took up the poker, and coaxed the banked fire back to life. The warmth came at her, and the room lightened into view. She did not see it. Her mind was starting to work properly again, for the first time in days, and it was like the resurgence of the banked coal fire. The thoughts were crackling, the ideas popping. There were possibilities; there might even be hope. Celisse's face receded. She worked her brain vigorously for hours, and felt the better for the mental exercise.

Shortly before dawn she returned to bed, and this time drifted off to sleep. The delayed rest served her well. The clock in the nearest bell tower was striking the hour of ten when she finally awoke. The morning was well advanced, and that was all to the good. She ached to put the morning behind her.

She washed and dressed, but never thought of food. Her mind stretched into the immediate future; a walk, and then perhaps a meeting. Or perhaps not, today. But there *would* be a meeting. She would insist.

She set forth from The Bellflower, with the not-distant past strong and clear in her mind. She remembered the way to The Cask in Cutter Lane. She remembered the warmth of Falaste's hand clasping hers. She remembered the talk, the laughter, the quiet music of his voice. She remembered it perfectly.

It was easy to find her way back. She walked, time and distance passed, and then she was there again in that obscure back street of an ordinary neighborhood. How long since she had last been here? Weeks? Centuries? Minutes?

At the top of Cutter Lane stood The Cask, an undistinguished wineshop of no discernible character. She went in, and it was just as she remembered, with its plain aspect, dim lighting, and equally dim patrons. Upon the occasion of her previous visit, she and Falaste had taken a small table at the rear. She seated herself at the same table now. She pushed back her hood and took off her mask.

That day, the two of them had ordered soup. She ordered

soup now, as if performing the ritual gestures of a magical ceremony. And then they had talked, and lost themselves in each other's eyes, and spooned their soup, and waited.

There was no one to talk to now. As for the soup, she could not swallow a mouthful. It was ordinary, perfectly decent bean soup, but the sight and smell revolted her. There was nothing to do but wait. She bowed her head to fix a sightless gaze on the tabletop. She sat motionless, while the schemes spun wildly in her head.

She had no idea how long it was before a shadow glided across the table, and the air moved, and the chair opposite her was suddenly occupied. She looked up to meet intelligent eyes in a bland, utterly nondescript face that she had encountered once before.

"It's you. It worked. You're here," she blurted, amazed.

"Maidenlady Noro Penzia." Lousewort greeted her in his undistinguished, unclassifiable voice. "That copper might have been left by any of several people, but my money was on you."

"Thank you for coming."

"I'm glad to see you at liberty and in good health. Perhaps you're in danger or want, though—it wouldn't be surprising. Is that why you've asked for this meeting?"

"I am in want—of information, above all things. You know that Celisse Rione was executed yesterday morning. Her brother Falaste Rione was not." She waited for his infinitesimal nod, then moistened her dry lips and forced herself to voice the question whose answer might devastate her. "Do you know if he's still alive?"

"Yes. He's alive in the Witch, and treated with exceptional favor, I'm told. Good food, extra blankets, candles, all that. And nary a beating."

Alive. The tears sprang to her eyes. She blinked them away and strove hard to keep her voice steady.

"I don't understand." There was only the slightest quaver. "He was condemned along with his sister. What's happened?"

"I don't know."

"But I thought that the— I mean, I thought that your people know everything."

"Not quite." Lousewort offered a small smile that was bland but somehow sympathetic. "We know a little of what goes on in the Witch, but the Rione situation is as much a mystery to us as it is to you. At least for now. Maybe we'll learn more, in time."

"Does Falaste have time?"

Lousewort shrugged.

"You and the others would do what you can for him, would you not?"

"Gladly. He's one of our best. What do you hope to do— send him a message, perhaps? This is something that might be arranged."

"My plan is a bit more ambitious. I mean to deliver him from the Witch."

"Really." Lousewort's brows rose. "You surprise me, indeed you do. Maidenlady, I admire your spirit and your devotion to our friend, but you must understand that the Witch is impregnable. The rescue of a prisoner is impossible."

"Tricky and dangerous, yes. Impossible, no. I've a plan."

"A plan. Of course. My dear young lady, if the matter were as simple as you seem to believe, do you think *we* wouldn't have come up with a plan, long ago?"

"Perhaps a fresh perspective was required. I've given it a good deal of thought, and I've devised a scheme that might work. I can't carry it out alone, though. That's why I've come to you. I need some people."

"People?"

"A good forger, for one. Then, a few women. Or boys who could dress up as women—either would do. Finally, an apothecary who knows what he's about. Could you get them for me?"

"Why don't I just pull 'em out of my hat? Maidenlady, I don't wish to wound you, but this is madness. You must abandon these dreams and accept reality. There's no plucking a prisoner from the Witch."

"No? Do you remember the last time I was here, Master Lousewort?" Leaning forward in her chair, Jianna eyed him intently. "We talked of Celisse Rione's resolve to remove Anzi Uffrigo. And I spoke up then to say that it was impossible. She was just a young woman on her own, with little of wealth, rank, or resources. She'd never be able to come anywhere near him—I thought. You and Falaste just looked at one another. Those looks expressed your opinion of Celisse. Neither of you dismissed the possibility that she'd somehow overcome all obstacles to achieve her aim. And the two of you were right. She did it, she found a way. If Celisse could do it, then so can I. Understand me, Master Lousewort. With your help or without it, I will save Falaste Rione. I'll find a way."

Lousewort studied her face. His own expression changed. At last he invited, "Tell me about this plan of yours."

Jianna complied.

SEVENTEEN

"What are you mumbling about?" Yvenza demanded, her tone peremptory yet hushed. In the opposite seat slumped Master Innesq Belandor, fast asleep. She preferred that he remain so. Master Innesq habitually employed waxen earplugs to exclude the world, and quiet conversation between his fellow carriage passengers would not disturb his slumber. Nevertheless, she kept her voice subdued.

She might as well have spared herself the trouble. There was no sign of comprehension, much less intelligible response from Nissi. The girl sat beside Innesq, very close but not touching him. The pallid little face was slack, the colorless eyes huge and blind. A thin drone of meaningless noise dribbled from her lips.

"What is this? What's the matter with you?" Leaning forward in her seat, Yvenza snapped her fingers. This produced no result, so she took the small jaw in her hand and jerked it toward herself. Nothing registered in the eyes. Sounds incomprehensible and alien issued from the mouth.

"Stop that. If you can't speak sensibly, then hold your peace."

The girl murmured a few nearly inaudible words that Yvenza strained to capture. Again she might have spared herself the trouble, for Nissi spoke in some language never meant for human ear or tongue.

"What do you hear? What do you see? When you are yourself again, you'll tell me all of it." No knowing when that might be. In the meantime Yvenza leaned back in her seat and stared out the window to watch the trackless hills flowing by.

By all standards of normality, such terrain was unnavigable by carriage. The combined skills of the arcanists in the party, however, had eliminated that difficulty, at least for the present. The six of them had contrived to create a short stretch of smooth, level roadway that somehow remained positioned perpetually beneath the wheels of the party's carriages and wagons. And very odd it was to witness the land resume its natural rugged contours in their wake. The sight never palled.

So they had proved themselves capable of working together, which augured well. Innesq Belandor had displayed a quiet contentment that was in no way affected by the Taerleezi boor Pridisso's attempt to claim the lion's share of credit for himself.

"When?" whispered Nissi, quite clearly.

Yvenza took note.

"Will they speak?" A profound, almost convulsive shudder rocked Nissi's slight frame. She gasped and recovered herself. Her eyes flew to Innesq Belandor, who slept on unaware. She then turned to find Yvenza studying her minutely.

"Tell me," Yvenza commanded.

"They . . . are coming. Soon."

"Who or what comes?"

"They are of It."

"It? The Overmind thing that Innesq speaks of, you mean?"

"They will be . . . seen. They are a . . . face of It, neither flesh nor spirit. They grow stronger. And They will be seen."

"Somebody or something is about to attack us? Is that what you're saying? Are they armed? Are they arcane? How do we kill them?"

"They are coming. Soon."

. . .

The day advanced, and in the late afternoon the shifting stretch of hospitable roadway brought the carriages and wagons to an inky tarn girdled with trees, occupying a natural depression among the surrounding hills. There they halted and set up camp for the night. The roadway under the wheels faded into nothingness, not to resume existence before morning.

It soon became apparent that the site was a treasure trove. The water that appeared so ominously dark was in fact clean and pure. Better yet, the place offered a rich supply of fresh food.

Dusk, and one of the Taerleezi servants drawing water at the tarn spied a small creature burrowing out of the muddy bank. He scooped it up and took a look. The animal resembled a newt, with a moist green-brown skin, stubby little legs, round yellow eyes, and a long, whiplash tail. It was far too small to make a meal, and he was on the point of tossing it aside when he noted a second newt emerging from the mud. And a third. Then more; dozens, scores, hundreds. Within moments, the bank teemed with newly hatched creatures scrambling for the water. Here was more than enough meat to feed the entire party.

They were easy to catch. Scooping them up by the handful, he quickly filled his bucket. While doing so he loosed a distinctive, tremulous whistle that summoned several of his fellow servants, both Corvestri and Belandor. Spying the prize, they ran for buckets of their own. Soon the containers were loaded with wriggling green-brown cargo.

That evening they collaborated on dinner, with Taerleezi and Faerlonnish cooks alike contributing ingredients to the communal pot. It was the first time in days that they were to enjoy fresh meat, and therefore something of an occasion. Ojem Pridisso's servant produced an impressive assortment of vegetables, together with Taerleezi wine to add flavor to the broth. The Faerlonnish chefs brought forth herbs, spices, and dried petals worthy of an aristocratic Vitrisian table. As night fell, a magnificent aroma filled the camp.

For the first time since the journey had begun, all of them were to dine together. There was no table or board large enough to accommodate the entire party, and thus they arranged their various collapsible stands and tray-tables, their jointed stools and folding camp chairs in a close circle about the central cookfire. For once the various households mingled. Even the nationalities mixed—something unprecedented.

Taerleezi Littri Zovaccio was sitting among the Faerlonnish Belandors for the first time. Yvenza and her ward sat at Ojem Pridisso's lavish table, with its new, very white linen cloth and its blindingly polished new silver candelabrum. Young Vinzille Corvestri was there as well, sitting beside Nissi. The Magnifico Vinz Corvestri and his wife sat alone together, served by their own attendants.

The Magnifico Aureste did not wish to observe Corvestri and his lady. Better by far to focus on his own brother Innesq, whose expression communicated exceptional satisfaction. Understandably so. Matters were finally arranging themselves in accordance with the middle Belandor brother's hopes. Aureste suppressed a smile. Innesq, that lifelong recluse, actually appeared to be enjoying himself. Even now, sitting there in the glow of the firelight and striving manfully to engage Littri Zovaccio in conversation, Innesq looked happy.

"Does it not appear to you, Master Zovaccio, that a shared meal of this kind is a particularly agreeable occasion?" Innesq essayed.

Littri Zovaccio inclined his head with a faint, mournful smile.

"We chat, we exchange ideas, we come to know one another, do we not?"

Littri Zovaccio nodded.

"The food and wine, the warmth of the fire, the conviviality—these things lighten the tedium of a long journey."

Zovaccio considered, then nodded.

At least they were not to be subjected to the aural scrape of the Taerleezi accent, Aureste reflected. He decided to help his brother.

"I've heard it rumored that Taerleez now requires her citizens to secure official safe-conduct in order to enter Faerlonne. Is there any truth to this?"

Zovaccio replied with a melancholy shrug.

Dinner arrived, served by a Belandor attendant. Bowls of the collaborative stew were placed before Zovaccio, Aureste, and Innesq.

Aureste swallowed a spoonful, and his brows rose in surprised appreciation. The stew was excellent, as finely flavored and subtly seasoned as anything he might expect to grace his table at home in Vitrisi. The vegetables were varied and perfectly cooked, each retaining a hint of a crunch, while the entire concoction was generously laced with shreds and small chunks of mild, tender white meat. It had been too long since he had tasted fresh meat of any description. He ate with pleasure, then looked up to gauge the reaction of his companions. Littri Zovaccio appeared as content as the lugubrious cast of his features allowed. Innesq, however, was not eating. He sat frowning down at his bowl.

Aureste transmitted an inquiry with his eyes.

"There is something here that troubles me," observed Innesq.

"You've always had a finicking appetite, but there's no cause for complaint here. You can't say it isn't appetizing and well prepared."

"I cannot say so because I have not tasted."

"Grant me patience. You don't like the way it *looks*?"

"I do not. What is in this dish?"

"I'm not certain. I think it's frogs or some such thing that the lads caught by the gross. They were altogether delighted with themselves. Do *you* know what this is?" Aureste addressed the question to Zovaccio.

Zovaccio shook his head.

Aureste raised a finger, and a servant was instantly at his side.

"What is the principal ingredient in this dish?" he inquired.

"Newts, so please you, Magnifico. Leastways that's what

we think. Maybe salamanders. Some were saying four-legged water worms."

"Are there any left whole?" asked Innesq.

"Plenty, Master Innesq. We're keeping a bucket of 'em alive in water, so they'll be good and fresh for breakfast."

"Bring me one, if you please."

The servant bowed and retired. Moments later he was back, small creature in hand. Innesq took the animal and examined it closely. His face changed.

The alteration caught Aureste's full attention. Never in all his life had he witnessed his brother's serenity so violently transformed. Never had he beheld such a look of unalloyed dismay, even horror, upon Innesq's face.

"Do not eat," Innesq commanded.

Aureste and Zovaccio set down their spoons at once.

"Poisonous?" Aureste demanded. One hand instinctively moved to press his belly. No fires burning there—yet.

"Worse." Bending from his wheeled chair, Innesq set the captive amphibian gently down on the ground, and watched it scuttle for the shadows. He straightened. "These creatures are the young of the Sishmindri. They have laid their eggs in this quiet spot."

"Oh?" *Is that all?* "But the meat—it's not toxic?"

"I believe not. But what of that? Surely you would not knowingly consume the flesh of their children?"

"Well. I must confess, I never considered it." Frowning, Aureste regarded his dinner. He thought of the adult Sishmindris of Belandor House, with their inscrutable golden eyes, their expressionless faces, their coincidental outward resemblance to humankind, and a spontaneous revulsion bubbled inside him. He managed to rise above it. "The creatures are far too valuable to put to such use. I'd hardly venture to guess the worth of tonight's stew pot—it's an extravagant feast indeed. That being so, we must savor it to the fullest."

"You do not mean that. Aureste, Aureste, these are intelligent beings. Do you not understand?"

"Many creatures upon which we feed possess a certain measure of intelligence, or instinct that doubles as intelligence. We devour them with pleasure, all the same. Mind you, I'm not in favor of employing Sishmindris as cattle—inasmuch as they refuse to breed in captivity, the concept is impractical. All I say here and now is that we possess a tasty pot of very costly stew, and it would be a great shame to let it go to waste. Come, reason favors me. You know this."

His brother cast a pained glance that Aureste hardly allowed himself to see. The thing was done. Innesq would have to reconcile himself.

Innesq did nothing of the sort. For the first time in all his retiring life, he lifted his voice to address a gathering.

"Friends, colleagues, fellow travelers, attend me if you will. We have unwittingly committed a grievous error."

His oratorical inexperience never revealed itself. His words winged strongly through the firelight.

"We have slaughtered hundreds of young Sishmindris. There is no undoing this, and the deed must lie heavy upon every conscience. But we need not add to our offenses. Let us stop now. Release the captive hatchlings, let them seek the shelter of the tarn. As for those already slain—pour the pot out upon the ground, let the dead merge with the soil, as nature intended, and then let us ask forgiveness. We cannot truly make amends, but this is the least we can do."

His words reached the ears of all, and registered in the eyes of all. But the listeners' reactions were difficult to judge. There was no immediate reply, and the fraught silence lengthened.

Into that silence smashed a massive volley of rocks. They flew from the darkness beyond the fire, and they were well aimed. One of the Taerleezi chefs engaged in ladling out stew was struck squarely in the temple. He fell without a sound, bowl and ladle dropping from his hand. Cries arose as stones thudded into heads, limbs, and torsos. One of the Corvestri servants went down, face bloodied. A whizzing missile grazed

Aureste's shoulder, and he loosed a curse lost in a sudden great gust of noise. A huge cacophony of hoots, croaks, grunts, and hisses arose on all sides. The invisible attacker unmistakably surrounded them.

For the moment no spoken command could be heard, but the Belandor bodyguards were well trained. Already they were grabbing for their crossbows and forming a circle, backs to the fire. The Pridisso and Zovaccio servants were there beside them. The Corvestri attendants, less efficient, were fumbling for their weapons. A rock struck one of them in the right arm, and the bow fell from a suddenly useless hand.

Aureste's eyes turned instinctively toward Sonnetia Corvestri. An attendant was hurrying her toward the shelter of the Corvestri carriage. She was being properly looked after. He turned to Innesq, who met his regard with an infinitesimal nod. The message was clear. His brother could and would employ arcane power in defense of the expedition. No doubt his fellow arcanists were similarly willing. But even among the most accomplished, results were far from instantaneous. They needed to fortify and prepare themselves. The mental exertion itself was often prolonged, and during this period they remained vulnerable. In the meantime, the rocks were flying.

Drawing a short-bladed sword, Aureste planted himself solidly before Innesq.

The croaks and hoots reached an impassioned crescendo. Out of the blackness beneath the trees erupted a mob of furious Sishmindris. They were broad and brawny, smooth of skin and flat of skull, with eyes of molten gold. They wore no garments of mankind, but did not disdain the weapons of men. Many bore slings, in whose use they had already demonstrated formidable proficiency. Others carried heavy clubs, sharpened wooden stakes, even chunks of stone chipped to an edge and bound to wooden handles.

Never had the Magnifico Aureste beheld Sishmindris bearing arms, although he had heard rumors of such in Vitrisi. Even without the rumors, however, he would not have been entirely surprised. The cowardice and docility of the Sishmin-dri nature were widely regarded as axiomatic, but a portion of his mind had always harbored suspicion. Something in him had recognized amphibian treachery.

Deceitful and duplicitous they might be, but still no match for men, and he would have expected little difficulty in defeating them, but for their numbers and their fury. There was no counting them. They were everywhere, on all sides, stabbing and smashing with their sticks and stones; crude weapons, but remarkably effective at close range. Only a few feet away, one of the Taerleezi servants fell beneath the onslaught and disappeared, instantly enveloped in a blur of flailing greenish limbs. To his left, one of his own men went down, pierced clear through with a sharpened wooden stake. Aureste found himself attacked by two of the creatures. He killed them both, and knew a moment's incredulity, for nothing in his past could have prepared him for the necessity of soiling his sword with the blood of Sishmindris. No time now to ponder the indignity, for another was upon him, swinging mightily at his skull with a club the thickness of a small tree. There was no parrying such a blow, so he dodged with nearly the agility of earlier years, lunged, and drove his blade deep into amphibian vitals. The creature's death cry was lost in the great surrounding din of croaking rage.

Aureste chanced a quick glance behind him, where Innesq sat motionless in his wheeled chair, eyes open and unseeing, face empty and at peace. He had seen that look many times and knew its meaning. Innesq was elsewhere.

A new note colored the uproar, a surge of excitement or triumph. His glance discovered the source. A hooting troop had taken possession of one of the supply wagons. Now they were emptying it, hurling sacks, barrels, and hampers off into the darkness, presumably into the arms of unseen confederates.

A rock streaking in at an angle missed him by inches, but clanged loudly on the metal frame of Innesq's chair. The rock was followed by a burly mottled female, stone ax uplifted, staccato cries bursting from her wide-open mouth. He halted her with a stroke that nearly severed her head from her body.

Something pale slipped weightlessly along the edge of his vision, circling toward his brother. He spun, prepared to kill, and confronted the girl Nissi. She was kneeling beside Innesq, clutching one of his lax hands in both of her own. Her uncanny eyes were closed, her pallid little face calm and still. Only her lips moved soundlessly in the midst of the tumult. No threat there, quite the contrary. Their conjoined power was greater than the sum of its parts. And the other arcanists—were they similarly engaged? His eyes swept the firelit circle, but he caught no sight of the Corvestris or either of the Taerleezis. Something like doubt or misgiving shot through him. He realized then that arcane intervention was essential. Without it, the vastly outnumbered humans would be overwhelmed—by Sishmindris, of all things.

A concerted assault took down another two of the ill-trained Corvestri guards. There was an obvious weak spot in the human line of defense, and the attackers bore down on it. He could marshal the guards if he could reach them, but a hissing enemy advance upon Innesq kept Aureste pinned. There were two, then four. They had clubs, and one of them wielded a steel blade presumably snatched from some dead man's hand.

A precise horizontal stroke sliced a Sishmindri throat, and a jet of alien blood sprayed Aureste's face. As he wheeled to plunge his sword into the nearest greenish belly, a glancing blow clipped his ribs, and his lungs seemed to freeze. For an endless moment he struggled to breathe. A sharpened stake drove at his midsection, and he shifted a slow, lead-weighted blade to parry the thrust. Another thrust, another parry, and still he could not catch his breath.

If he died now, Innesq would follow in an instant, and then all the others. *Sonnetia*.

It was going to happen. He could not defeat the amphibians. There were too many of them.

The Belandor guard fighting beside him fell, skull crushed. Croaking Sishmindris converged on the fresh break in the human circle.

He willed his lungs to expand and to fill with air. He willed his arm to greater speed and strength. For some seconds it worked, and twice more his sword thrust home. But renewal was brief, and he soon found his breath coming in gasps.

It might have been misperception, a trick of rushing blood and heated exertions, but it seemed to him then that the air he gulped down into his lungs was exceptionally cold. The atmosphere throughout the journey had rasped with the raw chill of early springtime, but now it stabbed with winter's malice. The sweat on his forehead was icy.

It was not imagination. The air had chilled to freezing in seconds. Despite violent exercise, his teeth were starting to chatter. The fingers of his gloveless hands were losing sensation.

The effect of the change upon the cold-blooded, unclothed Sishmindris was profound and immediate. Within seconds their energy flagged, their movements slowed, and they became delightfully easy to kill. Aureste dispatched several with gusto. His spirits, always resilient, had rebounded fully, and he enjoyed reinvigoration. When his latest adversary attempted to retreat, predatory instinct drove him forward a few paces in pursuit, and the air about him warmed and softened at once. Instantly he drew back to the frigid zone. No question, of course, what had happened. A bubble of freezing atmosphere—uncomfortable to warm-blooded humans, paralyzing to amphibians—had been created by arcane art. Innesq's art, or else Innesq's and Nissi's. Or perhaps the others, wherever they were, had joined in. It wasn't clear, and it didn't matter. The Sishmindris had been thwarted.

They had the wit to recognize as much themselves. Their wild vociferation sank to bitter hoots. They fell back. A low, maledictory hissing accompanied their retreat.

It was over. The campsite lay in shambles, littered with the dead bodies of men and Sishmindris. Aureste turned to his brother.

Innesq was again present and aware, albeit pale and drained. His eyes traveled the corpse-strewn vista and closed briefly. A muted whimper caught his attention, and he looked down to discover Nissi crouched beside his chair, arms wrapped tightly around herself. Her shoulders were shaking, and tears gushed from her eyes. He touched her spindrift hair consolingly.

"Innesq, what have you—" Aureste began. His brother's imperative gesture silenced him.

As Innesq wheeled his chair about, Nissi rose to her feet. She wrapped her hand in a fold of his cloak. Together they retreated in silence.

Aureste shrugged. Innesq was always exhausted and often melancholy in the aftermath of arcane endeavor. He would recover soon enough; he always did. In the meantime, practical concerns pressed. The chattering of his teeth and the numbness of his fingers told him that the frigid bubble enclosing the camp remained in place. Uncomfortable, but advantageous; so long as it lasted, they were safe from any renewed Sishmindri assault. There was time to muster the remaining able-bodied guards, post fresh sentries, patch and bandage the wounded, assess losses. These matters occupied Aureste's attention throughout ensuing hours. During that time, he glimpsed not a single arcanist of the group. Probably they had all contributed to the creation of the bubble, and now all required rest and quiet. Saving his own brother, he could happily have dispensed with them altogether, for they were an alien, peculiar, and generally unappealing lot. They had their uses, though—no denying that. But for arcane intervention upon this night, the peevish Sishmindris would surely have slaughtered the entire party.

And Sonnetia Corvestri? Nowhere in evidence. Probably safe in the family carriage along with her husband and son. That was certainly where she ought to be, but the thought was disagreeable. With some effort, Aureste pushed her face out of his mind. He worked on, and the hours passed. During that time he learned that the supply wagon despoiled by the Sishmindris belonged to the Corvestris, and it had contained all the provisions that the family had carried from Vitrisi.

In the last declining hours of the night, he managed to snatch a few hours of uneasy sleep. Around dawn a sentry roused him to report the dissipation of the cold bubble. The air formerly enclosed had resumed the composition and temperature of the surrounding atmosphere. Aureste rose and emerged from his tent to find that it was true. Early spring had returned, but the amphibians had not done likewise; at least, not for now.

The dawn was rising and the camp was stirring. The rose-gold light illumined neatly segregated stacks of dead men and dead Sishmindris. In all likelihood, some maudlin element among the survivors would agitate for traditional burial—a waste of time and resources that he would personally oppose. His eyes traveled on, coming to rest upon the empty Corvestri supply wagon. The Magnifico Vinz was likely to go hungry, now. This prospect would hardly have troubled Aureste, but for its inevitable corollary. Should Vinz Corvestri starve, so, too, starved his wife Sonnetia, as well as that adolescent brat she valued so highly.

Well, it was up to Vinz Corvestri to provide for his own family. Probably one or another of the travelers could sell him some supplies. The Taerleezis carried more than they could reasonably expect to consume.

Vinz Corvestri could scarcely afford to purchase anything from anybody. The Corvestri fortunes had dwindled long ago, and the proceeds from the sale of his wife's jewelry had gone elsewhere.

His arcane talents then. Surely they would serve to replenish the family larder.

His arcane talents, such as they were, must be conserved and dedicated to the collective endeavor. The purpose was all.

Aureste could almost hear Innesq's voice in his mind. He shook his head. His conclusions were regrettable but unavoidable.

When the camp was fully awake, he sought out Littri Zovaccio, by far the less offensive of the Taerleezi arcanists. He offered a proposal, and Zovaccio's nod conveyed definite acceptance. The Taerleezi arcanist would replenish the Corvestri supplies at a nominal price affordable to Vinz Corvestri. The difference between Vinz's meager contribution and the true sale price would be made up discreetly by the Magnifico Aureste.

He could only pray that Sonnetia would never find out about it.

The prayer might have been answered, had the transaction not been witnessed by a Taerleezi servant, who carried the news straight to the Magnifica Yvenza Belandor, and received a double handful of nuts and raisins in reward.

. . .

The morning departure was delayed by the burial of the slain human guards; a nicety demanded by certain vehemently sentimental members of the group. The digging of the communal grave, the mass interment, and performance of modest obsequies were extravagantly wasteful of time. But the proponents of burial were immovable, and debate pointless. The task was performed, the hours sacrificed. The most eloquent advocate in the world, however, could not have secured similar consideration in behalf of the dead Sishmindris. The amphibian bodies were left exposed to the elements, lying where they had been stacked.

Nobody ventured to suggest drying or salting a quantity of their meat.

Vinz Corvestri observed the proceedings with mild interest. The previous evening's exertions had left him depleted and listless. He had not taken part in the creation of the protective atmospheric bubble—that had been almost entirely the work of Innesq Belandor and Nissi. He had, however, contributed much to the essential maintenance and repair efforts, and he had done it on the spur of the moment, without recourse to artificial stimulants or enhancements of any kind. Difficult enough at any time, but he had worked effectively under the very worst of circumstances. He had good reason to be pleased with himself, and even more reason to be pleased with Vinzille, whose apparently boundless youthful energy had proved invaluable.

The group arcane effort had saved the expedition, but success had come at a price particularly burdensome to the Corvestri members. They had lost two of their guards, and all of their provisions. For a little while it had seemed inevitable that precious arcane energy must be used to replenish supplies. But then, quite unexpectedly, Littri Zovaccio had approached and tendered a written offer to furnish adequate victuals at a very moderate price. It had seemed a stroke of remarkably good fortune, and Vinz could only assume that these Taerleezi arcanists were more in need of ready cash than they were willing to admit. He had paid readily, and his despoiled wagon had been refilled.

The burial was completed. The shifting stretch of roadway was reconstituted, and the journey resumed.

The road beneath the wheels was impossibly smooth, and the ordinary jolting motion of the carriage softened to a not unpleasant vibration. Still deeply tired, Vinz drifted into slumber, and slept for an indeterminate span. He woke to find himself alone in a stationary vehicle. They had paused to water the horses. His wife and son were nowhere in evidence; presumably they had chosen not to disturb his well-deserved rest. The quality of the light told him that at least a couple of hours had passed.

He stretched and blinked. His fatigue had abated. He was awake, alert, and—for the first time that day—a little hungry. He climbed out of the carriage and surveyed his surroundings. The air was almost free of mist, and he could see clearly in all directions. They had come to the summit of a modest rise dwarfed by surrounding hills of greater height and girth. The sharp slopes were clothed in last year's brown-chalk garments of dead meecherhaven, zexxit, and woody tuphinney. Bright new growth poked through the countless rents in the drab mantle, and patches of green reared themselves everywhere. Here and there the low stands of early bellafrice beckoned like pools of blue water. In the hollow spreading below the rise, the dark conifers clustered like conspirators. Beyond them, the hills rose steep and stony.

Vinz stood motionless for a moment, clearing his mind of conscious resistance, opening the mental door a provocative crack, perceptions attuned to the slightest alien touch. There was none. The Overmind was not with him or in him, for now.

He expelled his pent breath in a sigh, half disappointed, half relieved. His stomach made its presence felt, and he remembered that he wanted food. Those provisions he had purchased from Littri Zovaccio must include some flatbread, or dried fruit, or something that could be wolfed without benefit of preparation. His eyes shifted to the Corvestri supply wagon. In between it and himself loomed the Dowager Magnifica Yvenza Belandor. She was making straight for him, striding vigorously, radiating buoyant good cheer.

Vinz's brows bent. He did not wish to deal with Yvenza Belandor at the moment. Not that he disliked her. She seemed an amiable creature, and her gracious formality struck him as engagingly quaint. Just now, however, he wanted to eat. No, it was something more than that. For some reason, her purposeful advance struck a chord of uneasiness, even dread within him. He could hardly account for it.

No escape without obvious rudeness, however.

On she came, all smiles, so affable and cordial that his own ill nature shamed him. He produced a smile of suitable warmth.

"Magnifico Corvestri." She halted before him. "Well met, sir. I have been longing for the opportunity to express my gratitude. But for your skill, your courage and coolness of yester-day evening, the Sishmindris would surely have murdered us all."

"Ah, Magnifica, you grant me credit far beyond my merit. Last night's arcane defense was a shared effort. Should any one of us deserve special recognition, it is surely Innesq Belandor." Despite his perfectly truthful disclaimer, Vinz warmed to the praise. It was good to be appreciated, even by an aging woman of no importance. He had been starved for appreciation, he realized. He received little enough at home. He regarded Yvenza with a kindlier eye.

"You are overly humble, sir." She shook her head in mock reproof. "You refuse to acknowledge your own excellence."

Excellence. How much he wanted to believe it, in the face of all evidence to the contrary! He could feel his lips stretching into a smile.

"Well. I do what I can," he returned, with a becomingly modest shrug. "And you, madam? How did you fare, last night?"

"Well enough. My natural terror was offset by my faith in the talents of men such as yourself, Magnifico. And behold, my confidence was not misplaced. You defeated our enemies, and most of us—for I would not have it said that I forget the loss of the brave guards—most of us survived to greet a new day offering twofold joy."

"Twofold?" Vinz was a little puzzled. Her expression of benevolent gratification threatened imminent sermonizing.

"To be sure. Last night, we withstood the attack of the Sishmindri marauders. And today witnesses the defeat of an enemy more insidious and perhaps more dangerous. I refer, of course, to internal dissension."

"Dissension?"

"Long-standing enmity. We have spoken of it in the past, more than once. Thus I am confident that your pleasure in this morning's fulfillment of our shared hopes equals my own."

"Forgive me, but I don't understand you."

"Come, come, Magnifico. It's no secret. For my own part, I'd gladly shout the news to all the world that the ancient feud between our two Houses has ended at last—and I hope, forever."

"The feud? Yes, I'd be perfectly happy to end it. I see no sense to it. But it's one thing to be willing, and another to actually—"

"But it is done, sir. Surely the Magnifico Aureste Belandor's large gesture of friendship admits of no other interpretation."

"Gesture? What gesture? What do you mean?"

"His replenishment of the Corvestri provisions stolen by the Sishmindris last night. What could be more gracious or open-handed?"

"You are misinformed, Magnifica. I'm sorry to dash your hopes, but I myself purchased supplies directly from Littri Zovaccio."

"Ah, you contributed something to the price? Excellent. That makes it all the more a joint endeavor between our two reconciled Houses."

"You mistake the matter. Zovaccio and I arranged the transaction. Aureste Belandor had nothing to do with it."

"Indeed?" Yvenza appeared astonished. "The Taerleezi servants tell a different story, and they should certainly know. If I may be so bold, Magnifico—how much did you pay Master Zovaccio?"

Vinz named the sum.

"Forgive me, but does that not seem a remarkably low price for all that you received?"

"How should I know? I am no household steward. What have I to do with the price of meal and onions?" An oddly sickening doubt was stirring to life at the pit of his stomach.

"Ah, Magnifico Vinz. I see that the best of intentions and circumstances do not prevent all misunderstanding. You should know, then—since it's spoken of freely about the camp—that the diostres you turned over to Littri Zovaccio amounted to a modest percentage of the sale price. The balance was paid by the Magnifico Aureste. I tell you this in order to impress upon you the genuine warmth of Aureste's new-minted friendship."

"No." Vinz shook his head. "Untrue, madam. There's no friendship between Aureste and me, and never could be. We might end the quarrel between our two Houses, achieving peace and civility, but nothing more. He has no reason to perform such a service for me."

"For your lady wife, then?" Yvenza appeared earnestly eager to solve the mystery. "She has long striven to repair the breach between Houses Corvestri and Belandor. Everyone among us has remarked upon her eagerness to seek out the Magnifico Aureste, to walk and to talk with him, apart from all others. It might be said that she has launched a full assault, and certainly she has conquered. Her charm and determination have overcome his resistance. He is her subject now, bound to undertake all in his power to please her. Almost single-handedly she has defeated the rancor of generations. Honor your wife, Magnifico—she is a most triumphant lady!"

The cold doubt at the bottom of his stomach was expanding. *Everyone among us has remarked upon her eagerness to seek out the Magnifico Aureste.* Her eagerness had manifested itself before the journey had ever begun. She had sought him out in Belandor House itself. And now, her behavior had drawn attention. People were talking about it. Laughing? If it was all true—if Aureste Belandor had indeed subsidized the purchase of provisions, for the sake of the Magnifica Sonnetia—then there was really only one conclusion to be drawn. Vinz's intestines writhed violently. The Magnifica Yvenza was smiling with an air of pleased expectation. Evidently a reply was required.

He said something or other to her—he hardly knew what. Then, his recent hunger completely forgotten, he stumbled blindly back to his carriage, with Yvenza's helpful admonition ringing in his ears.

"Ask your lady wife, Magnifico. She will be proud to explain the nature of her power over Aureste Belandor."

Ask his wife. Not a bad idea.

The journey resumed. Vinz Corvestri sat in his carriage, studying the face of the Magnifica Sonnetia, who sat opposite him. And he found himself wondering, as he had so very often wondered during the course of their married life, exactly what went on behind the fine features and the sylvan greenish eyes. It was not the moment to ask, however. Sometimes Vinzille shared carriage space with his parents; sometimes he preferred to ride horseback. Today he was in the carriage, and his presence precluded potentially disruptive conversation.

Sonnetia had her writing box open in her lap. She was engaged in musical composition, one of her favorite diversions. Absorbed in her work, she did not at first notice her husband's fixed regard. Presently, however, she twitched as if she felt an insect crawling on her skin, and looked up sharply to meet his unblinking eyes. Her brows rose in polite inquiry. He said nothing, and she returned to her work. Twice more during the next hour she looked up to discover him watching her. He said nothing, and after that, she ignored him.

Time passed as it had passed for what was beginning to seem endless days. The long, tedious hours in the carriage were enlivened from time to time by conversation with Vinzille, usually revolving about the technicalities of arcane procedure. Such discussions were enjoyable, but could not be sustained continually, and there were vast silent stretches that had to be filled with small pastimes, eating, and sleeping. He did not want to eat, and he could not sleep. No pastime could capture his interest. He sat and watched his wife.

Throughout the day there were periodic rest stops for the benefit of horses and humans. During such intervals Sonnetia and Vinzille invariably quitted the carriage. Vinzille was driven forth by an excess of youthful energy, while Sonnetia— she was glad of the chance to get away from him. Or so Vinz's suspicions ran. He would watch until her green-cloaked figure disappeared from view, then settle back in his seat with a sigh. He would not stoop to follow or spy on her. She might speak with anyone she pleased. She might step out of sight into the nearest grove or thicket and meet with . . . anyone. She might return to the Corvestri carriage—or not.

She always did return, though.

The day wore down to a nubbin. The tired sun sagged in the sky, and they halted to make camp. Darkness fell, the air chilled, and the space about them shrank to the diameter of a firelit circle. There was dinner to endure, and then a span of diffuse activity, and then at last he was alone with his wife in their tent. It was a fairly spacious tent, high enough to permit upright posture, and thus suitable to the dignity of a magnifico of Vitrisi. It contained two narrow cots, well blanketed, a small washstand, and a single small oil lamp. There were no luxuries, however—no partitions or compartments, no special lights or furnishings, no rare oils or perfumes, no remarkable refreshments. Quite simply, he could not afford such things. Others might afford them—Aureste certainly could—but what of that? Creature comforts were never truly important—or shouldn't be.

At last he could talk to her.

She was bent over the washstand, her back to him. She had stripped down to her shift for the night, but had wrapped a blanket about herself for warmth or concealment. All he could see was a long curve of dark wool and a tumble of auburn hair.

"Magnifica." He cleared his throat.

"Sir?" She turned to face him with her customary courtesy.

"I trust you traveled comfortably today?"

"As comfortably as a carriage allows."

"And you ate well? The provisions supplied by Master Zovaccio were adequately filling and nourishing?"

"Yes, of course."

"I hope so, inasmuch as those provisions came at a higher price than I ever dreamed. But perhaps you already know that."

"Magnifico?" Her expression was uncomprehending.

"Perhaps you already know that the purchase price of the supplies was largely borne by Aureste Belandor."

"By Aureste? Are you certain? Where did you hear such a thing?"

"Oh, it's spoken of freely about the camp. I daresay I'm the last to know."

"Not quite the last. This is the first time I've heard of it."

"Is it? Is it indeed? That's rather remarkable, madam, in view of the warm friendship you've cultivated with that man. Why, I'd have thought that the two of you tell each other everything."

"I don't understand you. What has put such thoughts into your head?"

"It's common knowledge. That shouldn't surprise you. You've not exactly striven for discretion."

"What need? True, I've spoken to Aureste Belandor from time to time since the journey began. Where's the harm in that?"

"Oh, no harm at all, certainly no harm, if you care nothing for your own reputation, or your marriage vows, or the honor of your House, or your son's welfare."

"But this is fantastic. You aren't seriously suggesting—"

"I am suggesting that Aureste Belandor must have good reason to pay for the food that you eat. He's not renowned for his altruism."

"Magnifico, listen to me. You distress yourself needlessly. I know nothing about the sale of provisions, but I know something of the Magnifico Aureste—"

"A triumph of understatement."

"He may not be renowned for altruism, but he's not incapable of generosity, and—if all of this is true—then I believe that his motives in this case are good. Still, if you're unwilling to accept the favor, then you might offer to repay him. If that isn't convenient here and now, then give him a note."

"Do you imagine that I'd place myself in debt to Aureste Belandor, of all men?"

"By your own reckoning, you're already in his debt."

"Not by my own will! It was done by stealth, without my knowledge or consent. The extent of *your* knowledge isn't clear, but one thing is. That man would never have put forth such sums save in payment for what he has enjoyed, or what he expects to enjoy."

"You insult me." Sonnetia's face froze. "You insult me without justice or reason. And your suggestions are vile."

"If my words are vile, then how much the worse are your actions?"

"I have never wronged you, never in all these years. You've no cause and no right to accuse me."

"No cause? I should like to believe that, but you stand compromised. Perhaps you are honest, but appearances suggest otherwise, to me and to others. You are my wife, and I'm still willing to trust in you, but the appearances must be altered. First and foremost, you are never to speak to Aureste Belandor again. You will not address another spoken or written word to him throughout the remainder of this journey. If he speaks to you, you will not answer. When we return to Vitrisi, the prohibition remains in effect. This course will display your virtue, and thereafter any tarnish darkening your reputation will be polished away by the hand of time. Now swear yourself to silence, and prove your constancy."

"I have nothing to prove." Her voice was very low. She was staring at him, and her expression was singular. "The character of my entire life speaks for itself."

"Well, then." Vinz hesitated. "Give me your assurance, then."

"First you forbid me to speak to Innesq Belandor, on pain of arcane enforcement. Now I am not permitted to speak to

Aureste. What next, Magnifico? Shall I be forbidden communication with servants? Acquaintances? Friends? Family members?"

"This is a hysterical exaggeration. My decision is based on sound reason. I expect your compliance."

"You shall not have it. Understand here and now that I will speak to anyone I choose, whenever or wherever I choose, and I will say whatever I choose. You do not rule my thoughts or my speech, you never have and never shall. And if you attempt to constrain me by arcane force, then we will see what our fellow travelers have to say about it."

It was incredible. She had never openly defied him before. He had thought her too well bred ever to do it. For a moment, Vinz found himself at a loss. He looked at her white, set face, and for the first time saw undisguised, unequivocal hostility there. *And disdain?* He did not know what to do, but one thing was clear—he must be strong.

"You're my wife. Must I remind you of your duty? You'll respect my authority."

"I respect legitimate authority when it is not abused."

"Oh, and you've grown so wise, you'll judge when to obey and when to balk? You'll be a proper wife—*when it suits you?*"

"A proper wife isn't to be mistaken for a beast of burden."

"This is absurd. I hope you won't oblige me to resort to threats and coercion; such things lower us both. For the sake of your own good name, and the welfare of our son, I demand only your promise to break off all communication with Aureste Belandor, a notorious character. Now then, madam?"

" 'For the welfare of our son'? Your tyranny clothes itself in hypocrisy. I've already told you, my thoughts and speech are my own. I'll employ both as I see fit."

"I see that you are lost to decency and honor. But I'll not allow you to smirch the name of House Corvestri. I want your promise of obedience here and now, else there will be no choice at all but to take steps. Yes, steps. I'll do it, too. I'll do what must be done to protect the family name. Do you understand me?"

"Oh, yes. I understand you perfectly. I understand your doubts and your terrors. I am sorry for you, but my life is no longer hostage to your weakness. Those days are over. I am my own mistress."

"Or Aureste Belandor's?"

She did not trouble to answer, but regarded him with a faint, pitying smile. The smile was unendurable. He slapped her face.

He had not intended to do it. His arm seemed to have moved of its own accord.

Sonnetia pressed a hand to her reddening cheek. For a moment she stood staring at him with an incredulity that matched his own. Then, pausing only long enough to snatch up a satchel of her belongings, she made for the exit.

"Where are you going?" Vinz asked.

"To sleep in the carriage."

"Unnecessary. You are making too much of this." *I'm sorry! Forgive me! Don't go!* he wanted to plead. But his tongue seemed endowed with a perverse will of its own, just as his arm had been, a moment earlier, and the words refused to emerge.

"I prefer it. I do not wish to sleep near you. I will never share a bed or sleeping quarters with you again." With that, she was gone.

Vinz sat on the edge of his cot, blindly regarding the canvas exit through which his wife had passed. For a time he seemed frozen, and felt nothing at all. Then the ice cracked and broke. *She was not coming back*. He recognized the significance of that brief but calamitous exchange, and misery filled him, but stronger than misery was rage. Not at Sonnetia, she was not to blame. He reserved his anger for the person truly responsible for all his woes.

Aureste Belandor. Always.

Perhaps she would bypass the carriage and go directly to him.

Vinz was almost startled to discover the intensity of his own hatred. It was vast and consuming, ravening inside him like some great beast. He had always hated Aureste, but never before had the hatred owned him.

He must find some outlet, else the hatred would eat him alive from the inside out. He considered. So often he had contemplated a world free of Aureste Belandor, and the thought had brought peace and joy. He had attempted to achieve that beautiful ambition upon one occasion, and failed through sheer mischance. It was time to try again.

The Magnifico Aureste was no arcanist. He was not essential to the success of the expedition. They could all do quite well without him.

It would be easy enough to remove him—any stout lad among the Corvestri guards could do the job. The trick would be to eliminate Aureste in such a manner that no suspicion could fall upon the Magnifico Vinz. Not Sonnetia's suspicion, and certainly not Innesq's. It must appear natural—an accident, perhaps, with nobody to blame. Any arcanism employed must go undetected by an entire gathering of accomplished arcanists. A challenge, to be sure, but not an impossibility.

Vinz sat motionless and blind to his surroundings, while the dark thoughts swirled in his head.

EIGHTEEN

Grix Orlazzu came to an open, flat stretch of ground, and there he paused. The scene before him was indistinct, half lost in the perpetual mists of the northern Wraithlands. He could descry an expanse of hardy, drab ground cover interspersed with rocks and patches of bare dirt; a dim palisade of dark conifers edging the clearing; and beyond, the suggestion of lofty hills. Little enough to see, but it was not with his fallible eyes that he was likely to view reality.

Drawing a deep breath, he closed his eyes and opened his mind. No stimulants or fortifications were required in this place; he had not needed them of late. The extrasensory perceptions poured in freely.

Energy roared through the soil, the vegetation, the water, and the air. It sang through his brain and danced along his veins. His surroundings almost glowed with power, so intense that he could only conclude that the slow, immutable underground circuit had carried the Source to this very spot; that it rotated upon its great axis directly below. Its proximity elated and awed him. He might almost have imagined himself merging with that great originator of power, losing his individual identity and becoming part of it, but for the odd sense of discord. It was as if he were hearing a mighty chorus sung slightly off key, and the wrongness jangled his nerves.

There was more. There was still the Other, always the Other, but now expressing Itself ever more insistently as They.

Many times he had nearly glimpsed Them with his eyes open. With his eyes closed and his mind receptive, They were closer yet, but still indefinite as to size and shape. He dreaded Them deeply, yet ached for knowledge. Here he sensed himself trembling on the brink of great revelation, and the lure was irresistible.

Orlazzu opened his eyes, and the vibrant hidden world faded. *They* receded as well, but reluctantly, and not far. He cogitated briefly and reached his decision. This desolate spot, seemingly quiet and empty, reeked to the arcane skies of power, purpose, and danger. If he chose to remain, the risks were great. He would need to construct solid fortifications, and he would need to maintain ceaseless vigilance; a daunting prospect. And yet the potential rewards—the insight, the knowledge, the understanding of the Source's essential nature—were too great to forgo. It might end in disaster, but he would make the experiment. He could hardly stop himself.

Accordingly Orlazzu prepared himself, ingesting a trio of lozenges. The task he contemplated was considerable. The power charging the atmosphere, though significant, was not enough in itself to sustain him—he needed more. He had not resorted to mental enhancement of any kind in days, and now the effect of a large dose was intense.

His mind broke free of its mundane shell, sprouted vast pinions, and flew. His trained power, heightened by means of the lozenges, buoyed by the energy infusing his surroundings, had never seemed so huge and so certain. The sense of rushing flight and unbridled potency was intoxicating. But for the discipline of a lifetime, he might have lost himself in stupid delight.

But discipline ruled yet. He steadied his breath, regulated his heartbeat, and prepared to commence creation of a vertical shaft destined to access an impregnable, stone-walled underground burrow.

Before the first yard of dirt and rock had been removed, however, an impingement caught his attention. His focus continued intact, but his vision shifted and he beheld a couple of undead humans standing a few feet away, staring at him with their milky eyes. Both male, barely covered in moldering rags; their age, condition, and origin unknowable.

His enhanced vision recognized vehicles of the Other—not nearly as pure and true as They, but capable of effecting Its desires. And It could hardly relish his presence in this place.

Orlazzu contained his surprise. He had seen animals of various species inhabited by the Other. He had seen a Sishmindri— an intelligent quasi-man—afflicted with the plague. But this was his first glimpse of truly human undead.

They were hideous and sad. Human bodies ought never to be subjected to such indignities. They were his own kind, and their exploitation represented his own potential ruin, together with that of every other man, woman, and child of the Veiled Isles. Moreover, they were dangerous. They would infect and absorb him, if they could.

No matter. He could rule them. A strong flick of his intellect shoved the undead pair back into the mists. They were out of sight, but hardly gone.

He could keep them out. Likewise he could keep Them out, and It out. Not easily, not without recourse to his best abilities, but he was equal to the challenge.

His full attention returned to the task at hand. Much remained to complete before the end of the day. Grix Orlazzu's mind embraced the Source, and excavation recommenced.

. . .

The dim and tangled neighborhood of Vitrisi known as the Briar Patch had long been recognized as the haunt of rogue Sishmindris. Here the fugitive escapees from plague-stricken palace, mansion, and town house had sought refuge and a kind of safety in numbers. Here they had banded together and, under the leadership of the great amphibian calling himself Aazaargh, they had established a tiny enclave of their own, which they defended with vigor and determination. There was nothing remotely secure, much less legal in their occupation of the Briar Patch. They had gone largely unchallenged by the forces of human order for two reasons. The first—that the maze-like warren they now regarded as their

own was difficult to attack and easy to defend. The second—
that the troops of the Deputy Governor Gorza were largely
busied with the struggle to control the riotous human element
of the city; the resistance fanatics, the ordinary criminal
predators, the desperate and unhinged, the infectious diseased, and the dead Wanderers.

Beyond doubt the long term of nearly undisturbed success
had bolstered amphibian confidence, perhaps to unrealistic
levels. It may have been for this reason that a murky afternoon
in early spring witnessed active implementation of the resolution restricting the Briar Patch to Sishmindri residency alone.
The passage of such a resolution was never announced, but
easily inferred.

There were still a few human denizens to be found lurking
in odd corners and courtyards of the old neighborhood.
Loath to abandon home despite all transformation of their
surroundings, they were largely inclined to silence and extreme discretion. All efforts to achieve self-effacement, however, were futile.

Shortly after midday, dozens of Sishmindri patrol teams
commenced sweeping the Briar Patch. Beginning at the perimeter and working inward toward the center, the patrols
hurried through the narrow little streets, checking building
after building. Any human encountered was immediately
taken into custody, regardless of age, gender, state of health,
piteousness of pleas, or vehemence of protest. No prisoner
was needlessly harmed, but those who resisted were forcibly
subdued. There were many bruises, but no blood.

When the sweep concluded in the late afternoon, some
three dozen men, women, and children stood packed into a
dense, scared mass at the center of the neighborhood. Their
captors surrounded them closely and, upon a croaking command, began to herd them eastward.

It was not a long journey. Quite soon they reached Hay
Street, which marked the boundary between the Briar Patch
and its eastern neighbor, the New Houses. Out onto Hay

Street the humans were thrust—so firmly that more than one landed facedown in the gutter. Those remaining upright gazed about in confused alarm.

"Ours." The amphibian commander's sweeping greenish arm claimed the Briar Patch. "Our ground. Sishmindri ground. This place is called Roohaathk. Ours now. No men here. Stay out." He gestured, and the Sishmindris melted back into the foggy shadows.

The human ejecta of Roohaathk remained closely huddled. Many of them clasped hands. None had been permitted to carry even the simplest belongings from their erstwhile homes. Several had been plucked from their firesides, and these lacked even so much as warm outer garments. They had no money, no belongings, no idea where to go or what to do.

Their sudden arrival and the attendant commotion attracted the notice of the solid New Houses residents, who began to converge on the spot.

Others were likewise noticing and converging. A trio of Wanderers shuffled north along Hay Street. A second trio was traveling south. Two more appeared at the mouth of a side street, and a moldering quartet had sprung up out of nowhere. So sudden, swift, and sizable a confluence was too great a coincidence for belief. Almost it seemed that they had been drawn by human distress and vulnerability, and it all smacked unnervingly of deliberate intention. The warier among the human observers withdrew. Hardier souls remained to watch, positioning themselves within easy reach of clear escape avenues. Some shouted warnings.

As they drew near, the Wanderers spread out to surround the clustered Briar Patch/Roohaathk exiles. They did not possess great speed or agility. Many of the humans broke free and fled before the circle was complete. But the elderly, the infirm, and a couple of young women encumbered with small children remained.

The circle closed, and the undead performed an action never before witnessed. They linked hands.

Shouts arose among the living.

The circle tightened, forcing the captives into a tight clump at its center. When they had reached elbow–to–rib cage proximity, the Wanderers moved in perfect synchronization, each seizing a horrified victim in an uncanny embrace, each pressing dead lips firmly down upon a living mouth. The captives struggled uselessly. The screaming spectators pelted the Wanderers with rocks from a safe distance, but these efforts were useless.

The grisly scene seemed to continue for hours, but in actuality it was only a matter of seconds before the Wanderers released their prey and turned their attention upon the shrieking audience. Advancing in close formation, they were plainly unconscious of flying rocks. One of them, a woman with a few waist-length strands of golden hair clinging to her bald skull, took a stone full in the face without breaking stride. Seeing this, the living fled down Hay Street. The undead followed at a slower but unflagging pace.

The Briar Patch refugees were left in disarray. Several were sobbing hysterically, the children were screaming, and one of the older men had collapsed in a dead faint. Among the adults remaining awake and aware, there was none who could fail to recognize the inevitable consequences of contact. Within days, or possibly hours, all of them would sport the carbuncles of the plague. In the meantime, their minds remained clear to contemplate the implications of this change in the Wanderers, who had never before displayed such clear organization, persistence, and purpose.

• • •

The Lost Zorius Stroll was an elevated walkway with an observation deck affording a fine view of the harbor and much of the waterfront. Here, in happier times, the citizens had repaired to take the air while watching the ships come in and depart. Here on the deck, they could sit at little tables of wrought iron, gossip and play cards, eat lunch, throw crumbs to the gulls and the Scarlet Gluttons.

These days the Stroll's popularity had declined, for the smoke-heavy, potentially plague-ridden outdoor air had lost much of its appeal. Even now, however, the place still had its devotees. A few young couples, walking arm in arm; a few sturdily active old people; a few boisterous youths. Most of them were masked; some were not.

Jianna had set her own mask aside, and felt almost naked without it. The acquired habit of concealing her face was difficult to break. Now she felt exposed, vulnerable—even hunted. Yes, her nerves tingled as if she were being watched and followed.

Ridiculous. She had worn that vizard too long, and it was beginning to warp her perceptions. Probably it would be good for her to go without it for a while; in any case, there was no choice. At the moment, recognizability was required.

The red feather lodged as if by chance beneath a stone at the foot of The Bellflower's front steps had summoned her to this meeting. Once, the medium of communication would have struck her as highly fanciful. Now it was simply practical. She had been summoned for a reason. She was here, and must be visible to her correspondent.

Both hands resting on the guardrail, she gazed out over the water at the Searcher, whose great bronze face and form were veiled in mist and smoke. In his upraised hand the huge lantern glowed, its light diminished but not yet extinguished. Her eyes shifted from the statue to follow the wheeling gulls for a while, then moved to the dock to settle upon a vessel moored at the dock and currently disgorging passengers.

Passengers? Surely not. Who would come to Vitrisi now? She knew little of conditions in the other great cities of the old Faerlonnish Alliance—Orezzia, Freni, Zicca Boste, and the rest—but she had heard that all suffered under Taerleezi domination, and that all had fallen prey to the plague. There seemed little to choose among them.

She studied the vessel, whose colors proclaimed Vitrisian origin. The name on the hull was *Swift Dispatch*.

"She was turned away from Posalli," spoke a voice that she knew, at her elbow. "Third ship within the week. The Taerleezis are no longer permitting Faerlonnish vessels to dock at their wharves. They want to keep the plague out."

"You mean, all of Faerlonne has been placed under a giant quarantine?" Jianna turned to face Lousewort. As always, his actual appearance failed to tally exactly with her recollections. It was all but impossible to keep his image in mind.

"In effect. Of course, there are ways around any quarantine. The big Taerleezi ports are guarded, but there are any number of quiet rural landing sites scattered along their coastline. Small boats could slide in easily. And of course, there's always a world beyond the Veiled Isles."

"Has it come to that, then? To save our lives, we must abandon our homes and seek refuge in foreign lands? And we need to do it by stealth, *sneak* in by night, because they don't want us?" She did not add the grim afterthought. *And that's the people with means to get away. The others will just sit here waiting to die.*

"Ah, Maidenlady Noro, don't be so quick to consign us all to doom. The folk of the Veiled Isles have survived pestilence in ages past. I'm willing to hope that we can do it again."

"Do you believe that the plague is part of something bigger, something even worse?"

"Don't know. Doesn't seem useful to sit around wondering and worrying about that when we've got solid, flesh-and-blood enemies with their boots on our neck to think of. Speaking of which, I've something for you." Lousewort slipped her a packet wrapped in coarse cloth. "Better get that out of sight."

She obeyed, stowing the bundle away in the pocket of her cloak. "This is—?"

"Just what you asked for. The documents have been prepared by one of our best men. The seals, the insignia, paper, ink, and penmanship—they're all as good as you'll find anywhere. The number of parties has been left open, so there'll be no trouble there. And the other thing, the brownish powder—that's a concentrate of kalkriole."

"Oh, yes, *kalkriole*." She nodded. "Then I'll need to mix a solution before I use it."

"You know kalkriole, I see."

"You might say so. And the people I need, the women?"

"Two so far."

"A few more would be better. Boys would do, if they can be trusted to wear skirts and pretend."

"I know some very accomplished pretenders."

"Then it won't be long, will it?" Jianna could hardly believe it. "Master Lousewort, I'm grateful for all that you've done. Of course, I'm ready here and now to make good on my debt to you. Tell me what I owe, and I'll pay you."

"Owe? Nothing. It's for Rione. He's one of our best, we'd all do what we can for him, and gladly."

"Thank you." The tears sprang to her eyes, blurring the world around her. Through the blur she discerned a figure approaching along the Lost Zorius Stroll. The individual moved haltingly, supported by a staff. Jianna was swept by a wave of revulsion that shamed her. It wasn't his fault that he was lame, poor fellow, and it certainly wouldn't do to stare. Turning away, she fixed her attention on Lousewort's conversation, which was worth hearing.

" . . . unchanged," Lousewort was saying. "He's still alive in the Witch, and receiving uncommonly good treatment. Ordinarily we'd just assume that a few palms had been greased, but Rione's got no money to speak of, and no family or friends with such resources, so far as I know."

"He's got his knowledge and talent," Jianna suggested. "Do you think they might have need of a physician inside the Witch?"

"Could be. That's as likely an explanation as any I've heard. If true, though, you know what it suggests."

"Desperation?"

"*Mine.*"

The voice behind her was low and hoarse. A large hand closed on her shoulder. Startled, angry, and curiously terrified, Jianna spun to confront the cripple whose advance she had noted moments earlier. She looked up into a single eye the color of bloodied slush, and the hot words died on her lips.

She was mad, else caught in a nightmare. A kind of sick, disbelieving horror froze her where she stood. Despite the dreadful burned-out eye socket, the scars, broken bones, and mutilations, she instantly recognized the ruined face of her husband, Onartino Belandor.

For a moment she stood staring, then the paralysis broke, and she pulled violently away from him. The hand on her shoulder jerked her to a halt. She had forgotten how fearfully strong he was. She could not tear herself loose—she would never escape him.

Her mouth worked, but no sound emerged. Her panicked gaze flew to Lousewort, who stood watching in patent surprise, and he responded at once.

"Friend, you are in error," Lousewort addressed the newcomer equably. "The young lady is with me."

"*Mine. Wife.*"

"I think not." Lousewort's eyes turned to Jianna's face, and what he saw there lifted his brows a fraction, but he continued smoothly, "Come, let's have no trouble here."

Almost absently, Onartino touched the tip of his staff to the other's chest, and shoved. Lousewort staggered back two or three paces, but kept his footing. Jianna attempted to wrench herself free, and Onartino's hold tightened until she gasped with pain. Interested spectators began to gather around them.

"Have a care, friend—you draw the Taerleezis down on us." Lousewort was back again, and lying. He gestured urgently. "See, they come."

Onartino's one eye followed the pointing finger. Instantly

Lousewort's foot shot out to kick the supporting staff aside. Onartino tottered, and Lousewort slammed a fist into his belly.

The pressure on her shoulder eased a little. Jianna twisted with all her strength, and suddenly found herself free. Picking up her skirts, she fled at a run. She was sound and fleet. Her crippled husband could not hope to overtake her. As she went, she cast a look back over her shoulder, to spy Lousewort hastening in the opposite direction. Her rescuer was safe, and she would meet him again soon.

She ran on without direction until exhaustion slowed her to a walk, and only then did she remember to don her vizard. She was anonymous again, invisible among Vitrisi's masked multitudes. He would not find her now.

He was a remarkably accomplished hunter. Determined, methodical, implacable. He would never rest until he tracked her down and reclaimed her—which, as her husband, he had every right to do.

Jianna shivered. She was breathing in gasps and drenched in sweat, but shudderingly cold to the core. The world had altered in an instant. Onartino Belandor was still alive. And he still owned her.

• • •

The Overmind was growing more insistent and obtrusive every day. The Magnifico Aureste felt it strongly. He was quite capable of excluding the Other indefinitely, or so he believed, but resented the necessity of continual effort. And it *was* continual; there was never an hour entirely free of that inquisitive, invasive, silently relentless pressure upon his mind. Sometimes it was immediate and demanding; sometimes it faded to the edge of detectability, but it was almost never entirely absent. He himself possessed the will and fortitude to resist, but what of the others, less richly endowed? Or perhaps burdened with the weakness of excessive sensitivity?

He did not fear unduly for his brother. Innesq possessed

strength to equal or exceed his own. But the others—those arcanist people? They were peculiar by nature, and now they were growing visibly more so. The girl Nissi—she was forever trailing around after Innesq like some starved white mouse angling for tidbits, and half the time lately she seemed lost in another world, head tilted to one side, eyes shut, lips moving to frame soundless inhuman syllables. The Taerleezi oddity, Littri Zovaccio—he seemed unable or unwilling to speak, and now his sight seemed to be going as well. In the evenings he stumbled about the camp, tripping over obvious obstacles, acknowledging no greeting, eyes wide and evidently blind. And the boy Vinzille muttered ceaselessly to himself, as if conducting unending internal debate.

When the moment arrived, would this irregular band of rickety eccentrics stand any real chance of completing their mission?

It was not a matter over which the Magnifico Aureste possessed an iota of control, and therefore he chose to ignore it.

They traveled on into a region richly clothed in black-green conifers, whose somber boughs were brightly dotted with yellow-green globes—the nests of the giorri, already veined with the fissures that would soon split wide, releasing hundreds of thousands of dream-winged creatures into the world. Bronze-colored vines of northern strangler looped from tree to tree, enclosing the groves in a great living net. The mists here were uncommonly dense, completely obscuring the sky. It was easy to imagine that the light of the sun never touched the ground in this place.

On they went, the mists turning afternoon into twilight, and Aureste felt the pressure upon his mind intensify. It, the Other, was here in force, perhaps stronger and more demanding than ever before. The press was so heavy that the demands of self-preservation drove all other considerations from his mind, for a while. Time passed—he had no idea how much time—and the internal struggles continued. He scarcely took note of the world around him. He ate once, without tasting.

People spoke to him, and he answered mechanically. At last came a moment when some instinctive mental twist or leverage that he had stumbled upon by chance thrust the invasive presence from his mind. He did not understand quite how he had done it. Probably Innesq would know and would explain. He did know, however, that It had not retreated far. It no longer impinged upon his consciousness, but surely remained close at hand, infusing the very atmosphere.

A great stir, shouts, imprecations, whinnying from the horses, and the world was with him again. The expedition had come to a halt. The reason was apparent.

Directly before them, only a few yards ahead of the front riders and a few inches above the ground, hovered a pair of spectral figures. They were tall, perhaps a couple of heads higher than a sizable man, and they appeared to consist of grey fog or mist, dark and dense, yet weightless. Their shape was impossible to judge, for it was infinitely mutable, now thin and attenuated, now squat and disk-like; sometimes similar to humanity in outline and disposition of limbs, sometimes reminiscent of a sea anemone with countless elongated tentacles, sometimes cloud-like and amorphous, but continually changing. Throughout the incessant metamorphoses, two features remained constant. The substance of the figures always displayed a confusing quality of slow, nearly imperceptible revolution. And every shape possessed a set of dark, almost black indentations, suggestive of eyes, but fathomless and empty.

Aureste knew beyond doubt that the forms he beheld were visible manifestations of the Overmind. This recognition had nothing to do with rationality. It was something that thrilled along every nerve in his body.

There was scarcely time for wonder or terror. The horse beneath him was plunging, rearing, and shrilling in a frenzy of fear. All the skill that he possessed was needed to keep his seat and to bring the animal under some semblance of control. Every horse present displayed similar terror. Their riders were occupied and, in several cases, thrown. One self-liberated, riderless creature turned and galloped away, vanishing into the mists within seconds. Nobody was able to give chase.

The carriages were immobilized. The expedition would bog down here and now if something were not done.

Aureste had regained tolerable command of his horse. Now turning to the nearest two guards, he issued orders. The guards took up their crossbows and fired. Two bolts sped for two hovering specters. Both were well aimed. Both struck their targets, and both passed through foggy insubstantiality. The visitants floated in place, unaffected and unchanged.

But no, there was a change. Ignoring the guards, both of Them turned the fathomless voids corresponding to eyes directly upon Aureste.

Their regard engulfed him. He was cold and lost in Their eyes, drowning in the empty dark.

With effort, he turned his face away from Them, and the world returned to him.

The two hovering figures vanished. Whether they had literally disappeared or simply withdrawn into the fog was impossible to judge.

In the aftermath of the apparition, the horses continued terrified and unruly. When urged forward, several of them balked, refusing the haunted mists. There would be no further progress that day. The afternoon was well advanced, and it was agreed to make camp in that spot.

Brimming with questions, Aureste sought out his brother.

"Yes, I have heard of Them and read of Them," Innesq explained. "They are a manifestation of the Overmind, and for some days past I have felt Their presence."

"You never said anything about it."

"To what purpose? I was not certain that They would choose to reveal Themselves in visible form. If They did not, and Their proximity was sensed only by me and a few other members of our party, what point in spreading useless alarm among all?"

"With adequate warning, we might better have prepared ourselves—there's the point."

"A just argument, but how would you have done so?"

"Perhaps there's little we could have done, but we wouldn't have been so taken by surprise. There would have been less confusion, less disruption. Tell me, did you catch a clear view of those things from the carriage?"

"Quite good." Innesq's nod conveyed a connoisseur's appreciation. "It was a rare sight indeed that I was privileged to witness. They were not communicative, however. They would not respond to my greeting or my queries."

"What are They?"

"It is difficult to say. They are beings neither flesh nor spirit."

"Can They be killed?"

"I think not. Nor would I kill Them if I could."

"Fine sentiment, but we must deal with Them, one way or another. They've already caused us delay. If They come back, there's sure to be more of the same, and we can't afford it."

"There is something in that. But it is with the power of our minds that we must oppose Them. No other weapon will serve."

"How can you be so sure? If good steel won't do the job, then what about fire? Has that ever been tried?"

"Certainly, and to no avail. You must not suppose that ours is the first human encounter with these beings. They are known of old. They have appeared, even within Vitrisi itself, when the Source has threatened reversal and pestilence has walked abroad. At such times, men have called Them the plague-wraiths."

"They seem formed of fog and vapor. Why don't you and your fellow arcanists get together and raise a great wind to sweep these plague-wraiths to the far side of Faerlonne? Or better yet, out to sea?"

"Ah, Aureste." Innesq shook his head smilingly. "That is rather imaginative, but I fear you must resign yourself to the use of mental weapons alone. Cultivate energy and determination. You possess both in abundance."

"So be it."

The conversation with Innesq was shortly followed by another exchange, less amiable in character.

In the evening, Squad Leader Xelli of the Belandor guards requested a moment of his master's time. The man radiated discomfort, and Aureste anticipated new difficulty.

"Yes, what is it?" he demanded discouragingly.

"It's the men, Magnifico. We've been talking." Xelli met his master's lowering black gaze and continued bravely. "After what happened today, it's clear that we're up against something that can't be fought. Arrows passed clear through; there's nothing we can do. That being so, there's nothing for it but to turn around and go home. We're not meant to be here, anyway. Everyone agrees to it, including the Taers. Why, even the horses are of like mind. You saw how the beasts wouldn't go forward today, and it will be the same story tomorrow. We've not much choice. So there you have it, Magnifico."

"So there I have it." Aureste nodded slowly. "Indeed I do, provided I am ready to accept the rule of my own servants. And the Taerleezi servants. Not to mention the horses. Perhaps it will surprise you to learn that I am not so inclined. Understand here and now, Squad Leader—nobody turns back. What, are my own handpicked guards so faint of heart? I haven't noticed the women among us whining for home and hearth. The Magnificas Sonnetia and Yvenza, even the little Nissi—none of them speaks of giving up and turning back. Are my guards weaker than the women? Answer."

"Could be that the women haven't the sense to know when it's time to pack it in."

"Or else it could be that they, unlike my precious guards, possess some courage. Well, before you lads think of slinking off, consider this. You're traveling among a nestful of arcanists. Do you really imagine that Ojem Pridisso, Littri Zovaccio, and the others will let you walk away? Use your head, man. If you attempt desertion, they've spells to find you wherever you hide, and magic to set your bowels on fire, to twist your bones like lengths of rope, to turn your brains to boiling soup. Depend upon it, they'll have their vengeance. On the other hand, if you do your duty, carry on to the end, I'll offer a ten-diostre reward at journey's end to every man of you, even the Taers. I trust we understand one another?"

"Aye, Magnifico."

"Tell the others. Now leave me."

Xelli bowed and withdrew. Quite possibly the guards' fears and doubts would resurface at some future date, but for now the problem had been contained.

Events soon demonstrated the error of this assumption.

Aureste retired and slept soundly, but some nameless instinct woke him early. For a few moments he lay wondering at his own pronounced sense of wrongness, then identified the cause. It was surely morning, but there was no noise, no familiar stir of human activity. He rose and emerged from his tent to discover a quiet, fireless, depleted camp. In the dark predawn hours, all the guards and servants, both Faerlonnish and Taerleezi, had silently departed. With them they had taken all of the horses and most of the food.

• • •

In an odd sort of way, Vinz Corvestri was almost glad of the servants' defection, for it added another item to Aureste Belandor's account, further justifying hatred. Somehow, in some manner that was not readily apparent but nonetheless real, Aureste had driven them away. Probably he had abused them, or alarmed them with his recklessness, or perhaps they had come to feel the degradation of serving an infamous kneeser. Whatever the specific cause, it was doubtless through Aureste's agency that the quality folk of the expedition now found themselves abandoned and adrift in the soggy wilderness, deprived of every comfort and forced to shift for themselves. And it was not as if they could call heavily upon their very considerable supply of arcane power to satisfy their immediate needs. No, that precious commodity was reserved for another purpose.

Without horses, the carriages were useless. Hereafter the nine remaining members of the group would walk. All of them, even the women, would carry packs of provisions and essential belongings on their backs. The countless possessions deemed inessential would be left behind, despite their value and desirability. The drudgery of cooking would theoretically be shared by all, but probably the women would do most of it. And all would assist in easing Master Innesq Belandor's way.

One of the abandoned Belandor wagons contained a sedan chair intended to transport Innesq, should wheeled transport fail. But the muscular young servants meant to carry the sedan had decamped, and the remaining aging, weak, or sedentary wayfarers were ill equipped to bear the burden. Thus it was agreed that Innesq would travel on in his wheeled chair. A modest collective investment of arcane energy would smooth the ground beneath the chair, in much the fashion that the trail beneath the carriages and wagons had lately been smoothed. Innesq lacked the physical stamina to propel himself over long distances, and therefore his companions would take turns pushing him along. It was a task that even the smallest among them could perform without great difficulty.

Vinz enjoyed pushing the wheeled chair. The exercise was useful, not unpleasant, and above all gave him the sense of compensating Innesq in some small way; of performing service to offset impending disservice. As he trudged along, the chair rolling smoothly over the impossibly level ground, he was able to study his companions as he never could when all had traveled within their respective carriages.

At the head of the group strode Ojem Pridisso and Aureste Belandor, side by side. Typical. No doubt each imagined himself entitled to leadership by natural law. The Taerleezi, while annoying, was essentially well intentioned, but Aureste was truly malevolent. Then there were the others—the Magnifica

Yvenza and her ward Nissi, both marching along uncomplainingly; Littri Zovaccio, somehow achieving self-effacement in broad daylight; and finally Sonnetia and Vinzille, strikingly like one another, both formed of finer clay.

He studied his wife covertly. She had not addressed a single word to him throughout the day. As she walked, she contrived always to maintain a nicely calculated space between herself and her husband, wide enough to free her of any need to speak to him, but not so wide as to call attention to a deliberate separation. How tactful she was, how perfectly correct. How infuriating. Soon, however, there would be no more reason to doubt or suspect her. He would trust her again, and all would be as it had been. After tonight.

The day crept on, blessedly featureless. The Overmind was present but not intrusive, and there were no spectral manifestations. There were only silent hills, dark conifers massing beneath an unwontedly clear sky, bare rocks, and an infinity of brown needles carpeting the ground. And then, in the late afternoon, one thing more—a slight, almost imperceptible vibration underfoot, scarcely more than a suggestion. Subtle though it was, it brought the expedition to a halt, but only for a moment.

"Friends, be easy." Ojem Pridisso turned to address his followers with the air of a reassuring father. "Here's nothing to fear, it's only the world flexing its muscles, and that's just natural. And we should be glad of it, too, since it tells us that we're getting near our destination. For certain, the Quivers aren't far off."

He was probably right. Within the next day or two they would reach that site, so famously infused with arcane energy, and then their real work would begin. Were the six of them equal to the task of cleansing the Source? Vinzille, for all his natural ability, was an incompletely trained youth. And little Nissi, whatever her potential, remained an untried and unproven talent. Nevertheless, Vinz realized, his own confidence ran high. After tonight, with a mind clear of doubt, misery, suspicion, and a heart at peace, his power would rise to any challenge. He would buoy the others up, if need be, with his own strength.

It was the longest, slowest day in the history of the world, a day stretching on into eternity. At times Vinz thought it would never end. But the centuries dragged by at their own pace, and the day dimmed toward its close.

They came to a small stream wandering among the trees, and beside it they halted to make camp. The task was pitiably simple, demanding little more than the gathering of wood and the kindling of a fire. There were no tents to pitch. The tents had been left in the abandoned supply wagons, along with the extra bundles of fuel, the heavier tools, most of the blankets, and all the larger barrels and sacks of foodstuffs. Henceforth all of them would sleep as best they could on improvised bedrolls.

The Magnifica Yvenza prepared a simple meal for them all. She worked competently, but the selection of ingredients was far more limited than ever before, and the end result unavoidably bland. Seated on rocks or folded squares of oilcloth ranged about the fire, the nine of them ate in glum silence. Presumably all dwelled with regret on lost comforts, and all considerately suppressed complaint. Ordinarily, Vinz might have shared the sentiments of his companions. This evening his mind was elsewhere. He did not notice what he was eating, what people said or did not say. He chewed his boring supper mechanically, and did his best to keep his overt attention away from Aureste Belandor. Should his eyes come to rest upon that detestable face, there was no telling what they might reveal.

And at last, *at last,* the minutes dwindled down to nothing, and it was time to spread out their bedrolls. Sonnetia, he noted bleakly, chose a solitary resting place far from him on the opposite side of the banked fire.

But still the waiting was not over, and would not be over until he could assure himself that every member of the group slept soundly. Feigning slumber of his own, he lay wrapped in his blanket, eyes shut, face slack, every sense alert.

When a low harmony of snores rumbled the air, Vinz judged the moment ripe, and sat up. The night was exceptionally clear and bright. The moon overhead was brilliant, and by its light he could easily observe the recumbent bodies all about him, could even discern the features of his companions. But that was trifling. He would do far better, presently.

Swallowing a tablet, he sat waiting for the familiar reaction. And while he waited, he recalled a certain analogous event in the career of his boyhood hero, the great arcanist Soliastrus. The relevant lines from *The Journey of the Zoviriae* rose up and marched across his mind:

Grey Soliastrus recognized the hour.
The hour so oft desir'd, so long delayed.
The Sword of Varis burned within his grasp;
The matchless blade born of the ageless fires
That heat the waters of the Well of Life.
The virtue of the flames imbued the steel,
Which ne'er submitted to a faithless hand,
But served a worthy master's righteous ends.
Thus armed, the mage staked all upon the hope
Of breaching the enchantments of his foe,
To end the monstrous tyrant's loathly life.

The poetry fired his blood. *To end the monstrous tyrant's loathly life!* His awareness expanded then, and his breath caught. Heart swelling, he stood up under the moon, readied himself, and spoke the requisite syllables, breathing them forth almost soundlessly. His mind and skill were at their height. The Source gave of itself generously, and almost he could have imagined that the camp, the sleepers, and the brooding conifers were flooded with a great light that radiated from the glory now blazing within him.

He saw the camp and everything in it in minutest detail. He could even see beyond, if he chose—through the stand of green-black trees, past the distant hills, on as far as the sea itself. But there was only one thing he cared to see now. He was ready. He *was* Soliastrus.

Tensing his intellect, he marshaled the power and sent it forth in the form of a Fume. To ordinary observers, it would have been invisible. Even accomplished arcanists would probably have detected its existence only by way of heightened perceptions. To Vinz, it appeared as a serpentine current, aglow with the ineffable colors of the epiatmosphere, flowing silently and swiftly over the ground to entwine the form of the sleeping Aureste Belandor.

Aureste tossed in his sleep, frowned and grumbled. The Fume slid through his parted lips and into his mouth. Insinuating tendrils of itself into his nostrils, it plunged to the depths of his lungs, thence finding its way into his blood.

It was done. Events would now proceed to their beautifully inevitable conclusion. Vinz allowed his connection with the Source to lapse, lest the surge of arcane activity in their very midst lure his colleagues from slumber. Spent, he lay down again, and drew the blanket up to his chin, but did not allow himself to sleep, did not so much as shut his eyes. Soon Aureste Belandor would wake, and Vinz very much wanted to see what would happen then.

He wanted to see it all.

• • •

The Magnifico Aureste dreamed. In his dream, he walked a dark and gloomy wood, a place of loss and loneliness. At first he walked alone, wrapped in despondent reflection. But soon others came to him, surrounded and pressed in close upon him. They were pale and translucent of face and form, and they moved with impossible lightness, as if their feet did not touch the ground. He understood that they were not alive, but did not know whether they were real or imaginary, whether he was awake or asleep.

Then he perceived that the faces were known to him. They came out of the past, both distant and more recent, and they did not come in friendship.

There before him rose his trusting cousin, the Magnifico Onarto Belandor, who had offered him hospitality and protection during the wars. Onarto, whom he had betrayed, ruined, and ultimately murdered. Onarto, whose fortune and title he had usurped.

And there beside Magnifico Onarto glimmered a woman, her face streaked with luminous tears. He knew those tears, he had seen them flowing endlessly from the eyes of his wife, the Lady Zavilla. She had been vastly wealthy and quite comely—it was from her mother that Jianna had inherited the exquisite alabaster complexion—but for all of that, a pitiful creature, weak and clinging. Within weeks of their wedding, he had come to despise her tears, her groveling pleas for affection, her whining reproaches. He had not troubled to disguise his contempt, and she had waxed melancholy and languid, then died in the aftermath of childbirth. Many women died in childbirth. But perhaps if she had been stronger, happier, allowed a modicum of hope—?

And there was Onarto's younger son Trecchio Belandor, his throat agleam with ghostly gore, shed at Aureste's command.

And there was an inhuman form among them—a Sishmindri. He recognized Zirriz, formerly of his own household. He remembered the ache in his arm from the violent exertion of the whipping. He remembered the smell of Zirriz's blood.

And then there was the stout albeit transparent form of the Magnificiari Flune Brulustro, whose false accusation and arrest he had personally engineered. He had witnessed Brulustro's execution.

And there was the old moneybags, Stizi Oni, strangled in his bed. If only old Oni had been more reasonable, if only he had died of natural causes as a person of his age ought, it would not have been necessary to arrange his removal.

And there were others, so many others. In some cases he had lost the names, but the faces were unforgettable.

A tide of grief and guilt overwhelmed him. Its intensity was extraordinary, and even in his dream he wondered at it. Occasionally, throughout the course of a long and interesting career, the pangs of conscience had troubled him, and he had learned long ago how to distance such qualms, how to neutralize and reject them. He was, in fact, an expert at such mental maneuvering. But never before had he suffered such an assault. He could not contain, evade, or stand against it.

Desperate in his dream, he snatched the dagger from his belt and thrust at the shape of Onarto Belandor. The blade passed through nothingness, and Onarto smiled upon him, but not in malice or triumph. It was the simple, kindly, trusting smile of old, and the sight of it shattered Aureste's defenses. Despair crushed him, pressing the tears from his eyes in streams. He was, he realized, a piece of vile human pollution, unfit to live.

The world would be a better place without him.

It would. He did not know where the voice came from, whether it spoke inside his mind or came from the outside. He did not know whose voice it was, his own or someone else's.

You are a criminal, a murderer, a traitor to your country, loathed and detested by all decent folk. Your very name is synonymous with villainy. You have brought shame upon a proud House, never before stained with infamy. Perhaps your daughter once loved you, but only because she did not know you for what you are. In any case, she is gone, dead or worse, because you failed to guard and protect her.

The tears were burning him, inside and out. The voice tolled like a passing bell—sometimes speaking in his own resonant tones, sometimes with the fluting notes of a woman, sometimes as an echoing chorus.

The phantoms crowded in around him, too numerous to count, but all of them his victims, all of them tallying the sum of his crimes.

You bring naught but suffering and ugliness to the world.
You are hated by all, and such is your just desert.
You hate yourself, and that is as it should be.
The world is a better place without you.

"*Enough!*" The cry wrung from his own lips woke the Magnifico Aureste. He gazed around him at a scene well illumined by moonlight. He walked a dark and gloomy wood, a place of loss and loneliness. He was barefoot and uncloaked. Evidently he had risen in his sleep and wandered from the camp. In his right hand he grasped his dagger. He was drenched in sweat, dizzy, and afire with fever. An iron band of the imagination seemed to clamp his temples. And the despair—the gigantic, killing despair of his dream—that was with him yet, deeper and darker than ever, permeating every fiber.

The ghosts were likewise with him yet. He gasped, and passed his free hand across his eyes. He was awake, or so he believed. But those floating phantasms were all about him— Onarto, Zavilla, Moneybags Oni, and all the others, all of them with their wounds and their knowing eyes that he remembered too well. And the fever blazed in his head, while the voices spoke on and on, and the guilt devoured his heart, and the dagger in his fist ached to drink his blood.

One stroke to atone and escape. One stroke, so easy and so right.

But there before him was another figure, one among many, but somehow different, less ethereal of substance, not unfamiliar, and watching with a look of simple pleasure. He knew them all, and this new one was no exception. Confusion clouded his thoughts and his eyes, and it took him a moment to recognize Vinz Corvestri, who—although wronged by the Magnifico Aureste—owned no proper place among the ghosts. But perhaps he did. Perhaps he had quietly died during the night, and now legitimately claimed membership in this company.

He had drawn very near, this happy Corvestri-figure. He

was watching avidly, and he was speaking, his tones somehow unlike those of the other ghosts.

"Do it. Do it. It is the only way."

Something within Aureste's burning brain rose in rage and revolt. Some confused recognition of trickery and treachery exploded, its force driving his dagger through flesh and vitals.

The mad moonlit world reeled. Gasping, Aureste dropped to his knees, and the dagger fell from his hand. For a time he knew nothing, understood nothing. Then, swift as a fleeing nightmare, the delirium abated. His surroundings had resumed their normal aspect. The conifers rose stately and somber; a night bird hooted nearby. The ghosts were gone, or perhaps they had never been there at all. Surely they could not have been real.

But one remained, its solid reality unquestionable. Eyes sightlessly staring and chest soaked with blood, Vinz Corvestri lay dead on the ground before him.

PAULA BRANDON is the author of *The Traitor's Daughter*, *The Ruined City*, and *The Wanderers*.